CELEBRATING

A TALE OF LOVE

NAKED

LOSS AND FAMILY

LINDSEY AVERILL

Self-Published
Made in the United States of America
1st edition, August 2020

You are the wind beneath my wings...

THE LAND

Beautiful,
opening.

They bought the land in Santa Fe in the 1970s, when no one else was interested. They borrowed the money from Elizabeth's father and were starting a life for themselves. Standing at the highest point of their newly acquired purchase, they squinted their eyes and just barely caught sight of human existence. Layers of sand and clay swelled out beneath them. Pinion trees stretched their branches over the chalky soil, creating streaks of shade for horny toads to hide in. Thirteen dry acres at the end of Old Pecos Trail. Thirteen acres, with almost no road access, that rolled and pushed its way to the arroyo on its northern border.

They chose the land because the sky was vast and magical from anywhere they stood. Floating above their crowns were huge three-dimensional clouds that danced like creatures, clustering together one moment and spreading out the next. They watched millions of stars rise in the evening, sharp little points of light that raced down from the sky to seduce them.

Looking up at a ceiling covered in duct tape constellations, they lay in a small-dilapidated blue tent and huddled. They laughed at the water that seeped through. In this little world, they constructed dreams of their home and their future. They speculated for hours about how many children they would have, and whether they wanted a kitchen that faced the sunset or the sunrise. They didn't know the winters would be raw and cold, or that the snow would pile high and leave them stranded miles from town. They spent their last pennies on an old beat-up Toyota truck that sputtered and kicked its way down the thump-ity-bump of the washboard roads and set out to build a family.

Even in the arid air and unfertile land, things tend to grow.

ONE

The lights were out, but the blue haze of the television crept around the room, flickering light, flickering dark. It was late, well after midnight. Cliff Gordon leaned against the doorframe that led into the living room. His wife, Elizabeth, nuzzled against the arm of the couch with her feet tucked under the cushions. Her breathing had been slow and steady for an hour or two, and the soft powdery glaze of sleep drifted across her face. Sissy Cornwall curled tight into the other corner of the couch, pulling a worn fuzzy Pendleton blanket closer to her chin. Although not related by blood, Sissy and her son Artie were as much a part of Cliff's family as the two children who shared his genetic code. He and Liz met Sissy before their son Michael was born, and now, after twenty-some-odd years, she was sitting on his couch slowly dying.

But Cliff didn't think of that now. He focused his eyes on the little tan man in the yellow bathing suit running across the television screen. The televised Artie couldn't have been more than two or three and his legs were chubby, his knees soft like Play-Doh.

"Cute, huh?" Cliff said, his voice vibrating through his chest cavity and rolling out into the stillness of the dark living room.

Sissy smiled, "Better than cute."

Ever since she got sick, they wanted to throw Sissy a party, but she insisted what she wanted most was to curl up with her family and watch movies of their life together. Cliff thought the whole idea was macabre, but he was wrong. True to form it was a celebratory night, a perfect night. The kids laughed and pointed at their former, shorter selves. Elizabeth fussed over everyone, like she always did, and they all felt good, which was exactly what Sissy wanted.

A little pot-bellied version of Cliff's daughter Clara waved out at him from the TV screen. She stood on the edge of the pool wearing a purple bathing suit that ruffled at the waist and shimmered in the sun. Gripping her nose between her fingers, she set out to test the buoyancy of the bright-orange, air-puffed floaties on her arms.

"Watch this, Daddy," she chirped.

When she jumped, droplets of water flew in his direction, and he heard his own voice, detached and faceless, "Careful, baby, don't splash the camera."

Her sweet young face showed little concern. Instead, gaps of baby teeth smiled out at him. "Come swimming, Daddy." The picture jumped for a second, and then the tape ended. Cliff could still see Clara's outline on the dark screen. Sissy looked over the back of the couch in his direction.

"I have one more," he said. "You up for it?" He tilted his head in Liz's direction, "Or, should I gather up my sleeping beauty over there and go to bed?"

Sissy tucked a chestnut strand of hair behind her ear and said, "No, one more." Her sounds had grown deep, hollow, almost sad, almost happy.

The only sealed video left in the pile of discarded cases was Artie's birth celebration. They had already watched all the birthdays and graduations, all the cookouts and trick-or-treaters, leaving what was either the most poignant or the most upsetting for last. Cliff knew it was not something Sissy could easily forget, and not just because she was the one who had the honor of huffing and puffing and bleeding and screaming.

He could still see the blue-purple color that came to Elizabeth's lips eighteen years ago when Sissy told her she was going to throw a party at which guests would be entertained by watching the "miracle of birth." The three of them were sitting around the coffee table, the same coffee table that Sissy was resting her feet on right now.

On that night eighteen years ago, Elizabeth was on the floor. She wore a white, embroidered, peasant blouse, and her wine glass, sticky with fingerprints and burgundy colored remnants, rested on the table in front of her.

"I wouldn't want to give birth in front of a gang of people, that's all," she said adamantly.

Sissy spoke around a Twinkie she had just stuffed into her mouth, "I think I wanna share it." She swallowed. "I mean how many times am I going to have a baby?"

"It's not really all that pleasant," Liz countered. "I mean the idea is beautiful and everything, but the action of giving birth is pretty grotesque, and... well, you certainly will not look your best."

Sissy laughed. "I'm not particularly worried about my appearance, but if you are, you'll be right next to me. You can touch up my lipstick."

Liz sternly pursed her lips, not laughing even though Sissy was funny. "It's personal, ya know? Do you really want all our friends looking at your," she lowered her voice to a whisper, "privates?"

Cliff sat on the couch just behind Elizabeth, twisting her blond hair in circles around his finger. He had been drinking but was more intoxicated by the looks on their faces, and he guessed he spoke just loud enough to be too loud.

"Oh come on Liz. Don't be such a priss," he said. "It will be fun. A big party. Lots of oh's and ah's and eww's." Neither woman laughed. They just looked at each other and rolled their eyes.

Sissy had only been living with them for a few months then and her sway over Liz hadn't even begun to grow to its full potential. The conversation went on for hours, days even. It had not been easy for them to convince Liz. He could picture Sissy perched against the kitchen counter, one hand rubbing the swell of her belly, her eyes fierce with the intensity of her argument. He could see her hollering through the bathroom door while Liz tried to shower. He remembered her trailing and droning behind Liz while they collected the laundry, and then finally one day at the breakfast table, Cliff watched Sissy push her fork back and forth through the scrambled eggs on her plate, while his wife gave in to her unyielding persistence. In between sips of coffee Liz sighed, shook her head and said, "Well I guess if you want to have a baby in front of all those people, it's your prerogative, but I was just saying..."

Before she could get another word out, Sissy cut her off, "Good. We're having a baby in the backyard Cliff-O." He was sure he smiled at that, and he thought maybe he had also winked at her, but he wasn't certain.

The preparations for Artie's birth had been ludicrous. You didn't invite just anyone to a "birth celebration," but they kept unusual company to begin with, and Santa Fe is a mecca for artsy, hippie, loving types, who might think a public birth is a great idea. Women in Santa Fe are constantly getting together to celebrate the passage into menopause or the arrival of a girl's first period, so why not Sissy's leap into motherhood? Of course, because of the nature of the event, no matter what kind of people you invite, they aren't quite sure they want to go.

As far as Cliff was concerned people came because it was Sissy. Something about her made people think, "Oh, Sissy's going to have her baby and she wants us to be there. Well then, that sounds fabulous." She had a spark that made people commit to things, much like a rollercoaster that makes you scream your heart out, pumps you full of adrenaline, and rattles your bones with excitement, until you're retching up cotton candy and corn dogs in a rancid smelling waste bin. She had even been able to convince Elizabeth that Clara and Michael should be privy to her outlandish presentation of human reproduction.

When all was said and done, Artie came into the world under the watchful eyes of nearly fifty people. In those days money was tight. Cliff had just opened his architecture firm and the cost of building Sissy's house still burdened their bank accounts, so all the guests received handwritten invitations. Each envelope included a detailed phone tree. Liz still had one of those invitations stuffed in a box somewhere.

Sissy had her first contraction, on a Tuesday morning in early August. Elizabeth was serving as the midwife. She propped Sissy's feet up on the chaise outside on the patio and they sipped icy lemonades, while Cliff, some boys from work and a smattering of other volunteers set up for the expected evening's entertainment.

The main attraction was situated at the bottom of the unfinished pool or a hole in the ground, depending on who was looking at it. Cliff decided the increase in possible vantage points made the pool a perfect place for the birth, even though it was not yet suitable for water. He built a temporary floor in the mud, propped an old mattress up on a platform, reinforced it to withstand the bouts of birth, draped it in white sheets, and christened it "Willamina, the birthing table." (They had laughed at that.)

Around seven in the evening, Cliff made the first in the line of phone calls. Sissy's eyes watched him through the patio doors, as Elizabeth helped coerce her awkward pregnant body down the makeshift stone steps of the empty pool.

"It's time," he said into the receiver.

Luminarios lined the path weaving around the Gordons' property and the edge of their two-story adobe rooftop. Each paper bag guttered with a warm golden glow. The sunlight slipped behind the horizon and the orange fiery streaks in the sky seemed to mimic the candles. Carrying a hodge-podge collection of used trays lined with glasses of champagne and colorful hors d'oeuvres, their friends' teenagers floated and weaved their way past the guests' apprehensive faces. Everyone stood frozen in wait, their necks craned, looking down into the depths of the unfinished pool. The smell of sage waltzed and spun through the crowd making the air smell fresh and unsoiled.

There was very little sound other than Sissy's struggle and Elizabeth's words of encouragement, cycles of clenched faces and fists, grunts and pushes, and then a child, a boy. Artie's lungs opened in their first ear piercing cries, and the crowd clapped and lifted their glasses in congratulations. With Elizabeth's hand resting on his shoulder, Cliff cut the cord that connected Sissy to her new man.

Eventually, Artie grew accustomed to his surroundings, and Sissy had each person in the room touch his fresh fingers and wish for his future. Cliff wished that Sissy's son would love him like a father and that in return he could be the father her boy no longer had. It was a spectacular sight, blood and all. When Cliff thought about all the moments that threaded together to become his life, Artie's birth celebration was quite possibly the most perfect and awe-inspiring memory he could call on.

But, that wasn't exactly the story the movie they were about to watch told. The guy they hired to film the celebration made an artistic choice, which failed to capture the essence of the event. His "choice" excluded the birth of Sissy's son altogether. He was barely in his twenties, an awkward pimply sort of a boy, perhaps not quite old enough to understand the power of a man's birth. He sat on the edge of the pool and filmed straight ahead, so most of the footage was crotch to ankle images of the guests, but all throughout Clara's tiny face was in the frame. Her wide eyes filled with terror and amazement.

Cliff's frail, blond, two-year-old chewed on her little fingers, pulling anxiously at her skin until it bled. She was wearing dress shoes, patent leather ones that reflected the hem of her skirt. You could almost track the happenings of the birth by watching her twisting expressions. Elizabeth tried to prepare her for the sight, but being so young, she couldn't understand. They probably shouldn't have let her watch. When the crown of Artie's head began to appear, pushing its way through the soft flesh between his mother's legs, she burst into hysterical tears.

After a few sob filled moments, the photographer suddenly turned the camera to the action. Cliff's swarming fingers, seeming larger than the baby's body, submerged Artie into the clear liquid that washed him clean, and for the first time Artie's little eyes squinted at the patio lights. Then, Cliff passed the infant to his wife and stood by smiling, as Elizabeth wrapped his tiny little legs and tummy into the warmth of an old soft blanket she had used to warm their children. Together they lowered Artie into Sissy's arms, and she nuzzled him for the first time, her bottom lying on the blood stained white cloth.

As if he finally realized the true importance of the event the camera man panned to Cliff pulling his two young children down into the pool with the rest of their family. The final frame rested on the panorama of the Gordons, all four of them, circled around Sissy and her new son, protecting them at all costs.

It was that image that flooded Cliff's mind as he slipped the tape into the VCR. He had done his best to be the good father he hoped and wished he'd be that afternoon, but he wasn't perfect. In the future he'd be better. If Sissy left them, he'd be better.

TWO

Morning nudged its nose through the systematically sealed windows of St. Vincent's Hospital. Sissy's bed was squeezed right up against the window, so she could look out at New Mexico's dry red dirt. She pushed the sheet back. One minute she was too hot, the next she shook with chills, but the miles of chimiso-speckled land and the rusty mountains in the distance distracted her, and every morning for a moment, she felt normal. The dusty soil reminded her of her first morning in Santa Fe; the sound of the truck door popping in her ears; Artie's father, Robert, mumbling something about taking a piss; lifting her head and watching the horizon fly away. In that instant she was introduced to New Mexico's unyielding beauty. At seven thousand feet above sea level, Santa Fe's ancient native heritage and muddy spires nestle in the clouds and the smell of juniper trees and the dirty clay soil always drifts in the air. Looking out at the vista, Sissy longed for that musty smell.

She would miss smells, but not just cookies baking or fat on the grill, but all kinds, good and bad. Things like, freezer burn or boxes that have been closed for too long; the sour of a working harbor, the sweet crisp of fresh cut grass and the murky musk of sex and sweat. She would miss rubbing powdery soil between her thumb and forefinger, the searing intensity of cold headaches as she bit into the end of a fudgesicle and the pure accomplishment of picking popcorn from her teeth. She would miss a lot of things, unexpected little pieces that once seemed like nothing, but she wondered more about the void her passing would create than the things she was leaving behind.

Sissy knew death. She understood how grief lingered; how it could bubble through the surface in an instant. In her life she had been blessed with the kindness of love – supported by the strength of true friendship. When Robert died, there was no reason Cliff and Liz should have taken her in, but they did. They loved her and Artie like family. They gave them a new world filled with laughter and spirit. Liz and Cliff provided everything Robert ever could or would but somehow the grief was always there, hiding in the dark. Sissy could picture Liz and Cliff going on without her. They were older, stronger, their life together existed before her. But Artie and Clara felt hinged to her, as though her death would brand them, burn clean through to the bone.

Clara and Artie almost never left the hospital. Artie slept in a chair, his left hand resting against his forehead, propping his head up. His other hand was nestled in Clara's hair. Sometimes, he looked so much like his father that it took her breath away. Clara sat on the floor next to him, her face resting on his knee, her forehead creased and her eyes squeezed tight with anxiety. Their sleeping bodies looked awkward in the sanitary surroundings. The hospital's acrid smells, plastic and metal, sweat, antiseptic covered decay, didn't belong near them. She could feel it all scrapping and clawing, trying to penetrate their young, teenage skin.

When they told her she was dying, she braced herself for a fight. She allowed them to poke and prod her. She listened to friends and saw all sorts of acupuncturists and New Age healers. She allowed an old Indian medicine man to dance around her shaking his prayer sticks, his beads bouncing, sweat running off his forehead and dripping into her hair. Then one morning, steam rising from a cup of deep red rooibos tea, Sissy realized she wasn't afraid of death's presence, and she put down her sword.

She didn't know where death would lead her. The Native Americans said she would go to the skeleton house and live with her ancestors, feeding on the odor and the essence of food. The eastern religions, Buddhism, Taoism and all their disciples said she would return to this world in some other form because she knew she was not enlightened. Christianity and Catholicism definitely were sending her to hell for her greatest accomplishment, her son, who happened to be born out of wedlock, making her a sinner.

What was a dying person supposed to believe? And how could she grab onto faiths she never believed in just because she was dying? Eventually, she would just know and there was comfort in that. The question that plagued all people would be answered for her. She hoped that good things were ahead, but she figured that when you died you were dead, gone, and put in the ground, energy neither created nor destroyed. Somehow she would go on, even if it were just to make richer, more fertile soil.

As a young girl sitting in the dark, Sissy had been consumed by the anxiety of being alive. She would curl her fists into tight knots, digging her fingernails into her palms, creating moon-shaped indentations, hoping the pain would distract her from the pressure to be something worthwhile. Everyone she knew then had no purpose or direction. They never struggled for happiness. They knew what they were: small town boys aiming for football scholarships, blue eye-shadowed blondes hoping not to get pregnant, beer drinking, wife battering, God-fearing people, who were just not sharp enough to be unsatisfied. Sissy knew she was someone, something more than Friday night football and a joint under the bleachers, but at the time she couldn't for the life of her figure out what. Clara had that same look, her age and her intelligence out of alignment, but at least she was growing up in a more accepting environment. Sissy had not been that lucky.

No one chooses to grow up in the boonies, especially if you're a weird bird; that's what Sissy's Daddy called her. He would say, "Sissy Wallace, I don't know where we found you." Then he would shake his head, smile as if he were mocking someone, letting the words, "weird bird" slip through his teeth. He didn't understand. She never expected he would. He owned the only hardware store for miles around, and he loved her, but Sissy just never wanted to sell tools or anchor chain or gaff tape.

Her mother, a striking woman, a tall glass of water, nothing but legs, was always disappointed by Sissy's lack of interest in what she considered the purpose of female existence: husband hunting. She would sit in the driver seat of her little red Firebird badgering away, the cool New England air rushing into the car, her left hand pushed out the window grabbing at the wind, one eye focused on the road, and the other eye on Sissy. She teased her hair up high on the crown of her head and wore a lot of pastel colors. They never had anything in common.

"Sissy," she would whine, her lips shining with frosty pink gloss, "Why can't you participate in school activities? You're so pretty. Boys would like you if you cheered or spent time with the other girls... You know make-up never hurt anyone... I was talking to so-and so's mother the other day, and her daughter..."

Her mother was a talker not a listener, and Sissy always understood that, or at least now, it seemed like she had. In her own twisted way, Sissy's mother taught her to be fearless when chasing what she most desired, which was how Sissy came to be with Robert, and how she finally found herself looking at happiness in the mirror. Sissy always thought she would leave something equally meaningful inside Clara. (Perhaps laughter in the face of tragedy or the passion for life that Robert inspired in her.)

Robert Cornwall crept under Sissy's skin and exhilarated her, set her off like a homemade rocket, spurting and sputtering towards adventure. He caught her eye the first time she saw him, all disheveled from working construction. They had been sitting at two different ends of the diner on Whistler Street. It was the kind of diner with olive colored vinyl seats that stuck to your thighs in the summer, and silverware that was always coated with water spots, but Sissy liked it because it had hooks by the door, so she didn't have to fret over where she hung her coat.

As usual, Sissy was alone. She drank tea, Lipton in those days, from a huge mug she carried in her purse, and skimmed the local paper thinking that journalistic endeavors about the high school homecoming queen were silly. Robert and his friends were laughing and talking. She watched them out of the corner of her eye, envious of their camaraderie. They were older than she was. At first she thought, maybe college boys home for Thanksgiving, but after careful inspection she realized they didn't fit the part. They had dirt under their nails. Robert sat in the corner, next to a stocky guy whose laughter was sprinkled with sharp, loud inhalations of air. He was wearing a long-sleeved green cotton T-shirt that was speckled with the white remnants of a printed slogan or picture. His sleeves gripped tightly to his biceps, showing off strength. Every few minutes he would lift a cigarette carefully from the ashtray, and placing it on his lip he would inhale, and then exhale without ever moving the cigarette away from his face. Wary of allowing her gaze to be detected, Sissy watched him over the edge of her mug. After a while she stood to go to the ladies room, and he looked up at her and smiled.

Men smiled at Sissy. They always had. She was pretty: thick, long, dark hair, full pouty lips, slim body, and smooth skin. Although Sissy's physical appearance was giving and delicious, they smiled because of her eyes; they were soft, inviting, and seductively quiet. They had no definite color, switching from brown to hazel to green at will, but always quiet. Her eyes defined her presence long before she spoke. Her eyelashes were long, always getting in the way, kissing the lenses of her sunglasses, forcing her to look sweet and demure. For most of her young adult life, Sissy battled off men who wanted the naïveté her eyes promised. So, when Robert smiled, she shifted her glance to the clock above his head and then proceeded on her way to the ladies' room. In the bathroom mirror she looked at her face while the water ran over her fingers. Her eyes never displayed her wild spirit or her racing intellect, but somehow they convinced her to feel peaceful too.

Later, when they became lovers, Sissy would learn that Robert had not smiled at her eyes. (Looking straight into her eyes scared him, or so he said.) He told her it was the mug that made him smile. She was so attached to the mug that she carried it to the bathroom with her and left her purse resting on the seat. It intrigued him that she felt the need to protect a cup of warm tea but had no attachment to the things in her purse. As she returned to her seat, he smiled at her again, but he never approached her that day.

She didn't see him for weeks, but she remembered his face, his well-defined cheekbones and strange golden eyes. He stayed with her even though they had never spoken. While customers milled about, she sat behind the counter at her father's hardware store and wondered who the group of young men were. How would she find him again? How would she entice him to know her? Whenever she could she sat in the diner on Whistler Street, sipping from her mug, hoping he would return. At night, lying in bed, she plotted and planned their future, trying not to toy with images of his hands running over her skin, and wishing she had not been so aloof that first day.

Robert never walked back into the diner on Whistler Street. One morning he came into the hardware store looking for her. The store was dark and dreary. Sissy never liked it; it smelled briny like rust and shipyards. It was as if a seagull might squawk through the silence at any moment, its wide feathered wingspan flapping, stirring the still air, but the only noise was the old leather belt lined with bells that jingled as the door opened. She heard the bells ring and never looked up.

In later years, she imagined his approach to the counter. How had his face looked? Had he been nervous? Did he clasp his hands in front of him or walk with them swinging by his sides? She would never know, but now that somehow mattered, everything, every moment mattered.

He stood in front of her, silent, with his fingers draped over the counter's metal edge that she and her father nailed up when she was a little girl. She lifted her eyes, her lips parted, and she drew in a deep breath that brought with it discomfort. "Can I help you?"

"I saw you from the street a few days ago." His eyes danced while he spoke, drifting from the floor, to the ceiling, and then back to her. "I remembered you from the diner."

"On Whistler Street?" Her fingers trembled in her lap, and she was thankful he couldn't see them.

"Yeah," he nodded his head slightly.

"Oh."

"I'm Robert."

"Sissy," the word bubbled up through her throat, caught on her tongue, and squeaked out through the space between her teeth.

"Are you always here in the mornings?"

She nodded, "It's my dad's place."

"Can you leave?"

"I could. I guess."

"Do you want to get a cup of tea?"

"Yeah," she smiled, tickled that he had noticed such a small detail. She slipped off the rickety stool, listening to its joints threaten to crumble and then decide it could withstand another day.

Sissy called out as quietly as she could, "Dad, I'm going out for a cup of tea. I'll see you later." There was no answer, but he wouldn't miss her. He was the only one in the store most of the time. A laminated sign taped to the countertop read, "Call out HELP for service," and enlisted at least a half smile from her father whenever he passed by it.

Walking out Robert didn't look Sissy in the eye. He watched his shoelaces so intently that she wondered if they had the tendency to try to break free from his boots. Once outside in the daylight, he looked up at her with that same intensity and said, "I want you to see something. I think you'll like it. I have a thermos of tea in the car. Do you want to go?" She watched as his nerves infiltrated his eyes and then again, his shoelaces became ever so interesting. "I mean, we can go to the diner if you want, but I..." She took a deep breath and ignored everything anyone had ever said about strange men.

"I'd like to go...yes."

His eyes lifted, and he grinned at her.

They sat facing forward in the truck, avoiding eye contact so as to ignore the uncomfortable silence. Sissy sipped eagerly on the tea he had poured for her, and Robert fiddled with a cigarette, rolling it back and forth between two fingers. Sissy looked towards him searching for something to say.

"Robert?" She was sidetracked by her own thoughts, "Is that what you like to be called or is it Rob?... or Robbie?"

"Robert's fine."

"Okay," she paused. "Robert?"

"Yep?" His left elbow rested on the open window and his right hand gripped tightly to the top of the steering wheel. He used his knees to steer when he needed to shift.

"Where are we going?"

"I can't explain it. You have to see."

They drove silently over old back roads. Sunlight filtered down through the trees, shattering on the windshield. It began to drizzle lightly, just enough to make the ground wet.

Sissy thought New England was at its most beautiful in the fall after it rained. The fire of colored leaves makes a soup of ooze that reaches out and slurps at your feet. Each step is a dangerous venture. Like wet toilet paper, the leaves glue themselves to the soles of your shoes. Worms and spiders, and other creatures with tickly legs creep out from their dark moist homes and make a game out of who can roam through the fiery paradise without being discovered by heavy feet. Brave, curious children remove their shoes and allow the disintegrating mulch to slide up through the crevices between their toes, but few adults are eccentric enough to enjoy the delight found in this squishy pleasure. Looking at Robert sitting quietly next to her in the truck, Sissy just knew that he would romp through the mulch with his feet bare and his heart high.

Robert pulled the truck over on the shoulder and parked. Jumping from the cab like a little boy, he hollered, "Come on, we're here!"

Sissy climbed from the truck slowly, not feeling as familiar with her surroundings. She looked both ways, not a car in sight, and crossed the street, following his lead. He hopped over the guardrail and was standing, looking back, waiting for her. When she stood facing him with only the rail between them, he looked her in the eye, smiled, and in one quick movement, he slipped his hands around her waist, and hoisted her over. Being so close to him made her hands shake. He slid her down, allowing her feet to find the earth, and then he turned and continued on his way. They walked through the woods, his arms swinging back and forth, his fingertips occasionally grazing a tree or grabbing at a leaf. The soil beneath them was soft and moist. She watched his feet lift and fall in the dirt and took notice of the prints they left behind. Abruptly, the trees cleared and Sissy saw the ruins of a small church just ahead of them.

"No one has used it in...Well, my guess is fifty some-odd years," Robert said.

Sissy walked out in front of him. The wall closest to her was still standing, but the doors had rotted from their hinges, allowing her to see right into the sanctuary. The ceiling and the walls behind and to the left of the pulpit had completely disintegrated, but the pulpit and the pews still survived. They were weather worn and grown over with weeds but fully intact. A partially shattered window created shards of multi-colored light. Droplets of water rolled down the cracked glass. Sissy walked between two pews, placed her hand behind her, testing the strength of the old wood, and then sat down and watched the little rainbows of light as they danced around her.

Robert stood in the aisle and looked out over the pulpit at the sky. The racing energy and childish rhythm that he had exuded earlier was replaced by an almost paralyzing calm. His breathing slowed. His hands dropped to his sides; he closed his eyes and lifted his chin. The noise of the road behind them was lost in the distance, supplanted by the soft rumblings of nature.

Sissy watched him, trying to slow down, trying to embrace his new soft pace, but her breathing stayed heavy and the more she tried to relax, the more she wanted to scream. She felt years of dissatisfaction pushing against the backs of her teeth. She wanted to shake her arms and jump up and down until the energy disappeared, but she didn't because they were strangers, because she didn't want to get in his way or disrupt his concentration, because he was something she wanted, which she didn't know exactly how to attain.

After a while he whispered, "Come here," motioning for her to stand in the middle of the aisle. She was slow to rise. Her hands felt jittery and her stomach bounced like she had ingested too much caffeine.

"Stand right in front of me and just do it," he said.

Sissy looked back at him, her eyes pinched in confusion.

"Go. Do whatever you need to do." He knew. He understood needing to scream it out, shake it off, break free and crow, so she did. She closed her eyes, faced forward and screamed until her body grew weak and she had to lean against him to avoid slipping from her feet. He kept her standing and then that pulpit with nothing but nature behind it calmed Sissy's mind leaving a clean white emptiness, and even now, that feeling was the only religion she ever knew, the majesty of nature, its endurance, its quiet strength.

After that there was no silence between them.

When the sun set later that day she thanked him and they were forever linked. It was simple. They were lovers, neither one for the first time, but it was new. It was passionate. It was fierce and consuming. Robert was a dropout. He was bold. He was a genius. He was a dancer and a dreamer and a man. He ignited her spirit, shaped it until she woke filled with life and peaceful excitement. For four years, they traveled together through their lives.

They only had one rule. Celebrate life, always. They celebrated ✕
by never settling down, moving from one place to the next, eagerly
searching for something new. It was perfection, well as close as it
gets. They didn't need anything but each other. There was no such
thing as a wrong turn, or a stress-filled sleepless night. If they had
no money, they would make some. They had no credit cards or bank
accounts. They were just happy. Nothing was ever worth tears or
sadness. That was their rule. Don't cry because stuff just happens. It
was bigger than *life is just a bowl of cherries* or *roll with the punches*;
it was more like, if life hands you lemons make lemon crepe suzettes.
Enjoy the ride. Robert mocked people who wallowed in their failures
and problems. Psychoanalytical sheep he called them. He said, "Why
waste your time crying? Move on, savor the memory and move on."
With him she was awake, and when he died, he left her alone and
alive in a way she hadn't known possible.

He was killed in a motorcycle accident. She was there. She watched
it happen. They both liked it in Santa Fe, the way the mountains ma-
jestically rose up from the earth and the way the clay dust crept under
your fingernails. It wasn't the same then as it is now. It was a sleepy
little town with history and culture. There were no movie stars, just
people. Everyone laughed and drank and smoked dope and delighted
in nature. They talked about staying there for a while. Maybe getting
married, but they never really settled on it.

He was drunk. He didn't have the lights on. It was a friend's bike.
He hit a rock; she could pick it up in her hands. The bike flipped. He
was thrown and broke his neck. She watched it happen. She didn't
stand or scream. She hoped that he would stir, but he didn't. She
took a deep breath and closed her eyes. She didn't cry. Of course,
there would be violent outbursts and unjust blame, but that all came
later. First, there was silence.

She could feel that same silence creeping in around her again. She
could see it in the way people had begun to look at her, the claustrophobic pity in their eyes. She could hear it in the timbre of Cliff's voice

and watch it resonate through Liz's knuckles. It was a black drowning feeling that hung on and suffocated anyone who came close enough to smell it. She remembered the taste too well, as if she had dined on death's silent sound just moments ago.

Life is never easy. When you're young the serious aspects seem to be off in the distance. They're something you step over and threaten each day, but somehow you never notice they're happening every minute. Sissy couldn't have done anything differently, but again, now, for the second time in her life, she wished she had learned that some things disappear in an instant.

She pulled air into her lungs, her chest heavy with dying. She watched her son's hand slip down through Clara's blonde hair to her shoulder. Any minute now, they would wake up and smile at her. They would begin their banter and make her laugh. They would go off in search of something to eat, and return grumbling about the crappy food downstairs. Artie would have his hands wrapped around a Styrofoam cup filled with steaming hot tea, Lipton again, and Clara would mumble that it was still too hot. God, they were so spectacular, but not like the decayed church that had inspired her all those years ago, sillier. They were goofy and immature, so full of life and dreams and dramas. She wished she could have the chance to see them through the rough spots. She hoped she had awakened in Clara the strength she would need. She looked again at their sleeping faces and hoped Artie would realize that loving Clara was what the future held for him. She hoped she had taught him at least that.

THREE

Elizabeth walked down the long familiar hospital corridor with a magazine in one hand and a white paper bag from *Tortilla Flats* in the other. She had stopped at the restaurant just before heading to the hospital and picked up a bean burrito with very little cheese and no chili because she decided that she was going to help Sissy feel normal one last time.

A few days earlier sometime in the late afternoon, she sent the kids off on some not so pertinent errands, pulled a chair close to Sissy's bedside and asked her what she could do to make it all easier. If Sissy had said she wanted to die, to be rid of the pain, Elizabeth would have mustered up all the courage she possessed, thrown everything she honored as a nurse into the garbage, and done what was necessary to make that happen, but even while she was asking, she knew that task would never be required. Sissy was the type who would suffer any pain for just a few extra instances of breathing. She loved too many people with too much generosity to check out early. Her request was simple.

importance

"You know what I want," she said. "You know what I really want?"

"Anything you want, you got it, baby."

"I want to sit on the freaking pot like a normal person." Elizabeth laughed and Sissy continued, "I want to feel the porcelain under my buns. I want to read a fashion magazine, and I want to go to the bathroom without any help. That's it. That would make it all easier."

Liz grinned and shook her head, "One plain-Jane, solitary bathroom experience coming up."

It was not a tall order, but it would take a little maneuvering. Liz knew that Sissy wasn't strong enough to walk to the bathroom on her own, and they would have to wait till the moment struck, but Liz would carry her and she would situate her and then she'd shut the door and wait until Sissy needed her again. It probably wouldn't go that smoothly. Liz knew it was hard for Sissy to go at all, but she would sit in that bathroom by herself, and maybe just for a minute, she'd feel normal again.

When she got to the door of Sissy's room, Liz stopped for a moment. She straightened her shoulders and bolstered her feigned strength. She knew Artie and Clara would be inside, and she would need all the power of her role as the matriarch of her family to get those two to bugger off for the entire day. With her eyebrows furrowed and her smile stern, she pushed open the door. Sissy looked up at her as she entered the room. She crossed right to the bedside table, and put her supplies down, without turning to look at the kids. For a moment while she could only be seen by Sissy, she relaxed her facial muscles, bit her lower lip, and let her eyes turn up in silliness. Hardened again, she turned to face Clara and Artie.

"Up," she said, "Up and out. You have been cooped up in here for days and I won't have it."

"Mom," Clara said in that indignant tone that is cornered by the teenage vocal cords, "we're not leaving."

"You are. The two of you are getting up and getting out of here. She's mine today and you can't have her." Keep it light, she thought and playfully stuck out her tongue.

"But..."

"No buts. Get up and get out." Elizabeth turned to Sissy for a little support.

"Your mother's right, Clara. You and Artie go home, clean up, watch a little T.V. Maybe take a nap. We'll call you and you can come back later." Artie sat still. His eyes were glazed over with exhaustion, but he was having none of it.

"I'm not leaving," he said.

Sissy pulled out the big guns, "I may be dying young man, but I'm still your mother and you will do what I tell you." Artie went limp with defeat. Elizabeth knew there was no retort. They would go now. She crossed the room and gathered their things from the chair by the door. She folded their dirty extra t-shirts and underwear and stuffed them in the backpack she had brought to them the day before. While they each bent to kiss Sissy and feel her frail embrace, Liz stood firm, holding the door open with her body, waiting to hand off the backpack in her arms. The kids moved slowly, fighting their dismissal with every stride. Liz handed the things to Clara.

"Just leave them in the laundry room," she said. Clara took them.

"Whatever." Her voice was bitter, icy, but Liz ignored it.

"I'll call you later." Elizabeth watched them walk down the hall, then she shut the door and turned to face Sissy, the doorknob still in her hand.

"I wasn't sure we'd get rid of 'em," she said. The corners of Sissy's mouth turned up ever so slightly.

"The death card works every time."

"No kidding. Talk about giving your kid a complex." They both laughed. Liz pulled one of the chairs close to the bed. "Okay," she took the white bag from the table and began to unwrap its contents. "The first piece to this quest is the lukewarm bean burrito I have here. Not as spicy as you desired in your younger days, but tasty all the same." Liz used plastic utensils to cut the burrito into bite size pieces and then she pulled the tray table over Sissy's bed placing the food in front of her. "Eat up," she said.

It took Sissy almost thirty minutes to eat barely a third of the meal, but Liz was not discouraged. She expected as much.

"I can't eat any more," Sissy said. Liz removed the food, put the lid back on, and put it back in the bag. She'd throw it away later, but she felt better pretending that Sissy might want to save it.

"So," Sissy said, "now what?"

"Now we wait."

"We might be better off if you had brought me a laxative milkshake."

Elizabeth closed her eyes and bowed her head, as if in prayer. "Trust in the bean," she said. "It will work its magic." Sissy exhaled little tufts of laughter through her nose.

"You're a cheese ball."

"You love it." She paused, drinking in Sissy's face, memorizing the lines around her eyes when she smiled. "Well, how should we pass the time?"

"My first choice would be a beer, a live band, and a little line dancing, but I guess the T.V. will have to suffice." Liz used the remote to click on the tube. They watched the news and then some soaps, and when the television lost its charm, they decided to play a few rounds of gin rummy. Liz shuffled the cards and dealt out two hands of ten. The first game went quickly and she dealt again. They played three rounds. Sissy won two of the three. She was always the better card player. Liz was shuffling, preparing to deal the fourth hand, when Sissy stopped her.

"I want to ask you something," she said.

"Ask away," Liz continued fanning the cards between her fingers.

"Do you regret having me in your life?" Liz's fingers froze and the cards cascaded to the floor.

"Of course not. Don't be ridiculous."

"No, you don't understand what I'm asking you. I know you love me, Liz. I know you're glad that you know me, and I know you love Artie, but we've made your life so different than you expected it to be. Do you ever wish that you just had a normal family?" Liz steadied her gaze and looked Sissy square in the eye.

"Never. I have a normal family. I have a wonderful family." Liz's voice began to shake, and she felt tears brimming. She took Sissy's hand in hers and squeezed it tightly, "It's been my honor to have you in my life. I wouldn't have had it any other way." Sissy nodded, closing her eyes for just a second. Elizabeth brushed the tears away and attempted to regain her composure. She gestured to the cards. "Look what you made me do, ya shit." Sissy was still serious.

"I need you to do something for me."

"Anything, you know that."

"Don't be sad in front of the kids. I want them to get past this as quickly as possible. They're too young for misery." Elizabeth hunched over and began picking the cards up one at a time.

"Sissy, they're going to be sad. We can't stop that."

"I know, but I want them to grieve the way Robert would have grieved." Liz felt the muscles in her neck constrict. She had never believed in the great and all knowing Robert, and she wasn't quite certain that his advice would be helpful in this situation. As Sissy continued to talk, Elizabeth focused on gathering the cards. "Celebrate me with them. Don't dwell in the sadness."

Liz kept her gaze on the floor. She was so caught up in Sissy being sick that she hadn't really thought about how she would act once Sissy actually died. In fact, even though she knew Sissy would die, she still had days when she was able to pretend this whole thing wasn't happening. She didn't think she could do what Sissy was asking of her.

She couldn't hide her emotions. She didn't know how. Even though there was a little part of her that felt it would be the right thing to do, the other part of her, the bigger part, couldn't imagine having one happy moment without Sissy. How could she pretend?

Her heart galloped, hammering against her ribs. She didn't want to disappoint Sissy. She didn't want her to feel like the kids were going to suffer. Her head began to pound. She needed to catch her breath, maybe get an aspirin.

"Can I think about it, just for the day? I mean, I think I can, but I don't want to promise you if I can't."

"Yeah, yeah you can, but this is what I want." Sissy smiled, a wicked goofy smile. "I'm playing the death card here."

Liz looked away and placed the stack of playing cards on the table. "Okay, well, give me the afternoon." She pushed her hands into her legs and stood up.

"Deal."

"I'm gonna go get a coffee. You want anything?"

"No, take your time. I'm tired. I think I'll sleep a bit." Her eyelids began to droop as she spoke the words.

Liz grabbed her purse and soundlessly slipped from the room. She drifted down the hall to the elevator and slid in behind two young nurses whom she didn't know. They were complaining about an elderly patient who refused to speak to anyone without his doctor present. It wasn't much of a conversation, but Elizabeth hung on their words, feeling their frustration and missing her fellow nurses. It had been almost a year since Liz stopped practicing.

With Sissy sick, Liz decided to stay at home instead of working. Cliff's success made her income unnecessary, so it was really no big deal. She thought she was going to miss the distraction and the purpose of her work, but focusing on her family was just as time consuming, and it filled her with a new purpose. She had always picked up and fussed over her household, but she rarely had time to just pause and treasure the idiosyncrasies of the faces of the people she loved. She had grown aware of all the amazing facets of emotion that flared and wilted around her house, and she was really proud of herself and the emotional strength of the kids, which was why Sissy's request seemed so unnatural.

When the two nurses got out on the first floor, Elizabeth wished for the first time all year that she was still a nurse. Maybe if she had never known the depth of her family's emotions, she would have been able to make Sissy this promise, but now it seemed impossible. Once the two women were gone, she pushed the button marked four and waited patiently while the elevator climbed, chirping as it passed each floor.

When the doors opened, she headed straight for the emergency exit and ascended the flight of stairs to the rooftop. Outside, the air felt unusually cool for early August. Elizabeth turned her face into the wind. The tension in her neck had doubled in the elevator. She slid her fingertips under the collar of her t-shirt and applied pressure to the area just above her shoulder blades. Carrying the burden of Sissy's death would break her and she knew it.

The bond between the two was the most intense Liz had ever known. Many believe that great love only grows between lovers. They believe epic love is lustful. But two souls seeking to become one through sexual gain and marriage cannot attain what they desire. Sexual love is needy. It must be complimented and consoled, coddled. Even if a couple grows close enough to finish each other's thoughts, they will never walk with the same legs. They are bound and stunted by their obligation to each other. The love between lovers can be strong and true, but it always requires compromise and submission.

Others believe that the protective instinct of a mother defines true, clear, clean, love, but Liz knew better. Mothers push their children into the light. They wish so for their success that they bend the path with judgment and good intentions. The love of a mother is not even. The mother hunches over her young, her back raw and exposed to danger and her children never once worry for her safety.

With Sissy, Liz knew a love that combined passion and nurturing. She knew a love that asked no confession but knew truth, a love of common rhythm and experience, the love of circumstantial twins. Only a love that demanded nothing, a love of carelessness, a love of friendship, could ever grow to be whole. Sissy was Liz's great love. She was her twin.

And so, she knew she couldn't do it. She couldn't bury the grief that had slowly begun to billow in front of her and she didn't want to. She couldn't pretend to Artie and Clara that there was a right way to deal with the sorrow they were about to face, and it broke her heart that she wouldn't be able to make this promise to Sissy. She slid down and sat cross-legged on the ground, closing her eyes and resting her head against the wall behind her.

About an hour and a half later Elizabeth awoke to the blaring of a car horn in the parking lot below. She glanced frantically at her watch and then raced downstairs back to Sissy. She smelled the stench as soon as she opened the door. Sissy lay just as Elizabeth had left her only a pale brown puddle of feces was seeping through her bed sheets. Liz's tears burst forth before she could even speak.

"Oh shit. Shit," she sobbed.

"You got that right," Sissy said.

"I fucked the whole thing up. I fucked the whole god damn thing up." Elizabeth put her head in her hands. Sissy gently shook her head from side to side.

"It's no big deal. I've done it before. I'll just hit the button and they'll clean me up." Elizabeth looked up.

"No, don't. I'll do it."

"You don't have to do that Liz. I'm not embarrassed." Sissy hit the button and Liz backed into the corner and let her weight collapse into the chair behind her. A nurse that Liz had known for years, Carol Meyer, came into the room. She was a nice woman with a gentle disposition and a cutting wit.

"Well that's certainly a mess," she said winking.

"When you got to go, you got to go, I guess," countered Sissy.

"Lemme get Susan and we'll clean you right up."

Liz sat quietly while the two nurses lifted Sissy into the bathroom, looking away from the brown stain that covered the seat of her pants. When the shower was running, the nurse Liz didn't know came back into the room and stripped the bed, pulling off the sheets and the plastic lining below. She put them into a laundry bag and carried them from the room, only to return a few minutes later with fresh linens. Once she had made the bed, she opened the top drawer of the bureau that sat against the wall opposite Liz, and pulled out a clean change of clothes for Sissy. Liz recognized the tattered cotton pajamas. She had given them to Sissy for Christmas a few years earlier. They were a soft lilac color. The woman reentered the bathroom and a few minutes later Sissy was lying back in her bed, good as new.

Elizabeth waited a few minutes before she spoke. "I fell asleep," she said.

"Don't worry about it. The same thing probably would have happened if you were here."

"I'm sorry."

"I said don't worry about it." Sissy's words were forceful. Elizabeth stood still.

"I should call the kids."

"Okay," Sissy said and looked out the window. When Elizabeth got to the door, she stopped and turned back to face Sissy.

"We could try again," she suggested.

"No, it's okay. I was just joking anyway." Sissy's hands lay flat against her sides and she didn't turn to look at Elizabeth. There was defeat in her voice.

"You sure?"

"Yeah." Sissy paused.

Elizabeth waited.

"Did you think about it?" Sissy asked.

"I did."

"Can you do it?"

"Yeah, I can. I promise." Sissy still didn't look at her, but Elizabeth saw her chest rise and fall as she sighed, expelling doubts and breathing in relief.

FOUR

Sissy Cornwall died three days after Artie's seventeenth birthday. From her perch off to the side, Clara watched Artie place his forehead on his mother's palm and rest quietly. In the end, Sissy's skin was sallow and her eyes were drowning in her cheeks, but if you could peel away the sickness, underneath it you would find her, beautiful as ever. Clara did not cry. Sissy told them she never wanted to see tears.

The dying celebration was a spectacular sight.   Men and women, who Clara had never known, came from around the country to pay their respects. The Gordons placed candles throughout their house and the thick hot air drove people into a frenzy of spirited delight.   A girl, who Clara envied in high school, ground her hips against Artie and ran her hands up and down his spine.   He smiled and laughed, his face alive with the fiery streaks of light flooding from the luminarios that lit the porch. The girl's lips glistened with softness as she whispered secrets Clara couldn't hear.   Weaving her red painted nails through Artie's fingers, the girl led him off into the darkness, and like their two half-empty beer bottles disregarded for more sensual sins, Clara was alone.

She leaned back against the coolness of the metal outdoor furniture, closed her eyes and felt the weight of her eyelids. Mourning with joy felt completely unnatural to her, so she decided not to mourn at all. But even so her body felt heavy with grief. For as long as Clara could remember, Sissy understood her when no one else did. Sissy knew Clara loved Artie. She even encouraged Clara's passion, agreeing they were meant to be.

All night Clara's mind flooded with memories of Sissy's understanding. Mostly she remembered one afternoon when she was little, maybe seven or eight. She was sitting on the kitchen counter, watching Sissy dance around the room. Sissy wore her hair pulled back in a ponytail cinched by a white scarf. Some sort of disco was playing, and Sissy poured drinks, swaying her hips to the upbeat rhythm. Clara sipped tea laden with sugar from a pink porcelain mug and watched smoke drift up in ringlets from the tip of Sissy's cigarette.

Turning to get the sugar out of the cabinet, Sissy looked at Clara and said, "You're so beautiful." Clara moved her fingers back and forth over her palm and watched her feet swinging above the tiles below. No one as exquisite as Sissy had ever told her she was pretty before. "In fact, you're the prettiest little girl I ever saw."

Clara watched Sissy stand high on her barefooted tiptoes and reach her arm over her head, searching for the bulky paper bag of sugar in the cabinet's depths. She smelled like sweat and primrose oil, sweet and dirty, like little boys. Hoisting her feet up onto the counter, Clara stepped over the stove, wrapped her little fingers around Sissy's neck and kissed her right on the mouth. When she pulled away, Sissy smiled.

Tucking one of Clara's blond curls behind her ear, Sissy said, "You look very grown up wearing my lipstick, squirt." Clara's eyes fixated on Sissy's fuchsia colored nails. Sissy was the most beautiful creature that ever existed, a princess or a fairy, something absolutely magical.

After that, they went outside, Sissy carrying Clara on her hip. Artie was playing on the swing set with Clara's older brother, Mike. Liz was reading a magazine and sipping on a grown-up iced tea. Clara remembered it as summer but it could've been spring. Before they reached the others, Sissy set Clara down and took her little hand.

"Do you love Artie?" she asked. Clara's young skin flushed pink with embarrassment. "Don't worry, I won't tell him."

Clara nodded.

"Good. That's good. That's how it should be."

Artie never realized how Clara loved him, but she loved him every day then and every day now. She pulled her knees into her chest and watched the people dance. They had always been too close for Clara to seem sexy or intriguing, but Sissy was sure Artie would realize he loved Clara someday. The question was when? Clara had turned nineteen, Artie was off in the darkness with someone else again and Sissy couldn't reassure her anymore.

Clara's parents wanted the best for her. They knew she was an intelligent girl, but her melancholy habits worried them. For their sake and maybe her own, Clara decided to postpone college when Sissy got sick. It wasn't something that was discussed in any real detail. She just didn't go. It seemed natural to her, and to them, that at this particular time everyone would be more comfortable if she stayed home. She was certain they wanted her to go to college eventually, but no one seemed to worry that she hadn't gone yet.

She took a job at a local pharmacy. The owner Mr. Balducci was a wrinkled seventy-year-old man who pinched Clara's cheeks, but he paid her well and never asked questions about why the high school valedictorian was not in college. Mr. Balducci came to celebrate Sissy's death; he drank himself silly and passed out on the yellow couch in the living room. Clara passed by him earlier, and as she draped a blanket over his comatose body, she wondered what happened in his life.

Sometimes, in the dusk hours before closing time, Mr. Balducci joked about burning down the pharmacy to pay his mortgage. One particular evening in a drunken intensity, he grabbed Clara by the shoulders and made her promise never to mention his musing about setting fire to the building. The fear in his eyes was deep and startling. Clara promised she would go to jail for perjury before she sold him out, and she truly believed she could compromise her own future to protect Mr. Balducci's reputation.

A cool wind ruffled the surface of the pool and shattered reflections of light over the last few dancers. Clara's parents danced with their bodies forming one continuous person. They smiled, touching each other's faces, their eyes bleary with love; her mother quietly hummed to the tune. Clara wondered if she would ever dance with love.

She had danced without love before. Two years ago she went to her junior prom with Artie's best friend, Jeff. Jeff was tall and lanky like a runner; he didn't talk much. Clara cuddled into his shoulders and waited for an emotion to spread through her chest but nothing happened. Jeff loved Clara. They dated for almost a year, and still she felt nothing.

One night in a brazen whirl of loneliness, fear, and jealousy Clara slept with Jeff. They had gone to a party filled with festering hormones. They laughed and danced like lovers until Artie arrived. Artie's presence distracted Clara's happiness. In a drunken haze, she watched Artie slip his hands under the skirt of a girl she didn't really know. He left with her, and Clara left with Jeff.

In the car on the way home, Clara said almost nothing. She tried to smile and be pleasant but her insides were turning. Jeff didn't seem to know the difference. She rolled down the window and let the wind awaken her face. The musky smell of a descending rain drifted in the car. Jeff walked her to the door and kissed her in a sweet and gentlemanly way, quiet tongue-less kisses. The rain began to fall. She pulled gently on his lower back forcing his groin to rub against hers, and his breathing quickened.

"Clara...?" She moved her other hand up to the base of his neck and ran her tongue over his lips, and he responded, gently pushing his own tongue into her mouth. It was as if she were someone else. Someone bold and outgoing. Someone young and reckless. She slipped her leg between his and allowed him to press tightly against her.

"Clara..." His lips moved frantically over her neck and collarbone, fluttering currents through her body. With her eyes closed she didn't care who was touching her. The feeling of his hands on her body eased her unhappiness. Silent tears, lost among raindrops, drifted over her cheeks, but she smiled.

"Clara..." His voice dripped coarsely from deep in his throat. He was someone different too. He was powerful and restless. And then he wasn't. "We can't do this here."

"Shhh...quiet," she whispered.

"They'll hear us."

"Quiet." She moved her hands slowly over the wetness of his arms down to the button on his pants. She didn't care who saw, or who heard, or who talked. The emptiness was gone.

"Clara..." His fingers ventured over her body and then pressed firmly into her thighs. She waited, moisture gathering beneath her dress. "Clara...I love you." Frustration raged in her chest.

"I know," she said, looking at his face, his eyes filled with disappointment. Her back was pressed against the earthy cement of her parent's house. She was guilty. "Kiss me," she said. His hand touched her face, softly cradling her chin. She pressed her lips against his palm, his wrist. The dirt under their feet had begun to grow soft, and Clara felt the heels of her shoes sinking into the mud. The smell of disintegrating nature and fertility had been awakened by the storm, and Clara wanted to fill her hunger without thinking. But Jeff couldn't understand that.

"Everyone can see us," he pleaded. She took his hand and walked around to the porch where there were no lights. Slowly, she slipped her sundress over her wet hair, exposing her skin to the night air.

"Look at me," she said.

"Is this what you want?" he asked, withering before her eyes.

"Yes."

It was a sad story really. Clara had used him, and she knew it.

41

They dated for many months after that night, but he was never the same. He went to college last fall, Ithaca. She didn't miss him. He wrote every now and then, but his letters were detached and pointless. Sometimes she didn't read them for days. Sissy was the only one who knew that the cause of Clara's depression was never Jeff.

Clara felt the warmth of a hand on her shoulder, and the voice of her older brother shook her from her thoughts.

"Dance with me," he said.

"I'm tired."

"But the party must go on," he smiled patiently. She knew he would pester her until she danced with him. They didn't bother moving towards their parents. They rested against each other beside the old metal chaise and moved slowly to the music. He was two years older. Following in Mike's footsteps had been a struggle for Clara, shy as she was, but she had always felt lucky that her brother's reputation forced her to be social. Clara loved Mike and was always eager to see him, even now.

Mike's relationship with Sissy had never been like Clara's, but he respected her and loved Artie. The boys were glued together for most of their childhood. Two little dirt devils stirring up trouble. Clara always wanted to be included in their malarkey, but she just didn't make the cut. Sometimes, on weekday afternoons they let her be a spectator but rarely.

As the song ended, Mike took Clara's face in his hands. "I know we're supposed to smile and dance tonight. And I know, no tears, but are you going to be okay?" Clara nodded her head. She was careful not to let her sadness flow forth.

"No worries. I can handle it...savor the memories, right?"

"What about Artie? Do you think I should stick around for a few days?"

"I don't know. Selfishly, I say stay. Rationally, your classes are starting. Go." Clara wished she could give definitive answers. She was always looking at every situation from all possible perspectives and confusing herself.

"We'll be okay around here," she smiled.

Liz had begun to pick up bits and pieces of garbage from around the pool. Her middle-aged body was rounder than Clara pictured her, and each of her steps had grown deliberate. Clara watched her hold the small of her back as she bent to the ground. Her hair fell forward and a small groan escaped from her lips.

"Clara," Liz called. "Would you and Mike eat some of that damn cake?" She walked closer to Clara and Mike spreading her arms as an invitation to hug.

"I'm not hungry," Clara said.

"Of course you're not hungry. I don't remember a single day in your life when you were." She kissed Clara on the cheek. Her hair fell into Clara's face, filling her nostrils with the smells of stale beer and frying grease.

The smell of frying grease was part of every celebration Clara could remember. A party was not a party without beer and coconut fried shrimp. Clara had always loved the sweet crispy taste of deep fried coconut shrimp. The thought normally made her mouth water, but she couldn't think of food today.

The last few days Sissy was alive she had no appetite. Clara watched Elizabeth bring her every dish she had ever liked and all the junk she could possibly desire, but nothing tempted her. She never complained of nausea or anything dying people complain about, but she grew frail and thin. Her beautiful dark hair was gone, so she covered her head with tied dyed handkerchief. Clara tried not to picture her that way. Everyone wasted words on the strength of Sissy's spirit. Even a spirit so strong couldn't keep her from wasting away.

Cliff appeared, romping through the patio door with a platter of tiny hot dogs and mustard, which had been neglected. His lips were perched in a smirk, and a dab of yellow mustard was caught in the corner of his mouth. He tried to convince his family to eat with him, but it was no use.

"Come on, one itsy bitsy hot dog won't kill ya," he chewed vigorously.

"Thanks, but no thanks," giggled Elizabeth.

Clara looked at her family. She always felt lucky to have such a strong support system. How could Artie ever survive without Sissy? Sissy wasn't even Clara's mom, and she was devastated.

"Clara, would you run inside and grab a garbage bag, so I can start dealing with this mess?"

"Don't worry about it, Mom. I'll take care of it."

"No. I'll do it. You look tired."

"Don't be silly. You have a gorgeous man smeared with mustard waiting for you," Clara winked, watching her mother's cheeks turn rouge.

"Clair-ra."

"Go on. Go."

"Thank you, sweetie." Liz shimmied into Cliff's arms, and they giggled their way inside like children. It was obvious Mike was also hoping to be dismissed from clean up. Avoiding all possible eye contact, he said, "How can I help Clar?"

"You go on to bed, too. I actually feel like being alone."

"You sure?"

"Yeah."

"'Kay, goodnight." He hugged her and headed inside.

Clara walked through the patio doors into the living room. Mr. Balducci snored rhythmically on the couch. A collection of sticky glasses, coated in an array of lipstick prints, covered the surface of the coffee table. With the music turned off the house was allowed to breathe its own noises, comforting Clara's thoughts. Parties cluttered her mind; they made the air grow stale. Even when they were fun, she felt uneasy.

She piled the cups into her hands, pockets, and armpits, holding the last glass with her chin. Being as quiet as possible and careful not to trip over the corners of the rug, she moved through the house into the kitchen. She stacked the glasses next to the sink, each one perfectly parallel to the next. The lights from around the pool filtered through the little window in the back door. She walked over and pushed the door open letting the dewy late night breeze move through the house.

A bottle of tequila had somehow found its way onto the floor next to the fridge. It was tilted on its side threatening to spill, but the contents had been drained, allowing it to lie comfortably without consequence. Clara contemplated moving the bottle but ultimately decided it looked happy in its current state. From under the sink, she grabbed two plastic garbage bags with red cinch ties.

It was easy to fill garbage bags after a party. People lose control of their littering etiquette. Clara moseyed around the pool gathering napkins, cigarette butts, and empty beer bottles. On her second trip around the patio, she noticed two beer bottles resting by the grate at the bottom of the pool. She considered ignoring them, but a warm wind lifted the hair around her face, and the prospect of the clean clear water rinsing her of grime became enticing.

Clara slipped out of her shorts and tank top, and in a moment devoid of her natural inhibitions, she dropped her bra into the pile of clothes. The layered sweat and thick grief were all the covering she needed. She perched on the poolside. Her lean and graceful muscles tightened in anticipation of diving and then she momentarily arched through the air before crashing through the water's surface. Coolness slipped in and around her crevices, electrifying her senses. Her pale skin grew rosy with energy. By scissor-kicking her legs, she escaped the trapping of her panties and allowed the water's movement to free her body. Diving through the watery silence, she retrieved the two beer bottles and broke through the surface, eyes closed, hands reaching above her into the night.

Clara often forgot to play, but now she did so without thinking. She climbed out of the pool and began to spin in circles, arms extended from her sides, blond tendrils floating towards the stars. Her toes gripped the slate patio leaving wet prints in their wake. Eventually, she wandered out on to the grass. The moon glowed, illuminating her young fresh skin. For a moment, she was Aphrodite, a goddess dancing alone. When she grew too dizzy to stand, she collapsed and hummed old Beatles songs to herself, pulling grass up from the ground in handfuls, stretching her legs above her body, wriggling her toes, and smiling to herself.

Finally, she lay quietly, on her side with her knees pulled tightly into her chest, watching the porch lights dance with the trees. Clara had never quite understood the celebration of a death, but naked in the grass, her scent and her sexuality meshing with the earth, she celebrated her womanhood and Sissy, by living.

She knew he had watched her for a longer amount of time than he would ever admit. When the sky began to lighten, Artie appeared above her, alone. His eyes sparkled with wonder, but his cheeks were puffy with sadness. Clara sat up and pulled her knees into her chest trying to cover herself. He stood in front of her without speaking. After a few minutes, she stood up, hands by her sides, and walked inside, leaving Artie and her clothes by the pool.

FIVE

Michael walked slowly through the living room, careful not to look back over his shoulder. When he cleared the door, his pace quickened. He took the stairs two at a time and covered his ears to avoid the giggles and sickening noises slipping out from under his parent's bedroom door. When he reached the bathroom at the end of the hall, he shut the door, turned on the shower, pushed his fully clothed body against the wall in front of the toilet, closed his eyes, and sank down to the floor. Being around them made him sick.

For as long as he cared to remember, Michael had defended his family, even though he found them as bizarre as everyone else did. When he was twelve, his parents threw him a birthday party and invited his classmates as well as their own friends. The kids ran around playing kick the can or something, while the adults got snockered. At some point after the sun went down, Michael and two of his friends walked into the living room. Sissy and Cliff were asleep on the couch. Cliff was sitting up, neck drooped against the cushion, Sissy's head lying in his lap and his fingers all twisted in her hair. Michael would have just kept moving, avoiding the sight altogether, but his friend whispered, "Do they always sleep like that?" Michael shrugged, and his friend followed with, "Does your Mom know?"

After that instance, Michael began to notice that his father's interactions with Sissy were too nice. He was too cuddly with her. He always had his arm around her or was kissing her forehead. As Michael got older things only got worse. Artie became the golden boy. He could do no wrong. When Artie got busted in his freshman year of high school for getting high on school grounds, not only Sissy, but his own parents laughed it off. Artists will be artists they said. If he got busted it would have been a completely different story. And then there was Clara and her years of idolizing Sissy and constant doe-eyed subservience to Artie's every wish. The whole thing made his skin crawl.

It wasn't that he didn't love them. Individually, they were the best. Artie was the coolest kid he knew. The four years between them had never been an issue, even when Artie was seven he was cooler then Michael's other eleven-year-old friends. Clara always made him smile. They had a classic cat and mouse/big brother-little sister relationship, and he loved it. As long as Sissy wasn't around, his parents were relatively normal, supportive parents. His mother more so than his dad, but not so much more so. He didn't like Sissy the way everyone else did, but he tolerated her, and he felt sad that she was dead. It wasn't a genuine sad. He was sad for Artie and Clara. He was sad for his parents.

He wouldn't miss explaining her to people. Since he started at Princeton, he just lied. When people looked at photographs of his family Sissy became his father's sister. Enough said.

Michael rubbed his eyes, and then dragged his hand up his forehead and through his hair. The steam from the shower sat heavy in the air. He stood up and wiped the mirror with his fingers, creating clawed streaks of clarity across the glass. Leaning his hands against the sink, he bent forward and looked closely at his face. He was handsome, all-American, good ole boy-handsome. He could be a president's son;

a clean-cut, khakis, golf shirt, athletic, kind of a kid. His hair was curly and dust colored, like his father, and he had deep brown eyes that were as symmetrical as the two sides of a scallop shell.

Years ago, *Time Magazine* published an article on the sexual appeal of symmetry. Supposedly, natural instinct drove both women and men towards mates whose bodies and features lined up the best. Symmetry served as some sort of external code for healthy genetics. Michael prided himself on his symmetry. And at Princeton it had served him well.

Besides being symmetrical, Katie Worthington, Michael's girlfriend, was wealthy, smart, and gorgeous. Michael spotted her from his dorm room window during freshman orientation. She was standing outside the building talking to a guy that lived down the hall from him. 5'7"ish, long legs, blond-bangs, short denim skirt with a pink cloth belt, and a red Ralph Lauren golf shirt with a pink polo player. She was hot, as only a Catholic schoolgirl could be. Your average, unsymmetrical eighteen-year-old, might have hoped to see her again, and left it at that. As it turned out, Michael definitely would have run into her because they were in the same English class and they both played tennis, but Michael wasn't average, and he wasn't unsymmetrical. He didn't take chances. He walked downstairs, opened the door, busted between the two, and said, "You're fucking gorgeous. Are you smart too?"

She tilted her head slightly to the left, almost smiled and said, "No, but I look better naked."

Sold! To the preppy kid with the freaky family! He hadn't so much as laid eyes on a girl since. For the record, she was smarter than she was hot, and she was smokin' hot.

Katie's family was not the product of American dreams. You could trace her money all the way back to the mother ship. Michael wasn't even sure if his family came from the same species. How do you tell your incredibly preppy, my father is twelfth generation Princeton legacy, and belongs to some hoity-toity country club, girlfriend that your family includes a fanciful free-loader and her son? You don't. Well, at least he didn't. In their two years of courting, meeting her family for brunch, making out in the library, falling in love and sharing their lives, Michael had never once told Katie about Sissy. He never even told her that Artie grew up on their property.

Sometimes, while they were driving in the car, Katie would hint that she wanted to meet his family. She would suggest that they go to Santa Fe for Thanksgiving or Christmas or maybe she could visit him over the summer, rather than him visiting her. Although he maintained a peaceful exterior, and consistently thwarted her suggestions, internally he was tortured because eventually she would have to meet them and he would lose her.

And then, his mother called. Sissy died, and he felt relieved.

Michael wiped his hand across the mirror again. He had dark circles under his eyes and his mouth felt pasty. He was going to throw up. He didn't remember drinking all that much, but it had been a long day. He knelt down by the toilet and rested his cheek on the seat.

SIX

Cliff's entire body burned with anticipation as he chased Liz's ankles up the stairs, but after a few minutes behind the barrier of their bedroom door, everything soured. At first they pulled hungrily at each other's clothes. Cliff's fingertips tingled with cool vibrations as they landed on her skin and his breath quickly grew thick and wet as though he were expelling the heavy humidity that hung in the summer air. Liz's passion was almost as intense. She nibbled fiercely at his lips and clawed her fingers through his hair.

By force of habit Cliff broke from her embrace, turned on the television and pumped up the volume to drown out the anticipated pounding of bed springs and the honeyed cadence of their climactic moans. It was a tactic they had used for at least a decade to hide their love-making from the children. Years ago the lack of spontaneity tortured Cliff, but now he hardly remembered what it was like to touch Liz without the drone of a news anchor somewhere over his shoulder. He had grown to embrace the comfort of their routine and saw no reason to stray from it, but in the few seconds that it took him to turn on the T.V., Liz's passion slipped away. Cliff didn't know he could lose her attention that quickly.

With the sound of the television billowing all around them, Cliff tried to return to his desires as though the page had not turned, but Liz was no longer facing him. He pawed at her hips from behind, pulling her to him, and dropped his lips to the curve of her neck, waiting for the sweet hum that originated in the back of her throat and the gentle release of the tension in her shoulders. Instead, Liz's shoulders inched higher, repelling his advances, and she said, "Cliff, stop." Undeterred, he slid his hand up over her hip and continued to gently nibble at her ears.

"Stop what?" He asked teasingly. Liz stepped away from his grasp, swatting her hands at his kisses.

"I mean it. Cut it out. I'm...I don't know. I can't." Liz's hands fluttered to her face, her shoulders curved, and the muscles in her back expanded and retracted with gentle sobbing. The emotional change was too sudden for Cliff to comprehend and the only thing he could think to feel was anger. The heat of his stunted desire flashed beneath his skin, and the air in the room felt thin. Instinctually, he clenched his teeth and dropped his arms to his sides, fists knotted.

He focused his attention on the little burp of freckled tan flesh created by Liz's bra strap and tried not to breathe. Liz didn't turn. She just stood there broken, the sound of her sobs clawing at his nerves like CDs skipping. He wanted to unplug her, reboot the whole system. He thought about opening the window, sticking his head out into the night and conjuring a fierce primal roar from somewhere deep in his intestines. He wanted to punch something, push it over and claw at its eyes until there was only blindness, but instead he stood still, feeling shackled and trapped. If he had been a cartoon his anger's impotence would whistle white puffs of steam from his ears.

Liz rocked forward and back on the heels of her feet and her sobbing quieted to a tight airy whimper that resonated with pain. It was almost as though she were silently screaming, a guttural noise, as if she were trying to shed her skin. It made Cliff think of women in darkness, forcefully pinned to the ground, the ripple of crow's feet when their eyes pinched in fear, the shearing sound of their torn skirts hiked, unwilling, above their knees, and finally, the soiled smell of their rapist's hatred, his lust. Like the reluctant beckoning of church bells on a spring morning, the horror of Liz's pain pulled Cliff away from his own selfishness and as quickly as his anger had risen it disintegrated. Stepping forward, he grasped Liz's shoulder and turned her so she was facing him. Her face was splotchy and she looked almost skeletal. At the sight of her pain, Cliff's insides grew solid and cold, and his own hurt began to pool beneath his breast bone. He pulled her into his embrace, trying to fill her with warmth and give her a sense of safety, but grief quickly made his arms weak, and within seconds, he found he could hardly stand.

Pulling Liz onto his lap, he collapsed on the bed. He nuzzled his face into the curve of her neck, circled his arms tightly around her, crushing her body into his and allowed a few of his own tears to escape. They stayed like that for only a few moments before Liz jumped up cursing.

"I can't fucking do this. I can't sit around and cry, like a baby." She shook her hands in front of her body, like Fosse jazz fingers. "You can just sit there and let me cry, when you know what I promised her?"

For the second time in moments, Liz's manic behavior startled Cliff. She flung her words at him, and he was inclined to block them like punches, raise his hands to cover his face, maybe stop, drop and roll. He felt as if his spirit stood up with her, as though he had lent her his soul for strength and she was whipping him with it. He sat half-naked and motionless, absorbing her unhappiness, feeling it blister. Her anger prickled his pores and suffocated his muscles. He watched the fire behind Liz's eyes surge.

"Say something, God damn it." She screamed inches from his face.

He tried to wake his vocal cords, but they shattered in his throat and all he could do was swallow the thick sour spit that had begun to collect around his gums. Liz's lower lip twitched and she pressed her fingers against her scalp, forcefully pushing her hair from her eyes.

"You're no help." She wiped snot from her nose with the back of her hand. "You can sit there and cry, but I won't. I promised we wouldn't, and I won't." Cliff reached in her direction, but she pulled away from him and stormed into their bathroom, slamming the door behind her. Outside the bathroom, Cliff pressed his palms against the door, waiting and listening. When only silence ensued, he rested his ear against the wood and called out to her.

"Liz, baby, are you okay?" She didn't answer. "I love you. I was just startled. I was...Liz, come out and talk to me, please." It was all he could do to keep from crying. The rush of the bathwater echoed from behind the door. Cliff sank to the floor. "I need you," he whispered. He couldn't stand. Instead, he scraped at the carpet with his fingernails and remembered sitting on the soccer field in high school pulling up clumps of grass. When she turned off the water, he didn't try to speak to her again, but he kept his ear pressed to the door, listening to the little ripples of water as she settled into the bath.

Dealing with Liz's emotions was beyond him. Liz was dramatic from the moment he met her. When they were young he mastered a steady quiet gaze that seemed to settle down her fire. He remembered saying, "Trust your instincts" a lot. He also remembered screaming brawls, but that was a long time ago. He thought she had grown beyond furious emotional outbursts, but it occurred to him that for at least a decade, he had resigned his post as her supportive confidant and allowed Sissy to carry the responsibility. Finding the forgotten balance of their early camaraderie would take work.

He figured that if he waited long enough she would come out, wrapped in a towel, and they would curl into each other and fall asleep, protected by the bond that had kept them together all these years. After about an hour he heard the hollow suction of the drain. He stood and stepped back from the door, waiting to embrace her, maybe apologize. He was patient, but she didn't come. He pictured her smoothing cream over her skin, cutting her toenails, tweezing her eyebrows, and still she didn't come. He moved to the end of the bed and sat down facing the door. He listened carefully and after a while he heard the slip of her feet against the porcelain tub and then to his surprise, the thunderous rush of the bathwater began again. All hope of curling up next to his wife slipped between his fingers and pooled around the drain at the bottom of the tub. Defeated, Cliff lifted his feet up and let his head fall to the pillow. He watched the closed door closely, letting the patterns of the wood grain come to life in his head, and finally without ever being aware of his utter exhaustion, his eyes dropped and he was overcome by sleep.

In the morning when he opened his eyes again, the bathroom door stood open, but the space in the bed next to him remained unruffled.

SEVEN

At dawn Artie was still sitting on his front stoop. The celebration had been forced for him, but he put on a good show. He danced, laughed and drank. Sometime around dusk, he and Liz lit sparklers and drew the word Sissy in the darkness with the sparks. For hours he kept seeing the glowing letters. Her whole name popped and snapped in front of his eyes, as though the tip of his sparkler had singed fiery burnt cursive into the empty air. Consciously, he knew there was nothing there, but the mere figment of the blazing letters made his skin feel too tight, and if he turned his head too quickly a faint hint of the sparkler's metallic burn wafted in his direction. All and all, the night was a blur of nauseous make-believe.

He attempted to avoid the seeping misery by focusing on Hailey Stuart, a young woman who had spent the entire night making it perfectly clear that she wanted him, bad. Hailey was tall, thin, popular, what his mom would have called a real-looker. She also would have called her either a spineless-slave of the American fashion magazine or a designer carrying case for a humming bird's brains, and truth be told, Artie would have found it easy enough to over look her lackluster attributes on any other day, but on this night her insipid nonsense was hard to ignore.

Initially, he figured the gods or god or the great punani owed him one, and maybe the heavens had decided to make his mother's funeral celebration bearable by giving the gift of a free, although ever so flighty, piece of ass. If not, at least her presence made onlookers believe he was having a good time. Artie danced with her, her hot sticky breath pressed against his ear, whispering all the sexual feats she could conjure in that unimaginative mind of hers, and when he couldn't stand to listen anymore, he suggested they sit.

They sat at a small glass table at the far end of the pool, looking back at the house. Within seconds of pressing their spines against the water resistant fabric of the outdoor furniture, Hailey began a vomitous rhythm of conversation that required a continuous stream of verbiage from her and the mere appearance of attention from Artie. Hailey covered the full gamut of frivolous and completely expendable conversation: the current status of so-and so's relationship, (with so-and so's identity ranging from those with whom she was actually familiar to famous actors and actresses, with whom she felt familiar;) or the great deal she got on a blouse just the other day and the ugly pumps a friend bought at the same time.

Artie lost track of her words quickly, but the sound of her voice rumbled in circles around his head, keeping him anchored to the velvety pleasantness he had plastered to his face. He used the cadence of her voice to dissolve his own thoughts, like a mantra. He focused on the movement of the sound waves as they entered his ears, and he imagined how they bounced through the darkness of the ear canal, until they finally cascaded, slipping and sliding like a speed skater gone out of control into the soft fleshy give of his ear drum. He pictured the small vibrations that they created and the signals that they triggered in his nerves. He followed those signals to the soggy black hole that symbolized the center of his brain. He imagined that when these signals reached that imaginary core of his emotional state, they would explode, obliterating his own thoughts and leaving a peaceful emptiness behind.

He stayed like that for a while, completely blanketed in the nothingness. When Hailey put her hand on his knee, stirring his mind from empty, and saying, "You want one?" he was startled to see her. Her lips looked waxy and unfamiliar pulling across her teeth and her appeal melted before his eyes, becoming uninspiring. He imagined she was a live version of Mrs. Potato Head, there was some excitement found in her interchangeable parts, but in the end that was all she was made of, colorful plastic parts. Blankly, Artie stared at her big blue and white googlie eyes.

"You want one too?" She asked again. He twitched his head, shaking his brain free from the trance like state.

"I'm sorry. What?"

"A Beer. Do you want one?" She lifted her eyebrows, like duh.

"Uhh. I guess. Sure." As she walked away Artie looked past her swinging hips and rested his eyes on Clara. She was lying on the chaise by the door leading into the house. She had wrapped her fingers so tightly around the metal rim of the chair that her knuckles turned white. Her eyes were closed, but they flittered quickly beneath her lids as though they might burst at any minute. Other than the motion of her eyes, the expression on her face was bland, flat and colorless, similar to overcooked vegetables. Like him, she appeared to have adopted a state of un-feeling, a state that rested somewhere close to sadness and nestled deep into the armpit of avoidance, but on the surface appeared more like indifference.

Michael leaned on a wall a few feet behind her, running his fingers through his hair over and over again. His eyes darted back and forth either with impatience or fear and discomfort. Thick dark circles spread out from Michael's nose, circling low and then turning up again towards his temples. His shoulders hunched forward and he dropped his weight deeply into his knees. Just looking at him had made Artie's tongue grow thick with exhaustion.

Artie did not really say a word to either Michael or Clara all night. Michael had tried to talk to him a few times. He wanted to offer his support. Give Artie a shoulder to lean on. Michael could never understand how inappropriate normal consoling was in this situation. Artie had been force-fed his mother's "Celebrate life" mumbo-jumbo for as long as he could remember. In honor of her and everything she wanted her friends and family to believe about her choices, he would do his best to brush off all offers of sympathy, even though he knew that secretly she hadn't always been a successful celebrator herself. He remembered hardly a night when the light whimpering sounds of his mother's tears had not drifted down through the floorboards and rocked him to sleep, but it didn't matter. He believed the saying should have been perception is 9/10ths, instead of possession, and therefore, talking to Michael was out of the question.

Clara was a completely different story. Artie was fairly certain that she had done her best to avoid him all night, and he had done the same. The sadness behind Clara's eyes was too much for him to bear. If he was going to honor his mother's theory and celebrate her life, then he certainly couldn't recognize his own true feelings and that was exactly what was hiding behind Clara's wilted spinach look. Just seeing how she gripped that chair, he felt her concentrating on constructing impenetrable walls around her sorrow, and when he closed his eyes, he could hear the shrill sound of nails pounding through metal, closing off his own feelings.

It was too much to even look in her direction, so Artie turned his eyes away, focusing on the table top in front of him. The glass was coated in the dewy wetness of the late night hours. He pressed his finger down on the damp surface and drew the smooth opposing curves of an "S." The thick puckering sound that accompanied the movement reminded Artie of long car rides. The three kids used to spend hours torturing Liz, Cliff and his mom from the backseat. They repeatedly blew raspberries and created that snapping sound by curling their lips over their teeth and then popping them together. Before Sissy got sick, the three of them still behaved that way, playing like children, pulling each other's hair, passing the blame for smelly farts, stealing each other's possessions, and reading each other's secrets. Artie was unsure whether that light-hearted banter would ever feel natural again. He closed his eyes and pressed his tongue against the roof of his mouth. His ribs felt tight and heavy, and he could feel the cool current of fear in his fingers. He knew he had to get away before he started to lose his cool.

Slowly, he moved to stand. He was unsure where he was going, and he wanted to slip away without being noticed, but before he could so much as clear the chair, Hailey returned. She placed the two glass bottles on the table in front of him. She had already sipped from hers and the greasy pink smudge of her lipstick circled the beer bottle's glass neck, reminding him of the first time he got a blowjob, which in turn got him thinking about popsicles

He remembered watching a purple sugary stream running from the end of the grape popsicle down over his thumb, and he remembered his mom pulling a napkin from her pocket or her purse and wiping his arm, his wrist, his fingers and lips, without even pausing her conversation. It was a moment out of the movie of his mind, filmed from his point of view as a child. All the people he remembered were legs and waists, with the exception of her face bending down into the frame, talking about things he didn't understand and gently cleaning his sticky spots. He wondered how old he was when she stopped carrying napkins or if she ever stopped carrying them. He had an urge to shift through her closet looking for crumpled tissues. Hailey closed in on him, sensing his imminent departure.

"Where were you going?" she asked.

"Oh. Well...Um..." No where, he thought, knowing he was trapped. "I was thinking I might take a walk out to the arroyo behind my house," he looked down at his hands, and then settled into his seat again, "but maybe not. It was a stupid idea." Hailey, who looked just a little more drunk than when she left, abruptly sat sideways in his lap and put her arms around his neck.

"A walk sounds like a good idea to me."

Walking with Hailey was not what he'd hoped for, but he didn't really know how to turn her down. So, she walked out into the arroyo with him, kissing his neck and his ears, pushing her hands into his pants. When he didn't respond, she pressed herself against him and pushed his hand up under her shirt. He felt the stiff rise of her nipple beneath the fabric of her bra, but his body remained unaware of her. He couldn't feel anything. His mouth was bitter, and he kept choking on the dust and the smell of pine in the air. She said she understood, but she assumed that the distraught look that was slowly overtaking his face was a result of his little guy's lack of performance.

"Artie, don't be upset, I mean your mom...well, you know." He knew. But he wondered how she could be so stupid. He couldn't stand her presence a minute longer. He tried to be pleasant, but it didn't work out that way.

"Let me walk you to your car," he said.

"I can stay here with you." He didn't want her there. He needed someone who understood him, someone who loved him, someone who he could stand to listen too, someone he cared for. He wanted Clara, not some stupid ditz with hot pink lipstick.

"No," he watched Hailey's eyes pull back, "you should go, Hailey. You need to go." She took her hand from his knee.

"I can walk back on my own," she said. Normally, he might have tried to make her feel better, but in that moment he didn't see any reason why he should.

He sat out by the arroyo most of the night, listening to the coyotes howl and scratching his fingers through the dirt. He wanted so much to go to Clara. He wanted to fall to his knees and wrap his arms around her legs and hang on to her and cry. But they were celebrating, so he sat by himself and cried, in the dark, alone. He knew Clara was the only person who loved his mother the way he did. The only person who loved him the way his mother did. He didn't think he'd been thinking of her in any other way, but now he didn't know.

He sat in the dark out by the arroyo until condensation started to form on his skin, and then he walked slowly back, paying no heed to the branches and the shrubs that scratched at his legs. He approached the house from behind and when the light from his living room shone on his skin, he noticed the blood and dirt pasted to his leg hairs. He decided to just jump in the pool. He walked around the side of the house, and hidden in its shadows, he saw her. He hadn't meant to watch her. She was so light and free. For what seemed like hours, he stood in the shadows of the house that her father had built for him, watching. When she curled in the grass, he couldn't hide his tears or his lust from her anymore.

He had just stood there, unable to speak. She looked up at him with such understanding, and for a second he thought she was going to put her arms around him, crush her small naked body against his chest. His hands anticipated encircling the smooth damp skin. His nose was already filled with the chlorine in her hair. He stood perfectly still and waited. She looked right at him and then through him, and suddenly, she was gone. He was left wanting to fall into her, to crawl up inside her and hide in her strength. And now, even with the sun high over his head and signs of stirring life in the big house across the way, he still couldn't bring himself to stand upright, peel his eyes from her window sill and go inside to bed.

EIGHT

In the morning Elizabeth pushed in the lock and turned the knob, but she waited before opening the bathroom door. She was sure Cliff would be sleeping, but she was uncertain where he chose to pass out. She pictured him lying on the floor between their two closets. She pressed her ear to the door, feeling the cool wood against her face, listening for raspy breathing. Nothing. Slowly she inched the door towards her hoping he wasn't about to fall backwards at her feet. He wasn't there. She tip-toed into the bedroom, and found him snoring on the bed, his back to her, still wearing only his pants from the night before, and hugging tightly to the pillow where her head should have been. She had no intention of waking him, but she stayed standing by his feet for a few minutes wondering what she would say if he suddenly awoke.

She wouldn't be able to say she was sorry for the way she had acted the night before. She wasn't really sorry. She kept picturing the shock on his face when she opened her anger and began hollering at him. Instead of feeling guilty, she felt sparks of joy. Making him suffer made her feel better. It made her feel strong and empowered like she would be able to keep her promise after all, like she was a dark ancient tree with a thousand lush limbs swooping and bending to protect scared little brown and white bunnies from a tornado.

Cliff gurgled and rolled over on his back, throwing one arm behind his head. His face was placid with sleep, but he still clung tightly to the pillow, the fingers of that one hand curled with tension, like a hawk gripping its prey. Elizabeth could smell him from where she stood. His odor was oily and salty, like kosher chicken soup. There were times in her life when she found his scent erotic. Times when she had buried her nose in his armpit, the fine soft hairs tickling her upper lip, but at that moment thinking about the intensity of his smell was rank and dirty. It was masculine and hard, like aggression. She couldn't look at him anymore, and the thought of hearing his voice made phlegm gather behind her tongue.

Rather than trying to quietly pull clothes from her closet, she trudged downstairs to the laundry room and made do with what was recently clean or waiting to be cleaned. Most of the clean laundry belonged to Clara. Yes, her teenage daughter's clothes fit her, but she felt foolish in them, like heels on the morning after a drunken stupor, so she settled on a pair of dirty jeans and a white undershirt that could have belonged to any one of the men in her house.

Before rushing out the door, she paused, noticing Artie sitting on his front stoop. She could tell he had been sitting there for hours, and she didn't have the courage to engage him on her way to the car. She considered pretending she didn't see him as she passed, but she knew there was no way to do that without looking frenzied or upset, and her promise entailed a façade of complete and utter happiness. Instead she stood, leaning against the kitchen sink, hoping she could telekinetically will him to stand and go inside before Cliff woke. He looked so little squatted in front of the house Cliff had built for Sissy all those years ago.

In flashes, Liz remembered Cliff, shirtless and sweaty, dirt on his face. Between Sissy, him, and the guys from work, they had the place built before Artie was born. They all had nothing then. It was that little high ceiling-ed adobe in her backyard that had gained Cliff his acclaim as a builder and an architect, but they built it because they had to. Sissy had nowhere else to go, and they wanted her and her little child with them. Her presence woke them, stirred them from the mesmerizing monotony of their routine.

Liz put her head in her hands and tried to focus. She walked over to the cabinet and poured herself a drink. She didn't care that it was the morning. Clara wouldn't be up for at least a few hours, and she didn't care if Cliff found her drinking. She wouldn't take the time to ask whether he understood. She might even enjoy the shock on his face. She would do anything necessary to appear happy and he could just deal. They were happy when Sissy first came into their lives and they could be happy now.

They met Sissy and Robert at a campsite outside of Salt Lake City, Utah. She and Cliff had taken two weeks off from work and decided to drive around the southwest, following their whims and enjoying each other's company. She was still a full-time nurse. Michael wasn't even born yet. In fact, she believed Michael was conceived on that trip, in the car behind a 7-11, the night before she met Sissy. It could have been earlier that week or in their tent later that night, but she always felt like it was in the car. She just felt him rise up inside her as they were pulling back on to the freeway.

The following morning Liz saw Sissy for the first time. Robert had gone off somewhere, and Sissy was sitting on a piece of wood next to a smoldering campfire, eating a peanut butter and jelly sandwich on Wonder bread. It was a mess. There was too much jelly and peanut butter filling and blobs of both were all around her. Liz watched her lick peanut butter off her fingers and smiled. Sissy, bright and vivid, waved, beckoning for her to come say hello.

"Hi," Sissy wiped her hand on her pant leg and poked it forward. Liz hesitated before shaking her sticky fingers, but her smile was so open and genuine that she decided it was worth the risk. "Sissy Wallace."

"Lizzy Gordon. Nice to meet you."

"Where ya from?"

"Santa Fe, New Mexico. You?"

"Nowhere really, at least not yet." She threw her head back and laughed. Liz could see little bits of peanut in her teeth. "I grew up in Connecticut, but I'm not from there anymore." She lifted her eyebrows and the jar of Skippy at the same time. "Peanut Butter and Jelly?" She offered.

"No thanks, I'm going to make breakfast as soon as my husband wakes up."

"You don't happen to be making coffee in that coffee pot you've got?"

"I was thinking I might. Why, you want some?"

"Well, no, but I have some great tea bags. If you want to heat up some water, we could have a cup of tea together."

"I could do that."

The rumble of a car made them both turn their heads. A cream-colored dodge truck with rust around the tires slowed and turned in their direction. The truck's roar made Elizabeth pull her wool cardigan tighter around her chest. A man, who turned out to be Robert, climbed out from behind the wheel. Elizabeth shivered at his rustic good looks. He walked casually, but with intent, in Sissy's direction. Kneeling down so he and Sissy were knee to knee, he smiled and leaned in like he was going to kiss her, but instead he attacked her right hand and gobbled up the last bit of her sandwich. Sissy squealed and giggled and then the two finally kissed.

And kissed, like they were alone, like the world had stopped, without shame. Even thinking about that kiss now made Elizabeth flush with embarrassment. Finally Robert lost his balance and fell into the dirt. He looked like a spider, his fingers stretched wide to support his weight, and his limbs sprawled out around him. Sissy just stood up and said, "Robert, this is Lizzy. We were just about to have some tea." He smiled, crawled to his feet, and nodded in Elizabeth's direction. As they approached Elizabeth's campsite, Cliff emerged from their tent, dusting his knees, his hair wet with sweat and in disarray from sleeping. There were some basic introductions, nothing to speak of.

Liz remembered they all got along well. They laughed and talked all day, but the details of their conversation had become a blur. By late afternoon they were all a little giddy from their day in the sun. The two men went off in Sissy and Robert's truck to get some beer, and the women stayed behind with the intention of making dinner, but Sissy had a different idea. She decided that they should swim.

"I'll race you there," she bellowed as she took off.

They ran down to the lake, untying their sneakers and hollering to each other. The water was murky and brown, but Sissy flew right in, splashing everything around her. They had fun. They held their noses and covered their bodies in mud. They played patty-cake like little girls. The density of the salt water made them weightless. It was freeing. Elizabeth drifted back and forth, gliding on the surface. She raised her arms above her head, her hands touching, prayer-like. She drifted and cut through the water, a sailboat, stiff and perfectly formed. Together they stretched out on the gravel beach and let the water lick their toes. The sun crystallized the salt on their skin and made them glitter. It was a magical moment. Liz loved her then. She was taken with her infectious freedom.

That night they all got drunk. They roasted marshmallows, savoring their sweet stickiness, and laughed. The campfire crackled and snapped as though it was dancing. Elizabeth watched it, mesmerized by its grace. Early in the evening Robert placed his head in Sissy's lap and fell asleep, and Elizabeth spent most of the night listening to Cliff and Sissy talk. She was lying next to them, her blonde hair in the dirt and her feet resting on Cliff's knee.

Cliff watched over them both all these years, kept them safe. He loved Sissy almost as much as Liz did. Liz was not jealous of their relationship. Friends wanted her to be uncomfortable. They questioned her indifference. They shook their heads and said she was foolish, that the love in Cliff's eyes was more than she imagined, or that the way he danced with Sissy was inappropriate. She chose not to get uneasy when they went off on one of their tangents. She knew that her love for Sissy was the same or greater than her love for Cliff, so why couldn't his love for Sissy be as powerful as his love for her without the intrusion of lust? If they had ever stumbled in those woods, it was a moment better left behind. She decided Sissy and Cliff were like siblings. They moved through the world in similar rhythms, which was why she loved them both.

When they left the campsite the next morning Elizabeth's stomach was knotted with desperation. She forced Cliff to linger a few extra hours, trying to think what she could do to impress Sissy enough that she would remember them but when they pulled away. She was certain she would never hear from Sissy again, but when they got home from their vacation there was already a postcard. It wasn't much. Just a picture of the Grand Canyon and a bit of scribble, but then Sissy started to send one every week, and eventually the postcards turned into long endless letters addressed to, *Elizabeth & Cliff, our family* and signed *Love, Sissy - P.S. Robert says, "Hi."* Robert never did say much.

It was about three and a half years later that Sissy wrote to say she and Robert might show up in Santa Fe, so look out for them. Elizabeth was so excited. She wanted so much for Sissy to see Clara's fresh, little newness. She thought that the feel of a delicious new baby might make Sissy want to slow down, stay for a while, or maybe, get married. She prayed that maybe they would love Santa Fe, like she and Cliff had, that maybe the land of enchantment would cast its spell, trap them in its net and they would stay. They came and they stayed for a while. And then Liz got her wish, but she never meant for Robert to die. Cliff and Sissy knew Robert was dead the moment it happened. No one had to tell them, they just knew.

The night Robert died, Cliff's boss, Peter, invited them to a bonfire in the desert. They went out to the desert to have fun. Elizabeth remembered waving at the baby sitter and then trying to squish into the cab of Cliff's truck, but her hips were just a fraction too wide, and she couldn't shut the door. Robert hoisted her up on to his lap and said something silly like, "Come here mama and sit on my lap." They laughed and Liz blushed.

It was so dark; there was no moon. The bonfire flashed, only allowing Elizabeth's eyes to see bits and pieces of what was going on around her. Everything felt hurried and perverted. Elizabeth hated it. She hated that grotesque flaming monster, climbing higher and higher, trying to seduce her, groping her thoughts, radiating with danger. She fought it like a living beast, avoiding its gaze. She saw Sissy on one side of the flames. She looked so small and fragile. Cliff was only a few feet from her, laughing, holding a beer in his hand. Elizabeth tried to keep her eyes on them. They were her quilt of safety. She was certain nothing could happen to her as long as they were both there.

When Sissy rose to her feet, Elizabeth thought she was coming to save her. She thought Sissy could hear the discomfort ringing in her ears. But Sissy just stood, looking past the flames in the other direction. Someone was playing a guitar and it stopped. Elizabeth turned her head to see what had caught Sissy's attention, and suddenly the flames slowed their pace and seemed to flash to the rhythm of Elizabeth's breathing.

She could see him, lying just beyond the mangled bike. He looked fine, almost smiling. His head was lying flat against the ground, and his eyes were looking right in her direction. Peter ran to his side and placed two fingers on his neck. Sissy held her ground and Cliff walked over and allowed her to fall into his arms.

Elizabeth didn't give up quite as easily. She waited. She believed Peter was going to say, someone call an ambulance, but he didn't. He just took those same two fingers and closed Robert's eyes. Okay, she had thought to herself, he's dead. The horror of it just seemed to drift above her head. She could only think of the practicalities. In those few moments, she knew Sissy would stay with them, and when Sissy realized she was pregnant she agreed to stay. What else could she do? She had no skills. It was just the way it was meant to be.

Elizabeth always wondered why Sissy loved Robert so much. Not that she had ever wanted anything to happen to him, but he was always such a punk. He never slowed down, never stopped to consider how his actions might affect others. Through all the years Sissy never even dated another man. Elizabeth had dug up some mighty interesting prospects. For instance, Roy Gibler, a dermatologist who had quite a witty sense of humor. Elizabeth invited him over for dinner a million times, but Sissy was so stubborn. She would smile and say hello and then go out back to drink beer and joke around with the kids, leaving Elizabeth to entertain Roy because Lord knows Cliff snuck out of there long before Sissy.

For eighteen years they had been a family. Three kids, a million diapers, endless dirty socks, and many broken dishes later, Elizabeth was sitting at her kitchen table at five-thirty in the morning drinking Scotch alone and Sissy was dead.

As if he had heard Liz complete the cycle of her inner monologue, Artie stood. He put his hands on his hips and looked longingly in the direction of the house. Liz wondered what was so captivating, perhaps a flock of birds or the last pink hues of the sunrise. There was nothing melancholy about his body language. His face looked more focused than sad. Trying to understand his behavior felt like exertion, and Liz was happy when he resigned from his thoughts, dropped his shoulders and went inside. Finally free, she took a swig of juice from the container, jotted down a note about going out for coffee, put on Clara's old beat up flip-flops, and left.

While leaving, she pictured herself leaving, felt the intensity, the dramatic flair of closing the door, the sun on the back of her shoulders as she walked the path to the car, the sentimental look on her face as she turned back towards the house. She meant to get in the car and immediately drive away, finalizing the seriousness of her departure, but when she shut the car door, there was a part of her that thought she might never go back again. She looked over her shoulder at the house. She counted all the windows she could see from the car and pictured the bodies behind them, sleeping in their beds. She closed her eyes and imagined kissing each forehead, Michael's, smooth olive skin bordered by dark hair; Clara's, creased ridges of anxiety; and Cliff's, tan, thick and more porous with age. Sadness or sentimentality pulsed behind her eyes, making her nose feel cold. Elizabeth rolled her lips in, covering her teeth, and then bit down, allowing the dull ache to stay her tears. Without looking back, she put the car in reverse.

She wasn't certain where she should go. She drove down Old Pecos Trail, but turned off into the hills before she got to town. The sputter of dirt and gravel under the tires felt more familiar than the smooth vibration of asphalt. She passed a few houses that either belonged to friends or had once belonged to friends. She passed a brilliant blue fence that reminded her of the blanket Michael had toted around for the first three years of his life, until he finally flushed the last few threads down the toilet by mistake. She passed the road that lead to Santa Fe Prep and wondered for the thousandth time if she should have sent her children there, and she passed about twelve stop signs without slowing down, until she was at the one on the corner across from Downtown Subscription. An influx of traffic forced her to stop. Downtown Subscription was an unusually popular coffee shop that carried every magazine anyone ever dreamed of, strong good coffee and a small assortment of pastries that came with great raspberry jam and cream cheese, if so desired.

Elizabeth couldn't believe how many people were already sitting outside drinking coffee and flipping pages. It was early still, not even seven. It was so crowded that one young man with long violet dread-locks was reading sprawled on the brick sidewalk. Melting into the anonymous crowd appealed to her, so Liz pulled into the parking lot. Much like the table space, parking was limited. After waiting, hope-fully, for about ten minutes, she pulled the car half onto the sidewalk, and thought, *go ahead copper, give me a ticket, see if I care.* She grabbed her purse off the passenger seat and slammed the door behind her, enjoying the rattling metal as it snapped shut. When she got a few feet from the entrance, Liz looked back at the car, deciding it was okay. People can walk around it, she thought. Deep down she knew if a space opened up while she was there, she would jump up and move the car.

When she got inside the crowd appeared to be thinning. There were only two people in line. Liz waited behind a woman wearing a floor length prairie skirt and a concha belt. The woman had fascinatingly long, unkempt blond hair. It seemed like each strand was a different color. Corn, yellow, ivory, cream, honey, a little russet a little mouse, birch, every time the light struck it, new colors appeared, like the reflective facets of a gem. Elizabeth had to control herself from taking a handful and pulling it close to her face. Years ago Sissy's hair had a similar quality, only brown, or maybe it didn't, but Liz felt like it should have.

The man who the coffee girl had been helping stepped away in a huff, and the woman in front of Elizabeth approached the counter. Elizabeth continued to watch her, waiting for her to speak.

"He was a trip, huh?" Liz couldn't see her face but she sensed the raising of her eyebrows. "Don't you just want to say, 'listen, it's just a cup of coffee, jackass."

"Tourists," said the girl, her voice dull and tired, as if she spent her entire day dealing with constant incompetence on the part of her customers. "Probably a New Yorker." The woman threw her head back and laughed. It wasn't as funny as she made it seem, but the gently sloping dips and climbs of her laughter smoothed the girl's face, forcing it to grow less vacant and Elizabeth found herself grinning.

Liz knew that Sissy would have jumped right into their conversation. She would have made the woman notice her. She would have invited her to have breakfast with them or invited them to have breakfast with her.

"Are you alone?" She'd say, leaning over the woman's table once she sat.

"Yes," the woman would have replied.

"Do you mind if we join you?" Sissy would have said, and then she'd introduce Elizabeth to the woman, and the woman would introduce herself to Elizabeth, and they'd all sit in the shade and talk over their coffee. But, Elizabeth was never like that. She couldn't just introduce herself to strangers that she found interesting, so she just stood there, feeling stunted, and watched the woman walk away.

When helping Elizabeth, the girl behind the counter was less chatty, and before Elizabeth could muster up the gumption to say something funny or at least force the girl to make eye contact, their entire interaction was over. She picked up her little tray, one chattering, bowl-sized, latte and saucer and one plain bagel, with both jam and cream cheese.

All the tables inside were full, so Elizabeth had to maneuver opening the door and carrying the tray at the same time. She was taken aback by the nervousness she felt about possibly dropping the food. She watched the chalky brown liquid slosh over the edge of the cup, as she slid one arm under the tray, cradling it like a baby, pulling it close to her body. When that didn't work, she held the tray with two hands again, and tried to push open the door with her hip, but the door was heavy, and she couldn't quite situate herself to throw her body weight into it without spilling more of the coffee. She looked around at the tables, hoping someone, watching her suffer, would catch her eyes and stand up to help. No one seemed to take notice of her predicament, and there was nowhere to place the tray down and try to hold open the door with her foot while she retrieved it. She was starting to lose all hope and thinking she might just leave without eating, when the woman with the multi-faceted blond hair pushed open the door and said, "They should have something to prop this thing open, huh?" Elizabeth was so relived that her eyes glassed over with tears. Completely embarrassed by the severity of her emotional response, she looked at the floor.

"Thank you," she said. Then she looked up and smiled even though she still felt completely defeated. The woman's eyes were silver, and she was about Liz's age. "You have no idea how glad I am that you opened that door." The woman laughed, full and heartily, like she had when she was talking to the girl behind the counter.

"It's pretty early to be having a bad day."

"I guess, yeah." Elizabeth let her eyes stray from the woman's gaze. "Happens sometimes, though."

The woman nodded, and then completely serious, in a new deeper tone that resonated with understanding, she said, "Sure does."

Outside, Elizabeth found that there were still no seats to speak of, so she started to walk to the car. She figured she could eat sitting on the hood or in the driver's seat. The woman called after her, "Hey, if you want you can sit here, with me." Elizabeth looked over her shoulder. A few minutes earlier she had been daydreaming about speaking to the woman, but now she felt overwhelmed at the prospect of talking to anyone. The woman smiled, baring slightly yellow teeth. "Come on," she waved her hand in gesture. "We don't have to talk. We can just share the table." Elizabeth nodded, and turned back, walking in the woman's direction.

"Thank you, again. I guess."

"No problem."

Elizabeth put down the tray, which left little red imprints of wood grain on her fingers. "No, it was really nice of you." The woman titled her head and squinted her eyes.

"You're not one of those subservient types, are you? 'Cause I didn't have you pegged that way, and I'm not usually one to share my space with the world's unholy opinion-less." She was funny. Liz liked her.

"Certainly not." She tried to sound very official, silly, joking official.

"Well good then. I'm Ruth." She sat and Elizabeth sat too.

"Elizabeth, but most people call me Liz."

"Am I most people?" She was straightforward in a weird and awkward way. It was almost forceful, but it fell off a little too early and wound up feeling protective, like being a mother.

"I don't know, are you?"

"Usually, not," she shook her head "by that I mean my opinions of what is beautiful or well-suited, usually differ from the opinions of those around me. I think I'll stick to Elizabeth, unless you like Liz better."

"Not really. You know 60 percent of the world's female population has a name that somehow derives from Elizabeth. At least, I heard that in a movie once."

"Really, I wonder if that has anything to do with Queen Elizabeth?"

"Maybe." Liz picked up the bowl and sipped her latte. Ruth reached across the table and broke off a piece of Liz's bagel. At first, Liz was a little shocked, and she felt her eyes widen.

"Do you mind?" Ruth asked. Elizabeth thought about it before she answered. Part of her mind kept screaming that a complete stranger reaching across the table and eating her food was absurd. She thought it was rude when Cliff or the kids did that, so a stranger violating her plate should have been ruder, but it didn't feel that way. It felt natural. Surprisingly, she was even happy to have Ruth eat from her plate.

"No," she answered, "take whatever you want."

Over the course of the day Elizabeth bought ten more bagels and sat happily talking to Ruth for hours. The conversation between them migrated and gave birth; it was alive. Ruth told her about growing up in Florida, realizing in high school that she had a special interest in her girlfriends, and more recently, swearing off relationships with the fairer sex after a particularly sticky heartbreak. "It's no different than a man," she said.

Elizabeth told Ruth all about her family, about Sissy's death and her promise. Ruth was vocal about her opinions, and she made it perfectly clear that Elizabeth's promise to Sissy didn't sit right with her, but she also seemed to understand that there was nothing Elizabeth could do about it. It was already done.

"Just don't let it cave in on you," she said.

"What do you mean?" Elizabeth asked.

"Well, you promised to be bright and cheery for your family, for your kids, but that doesn't mean you shouldn't have your own outlet."

"Like a shrink?"

"Maybe, I'm not really a shrink fan." Her voice was sarcastic. "They're always trying to get you 'in touch' with the problem," she used her index and ring fingers to symbolize the quotes around the words "in touch." "Sometimes you just need to vent, ya know? What about your husband? Why don't you talk to him?"

"No," Liz brushed off the suggestion and rolled her eyes, "Cliff is going to have trouble holding it together as it is."

"Well, how about your friends?"

"I don't know. Sissy was my girlfriend, ya know? There really is no one else I feel close to."

"That's sad."

"I think it's normal. How many really close friends do you have?"

"Point. Match," she paused, "I'll make you a deal. I'll be your friend, if you'll be mine." Elizabeth felt her eyes smiling.

"Deal."

About an hour later, Elizabeth stood and finally gathered her things to go back home. Ruth did the same. They crossed into the parking lot together, still talking. They came to Ruth's car first, and Elizabeth stood awkwardly, trying to visualize how it was best to say good-bye. She pushed the dry dirt around with the toe of her left flip-flop. Ruth was less awkward about the whole thing.

"Well, maybe I'll see you tomorrow," she said, then she spread her arms wide and crushed Elizabeth in a firm embrace. "It was a pleasure, Elizabeth."

"For me too."

Ruth backed her car out of the space and gave a little wave before pulling away. Liz waved back and stayed standing in the space until the dust from Ruth's car settled. When she was alone, Elizabeth dug through her purse for the keys and crossed the parking lot, amazed that she had completely forgotten about moving the car.

THE BIG HOUSE

They built themselves a two-story adobe home. At first, they thought they wanted something quaint, nothing lavish, but as the building progressed lavish seemed to occur. The house was big and littered with windows of all sizes. Light was their primary concern during its construction. They coerced the sun's rays by putting windows at different heights from the floor. In contrast to the light splashed walls, the dark brooding wood beams in the ceiling were exposed in classic adobe style, resulting in an intensely dramatic environment.

Outside, the gravel driveway slowed briefly by the front door, then it twisted its way on down to Sissy's house. A path of red and brown stones led visitors from their cars to the slate patio that wound around the house, and eventually led its followers to the pool. They had laid the slate themselves, armed with an aptitude for imperfection, so over the years weeds sprouted up through the unsealed crevices. They placed two worn rocking chairs on the right side of the patio and on the left side, they hung a swing from the structural beams.

The house's front door looked as though it was protecting an army. It was a heavy, oppressive slab of wood covered in black wrought iron metalwork that criss-crossed over its surface. It had once hung on the hinges of a great Arab sheik's palace, or at least that was what they told people. The doorknob was massive and always cold. More often than not the door sat open, a piece of wood driven under it, and no one ever felt unwelcome.

On the first floor there were five rooms; the living room, the kitchen, the dining room, the guest room and a bathroom. All of these, except the bathroom, were abnormally large and two of the kitchen walls were entirely glass. On the second floor, there were three bedrooms and two bathrooms. All of these rooms had skylights fixed with wood kiva ladders that allowed them to climb out onto the roof. They covered the roof in gravel, and in the summer the women donned bikinis and stretched out on its stony surface to bake their skin and offer their sun kissed images to the sky.

They didn't bother with decorative designing. They filled the house with a variety of colors, creating a space that felt clean and cozy. People hungered to visit them. In the summer the house smelled of garden-picked flowers and vegetables, and in the winter the never-ending fire burning in the living room filled the house with spicy smoke, making their clothes smell of oak. They had only the best appliances and the fullest down comforters. There was no uncomfortable place to sit and no glass you weren't welcome to sip from.

They decided most families congregated in the kitchen as night fell, so they built it to face the sunset, and in the evenings they often gathered there. Through the years, the view changed and became more complicated, but the sunset remained breathtaking.

They laughed together and drank their drinks; ice cubes rattling against their glasses as they threw their heads back and rocked with happiness. The sun slowly drifted behind the hills on the horizon and the sky lit up with the most vivid array of colors they could imagine. Bursts of red and yellow faded into pink, who whispered sweetly until purple crept up and shooed her away; then the stars and navy stirred from their hiding places, and it became night. And when night fell, they all gathered around the kitchen table and they ate.

NINE

Three months after Sissy's funeral, Liz sat in the kitchen waiting. Since Sissy died, her morning ritual had changed drastically. Sleep eluded her, so she spent most nights roaming around the house. She couldn't read or even watch T.V., so she paced, sifting through her memories, organizing and filing moments in her mind, so as not to forget them. Liz was living the life Sissy asked her to live, but it had grown to entail an empty, heartless, smile that froze her facial muscles and made her jaw ache. Right before the sun rose, when she was sure everyone else was sleeping, she locked herself in the kitchen pantry and let her jaw relax. She drank Scotch from a tumbler and stared at the cans and cereal boxes, counting the products like her life depended on it.

At 6:04 a.m. the timer on the coffee pot clicked on, replastering her so-called happiness to her face. As an actress enters a scene, she drifted from the pantry to the kitchen and began to set the table for breakfast. When the coffee was ready she poured herself half a mug full and then topped it off with the remains of her tumbler. Most days she immediately rinsed the tumbler and transferred it to the dishwasher, but occasionally, she forgot and then there was a scurry to hide the evidence before the kids appeared. She didn't hide her drinking from Cliff, so if she forgot he remembered. Every day the table was set about fifteen minutes before anyone came to breakfast.

She used those fifteen minutes to set the scene. It had to look like she had just gotten up, like she was sitting in the kitchen eating her own morning meal, only eating didn't come easily or feel natural. She made a game out of it. *What will I pretend to eat today?*, she'd think. She'd butter toast and spit two bites into the garbage pail or let a few flakes of cereal soak in a spoonful of milk at the bottom of a bowl.

Today she had chosen half a cantaloupe and some cottage cheese. She dug her spoon into the tender peach flesh four times, and dumped each bite down the disposal. Then, she strategically smeared a few cottage cheese curds into the center, watching the juice from the melon turn white. It was like art.

At 6:10, like clockwork, the sounds of Cliff waking began, first the alarm, then the shuffle to the bathroom. His feet on the floor above her were familiar, but she knew when he arrived in the kitchen his face would appear foreign and distant. He was not the same. She managed to put on a great show for the kids, all smiles and happiness, but he was half zombie all the time. Liz could hardly stand to look at him, but she was able to pretend that everything in their relationship was okay.

It wasn't hard in the mornings because when he came downstairs, Liz genuinely liked to watch him fix his breakfast, but not because it reminded her of a different, happier, more honest time. She liked to watch him fix his breakfast because once he and the kids ate, they would leave, and she could go upstairs, get dressed and run away to Ruth's house, where she could be herself.

Everyday was the same. First the kids would leave, then ten or fifteen minutes later Cliff would kiss her cheek and mosey out the door. After the kids were on their way, Elizabeth felt like loading him up on a dolly cart and rolling him out herself. Some mornings she grew so impatient that she felt like screaming, "Hurry up! Get out! Go!" But, she never did. She just picked up the dishes, listened quietly to his chit-chatty talk and smiled. Once he shut the door she raced up the stairs, threw off her robe, pulled on her clothes, and took down her hair, which she washed at night to save time. Before he even got halfway to his office, she was in the car and on her way to Ruth's house.

The first couple of weeks after Sissy died, she met Ruth at Downtown Subscription, then one morning Ruth talked about how the view from her house inspired her painting, and Elizabeth said she would love to see it sometime. The next thing she knew they were in the car driving into the hills.

Ruth lived minutes away, up in the hills behind the Steaksmith, and it was easy to understand why she found her view inspiring. The house faced away from town, so rather than human development, all you could see was the never-ending expanse of New Mexico. On that first morning, Elizabeth stood facing those hills dotted with endless junipers and thought, *I give up.* She wanted to curl up on Ruth's couch and never leave. Ruth convinced her to go home by promising that they could have coffee there the following morning. Now, it was Elizabeth's favorite place in the world. Ruth's house was her sanctuary and sometimes it felt like Ruth was her guide. So, from the minute the coffee pot turned on, Liz was counting the minutes until her family left for the day.

Like always, Cliff appeared in the kitchen dressed for work. He smiled weakly at her and asked, "Did you sleep at all?"

"Yeah, for a little while," she lied.

"Whatcha drinkin'?" He squinched his nose at her.

She attempted to smile, but failed. "Does it matter?" She asked. Cliff flinched. She hadn't meant to be cold, but his question irritated her. She tilted her head and shrugged, trying to redeem herself.

"Energy," she said, standing up. He crossed to her and tried to offer a hug, but the air between them felt dead, and they broke apart. He headed to the refrigerator and she went to pour him coffee.

She watched as he looked at the expiration date on the milk. "Another gallon goes bad before I even get around to drinking it." He put it back in the fridge and sipped from the orange juice container instead.

"Cliff, throw it away, so the kids don't drink it."

"Artie won't even notice and Clara always checks the date. She's just smart like that."

"Cliff." She forced a laugh to bubble up from her stomach, and she tasted acid as it crossed her lips.

"Did she get up yet?"

"No. She didn't get in last night until five. I wanted to catch her in the hall and yell at her, but... I don't know. It didn't seem worth it."

"What about him, is he up?"

"Nope. I've been watching the house all morning. I wish he'd just move in here. Why does he have to stay out there?"

"Because it's his home."

"Maybe Clara should move in there with him?"

"And let her ruin his bachelor pad?"

Elizabeth's stomach turned. "Does he bring girls there?"

"God, Liz. You're such a prude. The kids are adults for Christ's sake. We raised them to be that way." Liz waited for him to answer her question. "No, I've never seen him bring a girl there."

"Don't call me a prude. They're my babies." She sat down at the kitchen table. "Babies who I let come home at dawn without so much as an angry glance."

"What are you going to do?" He asked.

"I don't know but I feel like they're out of control."

"So tell them you think so. Did you eat?" Elizabeth could tell Cliff was finished with this conversation, and she let it rest. She didn't really feel like talking either. She nodded in the direction of the cantaloupe.

"Did you eat it or just put it on the plate?"

"What's the difference?"

"Energy."

There was no justifiable response, so she didn't give one. She just leaned against the counter and watched her estranged husband move around the kitchen, pondering what he would eat for breakfast. Like always, he would have two slices of whole wheat toast with butter and strawberry jelly, a banana and a glass of OJ, but first he would look through all the cabinets and the refrigerator like he might want something else. Like always, Liz tried not to focus on how this idiosyncrasy irked her.

TEN

Artie lay in his mother's bed watching an old re-run of the *Brady Bunch*. It was a stupid show. He didn't understand why people watched it, why it didn't fizzle and die like other shows of its era, and yet when he stumbled upon it, clicking through the channels, he couldn't help but get stuck staring at it. The way two families made one, it reminded him of his own family. The alarm clock buzzed over and over again from across the room. It was time to get up, to wander over to the other house for breakfast, but Artie didn't stir. He didn't want to smile or make conversation. He couldn't bear to answer another "did you sleep well?" or "how's school?" or any other pointless attempt at pleasantries. He only went to school so Liz wouldn't get on his case. That, and school provided infinite distractions.

In physics Artie would watch Christina Graves bend over her lab book, hoping to catch a glimpse of the soft buttery skin hiding beneath her bra. Christina had awesome tits. The kind of tits that made you forget about your own shit. Sometimes on Friday nights he would take her out to a movie or to dinner and then they'd park behind the gym. He never worried about getting into her pants; all he wanted to do was bury his face in her breasts, smell her skin. She smelled like raspberry tootsie-pops. He was pretty sure a man could go deaf, dumb and blind, if he spent too many hours buried in the depths of Christina's sweet smelling tits.

Once, he even snuck Christina into his house. He figured they would be more comfortable without the steering wheel and the seat-belts, but as soon as he shut the front door, he felt sick. All he could think of was that they could fool around in his house because his mother wasn't there, and his mother wasn't there because she was in a box in the ground with a stone above her head that read, mother of Arthur. Christina was completely unaware of his discomfort. She ran around the house talking about how awesome it must be to have a place all to yourself. She was a moron. Until recently, he had no idea how much he needed a girl's conversation. His girlfriends had always been eye candy, sweet treats, because when the night closed, his kisses still lingering on their doorsteps, he went home and bothered Clara.

He'd pull the truck into the driveway, and turn the key, so the engine stopped but the radio stayed on. After a few minutes she'd always appear, cross and usually in her PJs. She'd climb into the seat next to him, a stern look on her face. Tucking her feet under her, Indian style, she'd say, "Artie, you can't just expect me to get out of bed and come talk to you all the time."

"Why shouldn't I? You always come down if I wait long enough."

"Yeah, but it's rude, and it presupposes that I have nothing better to do."

"Do you?"

"Well...it's just not...," her balled fist always hit just an inch or so above his elbow. "Shut up," she'd say, smiling.

It was so easy for him to make Clara smile. The two of them used to spend hours talking about everything, but since the night of his mom's death celebration, she didn't come downstairs to talk anymore, but also he didn't really wait for her. These days, she was hardly ever home. She was different than she used to be.

Two years ago during summer vacation, they both got jobs in Nantucket because his mom said that everyone should spend a summer working in Nantucket. She and his dad spent a few months there when they first met. They lived on some old mariner's boat for something like ten bucks a day, and worked odd jobs. His mom's eyes always became hazy when she talked about the time she spent in Nantucket. She looked like that whenever she talked about his dad, but the Nantucket story was a particular favorite of hers. So, she convinced everyone that Clara and he should go there. She always wanted them to see stuff and experience things.

It wasn't as much fun as she said it would be. The Nantucket she remembered didn't exist anymore. He spent the summer working as a busboy, and Clara landed a job as a nanny. Lying on the beach and watching kids build sandcastles was way easier than busing dishes and it paid more, but Clara took everything so seriously that she didn't even really have a good time. The coolest thing about being there was being parent free. No one peering over your shoulder making sure you're following instructions. No one telling you that you look like you're not sleeping enough. No one scolding you for leaving your dish in the sink. The pure freedom of thousands of miles between him and responsibility made the trip worthwhile.

They lived in this shit hole that Liz and Cliff paid for, but it was cool. It smelled like rotting wood, and the toilet rarely flushed, but he could pee out the back door, so who cared? When they first arrived, Clara tied a handkerchief around her head, like someone's babushka and cleaned the entire place from top to bottom with a bottle of all-purpose antibacterial spray and a sponge. That was her nature, to mother. She took care of him that whole summer. She woke him up for work, made him eggs and bacon, and had dinner on the table when he got home, no matter that most of the time he was stumbling in at three in the morning.

He could see her sitting on the couch, just like Liz, waiting for him to come in at night. Her long blond hair tied in a tight knot at the nape of her neck. Her eyes weary with exhaustion. She got up at six-thirty to make breakfast for some rich woman's children, and still each afternoon she would run home to wake him and make him something to eat before he went to work. He was never late. Clara would do his laundry and darn his socks if he asked her to, she was just like that.

On Nantucket he first saw her act wild. One Tuesday night, early in the season before the hoards of tourists arrived, his boss sent him home early. All of his new drinking buddies were still working, so he figured he'd go home, eat some of Clara's food, and take a quick nap before he went out for the evening. He heard the music blaring from the end of the block, but it never occurred to him that it could be coming from their place. He stood outside and watched her through the window, banging her head, singing into a make-believe microphone. She had lipstick all over her mouth, and she was sweating because it was so hot. He burst in the door playing his air guitar, attempting to embarrass her, but she just laughed and kept going. For about twenty minutes they were a pretend rock band, and when the CD ended they both fell down on the couch panting.

She touched him that night. Leaned her head against his shoulder and rested her hand on his thigh. He was immediately aroused. He jumped up from the couch.

"You wanna smoke?" he said without making eye contact.

"Ummmmm...," when she spoke, he looked in her direction. She had stretched herself out, so that she was lying down. Her tank top was pushed up just a little bit and she was tracing her belly button with her left index finger. "I guess, if you want to." Clara almost never got high and her willingness to do so had made the entire situation more unsettling. As a matter of fact, he couldn't remember her ever getting stoned before that night in Nantucket, but he hadn't thought about that then.

Without saying anything, he went into his bedroom. His weed was in the top drawer of his night table, but he didn't get it right away. Instead, he sat down on the side of the bed and tried to think about anything other than Clara's belly button. He could still feel her fingers on his leg. He had to calm down before he went back into the other room. He dragged the back of his hand through the little beads of moisture on his forehead, closed his eyes and listened to the filling and emptying of his lungs. Through his own silence he could hear her moving in the other room. She was banging pans and slamming cupboards. She was cooking. The clatter of the water running, the pop-pop of the gas burner, and the puckering of the fridge door, magically returned him to the comfort zone. She wasn't sexy cooking. She was sexy dancing and lying on the couch. He could face her in the kitchen.

He pulled open the night table drawer, and packed a bowl. Back in the other room, he found Clara giggling to herself, smiling at her shadow, and cooking an outrageous meal of chicken scallopini, mashed potatoes, pasta with broccoli rabe and baked apples. She said if the munchies were going to make her eat too much, she wanted to eat something good. By the time she finished cooking Artie was so high he didn't need to go out. With placemats on the coffee table, they ate and fell asleep watching T.V.

After that night, every now and then Artie would come home from work and find Clara sitting in the living room, high. She'd curl up on the floor and flip through his photography portfolio, running her fingers over the edges of the photos, and crying. She was never hysterical or anything but her cheeks would be wet, her eyes dripping tears like a loose faucet. She'd barely noticed when he came home. At most, she would look up from however she had positioned herself over the portfolio and say, "They're so beautiful Artie," and then she would stare at them some more. She was so serious. It was rare that she had any fun at all. She was always scared, always holding something back. He had lived with her his entire life, and he had never seen her screw up. He had never seen her drop the basket and just let the fruit roll away.

Then this summer, his mother died, and she went bonkers. Since the funeral, he had seen her out clubbing, all crazy and dancing. Each night she left with a different guy, guys he knew from school. Jocks, jerks, drug addicts, punks, nerds, it didn't seem to matter. He wanted to grab her by her wrists and shake her, throw her in the truck, take her home, put her in a long matronly nightgown and force her to go sleep to by ten. But they weren't even talking, so he certainly couldn't tell her how to behave, and as much as seeing her out there in a crowd of people made him blister with rage, he couldn't stop looking. She was beautiful with her head thrown back, hair loose and curly, sweat glistening on her collarbone and arms waving around her head. He was tormented by her long legs and the rhythm in her feet. Watching her body move, he wanted her almost as much as he wanted her to stop.

Every time he touched a woman, he saw her naked by the pool, wet hair falling against her bare skin, the curve of her ribs sinking into her belly. He'd even begun to wonder if he always harbored feelings for her. He hated all her boyfriends. He'd lost friends over her love-life, but he assumed Michael would have felt the same way. His girlfriends couldn't keep up with her, so he never really had a long-term serious relationship. All the girls he dated were jealous and catty. His last girlfriend, Rachel, slammed a door in his face screaming. "Clara this, Clara that, I'm not Clara Artie! And I don't give a shit what she thinks!" Artie always figured Rachel was a bitch, and to tell the truth, he wasn't even sure how she roped him into dating her, but maybe she was right. Maybe he was obsessed with Clara. He certainly thought about her enough.

The *Brady Bunch* ended, and Artie stood up and crossed over to the clock. He absentmindedly scratched his neck, as he fumbled for the off switch. He picked his pants and fleece up off the floor and put them on. If Liz weren't constantly coming over to collect his laundry, nothing he owned would ever be clean. He fumbled down the stairs, stepped into his hiking boots, left the laces untied, and walked out into the snow that had fallen earlier in the week. Old snow turned everything on the earth gray, but the sky in Santa Fe was always blue, making things seem twisted and unbalanced. Artie shut the door behind him and immediately stepped into a cold wet puddle. All the reaction he could muster was to look down and sigh. He couldn't begin to care about the state of his shoes. He let his shoelaces drag through the wet muddy slush and almost took pleasure in the pins and needles of his frozen toes.

Every morning on the way to breakfast Artie had to pass the bronze sculpture, which was nestled in the garden between his house and the door leading to Liz's breakfast table. He made the sculpture for Cliff and Liz's twentieth wedding anniversary. It was a Native American boy. Little threads of snow gathered in the folds of the boy's loin cloth, and the metal left exposed, glistened in the sun. The musculature of the boy's arms and torso were well executed, but Artie knew that if he bent down to look at the boy's knees the same level of expertise had not been met. It was one of his first life-size pieces, and although it wasn't his best, it was his favorite.

His mom made such a big deal out of presenting the sculpture as a gift. She picked out a song to play, and she made him write a speech about why he had chosen to create this boy and what the boy symbolized for him. He thought the whole ordeal was going to be incredibly staid, but it was really nice. Liz was so touched she cried. The bronze boy's intense look of determination made Artie feel useless. He couldn't remember his reasons for creating the boy, and he certainly didn't know what it symbolized then, but now its sole job was to haunt him. To remind him that artistically he was as dead as the garden at the boy's feet. He had not created anything recently and he could feel the creative part of him becoming brittle, threatening fissure.

His mother's death assassinated his creativity. Initially, he thought sculpting would be his savior. He thought he could sculpt her, make her immortal, use his God damn talent for something, but it didn't work. He spent hours in his studio tossing clay and cement, chiseling stone, bending wire, but no medium did her justice. He couldn't capture her essence, the power of her grace. In his mind, her face never stilled. She had always looked horrible in pictures because her beauty was one of constant motion, one of vibrancy. His mother could not be three-dimensional. She needed life.

Suddenly, this "fourth-dimension," her life, was lacking in everything he designed. She had been the force behind his talent. She nurtured his creativity. In some way, she had been his muse. She created the hungered frenzy of the artist under his skin. She and Clara would sit in the studio and watch him. Her praise, her awe, her love and generosity, allowed him to burn with brilliance. Looking back, he hadn't paid them any attention, but without them the studio was too quiet. He missed their company and found he was nothing without his audience. Escaping into the wonders of television was a lot easier than talking to an empty couch, so he created nothing at all. Standing there looking at the bronze was the only creative thing he did all day, and he could only do it for a few minutes before he felt like choking.

Through the window in the kitchen door, he could see Liz and Cliff sitting at the kitchen table. They didn't appear to be speaking. Cliff looked older to Artie, weathered. The lines around his eyes were crevasses, deep dark circled chasms. His hairline was no longer receding; it was gone and what was left was quickly turning gray. There was grief in their expressions and in their calculated stillness, but it would disappear as soon as they saw him, replaced by an uncomfortably synthetic happiness.

As he approached the kitchen, Cliff waved, and Liz jumped from her chair to the sink. Artie couldn't understand why she needed to take care of them so attentively. She was always on top of everything; she never missed a laundry day. She was like Martha Stewart, only not nearly as holiday themed and a lot less nauseating. The kitchen table looked awkward without his mother in the third chair. She had always sat facing the window with her hands nestled around her tea. She was quiet giggles in the morning. Now, her chair was silent. Artie hated breakfast. He looked away from the table. Liz was standing at the sink rinsing a tumbler, which he assumed was there from the night before.

"Art, you want me to make you some eggs?" She was so chipper.

"Nope. I'll stick to cereal."

"The milk's bad."

"Okay then, toast and eggs it is." He got a glass from the cabinet and poured himself some OJ. "Cliff, can I take the truck to school today?"

"I told Clara she could use it. She has to run errands for Mr. Balducci, but I'm sure she'll drop you there."

"No, it's okay."

Liz cracked an egg on the pan behind him and it sizzled as it fell into the grease. She snorted at his attempt to escape a car ride with Clara, but she didn't know.

"Artie, don't be silly. Clara will take you."

"Well, I don't want to be late, and she's not even up yet, is she?" Clara appeared in the doorway. Her hair was wrapped up in a towel like a sheik. They looked at each other for a second, and then Clara twitched her nose at the smell of breakfast.

"Yum, I want eggs too, Mom." Liz nodded and headed back to the refrigerator for more eggs.

"Clara, will you drop Artie at school?" Artie knew she couldn't say no. He watched her face for the discomfort he felt, but she just sat down.

"Yeah, sure." Liz placed a plate in front of Artie, and he ate quietly. What could he talk to her about? He hadn't said more than five words to her in three months. Nothing more than, please, pass the salt. No one seemed to notice. It had been really easy to avoid each other. If it weren't so damn cold out, he would have just walked to school.

Artie went back to his house, gathered his books, and trudged back through the wet snow to meet Clara in the driveway. He looked down at his feet; the cold wetness seeped through his leather hiking boots and his socks felt moist. This car ride was not for him. Clara had turned the car around, and she was rubbing her hands together waiting for it to get warm. Her breath billowed in front of her face like his mother's cigarette smoke. He slowed his pace and approached the car window. His fingers ached with cold. He watched her shoulder lift and fall in the circular rotation as she rolled down the window.

"Listen, Clar, I'm just going to walk."

"Don't be such a wuss Artie." He tried to look at her blankly, but it didn't work.

"No really, I just need the quiet."

"Well, suit yourself." She shook her head and rolled up the window.

He waited a few seconds, thinking that she was going to pull out of the driveway, but she didn't. She turned on the radio, loud enough that he could hear the muffled noise, and stared straight ahead. Artie turned and started walking up the driveway. He heard the tires crunch on the gravel, and he moved over into the mud, so she could pass him. Only she didn't pass him. He looked over his shoulder, and the truck inched forward about twenty feet behind him. He turned around and continued walking. He figured that once they got to the main road she would tear out past him, kind of like screaming asshole, only not. But, Clara continued to follow him once he got out on to the road, and eventually he looked over his shoulder again. She smiled, waved, and then began to laugh hysterically. Artie stopped, and Clara pulled up next to him, leaned over and rolled down the passenger-side window. Still smiling. Still gigging.

"Get in the car, idiot."

He didn't say anything. She rolled her eyes and continued talking.

"I was thinking we should blow off our respectable responsibilities and play hooky. You know maybe go up to the ski basin." Or take a real drive to Abique, or something like that." She smiled at him and lifted her eyebrows in support of her evil plans. Scrunching her features together like a sneaky demon, she smirked at him. "Come on Art... Let's go have some fun."

"I..."

"I'll stop at Allsups and buy you a big, I mean B-I-G, Dr. Pepper and some beef jerky." She attempted to tempt him with a singsong voice and junk food, but what convinced him was the rosy color that had begun to flush through her face.

ELEVEN

Ruth had taken to rising when she arrived, so there was no need for Liz to ring the bell. She pushed open the door crossed down into the kitchen, filled the tea kettle and set it on the stove. Then she went into the bedroom, took the clicker off the night stand, lay down in the space next to Ruth, and turned on the morning show.

"What time is it?" Ruth asked groggily.

"A little after eight."

"You're later than usual."

"They chewed slower than usual." Liz joked.

"Was it a good breakfast or a bad one?" Ruth asked

"Cliff was a little snippy."

Ruth rolled over and faced her. Liz loved the way she looked when she first woke up. Her eyes were puffy, like a child's.

"Are you okay?" Ruth asked.

"Fine," Liz's voice was quiet almost inaudible. "I put the tea on." Ruth loved tea almost as much as Sissy.

"I should get up." Ruth said.

"You don't have to," Liz offered. "We can just lie here and watch Regis."

At Ruth's house Liz slipped into an alternative universe where sleep was possible, and television was a distraction. Lying in bed next to Ruth was comforting. Her body emanated warmth and she often laughed out loud at the bad jokes television writers work so hard to build up. Ruth also made Liz feel like she had genuine purpose. Liz filled the empty loneliness of Ruth's life. The fullness that came with two in bed was good for them both. Ruth stared at the television for a minute and then said, "I want to paint today."

"Then you should," Liz said still looking at perky little Kelly Ripa, but Ruth didn't get up.

The show cut to commercial and Ruth said, "I have to pee."

Liz laughed. "Then, go pee."

Ruth sat up slowly, stretching her arms above her head. She was wearing a big oversized t-shirt with a Georgia O'Keeffe flower on the front.

"Do you remember waking up and not having your whole body creak?"

"I hardly remember sleeping." Liz answered.

"Don't be so dramatic. You sleep on my couch, almost every day." Liz watched her cross to the bathroom. She left the door open and continued talking. "It's a shame you have to save all your melancholy for me. I can't tell you what a pleasure it is." Liz could hear her peeing. The toilet flushed. "I mean here I am doing you the favor of providing you a fake-happy free zone." Liz knew she was messing with her.

"Shut up, you know I'm happier here than I ever am there." Ruth came out of the bathroom with a toothbrush in her mouth. She paused in her brushing, and used her toothbrush to emphasize her words. There was paint on her leg and Liz wondered what new work she had done.

Ruth argued, "Do you see the conundrum in that? They're your family."

"Most people hate being with their families," Liz countered.

"Yeah, but you don't. Or, rather you told me you didn't."

Liz couldn't help but love when Ruth got on her case. It felt familiar and comfortable, like when Sissy used to tell her not to be so serious or to try not to worry about Clara. Sometimes Liz didn't even listen to her words. She just listened to the sounds of being lectured and smiled.

"True," she said, confirming Ruth's argument.

"I just think it was a stupid promise. I think she would understand, if you broke it."

"Do we have to talk about this again?" Liz took a deep breath and tried not to get upset.

"Am I making you upset?" Ruth knew full well that this line of questioning irritated Liz, but she did it anyway and Liz had started to get used to it. Liz learned that Ruth would back off as soon as she realized that she wouldn't get a rise out of Liz.

"No. Just bored." Liz teased.

"Oh, I bore you now?" Ruth rushed to her and started tickling her feet.

"Stoooop," Liz squealed. "You'll get toothpaste on me." Ruth stood up, smiled, turning back to the bathroom to spit. Liz turned her attention back to the television, and heard Ruth turn on the shower.

Liz knew Ruth was in love with her. Ruth told her. They were sitting on the porch a handful of weeks ago. It was early October and if you were wearing a sweater you could still sit outside comfortably. Liz was doing the *Times* crossword and Ruth was sketching. She looked up to ask Ruth what a six letter word for laugh was, and Ruth was staring at her. Liz knew what she saw in her eyes, and she was going to ignore it, but Ruth said, "It's my problem." Liz played dumb.

"What are you talking about?"

"Don't act stupid. It's unbecoming."

"I don't know what to say."

"Well, I'll say it then."

"I don't want you to."

"Too bad," she swallowed, "I love you." Liz immediately started crying. "Stop crying. It's selfish." Her tone was gentle.

"You're everything. You're my whole world right now," Liz whispered.

"And you can't lose that, but you don't love me."

"That's not true. But..." Liz didn't wipe the tears off her face but she stopped crying for a minute. A breeze picked up and the pages of the *Times* clapped in the wind. Liz knew that the interaction between them was tenuous, but like everything else in her life she reformatted it. She bent the rules and allowed herself to believe that spending time with Ruth was no different than spending time with Sissy.

"But you're a married straight woman? Is that what you were going to say?"

"Yes."

"I know that."

"So, what's going to happen now?"

"Nothing, like I said it's my problem."

Liz started crying again and said "All I do is come to your house and cry."

"That's my type. Needy beauties."

"I'm sorry," Liz said. Ruth turned to look out at the view and closed her eyes, letting the strong New Mexican sun wash the sadness from her face.

After a few moments of silence Liz asked, "What's a six letter word for laugh?"

Ruth sighed, "Cackle. Giggle?" Liz turned back to the puzzle.

They hadn't talked about it since, but after that conversation their relationship settled somewhere between friends and lovers. There was nothing sexual about their interactions, but there was a physical aspect. It was nurturing and supportive. Sometimes they slept next to each other or cuddled while watching T.V. They kissed each other's foreheads and brushed the hair out of each other's eyes. It was some kind of love. For Liz, it resonated with the same certainty as the love she lost when Sissy died. It was different for Ruth, but Liz didn't concern herself with that.

The tea kettle whistled in the kitchen, but Liz didn't move to get it. Ruth came out of the shower. She wrapped her towel around her head like Clara always did.

"You know the tea's ready."

"Yeah," Liz still couldn't bring herself to move.

"Do you want to see the painting?"

Liz stood up. Ruth came over and wrapped her arms around her.

"Breakfast was worse then you let on," she whispered.

"It always is."

Ruth held on and Liz closed her eyes.

TWELVE

Cliff sat at his desk and looked out the window at his view of the Santa Fe River. It wasn't exactly the most beautiful river, in fact, lately, it was more like a trickle of dirty water, but having an office downtown had increased business. The last few years had been tremendous. He built and designed stuff all over Santa Fe these days. He'd even heard rumors that Robert Redford mentioned his name when discussing the prospect of building a new restaurant in Tesuque. Work was good, but that was it. Home was a disaster.

Cliff noticed that Clara and Artie stopped speaking, but he shied away from mentioning it to Liz. Why worry her? He tried not to wonder why they had grown so quiet, but it just kept nagging at him. He busied himself with work. He never designed such beautiful buildings in his life, but there was guilt in that. For the last seventeen years guilt was everywhere he turned, feeding on him, draining him. He looked down at his desk at the picture of his family. Two strong beautiful men and one striking, confused girl, raised by him, and the only two women he had ever loved.

He couldn't remember when he started thinking of the two of them as one entity. They were the perfect balance. Now, just Liz seemed nothing but tired. Boring. In the beginning he tried not to be in love with Sissy. He played the role of friend, but it was a lie. He fell in love with her that first night in Utah. Liz was sitting right there, but she didn't seem to notice when he laughed too loud at Sissy's stories. She couldn't feel the warmth that spread through him when Sissy remarked that he was delightful, and she questioned if he was cold when he quivered from watching Sissy tuck her hair behind her ear. He forgave his feelings as they drove away from the camp site because he was never going to see her again, and he loved Liz too.

And then, he did see her again. He was sitting in the living room holding his brand new daughter, when Liz burst through the door, panting.

"She's coming to visit, Cliff!" she exclaimed with exuberance and shuffling through the pages, she read, "Robert and I were thinking we would come down to Santa Fe, so keep an eye out for us." She looked up at him, her eyes wide with excitement. He just looked at her.

And sure enough, they showed up. They were a semi-permanent type of guest. You never knew if you were going to wake up to their departure, or if they would be around for the next year. He found himself hoping they would stay. Sissy was such a light. She would stay up with him all night doing tequila shots and talking philosophically. Liz religiously went to bed immediately following the evening news. But not Sissy. She made him feel young and irresponsible. She and Robert were always dancing and laughing. Their desire was contagious.

During that time, he tried not to want Sissy, and he'd done a pretty good job, but then Robert died, and it got harder. Sissy was lonely and Liz wanted her to live with them permanently. Every bone in his body wanted her to live in his house, under his roof, forever, but he had to think about Liz and his family, so he let Liz be the shoulder she leaned on, and although he let her stay for the time being he refused to agree with Liz that she should stay indefinitely. Then, Sissy found out that she was pregnant, and Liz took her insistent arguing up a notch. She talked of nothing else. The solution to build Sissy a house of her own came to him in the middle of the night. It was perfect. Liz thought he was a god of compromise and he could protect Sissy without having her right on top of his family. He thought he could have his cake and eat it too, but of course he had been wearing the blinders of selfish need.

They built that house together, with their bare hands. He could see her straddling the beams, dirty, the beginnings of her pregnant belly poking out of her shirt. She was so full of life, and again, he was in love with her. At night, he crawled in bed next to his wife and felt the surge of guilt rise up and try to strangle him.

Some years, he had been able to completely avoid his feelings for Sissy, but not always. He treated them both like wives. At a party he danced with both and both cooked him dinner and did his laundry. He knew onlookers found it bizarre. Maybe it wasn't right. Maybe he should have moved Sissy off his property, helped her start her own life, but he couldn't. He wanted her near him.

It happened the first time when Artie was three. Liz and Sissy were supposed to take the kids to Florida for Easter. Cliff had to stay because the business was just picking up, and he had gotten one of his first huge clients. He was building a two million-dollar house for a dentist. Two days before they were supposed to leave Artie got the flu. Sissy convinced Liz to take the others to Florida, if for no other reason than they didn't want a house full of kids with influenza. Cliff took Liz to the airport, kissed her goodbye and thought nothing of it.

When he got home that night Sissy was in the kitchen cooking dinner and Artie was asleep on the couch in the living room. Cliff stood by the door and looked at his little sleeping face. He was holding tightly to the G.I. Joe doll Cliff gave him for Christmas, and his breathing was raspy with sickness. Sissy came up beside him, putting her arm around his waist and resting her head on his chest. They just stood there looking at her little boy, asleep in his superman underoos.

After a while they went into the kitchen to eat and drink. Cliff suggested they make margaritas, and they did, and they laughed. He couldn't remember how it happened, but at some point he kissed her. He didn't know if she meant to kiss him back or if they were both drunk, but they made love. They made love that whole week. As he rocked beneath her he brushed tears from her cheeks. He let her scream and punch her fists against his chest. Over and over he buried himself inside her, trying to vanquish the misery that ate at her spirit. They never talked. They just held each other and made love until it hurt. They went together to pick Liz up at the airport, and that was it. For thirteen years, they had lived along side each other and never touched again.

When Sissy found out she was sick she came to Cliff first. She walked into his office shutting the door behind her, sat on his lap and cried. He held her in his arms and rocked back and forth. When she turned her head and kissed him, he didn't understand it. He didn't know why she wanted him, but again he made love to her. Naked, she curled against him and said, "I'm dying." Cliff just stared at her blankly, the breath draining from his lungs, his fingers weak and shaking. She stood, dressed and left the office like nothing happened. Later that night she told all of them. Liz already knew everything, and Cliff pretended he knew nothing.

He had so many things he wanted to tell her but how could he? She had come to him, weak and frail and dying. Liz drove her to his office. He never knew what Sissy had said to Liz, but it didn't seem to faze her that Sissy needed to talk to him.

"Let's go for a drive," she said.

They drove out on Old Las Vegas Highway, towards Pecos, and for a long time they didn't talk. She rolled down the window and closed her eyes, letting the wind rush against her face.

"I don't know what I wanted to say," she said.

"You don't have to say anything."

"I do."

"It doesn't matter now." Cliff looked at the endless land ahead of him. He couldn't look at her. He missed her eyebrows.

"It does." She put her hand on his knee. "Thank you, Cliff."

"For what?"

"For everything. For raising Artie like he was your son, for giving us a normal life, for keeping us safe."

"It wasn't selfless."

"I know. I need to thank you for that too." He pulled the car over and put his head in his hands. His ears filled with the rushing sound that the ocean traps in conch shells and his eyes swelled with tears as she said, "Thank you for loving me all these years."

He looked at her, dropping his hands and shoulders. Beaten, he said, "I don't know what to do."

"I wanted to tell you that I loved you once before I..."

"Don't say it." And she didn't. They just sat there silently, and after a while, he drove them home and that was that.

Cliff could not understand how Liz never noticed. Sometimes he thought she chose to ignore his behaviors, and other times he was convinced that her love for Sissy, although not sexual, was stronger than his own, forcing her to turn a blind eye to his love. Sissy and Liz seemed to make each other stronger, braver, more balanced. Their bond was unlike his love for either. To him, they seemed to truly breathe as one even when they disagreed. Because of that connection he tried not to care that Liz drank scotch for breakfast, and threw himself into his work plagued by a new source of guilt, the guilt of knowing he couldn't help her grieve.

Cliff leaned back in his leather chair and breathed the stale re-circulated air that pumped into his office. He didn't need to feel guilty about loving Sissy anymore, but it would never go away. It wasn't like he didn't love his wife. He always loved her. He loved them both, equally. They were so different. He could picture them both in his kitchen, in his living room, dancing on his patio. They had both been his.

The phone on his desk jarred him from his thoughts. His hand looked strangely white as he wrapped his fingers around the receiver. It was Clara.

"Artie and I are running away today. I didn't want you to worry."

"Artie has school," He tried to sound authoritative but failed.

"Yeah, that's why I'm calling you. I already told Mr. Balducci that I wasn't coming to work, but I need you to call the school, so they don't call mom."

"I can't do that. She'll kill me."

"I promise it will just be this one time." Cliff thought about it for a minute and then decided that maybe they both needed to get away for a day. He hung up the phone smiling. It would be easier around the house now; it would be filled with their laughter and arguing again.

Clara & Artie

✦ ✤ ✦

THIRTEEN

Clara pressed the end button on her cell phone and looked past the truck into the convenience store. Artie was inside, passing a package of Twizzlers to the clerk. An unknowing onlooker would blame the harsh overhead lights for Artie's piqued complexion, but Clara knew his skin really was dull and dingy. Before Sissy died, Artie spent hours slicing slopes with his snowboard, careening down rusty rock faces, and basking under New Mexico's sky. These days he spent his free time locked indoors watching television. Earlier, sitting in the car, waiting for him to slouch out of his house, Clara missed his company and the physical presence of him. She thought he would play along, act like the past three months had not existed, but so far he couldn't look her in the eye. Everything was awkward.

Wrapping her arms around her body to block the searing chill in the air, Clara walked towards the door. She rubbed her fingertips back and forth over her biceps. The fabric of her shirt was soft and familiar, which made placing her hand on the cold metal door handle all the more difficult. Smiling intentionally, she took a deep breath and braced herself for discomfort. Artie was handing the clerk a few bucks, and piling a Halloween-sized collection of chocolate and gummy candies into a white plastic bag. The clerk, whose hair was slick, sat down on a stool he kept behind the counter and voraciously picked at a scab on the back of his hand.

Clara spoke, "Dad said, 'No problem.'"

Artie turned to her and smiled meekly. "So what's the plan? Where we headed?"

"Maybe we should drive down to the Santa Domingo Pueblo and see Adele?" Adele was an Indian woman who sold jewelry on the Plaza downtown. As kids they'd sit with her, helping her make Pueblo brace-lets and listening to her stories about the great Kachinas and the spirit world. Artie lost interest in beading bracelets before he turned ten, but they'd stayed friends with Adele, even after her daughters took over her trade, and she decided to stay home and care for her house. Clara figured Adele would be a good distraction for them both.

"I haven't seen her in years," Artie said, looking at his feet.

"Sound good?" Clara paused briefly, "or no?"

"No. That's a good idea." He didn't look up but Clara could tell from the movement of his eyebrows that he almost smiled.

They piled back into the car, and even though it was early, began noshing on junk and soda. The drive took about twenty minutes. For the first half of the ride, Artie looked out the passenger window, and Clara stared straight ahead, gripping the steering wheel at ten and two, trying to avoid dead air. The tension between them was rich and ob-scenely decadent like flourless chocolate cake. Clara's mind obsessive-ly sorted through her father's repertoire of cliché sayings. Things like, "Shit or get off the pot," "A man's gotta do what a man's gotta do," and "No time like the present" threatened to vibrate her vocal cords, but nothing fit quite right. Each cliché felt like jeans that are about half a size too big, they've become pouchy in the ass, but a size smaller is too tight. All Clara could bring herself to do was chew on the end of her soda straw, throw the wrapper from a Twix bar behind her, and get a new tooth decaying treasure out of the bag on the seat between them.

She turned the radio on. Trashy overplayed pop music filled the cab of the truck. Clara had always been fond of the Taylor Swifts and Britney Spears of the world. There was something about the fleeting yet obsessive nature of pop tunes that made her feel comfortable. Artie, on the other hand was repulsed by talentless entertainers. After a few seconds of pop torture, he reached across the gear shift and changed the station. His action was not unfamiliar, in fact, it was almost instinctual. He and Clara battled for control of the radio since they out grew *Free to Be You and Me*, but still, Clara had not expected him to stray from his perch at the passenger window.

For her, the whole thing happened in slow motion, his hand reaching out, touching the knob and rolling it between the thumb and forefinger, the quick change from the uncomplicated beats to the rhythmic hum of an acoustic guitar and the subtle bounce of his chin to the music that pleased him. Just by changing the station, he had reintroduced the status quo. In that one moment they were them, Clara and Artie. She felt like the road beneath the car was going to slip away from the tires, like the clouds overhead would part like the Red Sea and the sun would drop down and kiss their foreheads. A perfect moment. She did the only thing she could to preserve it. She leaned forward and rolled the knob back, returning to the repetitive beats of the top forty artists. Immediately, Artie looked at her and rolled his eyes.

"Why do you insist on listening to this shit?"

"I don't know. It's catchy."

"Catchy?" He said, his voice filled with that condescending whine.

"Yeah, I guess. Plus you hate it. That's pleasure in itself."

"You're a shit," he said smiling, laughter in his voice. Then, he leaned forward and changed the station a second time. They didn't talk anymore, but the air between them grew thinner.

Adele's house was an old adobe, nestled between hundreds of other old crumbling homes just like it. The floor was dirt and the only heat was from the fireplace, but it was warm with years of life. Adele always had a pot of fiery red chili on the stove. Her chili was so hot you choked on the air around it, but when armed with a drink and a homemade tortilla, it was delicious. The water from her sink had a brown tinge to it, but it didn't matter. The black cast iron pot bubbled with thick rust colored liquid. Little pieces of pork circled and bounced beneath the surface of the chili, and Clara's mouth watered at the thought of diving into a bowl.

Adele was tall and round, but she moved with agility through her kitchen as she heated up tortillas. Her dress was not traditional. She wore sweat pants and big T-shirts with pictures of things like winking cats or roses with rhinestone tears falling from their petals. Clara and Artie once saw her dressed in her full traditional dress at a ceremonial dance.

Men and women had marched in a circle, chanting and lifting their legs and arms to the never-ending pulse of the drum. As Clara watched, the dance took over her thoughts and hypnotized her. She felt the spirituality of the people she was watching. She felt the pulse of the drum rolling and rumbling in her breath. She felt their struggle and their history in her veins. Adele and her family marched past her, and Clara wished that she belonged to something as rich as their culture. They had a concrete injustice to tie their feelings of hatred and isolation to. It made the anger and isolation she felt feel foolish and floundering. Clara wanted to be part of something bigger than herself. She wanted to be the outcast on the outside that she felt she was on the inside.

At the ceremonial dances, Adele's long black hair had hung down free and radiant around her face. She tied feathers in it with leather cord, and the sun reflected its brilliance, but now it was pulled back in a purple hair tie that screamed Kmart, and it had a sheen of grease to it, but, still hiding underneath her layers of flesh and her dirty hair, was a vibrant and coquettish spirit. Clara looked up at her, and she smiled a gappy, missing tooth smile in her direction.

She served Artie first. She always served Artie first, whispering to Clara that women were more patient then men, especially young men.

Artie smiled at Clara, winked and dove his spoon into the chili. Clara itched to counter Adele's argument with her own feminist leanings but instead took a deep breath and let the moment pass.

"What have you two been up to?" Adele asked, air whistling as she spoke. She didn't know that Sissy had died, and Clara didn't want to talk about that.

"Nothing special really."

"Oh, come on now." Her wrinkles glowed. "Artie, something must be going on." Artie looked up and nodded. "Something big enough to bring you to my doorstep."

"My mom died," he said. Clara felt the color drain from her face.

Adele placed the ladle down next to the stove and crossed the room to Artie. A red glob of chili pooled on the counter, the color running free, staining everything it touched. Adele took Artie in her arms, pulling him close to her massive form. He began to weep, but only quietly. Clara looked away.

"It's okay, little one," Adele said, her voice smooth and sheltering, like cool water pouring over your skin. Clara kept her head down and chewed on her fingers. She stared at the dead gray wood of Adele's kitchen table. Artie's sobs grew and he began to grasp for loud breaths.

"It's okay baby, cry if you miss her." The raspy sound of her hand passing over his cotton shirt was loud and irritating to Clara like nails on a chalkboard.

"Only good things are happening to your mama now." Without lifting her head, Clara looked through her eyelashes at Artie. The tears ran down in streams over his cheeks, clearing paths through the dust on his face. He was holding tightly to Adele, his white fingers sinking into her copper flesh. Clara looked away again, curling deeper into her mind, wishing she could press her hands over her ears.

When Artie grew quiet, they all moved into the living room. The bowl of chili stayed on the kitchen table, the fat from the pork hardening as it grew cold. Adele sat in a big old wooden rocking chair that didn't seem to belong in the surroundings. It was the type of rocking chair that old men in plastic mesh baseball caps whittled wood in. The dirt floor beneath it was worn down so that it rested in two deep grooves. Clara and Artie sat across from her on a chocolate colored couch that threw dust into the air as they collapsed into it.

As she always had, Adele began to tell a story. It was a story they had heard before. It was a story about a young boy and girl crossing though their separate worlds, struggling to find each other. Encircled in the rich warmth of Adele's voice, Clara closed her eyes and out of habit she leaned into Artie's shoulder. His body was stiff and cold beneath her, unwelcoming, but she didn't move. The uncomfortable feeling of his shoulder pressing into her back helped erase the horrifying sounds of his sadness. Clara closed her eyes and focused on her breathing. As a child she had gone to yoga classes with Sissy and learned to count her breath. Breathe in to a count of twelve, hold to a count of twelve, breathe out to a count of twelve. She had never taken to yoga, like some do, but she often used this simple breathing technique to quiet her mind.

About halfway through the story, Adele paused. Clara's eyes flickered open and her face stood still, placid. Artie's breathing had slowed and grown rhythmic, his body had relaxed and now he cradled her against his chest. She knew he was asleep, and she felt safe and comfortable pressed against him.

"Go on," Clara said, "this is my favorite part." Artie stirred and Clara lay her hand over his. Adele laughed, thick and hearty, like the chili in her kitchen.

"Could have fooled me," she winked.

Clara had not realized her feelings for Artie were so apparent. She felt her cheeks grow hot. Adele sat contently. She didn't look at Clara, but she didn't look away from her either. Clara watched her lean back against the rocking chair.

"Always been that way," she smiled with her eyes closed.

Clara thought about saying something, but Adele became the storyteller again and the moment passed.

Later in the afternoon Adele drove with them up to the lake, and they all threw a stone into the water and said a prayer for Sissy. Because there was no wind the water lay still, silver and flat, like a mirror, allowing each prayer stone to ripple its surface and resonate with poignancy. It wasn't much, but Clara found the gesture warm and appropriate, a quiet way to celebrate. She wished Sissy good luck on her journey, wherever she might be. When Adele and Artie turned to head back to the car, Clara quickly picked up another small stone and made a second wish. She wished Artie would find the strength to honor Sissy's wishes, that he would stop wallowing in his own self-pity and celebrate his mother's extraordinary life.

Back at her house Adele wrapped some tortillas in tin foil for Clara's parents. Neither one had the heart to tell her they couldn't bring them into the house, so right after exiting the pueblo, Clara pulled the truck over to the shoulder, and they ate them in the car. They sat side by side in the truck, facing the sunset. Artie spoke first.

"Don't tell them I cried."

"I won't." Clara's voice grew husky with confidence, "I can't forget, though." She hadn't meant it as a threat. She was even surprised by her curtness, but her eyes flashed anger.

"What do you want from me? My mother died, remember?"

"No, Artie you misunderstood... I was... I don't know. It was so unexpected." She looked at him and then looked away. She hated that he cried, but she certainly hadn't meant to hurt his feelings. He reached over and touched her hand. She looked at their hands touching. She could feel every one of his fingers on her skin, little hot spots burning under his fingertips. He began to move them, drawing little soft circles on the back of her hand.

"She cried too you know," he said, "at night when she thought no one could hear her."

"She did?" Clara didn't believe him, but she pretended she did. She couldn't take her eyes off their hands. "Funny."

"Not all the time," he paused, and took his hand away. Clara looked up and saw anger in his eyes. "Only at my house, because God forbid anyone thought that every minute wasn't a celebration."

Clara's cheeks flushed. She wanted so much for everything to be normal between them, but she couldn't bear sitting so close. She wanted to cry out. Artie just looked so lost, his hands in his lap, chin tilted down, eyes unfocused. Her chest felt like it might implode, so empty. She had to hold him. She couldn't help herself. She squirmed across the cab and put her arms around his neck. She held him close for a minute, then cradled his face in her hands and kissed his forehead.

"I'm sorry Artie," she whispered. "I'm so sorry," she repeated and kissed his cheek. Slowly, he reached his hands up around her body, pulling her down, holding her close, touching his lips behind her ear.

Clara closed her eyes. She could hear her heart beating. He kissed the nape of her neck, slowly, a line of kisses moving towards her lips. Her mouth went dry. His hand snuck towards the hem of her shirt. Clara took a quick short breath and swallowed. When his fingers found the skin of her waist, she made a small whimpering noise, and Artie pulled his hand away.

Quietly, to himself, Artie said, "I can't do this."

"It's okay," Clara whispered, and put his hand back on her waist. He meekly pushed her away, but she didn't budge. "It's okay," she said again.

This time he was more forceful. He pushed her, and she fell back across the cab, knocking her elbow on the steering wheel. Embarrassed, she pulled her knees into her chest and hid her face behind them. Artie said nothing, and Clara began to rock gently, her back pushing against the driver's side door.

"I'm sorry," he said. Without looking up, Clara knew he wasn't facing her. She stayed silent, her teeth clenched. He shifted on the plastic of the seat. "Clara, I never should have done that. I shouldn't have touched you that way. I'm sorry." His voice was shaking. "It was inappropriate." Clara kept her face buried, but she unlocked her arms from around her legs and rubbed her elbow. "Did you get hurt? Did I hurt you?"

"It was an accident," she whispered. Artie inched closer to her, taking her arm in his hands.

"It looks okay," he said. Clara lifted her face. His lips were inches from hers, trembling.

"It's no big deal." She felt his breath on her cheek. He didn't move away. Clara bit her lower lip. Again her father's clichés popped into her mind. Breathe, she thought. "Now or never," Breathe in to a count of six, "Shit or get off the pot," hold to a count of six, "No time like the present." Breathe out to a count of six. Her hands were shaking and she lost control of her breathing, forcing her chest to rise and fall quicker than she thought possible. Tingling excitement coursed through her body. She lifted her hand and ran her fingers over his cheek. He closed his eyes and wet his lips. Then, he swallowed. Clara took a deep but shallow breath.

"Artie," she said, so quiet that only the "t" in his name made any real sound, "please kiss me."

He opened his eyes, searching her face. "Please," she said again, begging, hoping he wouldn't turn her away. She didn't have to ask a third time. He kissed her forcefully, cradling the back of her head with his hand and thrusting his tongue into her mouth. Their kisses were hard and intense, their teeth knocking together. Clara pulled her lips from his, looking for some sign that he wanted all the things she wanted. His body was positioned awkwardly, half bending over her knees so he could reach her lips. He ran his thumb over her lips, then he sat back, leaning his head against the head rest behind him, and closed his eyes.

"Now that," he said, pausing dramatically, "that was unexpected." There was confidence in his voice, and it made Clara feel awkward. She turned and faced the steering wheel. Her hands were still shaking. She couldn't tell if she was elated or petrified. She stared ahead at the pink and orange warmth that signaled the onset of night and tried to think of something to say but there were no words. When the sun had set completely, Clara started the engine and drove home.

In the driveway Clara climbed from the truck and headed towards her house. She stopped and looked over her shoulder expecting Artie to have disappeared through his front door, but he was standing in front of the truck, watching her walk away. Once she was facing him, he walked to her and took her hand. Then, with his fingers closed around hers, they walked through his door together.

FOURTEEN

Thanksgiving at the Worthington's was a huge production. It always seemed to Michael like the plethora of aunts, uncles, and cousins once removed was a test of his memory and endurance. Katie's family welcomed Michael with open arms, but he could never quite shake the feeling that he was using the wrong fork or ordering the wrong drink. Charlotte Worthington, Katie's mother, hosted but never cooked. The Worthington's South American housekeeper and her two sons dominated the kitchen.

The meal itself was pretty classic fare, turkey, yams, green bean casserole, however the presentation was more refined than any holiday meal Michael had ever eaten at his own home. There were silver platters, etched crystal, sprigs of thyme and intricate rusty colored flower arrangements that somehow made the house smell like a hearty fall evening. Michael was easily intoxicated by the lavishness of it all. He felt like being in their house made his laugh haughty. More than once Katie had leaned close to his ear and whispered, "You're clenching your teeth."

The table in the dining room was inexplicably long, forcing either pockets of intimate conversation or announcer-like monologues. Michael was seated to the right of Katie's mother, who was at head of the table, and Katie was on his left. Katie's Uncle Stewart, a quite prestigious plastic surgeon, was seated directly across from Michael, discussing the intense rise in elective cosmetic surgery among men.

"It's quite outstanding. I have a number of clients right now who are looking for calf or pectoral enhancements."

"Really," Michael said, as he felt Katie slide her hand up over his knee until she was gripping his inner thigh. Michael felt himself starting to blush and instinctually, glanced in Mrs. Worthington's direction.

"I can't imagine it," Katie said. Charlotte Worthington met Michael's eyes and smiled.

"...And more and more men are desiring face lifts." Stewart continued.

"You're kidding," Katie said.

"There are even procedures for...size enhancement."

"Oh, Stewart, stop," Charlotte said. "If you're going to talk about such things with my innocent young daughter, at least do it when I'm not sitting right next to you." Feeling like her words had a double meaning, Michael shifted, pushing Katie's hand away as stealthily as possible and focused his attention on his meal. Changing the conversation, Stewart began the torrent of questions that Katie's family members asked Michael year after year.

"I'm sorry, Michael. I know I've asked before, but where is your family from? Colorado?"

"New Mexico."

"Right, Santa Fe. Never been there but I've heard good things. Wonderful things, actually."

"Michael," Charlotte interjected, "we were so sorry to hear about your Aunt." Katie slipped her hand back into position. Again, Michael anxiously turned to Charlotte, who immediately made eye contact. Katie casually moved her fingers back and forth and Michael's breathing quickened.

"I'm sorry? My aunt?" Michael asked, looking to Katie for clarification. Charlotte looked fairly confused. Katie's eyes widened.

"Sissy, Michael."

"Oh, God. I'm sorry. I..."

"No, don't be," Charlotte said. "Sometimes it's easier to file these things away." Michael took a moment and then looked longingly into the faces around him and tried to camouflage the shame in his voice with artificial grief.

"I guess," he said. Then he paused strategically. "Thank you for your sentiments." He could tell Charlotte was fooled. She covered his hand with hers and smiled sympathetically, but Katie pulled her hand away as though she'd burned it. She hardly acknowledged him for the duration of the meal.

After dinner most of the guests moved into the den and sipped expensive cognac. Michael took a few sips before he realized Katie was not in the room. Excusing himself, he left the festivities and went to look for her. She was sitting on the landing at the top of the stairs, visibly distraught.

"You lied," she said.

"I'm sorry?"

"You lied at the dinner table." She was angry.

"What are you talking about?" He asked, feigning innocence.

"You did. That whole dramatic 'thank you for your condolences' bit. That wasn't real."

"I was just flustered because," he looked over his shoulder to see if anyone was listening to them, "you practically had your hand in my pants, and I swear she knew."

"Who knew?"

"Your mother," he said emphatically.

"Don't be ridiculous. She didn't know, and besides I wasn't doing anything."

"What was that whole bit about her young and innocent daughter?" Katie smiled.

"You're totally paranoid. You know that, right?" Michael sat down next to her and turned his face so he could look Katie in the eye.

"I thought she knew." Katie took his face in her hands.

"That was all," she said. "You didn't lie?"

"I was flustered." Katie kissed him and then she stood.

"We should get back before my mother thinks she knows something else."

Michael stood and followed her down the steps, trying to find comfort in the fact that he never said he didn't lie. Halfway down the stairs, Katie turned and looked at him like she had something else to say.

"What?" he asked gently, trying to appear as innocent and lovable as possible. She didn't say anything but her eyes were searching his face. "Katie, I love you."

At his words, she let the corners of her mouth turn up a bit. He walked past her, took her hand and led her back to the party. He knew she wasn't satisfied with his half-truths, and he hoped that maybe if he got just one aunt or uncle to give her a wink or a nudge-nudge about what a great guy he was that she might forget all about it.

Just a few minutes after they returned to the den, the Worthington's housekeeper's oldest son tapped him on the shoulder and whispered that he had a phone call. Excusing himself, Michael traipsed back up the stairs to the guest bedroom and picked up the phone, knowing full well it was his mother. She was not in a good mood.

"Why didn't you call?" Liz asked.

"You didn't give me a chance," he said defensively.

"You should have called this morning. We already ate and now no one is around." She was completely irrational and if he didn't know better he might have thought she was drunk.

"Mom, I was going to call." He waited for her to respond. She said nothing. Thinking about Katie and his need to keep her from thinking about his half-truths he said, "Listen, I need to get back to the Worthingtons. Can we talk about this tomorrow?"

"Go ahead, run back to the Worthingtons, Michael."

The venom in her voice startled him. He sat down on the bed, re-signed to the idea that they would be talking for a while. As always her timing was awful and he felt bothered and angry by her instability.

His voice was icy and stern when he said, "They're nice enough to welcome me into their house and I'm being considerate. Is that such a sin?"

"I would have welcomed you in your own home," Liz argued

"Is that what this is about? You're angry that I didn't come home for Thanksgiving?"

"You never come home," she spat. "You've been dating the same woman for three years and we've never even met her."

He couldn't stand this argument after his little altercation with Katie, it was too much. He started yelling, "How could I come home before this, Mom? How could I possibly bring my amazing girlfriend into that house and introduce her to that woman?"

Liz's voice shook asking, "What are you talking about?"

Still heated Michael said, "I certainly wasn't going to introduce Katie to my mother who lived in a house with my father's lover and her son, but maybe you're right, maybe I should have come home this year 'cause she's dead now. Isn't she?"

Michael heard the knock of his mother slamming down the receiver and then the phone line went dead. In the quiet of her absence, Michael hoped he hadn't yelled loud enough for anyone downstairs to hear him.

FIFTEEN

*Cliff's talk w/ Clara
about Artie & Katie re
Michael's — refusal to
reveal the situation
w/ Sissy to Katie*

Cliff didn't take lunch anymore. He found the empty office more re-laxing than the bustle of a restaurant. Gladys, his assistant, had tried to coax him into eating something, but he tricked her by offering to buy her lunch and then handing her his credit card. He had done this to her once before, a year or so ago, and she refused his offer. Today, she shrugged, shook her head and took the plastic he was handing her.

"You want me to bring you back anything?" she asked. Gladys was about thirty, maybe a little younger, and she was a good assistant, but being young and having a name like Gladys makes her appear and act older than she should.

"No. I'm not really hungry." He returned his glance to the work on his desk, hoping she would take his focus as a sign that she should leave quietly.

"You should try to be hungry every now and then," she scolded, like she was his mother. He sighed, but it was a lighthearted sigh, a sitcom sigh.

"You're right, but not today."

"You know hiding...."

"Won't help. I know." He rolled his eyes.

"Right." She dropped her shoulders, defeated.

"Go eat."

"I just care," she said. Cliff smiled at her.

"Which is why I haven't fired you. Go eat."

"I'm bringing you back something," she said as she shut the door. When she was gone Cliff let his eyes drift up towards the ceiling and leaned back in his chair.

"That one," he said making a fist and shaking his head. "I oughta..." He giggled a little, and then becoming aware of his happiness, he let his fist drop and his facial muscles relaxed to their home of vacant sorrow. He always felt guilty when he spent a few instances feeling relaxed. He pulled his chair back into the desk and focused again on the work at hand because as long as he was working he couldn't think.

Maybe fifteen minutes later, once he was deeply involved in his work and riding high on the peaceful emotion-free calm of the office, Clara called.

"I'm stranded," she said. Cliff could tell from her voice that she was a little frustrated.

"What happened?"

"The truck won't start. I tried to call Mom but..."

"She's not home."

"Right."

"Do you think it's the battery?"

"Probably."

"Where are you?"

"Parked in the lot at Tomasita's."

"I'll be there in a few minutes."

Cliff hung up the phone, grabbed his keys and pulled on his jacket. He was halfway out the door when he decided to go back and leave

Gladys a note. He wrote, *Gladys- Truck broke down. Gone to save Clara.* He paused and ran his fingers over the words on the page before adding, *I think I'll buy my daughter lunch, Cliff.*

Clara was sitting on the front of the truck, like she did when she was a little kid. When she was little she couldn't climb up there by herself, so Cliff had to lift her up and put her there. Nothing about her looked little anymore. Dressed for work, she was more ladylike than anything else. In her pink sweater and wool slacks, she had stretched out on the truck's hood, leaning back with her face skyward as though she were sunning, only it was winter so she looked a bit crazy. She wasn't wearing a jacket and even from a distance Cliff could see that her face and hands were red from the cold.

He couldn't park right near her, so he approached her on foot. When he got closer, he started to think she looked less crazy and more happy, which was utterly crazy in itself. She didn't realize he had approached, so when he spoke he startled her.

"Where's your jacket?" he asked.

Her eyes snapped open and she jumped to a sitting position, "God, Dad. I didn't know you were standing there." She hopped off the hood and gave him a big hug, pressing her cheek against his chest.

"It's cold," he said into her hair.

"I'm not cold. I'm good." She sounded good. She broke from their embrace and went to the truck cab to grab her jacket.

"Did you eat?"

"No. I was on my way but..."

He interrupted her, "You wanna eat?"

"You mean you'll take me to lunch, Dad?" She was cute, teasing. Cliff loved her so much. He played off her attitude.

"I don't know. I thought lunch with my daughter would be alright." He made a comical gesture incorporating his hands, his eyebrows and a slightly snarled lip, which made it look like he was feeling neither this way nor that about the idea. Clara laughed at him, and hooked her arm through his.

"Okay, Pops, you got yourself a lunch date." Joking, Cliff puffed out his chest and stretched his neck so that he was holding his head unusually high.

"You're such a dork, Dad." Cliff sunk his head and deflated his chest as though she had crushed him. She gave him a little smack on the arm. As they entered through Tomasita's two swinging doors into the darkness of the restaurant bar, Cliff returned to normal, put his arm around her and pulled her close enough so that he could kiss the top of her head.

Tomasita's bar was always filled with local characters in cowboy boots, throwing back smooth shots of high priced tequila, so much so that Cliff always joked that the owner must pay a monthly fee for these types to frequent his place, adding an air of "real" Santa Fe to his establishment. Cliff liked Tomasita's. The food was good, classic New Mexican fare, and although the restaurant was decorated in a slightly over the top gold, red and green southwest theme, it felt homespun and familiar.

The hostess sat them in a booth and they decided to forgo their menus because they knew what they wanted to order, roast beef burritos with red chile. Once the waitress had taken their order and walked away, Cliff started to regret suggesting they have lunch. Their conversation was stunted. It had been months since he and Clara had talked, and he really had no idea what to talk to her about.

"How's work?" he asked.

"Fine. You?"

"Work's good. Mr. Balducci?"

"Same old, same old. A little crazy but lovable."

Their conversation paused while the waitress set down their drinks. Cliff knew that once she was gone he would have to think of something else to say. He racked his brain for topics of conversation. Clara was looking at her lap and smiling.

"Why are you so happy today?"

"I don't know. I've had a good week."

"Do you live in our house?" he asked. Clara laughed but said nothing. There were a few moments of dead air that seemed like hours to Cliff. He kept looking at Clara who was clearly engrossed in her own thoughts. He couldn't get over how calm and peaceful she looked. Normally, her brow was intensely furrowed. He always loved her nature. He loved being her father.

Having a daughter blew Cliff away. It changed his entire perspective on women. He never had any sisters or female cousins, so Clara was the first girl he looked upon with no sexual undertones whatsoever. In fact, it was only when Clara was born that he realized how large a role sex and sexuality played in his relationships with women. Before Clara, it wasn't like he sexualized every woman he met, but he also didn't not sexualize them. He thought in terms of women and men, two very different separate entities. Being Clara's father had allowed him to see women as purely people.

Recently, he had started to notice that somewhere along the way Clara had gone from being the daughter he protected to being a woman who protected herself. He was acutely aware of this as he looked at her sitting across from him. He could tell that she was thinking about something that she wouldn't tell him, but he decided to ask anyway.

"What are you thinking about?"

"Nothing, really." She didn't make eye contact, and he could've sworn that she blushed a little.

"It doesn't look like nothing."

"Well, I've been thinking about asking you and mom if I could start staying in Sissy's house." Cliff knew that was not what she'd been thinking about. "He's so alone, ya know?"

"Yeah." He was disappointed, even though he had known all along that she wasn't going to tell him what she'd really been thinking about.

"And, I think if he had someone in there with him, maybe he would be less...I don't know, less lonely."

"It's not a bad idea, but you'll have to talk to your mother."

"She's pretty hard to get a hold of these days."

"Yeah." Cliff knew Liz spent her days somewhere but he wasn't sure where. It had occurred to him that maybe she was having an affair, but he quickly dismissed the idea, deciding that it wasn't her style, and truthfully, if she were he couldn't blame her. Their relationship was painfully superficial since Sissy died, but since Thanksgiving she had grow increasingly distant. Their conversation was stunted. Either they discussed the kids or they didn't speak at all. He couldn't imagine her sitting in the house all day by herself, so he was willing to accept whatever she chose to do with her days.

"Where does she go everyday?" Clara asked.

"I don't know," he admitted.

"I call her all the time, but she's always out. I worry about her."

"You don't have to worry about her. She's okay." Cliff needed to change the subject. He didn't want to discuss Liz's state of mind with Clara. He didn't want to discuss Liz's state of mind at all.

"Did she tell you that Michael's girlfriend called the house the other day?" He asked. The waitress arrived with their burritos. "She said something to mom about how sorry she was to hear about my sister."

"Your sister?" Clara cut into her burrito and took a bite.

"Apparently, your brother told her that Sissy was your aunt." Clara nearly choked on her food.

"What?!"

"Yeah, and your mom thought the whole thing was so ridiculous that she told this girl..."

"Her name is Katie."

"Right, she told Katie to let him suffer."

"What do you mean?" Clara had stopped eating.

"Well, apparently, Michael is pretty stressed out about Katie meeting us, and your mom figured it's because he lied about Sissy. So, she told Katie to just keep pressuring him to bring her here until he confesses."

"He should squirm," Clara hissed.

"Your mother totally agrees with you. She's furious at him. Kept ranting and raving about how no son of hers would be ashamed, blah blah blah... . You get the idea, " Cliff gossiped happy just to chatter.

"He has always been such a stick in the mud about Sissy and Artie, like there was something to be embarrassed about." Clara started to chew again. "I mean it's not like you had two wives." Now, it was Cliff's turn to choke. That was exactly how he referred to them in his head, his two wives. He started coughing.

"You okay, Dad? Take a sip of water." She pushed his glass towards him, and he took a sip. While he composed himself, Clara went back to her food, and then she looked up and said, "They're just really close *Clara* friends of ours. We're not related to them."

"Not by blood, but Clara come on, I can understand how it's hard for him to explain. Princeton probably felt daunting to him. He probably just wanted to fit in."

"Dad, we're not related. Things are only weird if you choose to think of them that way."

"True, but we both know that you're more open-minded then your brother."

"I guess. I just don't get him sometimes."

"Sometimes he's hard to get but he loves us."

"Yeah, I know and he's pretty lovable too."

The waitress came by to see if their meal was okay and Cliff asked for the check.

"You didn't really touch your food, Dad."

"I'm not that hungry. I don't really eat lunch that often so..."

"I know. Gladys told me on the phone the other day." Cliff laughed.

"She's obsessed with my eating habits. It's really nothing. I just have a ton of work, that's all."

"I figured."

When they were back in the parking lot, Cliff pulled his car up so it was nose to nose with the truck. He popped the hoods and connected the jumper cables. They leaned against his car while they waited for the truck to charge.

"You really don't know where she goes all day?" Clara asked.

"I'm just glad she isn't sitting in the house thinking up responsibilities for us all."

"Ain't that the truth." Clara fidgeted with her zipper, pulling it up, pulling it down.

"Par for the course, I guess."

"Maybe we're all a little crazy." Clara offered.

"Maybe."

"I just don't see why it's so hard for her," she stopped futzing with the zipper and her voice grew more intense. "She's so removed."

"She's just trying to move on, trying to be happy."

"So, then she should be happy. I mean when I start to feel scattered I just think about Sissy."

"What do you mean?"

"Well, her theory, ya know? If I choose to be happy then I can be. No tears."

"Tears aren't so bad Clara." Clara looked him in the eye, and he saw the same righteous anger in her stare that was in every one of Liz's glances.

"No tears, Dad. That's what she wanted. That's what she taught us." Her voice was stern and determined.

"I just meant that if you had to cry, then you could." Cliff could hardly look at her.

"No one has to cry." Her tone, her body language, her ideas, everything about her resembled her mother.

"Right, no tears," he said meekly. He turned and looked at the cables. "Why don't you give it a try?" Clara didn't move. He could feel her sizing him up. He felt as though those last few sentences had given her a reason to pull away from him, a reason to look down on him.

"You choose to be happy, Dad." He turned back to look at her, and immediately noticed that her brow had furrowed once again.

SISSY'S HOUSE

They designed the house like a sandcastle's tower. From inside the entire structure felt circular because the stairs, which began just to the left of the front door and wrapped around an elevated circular living room before continuing on to the upstairs loft. The ceilings in the center section were easily thirty feet high. Windows and skylights filled the space with light. The inside was painted white. They tiled the floor with Mexican tiles, being careful to avoid the ones with paw prints in them.

The first floor consisted of a bedroom, bathroom, kitchen, breakfast nook, and an extra space, which eventually became a sculptor's studio. The kitchen was small and galley-like. A large sub-zero refrigerator hovered in the corner, overpowering everything else, like a god. A small table, which they never used, was placed in the breakfast nook, under a large bay window, and over the years, it peacefully hosted vase after vase of fresh cut flowers.

The loft or rather the master bedroom, bath, and an unusually large closet, was sparsely decorated, keeping within the style of the house.

They chose whitewashed wood furniture. A four poster bed, a night table, and a bureau with a T.V. on it, and that was it. On the far side of the bed there was a break in the wall that led to the closet, a boxy space with walls that were four inches shy of the ceiling. These stunted walls held odd shaped shelves, space organizers, racks, drawers, a dream closet. The bathroom was marble, tight and long, but elegant. At the very end of the small space, they hid the toilet behind a half-wall.

There were two exits on the loft floor. One, which led to a small porch, was at the foot of the bed, and the other was down a tiny catwalk that over looked the living room. The second exit was accessible only by a kiva ladder and it led out on to the roof. They built ceilings of different heights, so the roof became a series of steps and planes. It was a place they went to when they were looking for peace.

The living room, which was the piece de resistance of the house, had built-in adobe couches, upon which they placed and replaced white canvas cushions. A kiva fireplace was built into the wall on the far side of the circle. At Christmas time they would set a large tree in the center of the living room and decorate it together.

Christmas was the only time that they all gathered in Sissy's House. They gathered around that tree, the house twinkling with tiny white Christmas lights, and they tore into their gifts one by one, allowing the piles of discarded wrapping paper to pile like leaves at their feet. And when the season had passed it would all be swept away and the room would be round and empty again.

SIXTEEN

*Clara models for Artie
in studio
"no one knew they
were lovers"*

The edges of Artie's ears and his nose were numb from the cold, but he was sweating. Liz asked him to clear the snow off the path that went from the driveway around past the kitchen and down to his house. It normally amazed him that he could sweat in the icy winter, but today he barely noticed. He just wiped his forehead on the sleeve of his shirt, pocketed his gloves and went back to thinking about Clara.

Clara was amazing. Sometimes she would pose for him. He began by studying her face. He'd sit directly across from her, his knees touching hers, her bare feet curled around the rung of his stool, and her hands holding the seat between her legs. She would close her eyes and stretch her neck towards him, like a plant leaning into the sun. His fingers would drift over her cheekbones and the bridge of her nose, his thumbs circling her mouth, moving back and forth over her lips. When her breath grew heavy, he would remove his hands and turn to the clay. Clara would lean closer before opening her eyes, lingering in his space.

The studio, like the rest of the house, had high ceilings. Artie designed huge canvas curtains with rope pulleys to cover the windows. The fabric was so thick that it simulated night. Assorted light bulbs hung curiously from extension cords, wherever they were needed. As Artie molded her features, Clara would glide from one window to the next, pulling slowly at the ropes, standing high on her toes, bending her body, and pulling again, until the room was pitch black. In the darkness, he would hear her move. She'd stand behind him, so close that the warm wetness of her breath would dance across his neck. Artie's pulse would pound in his ears. After what seemed like an interminable amount of time, one hand, the left one, would push down on his shoulder, and she would reach above him, pulling on the light over his head.

His hands would shake as she moved through the room and lit, a corner, or the couch, or whatever, as long as there was darkness all around her. Once the lighting was ready, she would catch his eyes, and remove her clothes without breaking eye contact. Sometimes the darkness would creep in casting shadows over her collarbone or her calf, and that part of her body, which never seemed significant before, would become the most sensuous. He would work furiously, producing small, feverish, abstracts. Nothing she modeled for resembled her. It couldn't. No one knew they were lovers.

Artie straightened, stretching the muscles in his back. He could see Liz through the window. She was sitting at the kitchen table reading the paper and drinking something in a mug. She looked up at him and smiled. He smiled back. After pointing to him, she wrapped her arms around her chest and shook her body, miming cold. He nodded, and then reconsidered. He put his hand out, palm down, fingers spread, and rotated his wrist back and forth, signaling that he was a little cold. She pointed to her mug and then at him. He shook his head. No, thank you.

Liz was so good to him. He felt so guilty about lying to her. They meant to tell them, but there never seemed to be a right time, and the longer they waited the more complicated it got. They didn't want to be regulated by the rules that would come with being upfront about their relationship. They didn't want to answer questions. Liz even supported Clara staying at his house because she hated the thought of him alone at night. She had no clue. He smiled again, shook his head and went back to work.

Liz's feelings about him being alone were right. He had hated being in the house alone. He loved having Clara with him. He loved knowing her habits. She flossed in the morning, but not at night. In the shower she always shampooed her hair before she cleaned her body. For some reason, she had decided his deodorant was better than her own. Little wet rings stained the night table, because she always needed water by the bedside. She had a way she laughed that was different from when she giggled, and the voice she used to be sexy was different than the voice she used when she wanted a favor.

His favorite thing was sleeping next to her. Clara always slept on her side, palm to palm hands pushed under her cheek. Giving him the opportunity to study the ridges of her spine, the spot where her waist curved in and became her hips, her nakedness, heels to scalp, pressed next to him. During the week, he woke before the alarm just to see her strong small body curled inches from his grasp. Without ever making contact, he would glide his hands over her curves, feeling the heat that emanated from her skin. Clara cooked. Her stomach and backside held heat like a furnace, hot and dry. The alarm would go off and she would turn over, curling into his chest, pushing her hips towards him. They'd make love until the last second, throw on their clothes, race to breakfast, and try to look innocent. On the weekends they would spend whole days in the house laughing and teasing each other. In the beginning their passion was a little embarrassing because they grew up together but once that melted, they just wanted to make each other happy. It didn't seem like a big deal until recently.

One Sunday afternoon they were cuddling in his mother's bed watching cartoons. He was naked and Clara was wearing a tiny t-shirt and panties. He had his hand resting on her thigh. He was even thinking about tearing her clothes off, when the front door opened. "Clar...

Art, Mom wants to know if you're going to hide out in here all day." Cliff walked right into the house. He was a flight of stairs away, while Artie lounged naked in bed with his daughter.

Artie jumped out of the bed, and then stood there like an idiot. His only thought was this is how someone feels when a plane suddenly goes vertical.

"Artie, what are you doing? Go in the bathroom or something," Clara whispered, her eyebrows pulled together in anger. She had pulled the sheet up over her legs so if you didn't know better you'd think she had pants on. Bathroom, he'd thought. Bathroom. Then, he bolted, went right over the bed and slammed the bathroom door. He shouldn't have slammed the door.

"Is Artie okay?" He heard Cliff ask.

"Yeah, he's been doing that all day. He's got a stomach bug or something."

"Should I get your Mom?"

"NO...um...he doesn't feel like having her fuss over him. You know how she can be."

"Are you sure he's okay?" He knew. Artie could tell Cliff knew. Cliff walked in his direction. Artie backed away from the door and hid in the bathtub.

"Artie, are you okay in there?"

Silence. He didn't know what to say.

"Artie?" Cliff asked again.

Artie cleared his throat. "Yeah. I'm okay."

"Should I get Liz?"

"No, I've just got the runs."

"Okay, if you need us just send Clara over."

"Okay."

"He's fine dad. He just drank too much last night and won't admit it...Right, Art?" Clara's teasing saved them.

"Shut up, Jerk-face," he hollered back. Cliff laughed.

When Cliff left, Clara opened the bathroom door and said, "The runs?

Gross, Artie." She thought it was funny. Artie didn't laugh. What if they had gotten caught? What would Cliff have thought? Would he hate Artie? Would he send him away? He could see his face in the mirror across from the tub. His lips were blue, and his teeth were chattering. Clara walked closer and sat down next to the tub. "Artie...are you cold?"

He couldn't say anything. She leaned over him, plugged the drain, and turned the faucet all the way to left. Scalding hot water poured forth thundering against the tub. She stood up, and he watched her slip off her panties and pull her T-shirt over her head. She stepped into the water one foot at a time. When she stood in front of him, he unexpectedly buried his face between her legs. He caught the back of her thighs with both hands, and her knees fell towards him. The muscles in his arms flexed, steadying her weight. He focused all his thoughts on her and waited patiently for her to vibrate at his touch. It was only temporary, but he hid in the smell of her, letting her prickly little hairs blur the growing numbness in his chest.

He could still go to that place now. He could still hide from what he'd done. He rested his weight against the shovel, and turned to look at the window. Liz had left the kitchen, but her mug, rested on the big wood kitchen table. Thinking of himself at four or five, his feet swinging, his nose just clearing his dinner plate, created just as much tension in his neck as Liz would have if she'd still been sitting there. Becoming Clara's lover had orphaned him. They were only her parents now. He was alone.

Artie scratched the shovel against the slate making an uncomfortable noise that sent shivers down his spine. He wiped his head on his sleeve again and huffed. There was no more snow to shovel. Every inch of slate on the property was cleared, even the path to the pool. He looked up in the direction of the big house. He could clear the driveway. While he walked, he rested the shovel on his shoulder and thought of the seven dwarves in *Snow White*. Hi-ho hi-ho it's off to work we go.

They never cleared the driveway. All their cars were four-wheel drive, but clearing the driveway without being asked felt good. Liz would appreciate it. She would know he did it because he was a good kid, understand that he was part of the family. He lifted the shovel back, gathered his strength and drove it hard into the snow. When he tossed the snow aside bits of dirt and gravel flew with it. He was wasting his time. There was no way to shovel a gravel driveway.

SEVENTEEN

The house was too quiet. It had been two months since Clara had come to Liz asking if she could move into Sissy's house. It was exactly what Liz had been hoping for. She thought Clara would keep Artie from going crazy, from wallowing in Sissy's death, but instead it seemed to be the exact opposite. They were both turning into hermits.

She actually missed the days when Clara tiptoed into the house at five in the morning, her face heavy with naughty behavior. She missed listening for Artie to be dropped off; the whir of an engine, the slam of some high school-er's car door and the trudge of his feet to the house. Now they never spoke to her, only to each other. They ate breakfast and dinner at her house, but they had nothing to say to her. They only made eye contact with each other.

Clara had started to fill Sissy's fridge with food, so they didn't even come to the house to snack. Last week Clara snuck through the kitchen door at three in the morning to get some milk. Elizabeth heard her and went downstairs. Clara was wearing clogs and an old shirt of Artie's, and reading the date on the milk in the light of the fridge. When she saw Elizabeth, she had almost looked embarrassed. She said, "Sorry Mom, I didn't mean to wake you. We...we just ran out of milk, and I wanted cereal." How had it gotten to a point where her daughter was embarrassed to be drinking her milk?

Elizabeth turned the T.V. on, trying to kill the echoing silence, but there was nothing to watch. She found the remote in between the cushions of the couch and pressed the buttons trying to get the damn thing to turn off. She could never figure out the T.V. or the DVD player. The kids laughed at her, but she wished that things still only had two knobs to turn. Finally, the television blinked and went off, making that high pitched plink-fizz sound as the picture disappeared. She sat, staring out at the driveway.

Headlights bobbed around the turn and moved up towards the house. Elizabeth recognized the shape of the lights instantly; it was the truck. She hadn't heard the kids leave. Maybe they went to the video store. Maybe she would go over to Sissy's house and watch a movie with them. No. Not maybe. She would. If her kids wouldn't hang out at her house, she could go hang out with them.

Since she had sunk deep into the couch, it took effort to pull herself up, but the sheer joy of her decision to spend the evening with Clara and Artie propelled her towards the back door. She knew Cliff was in the kitchen, and she wondered if maybe he would want to join them. It would be a pleasure to act like a family, even if it was only for this one night. Cliff was trying to balance their books, but he could leave that for later. The task would take him weeks to accomplish. She had told him to hire an accountant a million times, but he insisted on doing it himself. He said, "If I can build our houses, then I can definitely do our taxes." The statement seemed ridiculous to Elizabeth. One thing had absolutely nothing to do with the other.

Liz was aware of the void between her and Cliff. She had created it. His grief and behaviors were excruciatingly distasteful to her, but lately she felt more than just anger when she looked at him. It was a lack of knowledge. She felt like he was a stranger, in fact, being with him made the house seem more desolate. Michael's outburst on Thanksgiving had forced her to evaluate Cliff's interactions with Sissy throughout the years. She had turned a blind eye to their closeness without ever realizing how their behavior might affect the kids. She didn't believe that Sissy was truly Cliff's lover, but it shamed her that Michael perceived it in that way, and she was angry at Cliff because his interactions hadn't drawn a distinction between her and Sissy. She still loved Cliff of course, but he seemed more like an old annoying friend rather than the lover she had known over the years. There was no intimacy left. She never realized how Sissy's presence had anchored her marriage. Without Sissy there seemed to be no happy words between them. She often found herself wondering if their marriage would have lasted had Sissy not come into their lives, but not tonight. Tonight she would focus on the idea of family. She would force herself to really enjoy the moment.

She turned down the hallway to the kitchen and looked at Cliff sitting at the table. Like a fool, he was working only by the distant light from the hall. As she came through the door, he looked up at her.

"Do you need something?" he asked.

"I was thinking we could go watch a movie with the kids. Why are you working in the dark? Turn on the light in here for Christ's..." As she spoke she fumbled for the switch with her left hand, but then something caught her eye.

She could see Artie and Clara standing by their front door. She had been right. They were planning a night in. A familiar supermarket bag, probably filed with junk like microwave popcorn, hung from one of Clara's hands. Clara was facing Artie and smiling. Her other hand grasped aimlessly behind her, looking for the doorknob. She laughed, and Artie took her face in his two hands and kissed her. They were mingled together for a moment. Then Clara found the latch, and the door pushed open and they were gone. Everything was silent again.

EIGHTEEN

Cliff shut the door behind him. The distance between the two houses seemed to shrink. The night sky, tangible and black, closed in around him. He took a deep breath. The cold air burned in his chest. The snow was a few days old, and it crunched beneath his boots. Cliff didn't want to ruin it. He didn't want to be responsible for making them sad again, but there was nothing he could do.

He realized they were lovers on Christmas morning, but he didn't tell Liz. He hadn't even thought about telling her. She grew more and more militant each day. The girl he married was hiding behind a wall of routines and responsibilities. Her repertoire of emotions was limited to anger, discomfort, and repressed misery. Even when she laughed, he could see anguish in her eyes. If she would pause for just a moment and release all that stress, then he was sure her crow's feet would peel away and the vital, nubile Liz would reappear. Liz insisted they should celebrate Christmas in Sissy's House as they always had. They had to keep celebrating, she chanted. For the kids, she said.

On Christmas Eve, Liz and Clara decorated the tree. Liz had always been fanatic about Christmas decorations. They owned hundreds of glass balls and glittery snowmen, but the three Cliff liked best were odd shaped and fading. The kids made them out of construction paper when Artie was barely old enough to think. He kept picturing all three little faces sitting in a circle on the floor, scraps, crayons and dull scissors at their feet. Clara wearing pink pajamas with footies, gurgling, "Look, Daddy, Look. I made an onamint for the Christmas tree."

"Me too, Daddy Cliff," said Artie as his sticky hand squeezed Cliff's index finger.

"Mine's better than theirs Dad." Michael held his up for his father to see. "Look. See. My Santa has a face."

Sissy and Elizabeth had the kids make ornaments for years after that, but he still liked those first three best. Clara, like Liz, still enjoyed setting up for the Christmas festivities, but Artie had been hanging out on the sidelines with Cliff for a few years. Sissy had occasionally enticed them to hang an ornament or two but this year they just watched and sipped eggnog.

Cliff spiked their drinks, and he winked at Artie when he set the glass down in front of him. Artie was not in tune with Cliff the way Sissy had been, and he spit his first sip back into the glass, announcing, "The eggnog is awful. It must be bad." Liz smelled the carton, and Cliff elbowed Artie hard in the ribs.

The fire snapped and Cliff stood up to tend to it. He jabbed the iron poker at the orange embers in the fireplace for a while, and when he turned around, he noticed Artie had a funny look in his eyes. He followed his line of vision to Clara, who returned the gaze, her mouth half-smiling. He marveled at how Clara's expressions mimicked his own. She was teasing him. It was the way he looked at Sissy or Liz, but he didn't acknowledge where that thought led until the next morning.

Artie gave Clara Sissy's ring. It was a wide gold ring with an oval lapis set dead center. Clara peeled back the tissue, and said nothing.

She didn't gasp or coo. She looked straight into Artie's eyes, quiet and serious, and said, "I love you."

"Come on Clara, cut the suspense. What is it?" Liz asked.

But Cliff didn't care. He was watching Artie. Artie's cheeks flushed and his lips paled. Clara's expression from the night before came back to him. And snap, like a blaring car alarm over and over: ARTIE IS SCREWING MY DAUGHTER. He knew something was up the day Artie sequestered himself in the bathroom, but he was betting on green hair or a tattoo. It had never occurred to him that it was sex, but it made sense. Slowly, Artie's head turned in his direction. Liz and Clara had begun to gurgle over Artie's generosity. Liz was squishing his cheeks and kissing his face. Cliff just looked at him, and Artie stared back. It took him a moment to regain his composure, and realize how frightened Artie looked.

Cliff stood up walked down the three steps to the ground floor and crossed into the kitchen. He opened the cabinet, took out a glass and poured himself whiskey. He knew Artie was standing behind him. He thought that Sissy had always wanted this, so why not let it be. He rolled his shoulders, shook his head, and like everything else, he decided to forget what he knew. He took down a second glass and poured again. His eyes teared up, and he turned glasses in hand and said, "This celebrating shit is hard, when you pull a stunt like that." Artie looked blankly at him. Cliff looked down at his glass and then back at Artie. He offered Artie one of the glasses. "We always spiked our eggnog. You know...I miss her, kid." He raised his glass towards Artie's and said, "Merry Christmas, Sis. Wherever you are..." Clink. Cliff swallowed. Artie put down the glass and hugged him.

Liz's reaction was even worse than he expected. He didn't understand her. She kept saying incest and incestuous.

Cliff said, "They're not actually related."

"What?" Liz fired at him. "What are you talking about Cliff? They grew up together." She bit at the end of her words. The inside of his ears burned at her tone. "We're a family. They're siblings." Her voice was pressured and loud. "You don't understand." She was pacing. She continuously ran her hands through her hair leaving behind disarrayed knots and her cheeks were swollen and red from crying. She looked crazy.

"We'll deal with it in the morning," he said.

"No. Think of what they're doing. How can you not understand this? How can you just..." Her fists shook in front of her body and her face contorted with rage. "You're useless. I have to do everything."

She started to storm after them, but Cliff blocked her path. He grabbed her by the wrists.

"Let go of me, you bastard." She screamed and kicked him.

His shin throbbed. He could feel the blood running through his body to the point of contact. He flinched and let her go. Without hesitation, she ran for the other door. Her bare feet clapped against the floor. Cliff caught her by the back of her shirt, and she fell down. Her feet slipped forward and she drifted gracefully to the floor, like the tide clawing the shoreline. Cliff leaned over her, braced for her next move, but Liz just pulled her knees into her chest and stared blankly ahead. Looking at her curled on the floor of their foyer, withdrawn to somewhere hard and empty, Cliff decided to do whatever she wanted.

He used his key to open the door. He heard them laughing upstairs. Clara squealed Artie's name. Cliff wondered if Artie was tickling her or chasing her.

"Clara," he called, and they got silent.

"Daddy?"

"You need to come downstairs." He waited. He just stood there, arms limp at his sides. He heard them whispering, he heard their movements, he pictured her shimmying into her jeans, and then she appeared at the top of the steps. Her blond hair was tousled, and she nervously tucked it behind her ears.

"What's the matter, Daddy? Her voice was little, just a sliver.

"Your mom saw you."

"Saw me what?"

"Stop. I can't fix it. She saw you both." Clara sank down to the floor. In the blue moonlight, she looked emaciated. Cliff wanted to go to her, but he couldn't. His boots were wet. "You need to stand up... You need to go home. She's waiting for you in the kitchen."

"What about Artie?" She asked.

"He needs to do the same."

"What did she say?" She asked.

"She's mad. Come on, Clara, stop this." He raised his voice a touch. "Get up and go. Artie and I will be right behind you."

She stood up, looked over her shoulder to where Artie must have been standing, and like her mother, her strong controlled voice, said "It's gonna be okay. Don't worry." Then she started down the stairs.

"Let's go, Art." Cliff said loudly. He heard no movement, only crying.

NINETEEN

Michael – skiing with the Worthingtons

Michael loved to ski. When he was four Elizabeth drove him up to the Santa Fe Ski Basin, snapped him into a pair of blue skis that had two racing stripes down the center, patted him on the bottom, and said, "Well, you look like a skier, time to be one." Before he knew it, she was gone, barreling away from him towards the lodge. She only went about thirty feet, but just the thought that she was leaving him sparked his nerves, and he was after her. He fell a lot in those days, but by the time he was nine he raced on the basin's team and spent every weekend on the mountain.

Santa Fe ski basin was the thing he missed most about New Mexico. He loved it there. You could take the lift right to the tip-top, above the tree line about 11,000 feet, or as a kid, the top of the world. The wind whips hard and the snow rolls like a Jell-O mold, but the powder is perfect. When he got to high school, he and a few buddies used to go off the backside of the mountain, where there are no trails. It was awesome. Complete silence, except for the swish of your edges as you cut back and forth through the trees. Eventually, they would hit the road that leads back to the basin and hitch a ride.

Every couple of years a kid gets killed or lost in those woods, but Michael could never help himself. He'd try to talk himself out of skiing the bowl, and then swing off the chair lift headed in that direction. He'd stop at the crest, look down to the tree-line, and beyond to the road below. He'd make deals with himself, like if a car comes up the road in the next five minutes, I'll go, but when it didn't come, he'd always extend the deadline. Eventually, he'd give in and jump, whoosh, headed straight for the tree-line.

For Michael, skiing was a non-stop thrill, so when Bill Worthington, Katie's father, invited him to join the Worthington family at their house in Vermont for their President's Day weekend ski-a-thon, he had jumped at the chance. Without much effort, Katie convinced Michael to cut his Wednesday afternoon classes and drive up early, so they could have the house to themselves on Thursday. He had been looking forward to the trip for weeks. They were already en route when his phone rang for the first time. He looked at the caller ID, recognized his home phone number, and silenced the ringer. Since Thanksgiving he'd given up explaining to his mother where he was or what he was doing.

"Who was it?" Katie asked.

"My mom," he answered, "I didn't think I should tell her that I blew off International Economics and Global Marketing to sit in a hot tub with my girl." He smiled. Katie smiled back. Her cheeks were rosy.

"Is that all I am to you Michael Gordon, a piece of ass in a bikini?"

"Damn straight, girlie." He said without hesitation. Katie snarled at him, and then started lecturing, but she was happy.

"You shouldn't avoid your mother's phone calls. Just tell her you're busy. What if something bad happened or there was an emergency..."

"Then I'd call her back, after listening to the message."

"You never check your messages." Good point, Michael thought.

"I will. I'll check them right now. Will that make you feel better, your highness?" He wasn't sure if he was annoyed at her or not, so he tried to poke fun and joke, but his tone was not so fun. He knew he offended her. Lately, she was always pestering him to talk about his family, so when it came to discussing his relationship with them, he turned on her too quickly.

"I was just trying to help." She turned and pouted. They drove in silence for a while, and when he stopped for gas, she walked around to his side of the car and kissed him.

"Sorry," she said. "It wasn't really my business."

"No, I'm sorry. I was acting like a jerk. I just wanted us to have fun. Not talk to my mom." She kissed him again.

"You want a soda?" She asked. While, she was inside Michael dialed his messages. "You have twenty-two new messages," said the computerized operator. Most of the twenty-two were from Katie and his family and he quickly erased them. The second to last message was Steve, a friend from class. He wanted to know why Michael wasn't in class, and to inform him that the assignment for next week had changed. He listened to the message twice to make sure he understood the new assignment. Finally, he got to the message from his mom, only it wasn't his mom. It was his dad.

Michael's dad never called him. In fact, he couldn't remember once in his entire college career when his dad had called him. They spoke whenever he was near a phone call to Michael, which was often. So, Michael didn't really realize he never called until he heard his voice on the message.

"Umm...Michael. It's your dad. Give me a call. I'm home now, but I'm going into the office in a bit. Okay. Thanks."

Everything Katie said in the car flooded his brain. Michael had chosen not to go home for Christmas, again, and if something had happened to his mom, he could have never forgiven himself. If he had been thinking rationally he would have just called his dad back. Cliff sounded pleasant enough on the message, but Michael was so guilty about how he handled his family and Katie that he expected the worst.

He slipped the phone in the breast pocket of his shirt and focused on pumping the gas. By the time he climbed back into the driver's seat, the color had drained from his lips. When Katie shut her door, the first words out of her mouth were, "Are you okay?"

"It was my dad. My dad never calls," he said.

"So, call him back..."

"What if something happened?" The phone rang again. Michael looked at his pocket, as the phone shook against his chest.

"Answer it." Katie was annoyed.

Without looking at the caller ID, Michael flipped open the phone, and said "Hello?" It was his mother and she was crying. For an instant, relief spread throughout his chest, then his mind focused on Clara.

"Mom, is Clara okay?" He asked frantically.

"No. Michael, everything is wrong. How could this have happened? This never would have happened if Sissy were still alive." Elizabeth began to cry harder.

"Is she in the hospital, Mom? What happened? Is she going to be okay?"

Elizabeth's words were interrupted with sniffles and gasps but eventually he heard, "She and Artie....I saw them...I saw them kissing," followed by a loud sob.

"What?" He said curtly. "MOM, is Clara okay? And by OKAY, I mean is she physically ill?"

"No. I mean yes. Physically she's fine, but..." Sniffle.

"So, she finally slept with Artie, huh?" It had just slipped out. Right after he said it his eyes were popping out of his head, but he couldn't force his neck to turn in Katie's direction. "Listen, Mom, I have to go. I'm busy. Can I call you later or in a bit?"

"What do you mean, finally slept with Artie? Michael Timothy Gordon what the hell is going on?" Elizabeth's voice screeched at him, and he held the phone away from his ear. He could not talk about this now.

"Mom, Listen, I'll call you back as soon as I can." His voice had a slight sing-song quality. He put the phone in his pocket, and it began to ring again. He didn't answer. Gently, without looking at Katie, he turned the key and drove out of the gas station. Katie didn't say anything about Michael's conversation, but he knew she heard him. He wasn't quite sure how to broach the subject. She would eventually ask him, and he figured it was best just to wait for her inquiry.

The Worthington's "ski home" was awesome, a downright log cabin, nestled in the trees, a stone's throw from the slopes, furnished with red Navaho blankets and Elk heads, very posh-posh. It was a house where people drink hot toddies. They had stopped at the supermarket on their way up, and Katie suggested she make dinner, lasagna, while Michael unloaded the car.

Outside, Michael rubbed his hands together, cupped them around his mouth and blew his warm breath at his red tipped fingers. He had unloaded the luggage on the porch, and was now resting one foot on top of his suitcase. He needed to call his mother. Elizabeth would be sitting in the kitchen, growing angrier by the minute. He had often come home to find her tapping her fingers, pinkie first, the others in succession, like falling dominos.

Michael called Artie's house instead. Clara answered.

"Daddy?"

"What are you doing there? If Mom finds out she'll kill you."

"Mike?"

"Yeah, I was trying to get Artie. I thought he might be freaking."

"She told you, huh? He is. He's been crying the whole time. Won't talk to anyone, but Dad. Not even me."

"What are they going to do?"

"She's acting insane. Like I'm a delinquent. She threatened to send us off to military school. I graduated already, for Christ's sake."

Michael laughed, "Goin' for a buzz cut." He realized it wasn't funny. "She could do that to Artie."

"I know. I'm scared for him. He's been all freaked out about not having a family for weeks. He thinks that because we're together Mom and Dad won't love him anymore...Or something like that." Clara was acting cool, but every now and then the timbre of her voice sounded like she was going to cry.

Michael was pacing back and forth on the Worthington's porch. He kicked snow off the edge and watched it fall. He was no good at girl-counsel.

"Don't worry. She loves him as much as she loves us. She'll get over it."

"But I won't..." She started crying. "I love him. I want to be with him."

"Forever?"

"I don't know, but I want to find out."

"It'll all work out. Stop crying." She took a deep breath and sighed.

"I just feel help...hold on... someone's calling on the other line."

He sat down on an evergreen rocking chair by the door. It never occurred to him that his mom would be upset by Clara and Artie finally coming together. He had always assumed that someday something would happen between them. It was always obvious how Clara felt. He'd never discussed it with her, but he knew. He thought everyone knew. He couldn't imagine how Artie was feeling. He walked through the sequence in his mind. Because Sissy was dead, and his Mom was so shocked, Artie had traded the only family he had left to sleep with Clara. Michael's chest constricted a bit. It would have been better if they crossed the friendship-wall while crazy Sissy was still alive. Sissy could have calmed his Mom down. Clara clicked back.

"Llo..Hello?" Clara always said hello while she was pressing the flash button on the phone, so you heard her say hello or parts of hello twice.

"Hi."

"Listen, it's Dad. I have to go."

"Okay. I'll call you later. Wait...tell Dad I got his message, and I'll call him later. Also, tell Artie to call me if he feels like it. Okay?"

"Yeah." She was getting all blubbery again. "I love you, Mike."

"Me too. Talk to you later." He hung up. WOW, was he glad he wasn't there. He missed them though. He would have to talk to them all weekend. They would call. He had to explain everything to Kate. There was no getting around it.

He carried the bags into the front hall and walked straight into the kitchen. Katie was wearing an apron that had "Queen of the Kitchen" printed on it and the "I" was dotted with a crown. She was wiping the hair out of her eyes with the back of her hand because her fingers were covered in spaghetti sauce. God, she was perfect.

"I love you," he said.

Kate smiled. "You're kidding?" She quipped sarcastically. She always said that. He liked it. It made him feel like he was good to her. She always followed it with, "I love you too," but he didn't give her a chance.

"I lied to you."

"No, you sort-of lied. Basically, you omitted the truth. That's different." She didn't look at him.

"What?"

"Because if you lied, then I lied too...," she paused, looked at him and looked back at the lasagna, "and really, I don't think I should get in trouble for what I did, so it would be unfair for me to be mad at you."

"Katie, what are you talking about?"

"I called your mother."

"What?" He wasn't mad. He was shocked. "How? How did you get her phone number?"

"I was starting to think you were crazy, or that your whole family was killed in a house fire or something." Her eyes worked harder at apologizing than her words did.

"Go on."

"Anyway, I got the number from your cell phone, and I called her."

"What did she say?"

"That she wanted to meet me. I told her that I was constantly trying to get you to take me to Santa Fe, but I understood that she wouldn't want us so soon after her sister-in-law died, and she said she didn't have a sister-in-law...You get the idea."

"When?"

"Right after Thanksgiving."

"Why didn't you tell me?"

"Your mother told me to let you suffer," she half smiled.

"You must think I'm such a jerk." He ran his fingers through his hair. He looked up at her and watched her wipe the sauce off on her apron.

"No." Her voice was quiet. She came close to him and put her arms around his waist.

"I didn't feel like explaining it in the beginning, and then it was too late."

"I know," she said and rested her cheek on his chest.

"Thank you." He buried his face in her hair. He could feel that she was a little fidgety "Katie, are you sure it's okay?"

She looked up at him, took her arms from his waist, faced the stove again, and said, "Oh yeah. That's fine. It's just...I also told your mother Clara could stay in the apartment my dad owns in New York..." She turned, her nose was scrunched up and her fingers were close to her face like she was going to bite her nails. "I just wanted her to like me, ya know."

"When? Wait, what?" Michael threw his head back and laughed. "You spoke to her today. You called her to explain why I hung up on her. Didn't you? You sneaky little devil. You called her while I was unloading the luggage." Katie bit her lower lip.

"I just didn't want her to be upset."

He grabbed her and kissed her hard. "You amaze me. You meddle and things get better."

TWENTY

Liz was so completely embarrassed that it took her almost a week to tell Ruth about Clara and Artie's indiscretions. Ruth had been pestering her to talk about what happened since the morning after the incident. Liz knew how she looked when she showed up that day, and she was a good hour and a half early, but it wasn't her early arrival, her dirty hair or the fact that she was wearing the previous day's clothes that gave her away. It was her silence. She was so angry she could hardly talk at all, let alone confess her failure to notice what was both disgusting and infuriating to her and yet somehow obvious and inevitable to everyone she loved. Katie's offer prompted Liz to talk.

Liz was lying on the couch in Ruth's studio watching her paint when Katie called. Her cell phone jingled a computerized version of "Superstitious" by Stevie Wonder, and in response to the noise Ruth turned and lifted a curious eyebrow at Liz's ring choice. She was wearing her artist's uniform, a navy blue jumpsuit that she bought off some guy who worked at Jiffy Lube and a black smudge of paint on her face made her look like a football player or a solider. Liz feigned embarrassment. She didn't want to disturb Ruth's creative concentration, so she got up, motioned that she was going in the other room, and proceeded to pace the living room while Katie explained why Michael had dismissed Liz so abruptly.

Katie was so easy to talk to, and she had already overheard the sticky parts. Liz expressed a need to separate Artie and Clara, and Katie offered up a solution. Send Clara to New York. Katie was so confident that a spell in New York would be a mind expanding opportunity for Clara. She talked about NYU, the classes Clara could take, the bohemian-chic of Greenwich Village, and the independence New York could provide. She was so utterly enthralled with her solution that Liz was inclined to agree. Clara put off college because Sissy was sick, and now that Sissy was gone there was no reason she shouldn't get on with her life, so Liz hung up the phone smiling, feeling for the first time in months like things were back in her control. She turned to head back into the studio, but Ruth was standing in the doorframe. She had her arms crossed and her nostrils flared.

"You're sending your daughter to New York City without even asking her if she wants to go?" she asked.

Liz immediately felt defensive, "What nineteen-year-old wouldn't want to move to New York?"

"Oh, I don't know," Ruth said, throwing up her hands, "one who just lost a family member."

"Don't patronize me."

Ruth's voice softened, "Don't you think she needs you right now?"

"Clara has clearly proven that she doesn't need me in the slightest."

"What are you talking about? According to you, your daughter has been 'acting up' since Sissy died." Like always, she used her fingers to symbolize the quotation marks around acting up. "What the hell happened last week that was so bad you're willing to deport her?" Ruth had begun to raise her voice again, and Liz felt attacked.

She shouted, "It's none of your fucking business!" Ruth's mouth hung open and she looked stung. Liz immediately regretted yelling. "Ruth, I'm sorry."

"No, you're right. I don't even know her, how could I possibly know what she needs."

"She had an affair with Artie," Liz confessed.

"They slept together?"

"I didn't ask, but I assume so."

"And you had no idea..." Ruth's voice was calm. Liz could see her processing.

"They're like siblings. It disgusts me." Liz sat down on the couch and ran her hands through her hair. Ruth moved to sit next to her.

"They're not siblings." Ruth said, shaking her head and crossing her legs Indian style so that she faced Liz.

"That's exactly what Cliff said."

"You don't see it that way."

"I can't."

"Maybe you should try. Maybe you should trust them."

"They don't know what they're doing. They don't understand the repercussions."

"So, you're going to send Clara to New York to save her from herself."

"Something like that."

"Are you doing this for her or for you?"

"What do you mean?"

"Well, don't you think it's a lot easier to send her away than try to deal with the problem at home?"

"I think we should end this conversation."

"You feel I'm overstepping the boundaries of our relationship?"

"Honestly, yes."

"Fine." Ruth was very matter of fact, but Liz knew her well enough to hear the sorrow in her voice. She stood up and went back into the studio without saying another word. Liz stayed in the living room, curled on Ruth's couch. She looked out the window. The clouds were turning gray like it might storm. Liz tried to will it to rain, rather than think about Clara or Artie or fighting with Ruth for the first time. After a few minutes Ruth returned to the door frame. She looked at Liz and smiled sadly.

"I didn't know our relationship had boundaries," she said.

"Me neither." Liz said regretfully, letting her eyes drift back to the clouds, suddenly aware that her relationship with Sissy had no limits.

"Are you going home soon?" Ruth asked

"In a bit," Liz said turning to look at her and hoping that if she stayed a while the peaceful feeling of Ruth's company would return.

"I'm going to close the door." Ruth said.

"Yeah, okay," Liz said. Ruth didn't look at her. "I'll see you tomorrow, then." The peace was lost. The maudlin French sound of Carla Bruni whispered behind the door and Liz wondered if she had made Ruth cry.

TWENTY-ONE

Cliff
Liz *its ok! I*
don't love you
as much
either w/o her!

Three weeks before Clara left, Cliff was sitting in bed watching Elizabeth begin her "going to bed" ritual. She always began by taking off
her clothes and draping them over the chair at the far side of the room.
First, she removed her blouse, and then her pants. He heard the cold
sound of her pulling at her zipper, and he watched as she balanced on
one foot, pulling at a pant leg, then the other foot and the other pant
leg. Standing with her back to him in her bra and underwear, she always seemed old. The skin on her body just hung there.

He didn't want to send Clara to New York, and he wanted to hate
Liz for even suggesting it, but he didn't. She nonchalantly announced
her plans for Clara over dinner, as though it was just another bit of
information that might kill the awful silence between them all. They
played the roles they had become so comfortable embodying. Clara
flew into a rage, Artie crawled into his own skin, and Cliff just sat
there, dumbfounded. Even now, two weeks later, he wasn't sure how
he felt about sending Clara to New York.

He knew he wanted to keep his daughter close to home, so he could protect her, but their house had become so claustrophobic that he dreamed of escaping, so maybe the best way to protect her was to send her away. He also hoped that if Liz didn't have to focus on keeping her inane promise to Sissy, then maybe he could get to her. Maybe he could make her see that the kids needed her and each other, not just fake smiles.

Liz turned to face him. She looked at him, and he knew the look. It was a look that crossed her face more often in the last few months than it had during the entire duration of their marriage. She was going to say something he didn't want to hear, and she was going to make him listen.

"You don't love me anymore." Her face was hard.

"What?"

"I don't know if you ever will, but I can live with that."

"Liz, don't be ridiculous. I love you."

"No. Well, yes, you do love me, but it's not the same as when she was alive."

Cliff just looked at her. He looked at her aging face. Lines spread out like a fan from the corner of her eyes. He loved her, and he knew she was right. He spent everyday dealing with the fact that he loved them as one entity, two halves making one wife. He only loved her half as much, but he hadn't wanted her to feel that. He wanted to push it down. Drive it hard and deep inside of him, so no one could tell.

She said, "Cliff, with Clara leaving and Michael at school it is just going to be the two of us and Artie now..." she paused.

"Liz, I love you," he swallowed controlling an illegal swell of sadness.

"Listen to me for a minute because I can't watch you look at me like I'm broken. I think we should take turns spending time with Artie. I know he's much closer to you right now, and really, our silent meals are not helping anyone. In time, we'll figure out how to get back to normal. Okay?"

"We can do whatever you want, but stop please stop this nonsense about me not loving you."

"It's okay." She brushed a hair away from her face. "I don't love you as much without her either."

He turned his eyes away from her. It never occurred to him that she could feel that way.

TWENTY-TWO

At about ten–fifteen on the night before Clara left, Artie pushed his hand through the sleeve of his winter jacket. He pulled the zipper all the way up so that the collar covered his chin. He took his gloves from his pockets and pulled the itchy wool of his hat down over his ears. Once he was dressed he stood in the kitchen, listening to the silence of the empty house. He closed his eyes, pretending to hear the movements of his Mom in the bathroom above him. He listened for the faucet as she bushed her teeth, the patter of her feet as she moved to the closet to get her nightgown, the rumbles of the television when she got into bed. When he opened his eyes again, he filled a small glass with water and sipped it slowly, feeling each cool swallow pass over his lips. He placed the empty glass in the sink, took a few deep breaths and made his way onto the roof.

It was cold and a smattering of clouds covered the moon, hiding him in the darkness. He sat cross-legged on the edge of his house, facing Clara's room. The light was on and she was packing. He watched her. Her face was splotchy and swollen from crying. After each pile of sweaters or pair of shoes was loaded into the suitcase, she would stop and silently weep, her face cradled in her hands, the round tip of her nose peeking through her fingers. She moved methodically, back and forth from the dresser to the bed, like pacing, only more robotic. Eventually, she folded the edge of her comforter up over her shoulders and she fell asleep curled in a ball next to her suitcase. He watched her sleep. She left the lights on. She didn't toss or turn. She just curled tighter and tighter into herself, as if she were hiding, fleeing or about to disappear.

He forced himself to stay awake, savoring the sight of her. All he did was watch. All night. He watched her longer than he had the night she was naked by the pool, the night of his mother's funeral. He never stood to pee or to get a glass of water. He hardly made the effort to breathe. He just watched, wishing he could feel the smooth even rhythm of her heart beating. He watched until her sleepy hand drifted from under the covers to smother the blaring page of her alarm clock. He closed his eyes and imagined the sweet and sour warmth of her breath and the tickly stubble of the little hairs on her legs. When the early morning reach of the sun began to warm his cheeks, he allowed the dry sadness of missing her to well up in his throat and he swallowed, turning to go inside.

He showered upstairs, leaving his clothes in a pile on the bathroom floor. He turned the faucet all the way to hot and let the water scald his skin. He stood limp, never reaching for the soap or the shampoo. After a while the hot water ran out, and still he stood there, piercing cold rivulets running through his hair. The alarm clock in the bedroom finally pulled him from the shower, and he walked naked over the tile leaving little wet puddles of water wherever he stepped. He pulled the sheet from the bed and wrapped it around his shoulders. He heard the door downstairs open but he didn't move.

"Artie?" It was Cliff. "Artie are you up there?"

He didn't answer. Instead, he listened to the sound of Cliff's feet as he climbed the steps, slowly and deliberately. Artie never turned to face Cliff. He just stood there, the water seeping through the white cotton of the sheet.

"She'll be leaving soon," Cliff said from the top of the stairs. Artie pulled the sheet tighter around his body. "You should come over to the house, maybe sit and eat a little breakfast." Artie nodded his head. "You should at least say goodbye, Artie." Artie still didn't turn, but he spoke.

"I'll be there, just give me a minute." Cliff turned, leaving, and Artie listened again to the sound of his shoes on the steps, only this time the noise was moving away. Once Cliff was gone, Artie dressed quickly and crossed the yard without looking back so as not to lose his nerve.

Liz made Clara's favorite breakfast, goat cheese and banana stuffed French toast, but she didn't come down to eat. The three of them, Cliff, Liz and Artie, sat in silence, the clanging of their forks echoing around the room. When they were almost finished, Liz pushed back her chair, angry.

"This is ridiculous," she said throwing her napkin into the sticky maple syrup on her plate. She strode out of the kitchen and stood at the bottom of the stairs hollering about learning to take responsibility for your actions and showing your family some respect. Artie quickly put his plate in the sink and went outside to wait for the anger and the guilt to pass. He couldn't stand watching Liz berate Clara for the choices they had made together, but he didn't have the nerve to stand up and let the truth spill from his mouth. The truth was he should be sent away. He was the one who didn't belong.

Artie paced back and forth in the driveway pushing his thoughts from his head. The night Elizabeth announced that Clara would be going to New York, Artie smiled. He hadn't meant to, but Clara saw him. He knew she did. It was his first reaction. He was just so relieved that they weren't sending him away, holing him up in some boarding or military school. If he had thought about it for even a second, he wouldn't be having the feelings he had now, feelings of grief and responsibility. Somehow, he had become so pathetic, so alone in the world, that he had forced Liz to turn out her own daughter.

Cliff came outside carrying Clara's suitcase. He passed Artie and put the bag down next to Elizabeth's car.

"I can't believe she's really doing this," Cliff said. "I was sure she would change her mind."

Artie didn't say anything. He just shrugged his shoulders and pushed his hands deep into his pockets. They walked back into the house together. Liz was sitting at the kitchen table, eating again, as though it were any other day. She looked up at Artie and smiled. "You'd better get moving or you'll be late for school, Artie."

It hadn't even occurred to him that he had school. He looked at her. His eyes were wider than they should be, and he thought he might cry. Clara had not come downstairs yet. He knew he couldn't pull her to him and hold her before she left, but he at least wanted to see her.

"Um…I wanted to…" He couldn't say anything.

"CLARA. ARTIE HAS TO GO TO SCHOOL," Cliff hollered.

She didn't run or clamor down the stairs, but after a minute or so he heard the pounding of her bare feet above his head. When she came into the kitchen, she looked tired. Her hair was piled on top of her head and she was wearing a beat up T-shirt and a pair of boxers, his boxers. She bit her bottom, then her top lip, and finally said, "Bye, I guess."

Liz stood up and crossed the kitchen. Her face was tight and her teeth were clenched. She put her plate in the sink and turned on the faucet. Artie crossed the room and put his arms around Clara for just a second. He didn't say anything. He should have said something. He could have whispered, "I love you" or "Sure hope the plane don't crash," or "I miss you," or "I need you," or "Don't go." But all he did was hug her for a split second, and turn to leave.

"Take care. See ya later," he said as he walked out the door. He didn't look back because he was crying and he couldn't upset Liz. He couldn't risk losing anything else. Once he was out the door he ran for the truck. He knew he couldn't go to school, but he certainly couldn't stay home.

He reversed out the driveway and hit Old Pecos Trail in a matter of seconds. It felt like if he didn't see her leave, she might still be there when he got back. He turned the radio on and clicked through the channels as if he cared what song gurgled through the old speakers. He headed out towards the Santa Fe Airport. There was a clerk at a little convenience store out there who sold beer to underage kids. He couldn't think of anything he'd rather do than drink himself into a stupor, except maybe get high until he couldn't think anymore.

He pulled into the parking lot of the mini-mart and was surprised to see Christina Graves pushing open the store's door with her hip, two six packs in hand. For a minute he thought about putting the car in reverse again, but she spotted him right off and lifted one six-pack in greeting. Artie turned the key and the engine stilled, the sound of the cooling fan taking its place. Slowly, he climbed out from behind the steering wheel and walked in her direction. Christina lifted the beer through her passenger window, placed it down on the empty seat, and then turned, leaning her tush against the car, her arms crossed over her breasts. She wasn't wearing a jacket and the deep v-neck of her sweater left most of her chest exposed.

"Hey, stranger. What brings you here so early in the day?" Artie shifted his weight from one foot to the other. He knew she was flirting with him and it almost felt good.

"I don't know," he said. "Thought I might drown a sorrow or two. How 'bout you? What drives you to drink so early in the day?"

"A couple of us thought we'd ditch and get wasted up at Will's house. His parents are out of town."

"Good deal. Sounds like fun"

"You're welcome to join. Craig, Ben and Marti are gonna be up there and Will's got a hot tub." Christina uncrossed her arms and for a second he rested his gaze on the smooth curve of her cleavage, remembering how the sweet scent of her skin used to calm his nerves. The candy smell of Christina didn't mean anything anymore, not now that he could picture the little pieces of hair that escaped from Clara's ponytail at the end of the day or pretend to feel the sensation of her nuzzling her nose against his neck when she was cold, but it didn't matter.   Clara was gone, already on her way to New York.

"Ah...I don't know. I'm kinda a bummer these days."

"Come on Artie. It'll be fun, like old times. We'll get high, maybe have a beer or two." She stepped closer to him, reached out her hand, straightened his collar, parted her lips and turned two doe eyes up at him. "I'll make it worth your while."

TWENTY-THREE

Clara stood in line at the Albuquerque airport waiting to check her luggage. Airports made her stomach curdle. A movie she saw when she was a kid portrayed airports as purgatory. In the movie, dead souls drifted through the mist, until they stood facing a stretch of glass windows punctuated by revolving doors. Waiting behind the glass at the end of a rope maze and in front of a five-foot desk, stood a stiff suited woman. A woman who never looked up, never smiled, and never left the house unpainted. Her makeup was thick and dry, a dehydrated symbol of misery. A nasal voice echoed over the loud speaker, "Flight 666 now boarding at gate 10. Passenger Adolf Hitler, please report to Gate 10." It was not a great flick, but Clara could never quite get past the idea that planes delivered you to heaven or hell. Planes equal dying. Mention airports, airplanes, anything airport related, and Clara was immediately channeling the grim reaper.

Clara pressed her hand against her tummy where a nervous pressure was building. She had to go to the bathroom. Every plane trip she had taken until this morning incorporated a series of rituals. Normally, she was not the superstitious type, but going through the motions calmed her nerves. She had a good luck charm she carried with her, a small bronze frog Artie made for her thirteenth birthday. She ate gummy bears during takeoff while quietly chanting, "Up, up boy." Finally, before getting on the plane she called her parents and Sissy to say, "Sure hope the plane don't crash," and they would each reply, "Yep, sure hope the plane don't crash." It was this final aspect of her ritual which she had not attended to today.

Clearly she couldn't call Sissy because she was dead, but she could have gotten around that if she was speaking to Elizabeth. Clara yelled at her at least once a day, but nothing normal passed between them anymore. She didn't even allow her to come into the airport. Clara just shut the car door on Elizabeth's goodbye and walked away. Clara felt like hating her, blaming her for Artie's behavior. Artie was polite, spoke when spoken to, and always smiled. He never approached Clara, never fought for her, never showed one ounce of courage. It was as though they were never friends, let alone lovers.

Standing in front of Clara on line was a mother and her two young children. The older child, a little Hispanic girl, plopped down on the ground. Her legs were tan and chubby, and she had a long shiny braid down her back. She couldn't be more than two. The mother leaned toward her, and pulled her back to her feet, using her one free hand. In her other arm she cradled her infant. Between the three of them they had one suitcase. The mother was Clara's age, maybe a year older or a year younger.

Clara pictured the three of them on the plane, the mother buckling the older child's seatbelt, while struggling to support the infant on her lap, the little girl crying from the pressure in her ears, the plane tilting up heading to thirty thousand feet. In her mind, the child bounced in her seat as the plane angled back to the earth, and the three together emerged from the gate, the mother smiling, glad to be wherever she was. Maybe home.

Clara had six hours and a layover in Dallas between her and LaGuardia Airport. She had never been to New York before, and she didn't know anyone there. Katie, who Clara had spoken to but never met, was picking her up. Michael was supposed to come with her, but he called last night explaining he was held up at school. On the phone Katie had described herself as thin, blond and preppy, which made Clara a little dizzy.

Clara didn't know how to feel about being sent to Katie's father's apartment. On the surface, she was furious, but deep down part of her was thankful to escape from Santa Fe. The last few weeks had been more than hard. Both Clara and Artie were grounded "until further notice." Their only interaction was supervised, breakfast and dinner, under Elizabeth's scornful eyes. Elizabeth was insane. She called Mr. Balducci's Pharmacy first thing in the morning to confirm Clara's arrival, she drove Artie to school herself, and she devised a system of random checks. In other words, she popped into work at least three times a week. She didn't sleep at night. Clara would wake up and find her surfing the net, or watching the late-late movie. If Clara so much as went to the kitchen to get a snack, Elizabeth was there. She was everywhere.

Clara would have happily put up with her mother's wacko behavior if Artie gave her one inkling that he wished things were different, but his mood was heavy and serious like a blood soaked towel. He couldn't so much as glance at her. She was sure he was starting to buy the "incest" theory, which coming from Elizabeth was dumb, but coming from Artie made Clara feel ashamed.

Every night lying in the bed, she'd slept in since she was two, Clara thought about her family, Artie and Sissy. She'd thought about all the things Sissy had taught her, she thought about all the years she spent pining for Artie, and how he had lived his whole life except for the past few months without the burden of loving her. She thought about the things she had never done, and the adventures she hadn't taken. These thoughts, which were at first pleasantly distracting, quickly grew plaguing because she had rarely looked beyond loving Artie. Clara wasn't even really sure what she enjoyed doing. She had never lived on her own, or ventured far from Santa Fe for a long period of time, so she had no idea what New York would be like. Now, she didn't have any choice.

One night at the dinner table Elizabeth said, "I decided Clara should move to New York."

"What are you talking about? Where would I live?" Clara asked.

Elizabeth ignored her, directing her conversation to Cliff. "Katie has offered to put Clara up at her father's corporate apartment for a while, and it just seems like the best solution." Cliff looked almost as white as Clara. Artie never looked up from his plate.

"Who's Katie?" Cliff asked.

"I've never even met her," Clara said. Clara was ignored a second time.

"Cliff," sighed Elizabeth. She was disappointed, "Try to pay attention every now and then, okay?" She shifted in her chair and sat up straight. "Katie is Michael's girlfriend for the last three years." Her voice was hard. Cold.

"So that's it huh, you decide my fate and I've got to listen to you." Clara's voice dropped a notch, hinting at the idea that she was talking under her breath, but too loud to be secretive. "I hate you." She glanced at her father who had also retreated to the safety of his plate. She stood up, threw her napkin on the table, and looked at Artie. He didn't look up. She let the anger melt from her voice and coolly poured her bitterness in Elizabeth's direction. "Whatever you say, Mom. You're the boss." After she tore out of the kitchen, Clara waited for a reaction, but none came. No one yelled. No one fought.

A slim airline employee who was barely tall enough to see over her computer called forward the next passenger, and Clara watched the girl struggle to move her children and her suitcase. The two year old dropped to the floor again, and the girl closed her eyes like she might cry. Her chest rose and fell as she took a deep breath, forcing her frustration elsewhere. She adjusted the baby, picked up the suitcase, looked at the older child on the floor and said, "Let's go Mercedes. Come on." The little girl smiled at her mother and crawled after her on all fours.

Sissy would have helped her, but Clara always felt awkward helping strangers. Sissy believed in the whole karma bit, give, receive, give receive. Clara was big on self-reliance and didn't feel the need to put herself out there. Before Sissy died, Clara would have helped the girl. Now, she just wanted people to respect her space. She didn't want to make idle chit-chat with strangers or smile at the pushy sales girl and say, "I'm just looking, thank you." She wanted to be the person who told the truth. "If I needed your help I'd ask for it, you corporate drone," or, "Why would I want to see pictures of your kids? I don't know you." Unfortunately, Clara found that her quest towards truth-sayer resulted in a lack of common courtesy, and Clara detested rudeness. The man who checked Clara in was an embodiment of this exact conflict.

Acne scars covered his cheeks and forehead, and even though Clara's skin had always been clear, she feared acne, and she knew she would be unable to conceal the combination of pity and revulsion his appearance raised in her. If she looked him in the eye, she would have had to explain the look on her face. She would have to say, "The man behind me smelled awful." Or some other quickly devised lie, and the man would think she was cute or funny, and that she assumed a sense of camaraderie with him, when really he repulsed her.

Or, she could ignore him completely, like she was better than him because she was a passenger, and he was a lowly employee. Creating a scenario where she did not lie, but she also failed to offer up the truth, which was just mean. That was the choice, lie, be rude, or tell the guy his face looked like rotten fruit.

Clara heard people in New York were rude. Crazy bird-throwing drivers, who would run you over when the light changed, so they could get their extra-hot, non-fat, no-foam, half-caff, latte one minute before the next guy. So, as a tribute to her new home and future cohorts, Clara swallowed the truth and was rude. She talked without looking him in the eye, pretended to look for something in her purse, took her ticket, thanked him while she was walking away and didn't look back.

She tried on the ego of rude behavior. Acting important made her feel important. She carried her head high as she walked down the peach and turquoise hallways that led to the gate, stopping only to buy gummy bears. She boarded the plane without making eye contact with anyone. Flashing a forced fake smile at the stewardess, she pushed her way to her seat, and began to read a fashion magazine. On almost every page there was a reference to New York. Where to buy designer clothes in New York, hairstylists in New York, chic places to eat in New York, funky shoe stores in New York. New York was littered with opportunities, and according to Katie, Clara was living in a great part of town.

The plane taxied out onto the runway. Clara held tight to the armrests, preparing for takeoff. The bag of gummy bears rested in her lap. "Sure hope the plane don't crash," she said quietly, glancing at Sissy's ring on her left hand. Out the window, Albuquerque airport, in all its cheezoid-tourist's-idea-of-what-the-souwthwest-looks-like-glory began to disappear, the same way her and Artie's houses had earlier that morning. She tried to be excited about New York, but all she could think was that Artie had hardly looked at her when he said good-bye.

TWENTY-FOUR

Liz' mtg with Cliff

The door slamming had startled Elizabeth. She should have expected it. Nineteen year old girls slam doors when they're angry at their mothers. She watched Clara pull her suitcase over the curb and through the revolving doors. She was wearing an oversized sweatshirt that once belonged to Michael and a beat up pair of jeans. The denim fit snugly on her hips, which were fuller than Elizabeth remembered them. She headed for the ticket counter, and never looked back.

Elizabeth took a deep breath, started the car, and turned on the radio. She flicked through the stations, settling on 96.3 WRNM, Classic Rock. Elizabeth wasn't a music buff. She understood music possessed artistic and emotional power. It could make you feel sexy or proud. Slow sweet melodies could touch you, make you cry or give you shivers. Movie previews used epic ballads to suck in drama lovers. Elizabeth was aware of all these things, but for her music served a specific purpose.

Songs were kernels of the past. They triggered memories and broke down the barriers of time. A song from the fifties could instantaneously transport her to her Mother's living room in Palo Alto. When she became a mother, she started to manipulate what song reminded her of what event. If she wanted to remember something, she would pick out a song and play it two or three times at the event. For example, she played the title song from *Free to be You and Me* at Clara's fifth birthday and still put it on mixed tapes because it was a great memory. She tried to pick songs that were current to the era of the event, but it didn't really matter.

The classic rock station served the opposite purpose. She knew the music they played, and their songs already reminded her of something. Forgetting about today, ignoring the fact that she had just ostracized her own daughter, and thinking about yesterday felt like a good idea. After about ten minutes of ads and DJ babble, Mick Jagger's voice rumbled through her speakers. The Rolling Stones reminded her of college.

She remembered dancing in her dorm room with her roommate Evelyn, wearing nothing but panties. Elizabeth jumped around swinging her head and singing lyrics at the top of her lungs. She put on a lime green halter that tied low on her hips, so her whole back was exposed. She never wore a bra, which wasn't unusual then, but she looked great without one. She had perfect breasts when she was nineteen. They weren't very big, but they were strong. Evelyn called them terrific titties. She joked that Elizabeth could be used as a compass.

Evelyn had set Elizabeth up with Jeremy Olsen. They met him together at a party a week earlier. He was a twenty-two year old architecture student. He was about six-three, long blond curly hair that naturally looked like the pin curls of actresses from the forties. Elizabeth thought he was really cool. At the time, Evelyn had been on a few dates with an architecture student that Jeremy was friends with, and she suggested the four of them could go dancing together.

"Call us," she tossed over her shoulder as they left the party.

Elizabeth was pretty sure Jeremy Olsen was interested in Evelyn, but when he called she agreed to go out. The boys came to pick them up at 8:30. At first, they didn't hear them knock because the music was so loud, but eventually, their banging and screaming caught Elizabeth's attention, and she answered the door. That was the first time she saw Cliff. He had a man's face, strong and angular. His eyes were brown, like his hair, which was unfashionably short. He was wearing bell-bottom jeans, a brown leather belt, boots, and a white shirt that he left partially unbuttoned. If he wore that outfit today she would laugh at him, but that night she thought he was gorgeous. He made Jeremy Olsen look sleazy.

Jeremy Olsen was pretty sleazy, and Elizabeth had been right, he was more interested in Evelyn than he was in her. He pretty much ignored Elizabeth the whole night, but she didn't care because all she wanted to do was talk to Cliff. The date was messy. Laughable, even. Cliff seemed hurt and shocked by the whole thing, so Elizabeth didn't give him her phone number even though she wanted to. Jeremy called the following day asking to speak to Evelyn. They got married a couple years later and in 1983, Evelyn divorced him for sleeping with their seventeen-year-old babysitter. Elizabeth saw Cliff for the second time at their wedding.

That time he was wearing a three piece brown suit, and he approached her. He came up behind her and tapped her on the shoulder.

"I could be wrong, but I'm pretty sure that if you and I weren't so boring we wouldn't be here," he said.

She smiled. She'd been drinking since early in the day, and her insides were warm. "Cliff Gordon," she said before she turned around. She knew she looked beautiful. Her hair was streaked with white from sitting at the pool all summer, and she was wearing a pale yellow lace dress that was so light it could have been a nightgown. "I was pretty certain that your broken heart would prevent me from seeing you here."

"Who am I to stand between a man and his bride?"

She laughed. "You wanna dance?" She asked.

She was so hot for him. He was funny and bright and a little shy. She could still feel excited by the memory, sitting in her car at a red light, decades later. They danced together all afternoon, and then he walked her to her car and they started kissing. His kisses were warm and burly. His strong hands pulled her closer and she felt her nipples pressing against her dress. She couldn't remember what his mouth felt like when he kissed her good morning, but she could taste the champagne on his tongue in 1974.

She turned right and pulled into the parking lot of the only restaurant she'd ever been to in Albuquerque. She didn't like Albuquerque at all. Never had. Cliff's old boss used to say Albuquerque is what you'd get if a *K-mart* blew up. She wasn't sure if she would go that far, but she never really felt the need to know about Albuquerque's haunts.

The Owl Diner was open late, and that was its appeal. They always stopped there after they picked someone up from the airport. It was a joint with plastic table tops and neon lights, but the green chili cheeseburger was surprisingly good and the fries were homemade. It was the first time she'd ever set foot in the place during the day, and apparently she wasn't alone. A handful of men were sitting at the bar, but she was the only lunch customer. Elizabeth was glad the restaurant was empty. She didn't like sitting by herself because people stared at you. People pity a woman alone.

Elizabeth asked the hostess to seat her as far away from the bar as possible. The clock on the wall above the girl's head read 11:08 Clara's plane was scheduled to depart at 11:10. Elizabeth pictured her, scared, holding tight to the arm rests, eating gummy bears. "Sure hope the plane don't crash," she said quietly, so the hostess wouldn't hear her.

She ordered green chili cheese fries and a diet coke. There was a bowl filled with long tubular sugar packets on the table. Elizabeth picked one up and tipped it back and forth, listening to the granules roll from one end to the other. She couldn't remember the last time she ate in a restaurant by herself, or for that matter drove to the airport by herself. There was always someone to go with her until today. Granted, the list of possible traveling companions was significantly shorter this time. Cliff had to work, and Artie had school.

When she thought about it, Elizabeth was glad they weren't there. She couldn't think with them around. Cliff was so mopey and miserable, which was not only infuriating, but also forced Liz to talk non-stop to avoid being dragged into his depression. Artie had become a Ken doll; it was like someone unplugged him. Cliff explained to her what was going on with Artie. She understood how he could think he had mistakenly orphaned himself, but nothing was different in her heart. She loved Artie as she had always loved him, as her son. That was the thing that bothered her most about what had happened between Clara and him. Their choice was forcing her to acknowledge what she'd been avoiding since Sissy died.

Her family had changed. Artie was not her son. Sure, she changed his diapers, cleaned his scraped knees and took pride in his accomplishments, but she did not give birth to him. She couldn't be his mother. Elizabeth was not prepared for that. She had assumed that when Sissy died there would be a great sadness in her house, and there was, but she didn't realize how that sadness would burrow through her family, leaving nothing but disconnected empty shells in its wake. She had tried to do what Sissy asked of her, but nothing was right and no one was happy, no matter how much she smiled. It had never occurred to her that she would not be able to carry the torch.

Just a year ago, the house was a bustling vibrant place, a safe and love-filled place for everyone who lived there. Now, no one lived there, at least, no one who felt comfortable. She wasn't sure she had done the right thing sending Clara to New York. She kept wondering what kind of mother sends her own daughter away? She missed her so much, but she'd been missing her for weeks. She felt so mad. So mad that Clara and Artie were not babies that could easily be controlled, so mad that Cliff wasn't the young man in the brown suit, so mad that Sissy left her to take care of everything. She felt pressure everywhere. Each one of the people in her life was like a living pulsating source of stress. There was no one to talk to, no one to trust, no one but Ruth. She pulled out her cell phone and dialed Ruth's number. The phone rang twice before Ruth answered.

"Hello, there," she said, her voice was sweet, caring. Elizabeth could tell she was smiling.

"Hi." Elizabeth steadied her breath and tried to smile too.

"Did you drop her off already?"

"Yeah," Liz swallowed, "I feel terrible about it." Liz paused, gathering her thoughts. "Ruth?"

"Yeah?"

"I think I did the wrong thing. I think Clara needs us and I pushed her away because I was scared."

"You can change your mind. You can always change your mind, Liz."

"Maybe." It had been a long time since Elizabeth questioned her decisions, and she was afraid that if she altered any one part of her plans, everything would crumble and fall apart. But she wasn't sure that mattered because everything seemed to be falling apart with or without her decisions. "What would you do?" She asked.

Ruth sighed, "You want the truth?"

"Yeah."

"I never would have sent her in the first place. Call the airlines. Change the flight. Bring her home."

"I think you might be right."

"Where are you?" Ruth asked.

"The Owl Diner. I stopped for coffee, but now it looks like I'll be in Albuquerque for a while. What are you doing?"

"Me? Ruth paused, then laughed, a little snarky air filled laugh, "I'm driving to Albuquerque."

"What do you mean?"

"I thought you might need me. I'm like twenty minutes from there."

Elizabeth felt startled. "You didn't have to do that," She said.

"I know, but I did."

"Listen, my food's here." It wasn't but Liz wanted to hang up.

"Whatcha get?" Ruth was being, cute and supportive.

"Green chile-cheese fries." Liz mumbled

"New Mexico's answer to comfort food."

"You want anything? I can order it." Liz offered.

"Nah, I'll eat yours."

Again, Ruth's intimacy made Liz's skin crawl. She managed to sound normal, "I can't promise you they'll be any left by the time you get here."

After they said their goodbyes Liz set the phone down on the table and tried to figure out why her interaction with Ruth was so unsettling. Liz did need help. She just wasn't sure it was Ruth's help she needed. Liz wanted Sissy or someone in her family to lean on, someone who knew her history, someone she understood. She felt uncertain that she would ever be able to reignite the spark that held her family together, but suddenly, it was clear that they needed each other not new places or new experiences. Clara was coming home.

The waitress clunked the gooey yellow and pale green coated fries down, and Elizabeth nodded thank you. Steam rose up from the plate. The cheesy grease glistened and the intensity of the spice wafted to her nose. She used her thumb and forefinger to pluck a fry from the pile. Pulling back her lips, Elizabeth tentatively nibbled. It was hot, but not burn your taste buds hot, so Elizabeth popped the whole thing in her mouth.

She lived for green chile. Green chile exists nowhere but New Mexico. It is not chili as most Americans think of chili, no kidney beans, beef or tomatoes. Just stewed hot green hatch chile peppers. Elizabeth wasn't sure if it was how they roasted the chilies, or what, but the flavor was a feverish spice. Normally, when people eat something spicy their mouth, throat, and tongue light up, but green chile is different. It clears your head and makes you sweat. When they first moved to Santa Fe, a girl Elizabeth worked with swore a bowl of green chile and a good shot of tequila could cure all ailments. She didn't know about tequila; it had caused her more trouble than comfort, but there was sanity in green chile. Especially if you poured it over greasy, cheesy fries. As the heat lit up her sinuses, Elizabeth felt like everything was starting to make more sense than it had in a long time.

TWENTY-FIVE

Drive home from airport w/ Clara
Clara finds Christina
in Artie's bed

The drive from Santa Fe to Albuquerque takes about an hour, but when you're headed back to Santa Fe, it always feels longer. The landscape outside the car window builds slowly and it seems to take all of the car's strength to shake free of the dull pre-fab city, and make the exhausting climb into the mountains. Clara had been riding shotgun in the car for almost fifty minutes, and even though the night sky had long ago blanketed her view of the city, she still felt Albuquerque lingering on her clothes. Elizabeth was driving, talking way too fast, and constantly sniffling to avoid tears. Her dramatic behavior and sudden change of heart made Clara's throat itch.

"I never should have let you go." Clara said nothing, so, Elizabeth continued, "I can't believe I did that. I shouldn't have. It's going to be okay. We're going to make it okay now."

Clara felt Elizabeth turn her head for a split second, looking for affirmation, and Clara intentionally turned to look out the window. She had seen Elizabeth like this before. Both hands on the steering wheel, spine straight, voice strong and steady, determining the outcome of something that had no guaranteed certainty. It was ridiculous. All Clara cared about was getting home. She couldn't believe that she was going home.

The flight to Dallas had been nauseating. Marching twenty gate-lengths through the Dallas airport was nauseating. The sign that re-minded Clara of her *Lite-Bright* and read "New York/LGA" was nau-seating. The perky man in the red and blue standard issue American Airline suit was nauseating. Waiting in line to talk to him was nause-ating, and then suddenly as he spoke, telling her it appeared her tick-et had been changed, he became the most handsome, wonderful guy Clara had ever met. She ran back past those twenty gates so fast that she deserved a medal. She had to sit there and wait for like eleven hours, and it never even occurred to her to be frustrated or bored. She was just elated. She wasn't even afraid when the plane took off.

Liz was waiting at the gate when she disembarked, and Clara almost hugged her. Well, she thought about hugging her when she saw her standing there, her eyes all red and tired, but it just didn't feel comfort-able. Clara was still mad. Even though she decided not to send Clara to New York, Liz was still never going to accept that Clara and Artie loved each other more than she wanted them to.

As soon as the car was in the driveway, Clara would jump out, so fast that Elizabeth wouldn't even have time to think about stopping her. She would run full force to the front door of Artie's house. Right through the flowers because the shortest distance between two points is a straight line. When her finger tips touched the door knob she would slow, turning it quietly, tip-toeing through the darkened living room, and up the stairs, until she could see him curled tight like a little boy, whispery breaths all around, long eyelashes resting on his cheek-bones. The sheer anticipation of seeing him was enough to make her lightheaded, but what she wanted most was to see the relief that would pass across his face when he realized that Elizabeth had decided not to ostracize her.

Clara knew he would be relieved, even though he had acted so awful these past few weeks. He would be relieved just like she was, even though on the plane she had a few moments when she thought maybe New York was going to be an adventure, but it wasn't an adventure she wanted. She wanted to stay in Santa Fe with Artie, and as soon as he saw her, he would feel relieved. She understood that he felt caught between a rock and a hard place, but they would change that. Maybe they could get their own place, and then they wouldn't even have to concern themselves with her. They could just live cozy and comfortable, together. Maybe her dad would help them. They would figure it out. It was going to be okay now, whether or not Liz said so.

As they exited the highway, the car's headlights bounced off a reflector, producing a glare that forced Clara to turn back and look at her mother. Elizabeth had finally stopped blabbering, but Clara watched her eyes dart back and forth, and she knew Elizabeth had continued talking to herself in her head. Whenever she thought about anything intently, her eyes raced back and forth.

"What are you talking to yourself about?" Clara asked. She wasn't particularly interested, but she couldn't stand to see her mother silently agonize. Clara found her silent conversations more irritating than the ones she had aloud.

"Well," Elizabeth paused, took a deep breath, "Clara, I don't know what to do about you and Artie, but when we get home I'm just going to go into the house, and go to bed." Clara's fingers started to shake and her eyes felt dry.

"Mom, I..."

"Don't say anything." Elizabeth's face was hard, her lips pursed tightly so you could see all the deep wrinkles in her face. "Go tell him you're home, and in the morning we'll set some ground rules." Clara couldn't look at her mother. Her cheeks felt hot. She cracked the window and let the wind rush against her face.

When they pulled into the driveway, Elizabeth got out of the car first. She shut the door behind her and headed to the main house without looking back. Clara stayed where she was, pulling on the plastic trim of the front seat. She looked through the windshield at Artie's house. There were no lights on. He was probably sleeping exactly as she imagined, buried in the folds of his mom's old comforter.

Slowly, she opened the car door and settled her backpack on one shoulder. She took small steps towards Artie's front door, stopping frequently to feel the burn of the cool night air on her cheeks and nose. She wasn't sure what leeway Elizabeth had given her and not feeling guilty about loving Artie was so unfamiliar. She digested the idea slowly. Even if Elizabeth had only given them this one night, the gesture was enough to make Clara think about following her inside, and letting Artie realize she was home over orange juice and eggs. She decided that she would tell him herself, and maybe they'd talk like they hadn't in weeks and then she would trudge up the hill to her own door and curl up in her own bed.

The doorknob was so cold it felt hot, and Clara had to pull her jacket sleeve down over her hand to touch it. The door creaked, but not that loudly. The blue haze of late night television drifted down from the loft. Clara wondered if Artie was still awake. She tiptoed quietly up the stairs, just like she imagined she would. When she was almost at the top, she paused. A little tingle of nervousness coursed through her chest. She was so excited to see him, to be alone with him. A smile spread across her face, she climbed the last few steps, and turned to face her sweet sleeping Artie.

Artie was lying perpendicular, on his side in his boxers, his back facing Clara, his head resting on the taut tummy of an almost naked Christina Graves. Clara's mouth opened slightly and her eyes started to burn, but she didn't move. A chill wrinkled her stomach, and she swallowed hard to still it. Christina saw her immediately and giggled,

"Holy shit, this is embarrassing." Then she smiled and nudged Artie, nodding for him to look in Clara's direction. He was standing, instantaneously. His eyes were wide and you could almost hear his bones shaking. A beer can scattered across the floor.

"Just wanted to tell you I was home," Clara said. Then, she turned running full-force right through the flowerbeds to her own door.

TWENTY-SIX

Cliff lay his pencil down on the kitchen table. He had been up late every night that week trying to revise a design for a five and a half million-dollar home in the hills just outside of town. He always started by using the computer, but he consistently reverted to a pencil. There was something about drawing the lines that tuned him into the design. His hands knew; they could feel where the graphite belonged.

The client was a pretentious Hollywood bigwig whom no one had ever heard of, but his name was in the credits of every movie ever seen. He had changed his mind three or four times already. His high-pitched voice, trapped somewhere behind his nostrils would whine idiotic suggestions through the speakerphone,

"Listen, Cliff-y, I'm thinking the master should be on its own floor. What do you think?" A rhetorical question. "Fabulous, right."

The guy was an ass, but he was a great connection and the deal was a pricey one, so Cliff suffered with a smile.

These particular revisions should not have been that complicated, but he couldn't seem to keep his mind on his work. He was so worried about sending Clara to New York, but he knew there was nothing he could've said to change Liz's mind. When they left earlier that morning, he swallowed his anger and his pride, he hugged his daughter, and he kissed his wife on the cheek. He hadn't spoken to Liz since, but he wasn't sure what he would have said to her if she called, and she had left him a message that she wouldn't be home until late, so he wasn't worried. He missed her though. He missed her all the time lately. A few nights earlier, around one, Liz had shuffled down the stairs in an old T-shirt and sweats and completely distracted him. He heard the squishy shuffle of her socks as she headed towards him, and he held his breath. Took in a gasp of air and locked it in his chest. The tight bubble stilled his movements, like he was afraid, but he was anything but afraid. He was anxious. He couldn't wait to see her.

They rarely slept in the same bed these days. Some nights she would move to the couch downstairs or to Michael's bed, and on other nights he would move. He wasn't sure about Liz, but he tried to stay. He wished he could stay. He'd lie there looking at his night table, picturing the space between them. It was a human space, like the space that starts between your eyebrows and drifts down the bridge of your nose. He could draw the shape of the space, and he could describe it, but he couldn't claim it.

In the beginning, it was nameless like a lab rat. He was afraid to grow attached to it. Afraid he might enjoy the freedom of not touching, so he would move to avoid the fear, to avoid the space. Eventually, that fear evaporated into raw anger, and the space became a bitter, putrid taste, like biting through a worm in an apple. Again, avoiding the space meant avoiding the anger. The other night, the space had begun to set roots, and he felt no freedom in the chasm between them. Some nights he felt loss and other nights hunger.

Elizabeth had never been a frilly woman. She didn't wear perfume or buy negligees, but she was a sexy woman. She was tall and long. Athletic-looking. She had thick blond hair that escaped from fastenings and fell in rings around her face. She had the kind of beauty that grew when she moved. Dancing, running, washing dishes, Liz was at her best when a thin film of sweat brought color into her cheeks. Her laugh was sexy. When she laughed it was whole. He missed hearing her laugh.

He knew why he'd chosen to forgive Liz for her insane behavior, why it didn't tear holes in his ego when she yelled and cursed, when she called him weak. He deserved to be punished. He never should have jeopardized their life together. He shouldn't have touched Sissy, even if he still allowed her to live on their property. He should have been able to control his lust. He should have known better. He wasn't certain that anything would be that different, but maybe they would have been an impenetrable team. Maybe if he hadn't split his love between the two of them, then his relationship with Liz would be stronger now, and maybe that would have made all the difference.

One thing he did know was that he still loved Liz, even if his love was different than it had been for all those years of his life. When they were young, back in the beginning, when they decided to raise a family in Santa Fe, it was only them, and he was happy then. There were wonderful times in his life when he could remember only Liz, only the two of them. He wanted those times back. He felt almost sure that they could find that place again.

Cliff heard the car pull into the driveway. One door shut. He waited hoping to hear a second door, hoping she had suddenly changed her mind. Nothing. Everything was still. He could hear Liz's feet as she approached the door. Slowing down the ball once Liz started it rolling was impossible. There was always a part of him that thought he should let Liz run the show the way she wanted to because then everything would work out. Things used to run smoothly when Liz took charge.

He believed she would change her mind, if he just gave her some time to figure everything out. Suddenly, he knew he didn't want to send his daughter to New York. Clara didn't want to go there. He should have stopped it. He rubbed his hand across his forehead and whispered to himself, "Fuck."

If he opened his mouth to speak to Liz anger would fly out. He stood up and went to let her in. Maybe if he hugged her hello, he could avoid speaking to her. He'd just nod and listen, never make a sound.

Liz was standing facing the door, but she hadn't tried to open it. Tears were running down her face. He pulled open the door and started to say hi, when the second car door pushed open and Clara stood up. She stood there for a second, holding the rim of the window and then she closed the door and headed in the direction of Sissy's house. Over Liz's shoulder, Cliff watched Clara walk slowly and intently, across the lawn. He felt a smile wrapping his face from ear to ear. He crushed Liz against his chest.

"Thank you. Thank you. Thank you. Thank you. Thank you. Thank you." He whispered first into her hair and then up into the night.

"I couldn't do it," she said quietly. "I put her on the plane, but then I wanted her back."

"I'm glad. Jesus Liz, I'm so glad." He took her face in his hands and kissed her forehead. He could feel her resisting him, but he didn't care. He was just so proud of her and so happy. Liz pushed away and walked past him into the house.

"You want tea?" she asked.

Not really, he thought to himself, but he wanted to sit across the table from her and talk, so he said, "Sure."

"Apple with milk and honey, like you like it?"

"Yeah," he nodded and sat down at the kitchen table, watching her move, comfortable and soft in the kitchen they designed before anyone else was there to give them input. She filled the tea kettle and turned on the burner, then she passed him and went into the pantry to get the teabags. When she came out she closed the door behind her, glancing over her shoulder, and smiling a sweet little flirty smile in his direction.

He felt heavy and a little old, sitting there waiting, his hands resting on his knees, his buttocks spread against the wood chair. He was particularly conscious of the dark puffy circles under his eyes and the creases in his forehead, but he also felt good and strong, like something was different, like something new had begun.　He looked at the back of his wife, and for the first time he liked that she was older too, that they were lucky enough to have been young together.　He liked that he knew her first lines were the ones around her mouth and that she got them from laughing.　He liked that they were both still toned and strong because she insisted they stay healthy, exercise and eat five servings of veggies and fruits a day, and that their time walking or biking in the sun together had made their skin tougher and tanner.　He liked that their children looked like them and that they were making their own complicated decisions.　He liked everything about the life they built together, even when it was complicated.

"You want to marry me?" he asked. Liz looked over her shoulder, with her eyebrows raised.

"Already did that," her voice was stern, but she smiled.

"So, let's do it again."

"Cliff..." The door opened and Clara walked in.　She looked drawn and pallid, like she wanted to run, but her feet moved slowly, trying not to call attention to the emotion that was all over her face.　"Clara? Are you okay?" Liz asked. Clara nodded, but kept her teeth clenched. Cliff stood up and crossed to his daughter.　He placed his hands on her shoulders and tilted his head, examining her eyes.

"You sure, kiddo?　You look a little piqued."

"Fine. I'm completely fine," she kept her jaw tight. Cliff hugged her.

"I'm glad you're home," he said.

"Good to know someone is." Clara spun a bitter look in Liz's direction. Liz gasped a little, clearly not expecting Clara's anger. Clara narrowed her eyes and said, "I'm going to bed, good night."　Her words were fraught with tension.　She crossed the kitchen keeping her anger locked on her mother for as long as humanly possible. Cliff turned and watched her walk away.　He drew a deep breath into his lungs and sighed. They were alone again, just him and Liz, but Cliff knew that when he turned around things would be different then were just moments before. He thought about following Clara up the stairs and locking himself in her closet, but he knew he couldn't. He knew he had to turn and face her, and he knew she would yell.

Liz's face pinched with anger. "She's incredible. Your daughter is out of her fucking mind." She was always Cliff's daughter when she acted obnoxious to Liz, which Cliff always found just slightly humorous because Clara's dramatic aspects were clearly something she learned from her mother. "I did everything right by her today. I had even started to consider the idea that maybe they loved each other. Maybe, I was the problem with their relationship, not them." Surprisingly, Liz wasn't yelling at him. She was just yelling, "Or maybe, like everyone kept telling me, they needed to figure it all out for themselves, but no. She's not even home fifteen minutes and I'm a demon, again."

"Well, maybe it's going to take time Liz." He paused, and Liz looked at him as though she had forgotten he was there until he spoke. "I mean you tried to send her away. She's got to be angry about that." Before he had finished getting the words out, he knew he shouldn't have said them.

"Did anyone ask you?" Cliff closed his eyes and the muscles in his arms started to twitch. "Well, did anyone ask you?" Liz's voice was deep and strong. "Does anyone ever ask you?" She emphasized each word, making his head spin with her anger. "You and your pansy-ass bullshit. 'Let's get married, Liz,'" she whined mimicking a child. "As if everything can just fix itself. As if it's just going to be okay because you decided it should be. Fuck that. Fuck you and your sappy wedding ideas." Cliff kept his eyes closed and tried not to listen. Maybe if he didn't hear her, he could keep himself from leaving the bed later.

TWENTY-SEVEN

Elizabeth threw the piece of paper towel in her hand into the sink and followed Clara upstairs. As expected, Cliff didn't move. He sat limp and lifeless, with his eyes closed as she buzzed past him. Talking to Cliff was nothing but frustrating, and it occurred to her that telling Clara off might do a mother good. She could not understand Clara's behavior. In the car when Liz told Clara to go tell Artie that she was home, Clara had forgiven her. Elizabeth had seen it in her eyes. She watched her turn her head and saw the hard muscles in her jaw smooth out. She saw her eyebrows lift and lips part. She felt the wall of anger wash away. At least, Liz thought it had. She thought she saw her little girl looking up at her, feeling both guilty and thankful. She thought her eyes had said, "Thank you, Mommy." Then, in the kitchen, Clara had cornered her, slapped her with hatred. She couldn't put it together.

At the top of the stairs she slowed, gathering her thoughts. She knew better then to storm Clara without first composing herself. Clara had always been her most worthy adversary. As a parent, Elizabeth could force her to do anything, but she could not bend her will. She had flare for the dramatic, but her arguments were thought out and strategic. She did not often speak without thinking, and Elizabeth often walked away from their battles wondering whether she had won or been duped into thinking she'd won.

Elizabeth needed Clara to understand that she was not the enemy, at least not any more. She took three deep breaths and forced her nostrils to unflare. Rather than barge through Clara's door, she knocked, attempting to make an example of herself as one who respected the people she loved. Clara didn't answer, so she knocked harder, hard enough to feel little bursts of pain shudder through her hand.

"I don't want to talk to you," Clara called from inside the room. Elizabeth inhaled and exhaled through her nose, pushing the air out like a bull.

"Too bad because you're gonna. You can't act like that in my house."

"Just leave me alone." Clara's pitch was whiney and frustrated. Elizabeth turned the door knob, thinking it would be locked and feeling a little giddy when she discovered it wasn't. Clara was sitting on her bed, turned away from Elizabeth, looking out the window at Sissy's house.

"Clara," Liz shook her head. Standing in Clara's bedroom, it was so hard to see her as a grown woman. When Liz looked around at the years of memories that hung from every shelf and nail, she saw flashes of three and six and twelve, but not nineteen. She sighed and tempered her voice, making sure to express how much she cared. "Clara, I can't have that kind of anger in my house. Especially, when there is no reason for it." Clara turned to face her. Her eyes were hollow and the tension had returned to her jaw. She licked her lips and nodded her head, sarcasm overtaking her face.

"You'd like to think that wouldn't you? You'd like to blame me. Act like my choices and my actions are the reason for all of this, like my behaviors are making a freaking mess out of YOUR family." Elizabeth let her speak, hoping she would burn off steam. "I have news for you Mom. You're the problem."

"Clara, nothing is anyone's fault here."

"No, you're wrong. It's someone's fault. Yours. You're the reason Artie's become a God damn ice sculpture." Clara's eyes flickered for a minute like she might cry and her voice shook, but she instantly grew stern again. "You're the reason dad skulks around like a mute coward." Clara's words did exactly what they intended to do, and Elizabeth felt her lips trembling.

"Clara, I think that..."

"Do I look like I care what you think?" Clara pointed at her own face. "DO I?" Elizabeth didn't speak. She stared at her, trying to outwit her anger with silence. She concentrated on the little noises, her breathing, the quick pace of her pulse, the rush of her blood through her veins. Clara went to speak again, but suddenly, there was screaming.

Liz turned her head, her ears acting like radar, searching for the source of the noise. The sound was muffled, a woman's voice coming from outside and getting closer to the house. Liz moved past Clara, throwing open the window, as someone began to pound on the back door. It was black outside, the only light a misty bleeding haze from the kitchen windows. Liz leaned over the ledge, trying to see who was bawling beneath her. She could hear the low steady rumble of Cliff's voice. She had flashes of car accidents, glass and blood splattered on the road, a woman running for help, and then she heard Artie, and looked up. He was on the roof across the way.

He was bare chested, his arms stretched wide, his face and palms turned up towards the dark sky. "What do you want from me?" he hollered, his voice deeply resonant, but frenzied. It was so dark that he appeared to be a shadow, spinning in a slow circle, moving closer and closer to the edge. He was like the bright lights of the Ferris wheel, whirling out of control, so quickly that the colors seemed to trail behind the people and their dangling feet. Elizabeth's nose twitched and her throat constricted, as she watched him. "Do you want me to die too?" Like Tarzan he pounded his chest. "I can die too. Hell, I'm dead already." Elizabeth began to weep. She knew she couldn't fix this.

"Cliff," she whispered hoarsely, suddenly, shocked by her own panic. "CLIFF!" She screamed, looking down and realizing he was already moving, halfway across the lawn. He would be in Sissy's house soon, sheer strength, force and muscle barreling up the stairs. His heart racing, but his mind steady, focused and clear. Cliff would be on that roof saving Artie before she could even gather her thoughts.

Elizabeth turned from the window and rushed past Clara, down the stairs. She slid into the doorframe as she raced into the kitchen, but she didn't stop. Outside, barefoot on the still frozen grass, looking up, shaking, crying, covering her mouth with her hands, she watched her husband take action.

Artie stood, his arms crossed tightly over his chest, holding his own shoulders. Sadness vibrated his vocal cords, not words, just thin high pitched noise. She watched him teetering and pictured him falling with a grin on his face. He was so near the edge that Elizabeth wondered if she could break his fall. Cliff moved quickly and he didn't speak. He wrapped his arm around Artie's waist from behind, and at his touch Artie melted into a ball. He curled tightly against Cliff, wrapping both arms around his neck like he did when he was a child. Liz could hear him begging, "No more, Cliff. I can't do this anymore." Cliff cradled his head against his chest, smoothing down his hair and kissing his forehead.

Elizabeth fell to her knees, and the shaking in her chest subsided, but she couldn't stop crying. She felt how alone and scared Artie was up there, how angry and lost. She watched him curl into Cliff's lap like he did as a child, his long manly legs spilling out over Cliff's knees. She watched Cliff rock him back and forth, repeating, "It's okay kiddo. It's okay," and the sadness she constantly avoided poured forth.

Looking to wrap her arms around Clara, to feel the strength of her family unit, Elizabeth turned to her left. She had been aware of a hysterical presence next to her the entire time and assumed the sounds had come from her daughter. In her own panic she had completely forgotten the girl that came screaming across the lawn, so she was surprised to see her standing there. The girl was Artie's friend. Elizabeth knew her. Her name was Christina. Christina, not Clara, was standing next to her wearing a deep purple bra and panties. Christina's face was fraught with fear, and her skin was gray and coated in goose bumps. Elizabeth's mouth went dry as she suddenly understood Clara's anger. Slowly she turned her head scanning her surroundings for Clara. She stood a few feet behind Elizabeth, just paces from the kitchen door. Her posture was stiff, her arms wrapped tightly around her waist and her face stoic. She had not cried.

"Clara?" Liz asked, confused and concerned.

Clara lifted her chin and acknowledged her, but she didn't speak. Elizabeth watched her close her eyes and let the air out of her lungs, then she turned, slowly, one foot in front of the other and headed inside. Before she reached the door, she looked back at Elizabeth. "He's gonna be sick," Clara said, her voice even and devoid of emotion. "He likes ice when he's sick. Ask Dad. He knows." Elizabeth nodded

TWENTY-EIGHT

Clara closed the door to her room. She looked around for images or things that might remind her of Artie. She knew there was a photo album packed in the suitcase she left in the car. The pictures on its pages went all the way back to her fourth birthday party. They were sentimental pictures that she had gathered over years, moments when he had been caught kissing her cheek in congratulations or blowing out her candles for her. She was glad the album was in the car because she couldn't trust herself with it now. In the morning she would pass it off to her mother, telling her to banish it from view.

The window in her room was still open and Clara could hear her mother trying to calm Christina down. Clara had never liked Christina but not because she was slutty. That was her prerogative as far as Clara was concerned. Clara didn't like that Christina used sex to get what she wanted. Artie always had a thing for her. Once two or three years ago, he called Christina "choice," like choice meat, and in turn Clara didn't speak to him for a week. Sissy noticed they weren't speaking and confronted Clara about it.

When Clara explained the situation, Sissy told her teenage men were vulgar. She said they had "trouble harnessing their sexuality." She told Clara it was her job to explain to Artie why she was upset, to make him understand that he couldn't say those things, and not just in front of her. She had to make him understand that looking at a woman that way was disrespectful no matter whom you said it to. Confused, Clara had asked Sissy why it was her job? Why wasn't it Sissy's job? Sissy donned her all knowing voice and said, "Because he already respects me as a woman." Clara thought she had gotten through to him, although she was fairly certain that Artie never learned to respect Christina, but she thought she had taught him to respect her.

Christina continued to whimper outside, so Clara crossed her room to close the window. She could see that her dad was still on Sissy's roof with Artie. She could barely make them out. They were just shadows, but even knowing they were there made her bite her lower lip. She turned to look down at her mother, who was openly crying and at the sight of that she immediately pulled down the shades, hiding the fiasco outside.

She felt her hands and knees shaking, so she focused on her breath. First, she tried to breathe in to a count of twelve, hold to a count of twelve, out to a count of twelve, but she couldn't focus enough to get the rhythm, so she breathed into her diaphragm and then released as slowly as she could. Every time she got close to relaxing, her mind would drift away, wondering things like why no one else had come inside or what her mother was thinking now that she had seen Christina. Clara felt no need to dwell on Artie's rooftop display because it was all a show to her. Rule breaking was Artie's greatest talent. For the first time in her life, part of her hated him. She hated that he couldn't control his emotions. She hated that he drank too much. She hated that he had no fight in him. She hated that it was hours since he hugged her this morning, and she could still smell him on her clothes.

Clara heard the door beneath her room open and close, and she stood up. She didn't feel like talking to her mother, but it would be hard to avoid. She got undressed and grabbed her bathrobe, thinking if she could get into the bathroom before her mom got to her, then she could dodge the conversation altogether, and if not she would act as though everything was completely normal. Before exiting her room, she slipped into her slippers and grabbed her bag of toiletries out of her carry on.

When she opened the door to her room, Liz was standing at the end of the hall. The knees of her pants were black from kneeling in the dirt. She made no effort to approach Clara. She just stood at the end of the hall, one palm pressed against the wall to support her weight. Clara couldn't remember the last time she had seen her mother genuinely shaken.

"I'm gonna shower," Clara said.

Liz nodded. Her eyes were wide and glassy, making Clara feel even more uncomfortable than anything she might have said. Clara turned from her and started down the hall. Liz called after her.

"CLARA," her voice was a hoarse whisper of a yell, the panicked call of a horror film heroine. Clara couldn't help but think it was absurdly dramatic, but she paused turning slowly to face her. Here it comes, she thought.

"Yes, Mom," she replied, keeping her lips tight and stern.

"Are you...I ..." Liz stuttered, and Clara was aware that her mother's usual strength, the cold stare that fueled all their arguments, was lost to her. Clara thought there's no fight left in her either, and as though Liz could hear her thoughts, she gave up trying. "Do you have soap?" she asked.

Clara lifted her toiletry bag and said, "Yep," in such a way that she made sure Liz knew she could see her weakness, and she didn't appreciate it. For the second or two of silence that followed her one syllable answer, Clara made no move, and then when Liz failed to say anything else, Clara turned and continued her trip to the bathroom.

Once she shut the door, she focused on the tasks at hand. She thought, turn on the shower; hang your robe on the back of the bathroom door; unzip the toiletry bag; take out the body soap, shampoo and conditioner; test the water temperature; adjust the water temperature; climb over the edge of the tub into the shower; wash and condition your hair; wash your face; wash your body; take the razor, which you forgot to pack, off the side of the tub; shave your armpits; think about shaving your legs, realize there's no reason anymore; no one will touch them but you; put the razor back in place.

When the tasks were complete she stood under the shower head. At first her mind, stuck in task mode, echoed step over the edge of the tub and dry yourself off, but the water felt good, so she stayed, abandoning her focus. First, she wondered if maybe she should just get out and go watch TV or something equally mind numbing, but then she realized that she needed to think. She needed to stand there until the water ran cold and figure out the answers. How could she stop the torrent of unhappiness that threatened to penetrate her daily existence?

It didn't take her very long to come up with a valid solution. In the morning, she would ask her mother to send her to back to Dallas, and then after a two or three hour layover, she would board the plane that would take her safely away from purgatory to the heaven of New York.

TWENTY-NINE

Elizabeth sat in the kitchen listening to Cliff's alarm go off upstairs. The sunlight streamed in the kitchen windows, making her squint, but she didn't move to set the table or make breakfast, and for the first time in months, she didn't reach for her tumbler. She had decided that from now on she wanted to feel everything. She wanted to know that she was too tired to think anymore and so feeble that she might cry if someone near her raised his or her voice ever so slightly.

A few times during the endless hours of the night before, Liz had gone across the lawn, braving the wet cold of the night air to stand in front of Sissy's door. Finally, on her third attempt she snuck inside and listened at the bottom of the stairs. She couldn't hear much. She figured they were in the bathroom with the door shut. Inspired by Clara's words, she filled a glass with ice in Sissy's kitchen and tried to bring it to them, but before she mounted the stairs, she realized exactly what Clara had said, "Ask Dad. He knows." If Artie needed ice, Cliff would've gotten it for him. It occurred to her that what Clara was really saying was that Liz didn't know what they needed. She hadn't been paying attention to them at all. Losing her nerve, she put the glass down and walked out of Sissy's house, back to her own kitchen to wait.

Since then she had been sitting at the kitchen table, tracing the grooves in the wood with her fingers, trying to figure out what to say. She felt like she needed to apologize, but there were no words that came naturally. She went over all the things she had done wrong since Sissy died. She could come up with a thousand moments that could have gone differently. There were little cold conversations with each member of her family and missed opportunities for joy at every meal, but the moment which stood out the most was telling Cliff she didn't love him as much as she used to.

Michael's tirade on Thanksgiving, his embarrassment about their life and Sissy sat at the forefront of her mind. Her son had spent his whole life being aware of something she avoided. Cliff's love for Sissy was too big. What Michael didn't see was that Liz's love for her was also disproportionate. They had focused on loving Sissy rather than loving each other. Like a child, Sissy needed them both, and they were taken in by her silly, infectious whimsy. She kept them laughing and created the vibrancy in their house that people of their strength and spirit hunger for. They weren't wrong to have her in their family, but it did change the dynamic of their growth as a unit. Liz didn't know if they would ever be able to find each other again, and it felt like it was her fault because she hadn't tried to love him. She kept thinking that maybe the problem was that she didn't love herself, or that she had all the love she had felt for Sissy boiling in her, and rather than direct it at Cliff, she had chosen to direct it at Ruth.

Watching Cliff on Sissy's roof reminded her how strong he was. His strengths were different than hers. He was quiet. He fixed things by lending of himself physically, whether it was the comfort of his embrace or sheer strength in his muscles. He often took action to solve a problem rather than discuss solutions. She started thinking that maybe he had kept quiet since the night of Sissy's funeral because she didn't want to hear what he felt or what he was thinking. She didn't want to lean into him and lose control. All these months she thought he wasn't there for her, and maybe he wasn't, but in truth she wasn't there for him either, and he had tried to be there for her more than she had for him.

Like every other morning the sounds of the house moving began above her head, but they were not Cliff's sounds. They were the sounds of Clara, lighter, more nimble sounds; Clara turning off her father's alarm; Clara flushing the toilet; Clara running the water in the kids' bathroom. Most mornings Cliff was already in the kitchen when Clara began her movements, and Liz would have stopped listening to what was happening above her and started focusing on what was happening in front of her. She noticed that Clara didn't shower before coming downstairs.

Liz turned her head towards the hall door and waited for her to appear. Clara's behavior the night before was almost as startling as Artie's. When she saw Christina, Liz immediately knew that the half-dressed, crying girl was the source of Clara's anger, but she had been unprepared for Clara's emotionless response to Artie's breakdown. It hadn't taken much consoling to get Christina inside, but Liz could hardly look at her, so the moments were excruciating. Christina was less than happy to know that she had to call her mother to come pick her up in the middle of the night. Liz left the two arguing on the phone when she went to find Clara. She climbed to the top of the stairs and stopped to steady herself, like she had earlier in the evening. It was harder to compose herself the second time and before she could rein in her nerves, Clara came into the hall, smiling. Looking at Clara, so calm, in her bathrobe, headed for the shower with her slippers on her feet, pulled the breath right from Liz's lungs. As far as Liz could tell the only emotion Clara had access to was anger, which of course was unsettlingly familiar.

When Clara appeared in the kitchen, her behavior reminded Liz of ballroom dancers. She was light on her feet and her grin was devilishly wide. She glided to the refrigerator for the juice, she did a quick spin to the cabinet, and she delicately poured the orange liquid, holding it too high so that the stream from the container swished like a waterfall as it splashed into glass. Liz was surprised when Clara sat across from her in Sissy's seat, rather than next to her in the seat she had claimed for the past nineteen years.

"Good Morning," she said with a cheery lilt.

Liz looked across the table, but didn't speak. She was too tired to speak.

"Cheer up," Clara said. "It's a new day."

Liz tried not to resent Clara's joy. She stood and walked to the coffee pot, which had percolated on its own at 6:04, like every other day. Only last night Liz had forgotten to add the grounds, so the only thing heating was water. She used the water to make herself tea. Clara talked to her back.

"Mom, I was thinking." Liz glanced at her for a second. Clara caught her eyes, and she looked back at the selection of tea boxes. "You were right. I should go to New York."

Liz thought she was going to lose her balance. She steadied herself by grabbing the counter's edge. At this point, she couldn't think of one good reason for Clara to be in New York. Tea in hand, she turned and made her way slowly back to the table. She knew she had to say something.

"New York, huh?"

"I mean it actually makes perfect sense." Clara's words were steady and rational, pre-planned. "I've never really been on my own, and it would be a real eye-opening experience."

Liz tried to listen to her, but all she could focus on was how Clara was holding her orange juice. She had clasped both her hands around the glass, intertwining her fingers. Liz interrupted her. She nodded in the direction of Clara's glass and said, "That's how Sissy held her tea." Clara immediately dropped her hands. Liz looked up at her face and she saw Clara's composure shake momentarily and then resituate.

"I could take classes at NYU, like Katie said, or at another university. There must be tons of schools in New York."

"Did you know that?"

"What?" Clara asked, irritated.

"That you hold a glass exactly like she did." Clara did not respond, and for a minute Liz thought she was going to stand and storm out of the kitchen.

When she finally spoke she asked, "Can we talk about New York, please?" She didn't make eye contact.

"You want to go to New York," Liz rolled the words like she was considering the idea.

"Yes." It was clearly meant to be a strong resounding answer, but Clara was shaken by her discussion of the glass.

"Why?" Liz asked.

"The opportunities?" Clara had phrased her answer as a question, which seemed strange, as though she thought Liz would be more inclined to let her go if she provided the right answer.

"No other reason?"

Clara sighed, "Of course there are other reasons," she said bitterly. She closed her eyes and looked pained and frustrated as she said, "I think I'll be happier there."

Liz didn't speak. She sipped her tea and considered the idea. If she let Clara go to New York, then she would be allowing her to run away from her problems, but watching her struggle with them seemed like more than Liz could handle.

"Maybe there's another solution, Clara."

"No, there isn't. I need to get out of here."

The door opened behind them, and Liz turned to watch Cliff walk in. He was still barefoot from the night before, but he had put on a sweatshirt of Artie's somewhere along the way. The sleeves were pushed up, bunching tightly in the crooks of his elbows. His skin looked gray and the circles beneath his eyes were so dark it was as though someone had punched him. He crossed to the coffee pot and stood staring at it.

"I forgot," Liz said.

He nodded crossing to the cabinet and taking a mug down to make tea. Liz stood.

"Cliff, sit. I'll get it."

He set the mug on the counter and moved to the table. He collapsed into his chair with a thud, and grunted, "Caffeinate me, none of that herbal crap."

Clara made no move to speak to her father, so while Liz was fixing his tea the kitchen was silent. Liz set the tea in front of Cliff, touching his shoulder before she sat again. Cliff looked up at her and smiled a tired sad smile, the kind of smile that had not passed between them in months. It made Liz want to cry.

Once she was seated, Cliff eyed Clara. "You're in the wrong seat," he said.

Clara was visibly flustered by his comment. "I sat here so I could talk to Mom."

"You couldn't talk to her from your regular seat?" He didn't really sound angry, just tired and confused.

"I wanted..." Clara looked at her hands and started picking her cuticles. Liz realized she was afraid to tell Cliff what she wanted.

"I don't have patience for this, this morning," he said, "and really, right now, I don't care what you wanted to tell your mother that was so important you needed to look her in the eye. We all had a long night, and I'm tired."

"She wants to go to New York," Liz said.

Clara looked as though she'd been betrayed. Cliff put his hands over his face and furiously rubbed his scalp with his fingertips.

"I decided it would be a good opportunity, Daddy." Clara's voice was not much more than a whisper. Liz felt Cliff's rage building. "I could take a class or something." She could see the anger. His skin was turning red and the veins in his neck had started to pop. She couldn't let him unleash his fury at Clara.

"She thinks she'll be happier there," she said.

Cliff took the bait. When he lifted his face from his hands, he turned to Liz instead of Clara.

"And you think that's a good idea?" His eyes bulged.

"I want her to be happy." Liz maintained eye contact, thinking that as long as she kept him focused, she would be the target.

"It's not always about happy, Liz!" He raised his voice now. "Sometimes, it's about what's right. Clara is not going to New York!"

Despite Liz's best efforts, Clara put herself in harm's way. She whined, "Daddy..."

He turned to her, "Ab-so-lutely not. I'm done, DONE, with every-one in this family hiding, and pretending nothing happened." He was yelling at her, "Right now, you are going upstairs, taking a shower and going to Mr. Balducci to ask for your job back, and if you want to take a class or *something*," he mocked her, "then you can do it right here at the College of Santa Fe." He paused, took a breath, quiet-ing and turned to face Liz again. "You," he pointed at her, "are going across the lawn, and you're going to take care of Artie, while I rest for an hour or two. And if he wakes up you're not going to say a God damn thing to him. You're just going to love him."

Liz nodded, "It won't be a problem."

"Good." Cliff rubbed his head, picked up his tea cup, downed it, and left the kitchen.

When he was gone, Clara turned to Liz, bitter anguish in her eyes.

"How could you do that to me?" She asked.

Liz stood and took Cliff's cup to the sink." I couldn't very well agree to send you to New York without talking to your father." Liz was sur-prised by the cattiness in her own voice.

"Really, because I'm fairly certain that you did exactly that a few weeks ago."

"It's different now."

"Sure, it is. The rules always change to your advantage." Clara stood. "God damn it," she said, turning to leave the kitchen.

Liz stopped her, "I'll talk to him Clara. We'll figure something out."

"Yeah, sure ya will, mom. You've been such a big help so far." Clara's words stung, but Liz controlled herself. She crossed the room and tentatively moved to hug Clara.

"Don't touch me," Clara said.

"Okay," Liz nodded and let her leave the room.

Liz rinsed all three glasses, waited to hear Clara turn on the shower, and headed for Artie just like Cliff asked her to. Halfway between the two houses she remembered Ruth, and turned back to retrieve her cell phone from its charging perch on the kitchen counter next to the answering machine. When she was back outside, she called her. She expected the phone call to wake Ruth, so she was surprised when her voice sounded alert.

"I thought you'd still be sleeping," Liz said.

"It's almost nine." Liz had obviously worried Ruth.

"Right."

"What's the matter?" Ruth's voice was filled with concern.

"I can't come there today."

"Is everything okay?" Ruth asked.

"Not really." Liz didn't know where to start, but more surprisingly she didn't want to start.

"What can I do?"

"Nothing. I got this one."

"Okay," Ruth sounded disappointed.

"I'll call you later."

"Do you think you'll come tomorrow?" Ruth asked, there was desperation in her voice.

"Maybe." Liz was fairly certain that she would not go to Ruth's house tomorrow morning either.

"I love you," Ruth said.

"Me too. I gotta go."

Liz hung up the phone and looked longingly at the key pad. Things with Ruth would be different now. There was nothing she could do about that. She put the phone in her pocket, went into Sissy's house, and turned her mind to thoughts of Artie.

THIRTY

Artie woke up, but he didn't open his eyes. He could still feel the dizzying spins from the night before, and his head was pounding. Sweat clung to his skin, making the sheets clammy and bringing to mind the warm discomfort of urine soaked denim sticking to his thighs. The roof of his mouth felt pasty and the residual taste of bile lingered on his tongue. If he could have willed himself to open his eyes, he might have reached for the glass of melted ice on the night table, but opening his eyes meant acknowledging that he was awake, and waking meant facing his actions from the night before.

After a harrowing reintroduction with the evening's stimulants, Artie finally got into bed and Cliff pulled a chair up next to the bedside. He told Artie the story about the first night he met Sissy. He talked about the glow of her hair by the firelight and the song in her laughter. Artie thought he remembered the sound of Cliff crying, but he was unsure whether the sniffling sounds and the shaking voice were real or imaginary. The strength Artie felt when Cliff touched his brow

and whispered, "It's okay, kiddo. Sleep," was real and it still resonated under his skin, but he couldn't channel it towards positive action.
Instead, it hung heavy in his mind, an albatross of his own weakness.

He took a few deep breaths trying to quiet the noise of his hangover,
and as his mind grew less heavy, he became aware of the warmth of
someone else in the bed. For a second he entertained the idea that his
mother had never died. He pictured the long, fine bones of her hands,
the fiery pink color of her painted nails, her ring spun halfway upside
down, the knobby bulge of bone at her wrist   He felt the whisper of
her fingers as she tucked his hair behind his ear. His mind moved up
her arm to her shoulder, then the soft pocket of skin between her neck
and her collar bone, the uneven line of freckles on her jaw, but no matter how hard he tried he couldn't focus on her face. He had too many
memories of her face, she had too many expressions and they had all
grown distant and blurry since she died.

He was certain that the presence lying next to him was female, but
he knew it wasn't Clara. It didn't smell or breathe like Clara, and he
was certain she would not be allotting forgiveness that easily. Clara's
anger was fierce, and if she was going to forget what she thought she
saw, it wouldn't be because he gave in to his sorrow and cried out for
help. He was certain that Clara had digested his behaviors as a weakness of spirit, truly believing that his emotions enabled the horrors of
Pandora's Box, and in an effort to avoid the terrifying sadness of grief,

she would dismiss him as a relic that threatened to darken her pursuit
of life's celebrations. When she stood at the top of his stairs the night
before, he saw shock, but he felt change. She had slipped emotionless
from his grasp, like a stray cat that had eaten its fill.

If he could remember how Christina wound up in his bed, he would
have never let it happen. He had no memory of returning to the house.
He remembered being in a hot tub in the hills north of town. He remembered thinking about Clara even when he was trying not to. He
remembered how heavy his head felt. He remembered leaning back and
resting his weight against the cedar patio behind him. He remembered

the whirling puff of steam floating above him, and he remembered closing his eyes.

After that a whole lot of nothing. He woke up and it was dark and he was lying in bed. He had fallen asleep dressed. Smelling stale smoke on his clothes, he stood and peeled down to his boxers. He thought about showering. There were two beer cans on the night table, one un-opened, the other barely touched. He took a swig from the open one. It was warm, flat and sour, but he was so thirsty it didn't matter. When the liquid was gone, he tossed the can on the floor. It chattered when it hit, and then seemed to laugh at him as it rolled away. The room began to spin a little and he realized he was still tanked. Only then, did he turn and see that Christina was in the bed with him. She was lying with her back to him, wearing only a bra and panties. He rubbed his eyes, but she was still there.

"Fuck," he said.

"Not even." Christina turned to face him.

"I didn't know you were awake," he said his voice gruff with the rumble of too much smoke.

"Someone had to be," she sounded insulted.

"Did we....?"

"We could have but you were too busy crying about Clara."

"Nothing happened?" He tried to sound nonchalant but inside he prayed.

"No."

"Why are you undressed?"

"You can't knock a girl for trying." She sat up. "Pass me that beer." He was too tired to reach, and he knew he wasn't in full control of his equilibrium, so he sprawled back on the bed to hand it to her. They sat there half dressed and quiet until Christina said, "You're pretty screwed up about her, huh?"

"Looks that way," he said. Uncomfortable with any talk of Clara, he nervously laughed, "I'm still wasted."

"No shit. You consumed more than I thought humanly possible."

She handed him the beer. He downed it and tossed it onto the floor, so not to leave its partner lonely. Christina continued, "I always thought you had a thing for her."

"I didn't. I mean I didn't know until it happened."

"Sorry she left."

"Sorry about...." he gestured to their lack of clothing, "this."

"Doesn't matter," she said, but he could tell it did. He could tell she was close to crying. He turned to her and laid his head on her stomach.

"You're a really great girl Christina."

"If you like sluts," she said with a tearful smile.

"You're more than that." He hoped she wouldn't realize they were futile, empty words because he had always spent time with her for the wrong reasons, and he really had no idea what kind of girl she was.

"No one ever loved me like you love her." She wiped tears away from her face, and Artie noticed she had short fat little fingers, and her nails were bitten to the quick.

"Someone will. High school will end and something new will happen."

"I got into Arizona State."

"You did?" He was genuinely surprised that she had even applied to college. For him, she was the kind of person whose existence was so tied to his high school experiences that he never imagined her beyond graduation.

"Yeah," she smiled.

"That's great."

"Maybe there, I'll be more than a great pair of tits."

"I don't know," he teased, "they're pretty spectacular tits."

She looked down and cupped one of her boobs in her little chubby hand. "Yeah, they are," she laughed.

"They always smell amazing."

Christina's cheeks lifted and she grew coy. "I spray them with kids' perfume. It smells like..."

He interrupted her, "candy." He could tell it meant something that he noticed. Her insecurities and her need to feel wanted echoed his own desperation so loudly that he felt like they were twins. They each carried adult burdens without the wherewithal to handle them, and he thought that maybe if he could still her fears, even for a moment, then he would understand how to conquer his own. He took her hand and held it tight, saying, "We'll be okay," but she wasn't looking at him. Christina was looking towards the stairs.

She giggled, "Shit, this is embarrassing," and Artie knew someone was standing there, but it never occurred to him that it could be Clara until her eyes locked on his. The drafts in the room seemed to converge on the spot where he was standing and goose bumps popped up all over his body. What seemed like harmony just moments before showed its true and evil face, as it surged across the darkened room igniting Clara's shock. He couldn't hear her words above his own dissonant panic, but he saw Clara's lips move before she clamored down the stairs and slammed the front door. Snared by his mistakes, he stayed frozen next to the bed. Christina moved to her knees and faced him.

"Shit. Shit. Artie, I'm so sorry. Are you okay?"

He didn't say anything.

"I'll tell her. I'll tell her nothing happened."

Artie felt his jaw drop and sat down on the floor, pulling his knees into his chest. He started crying. Christina moved towards him.

"Don't touch me," he spat.

"I'll get you a beer. You want a beer?" She jumped up and headed downstairs.

Artie remembered crossing his arms over his chest and feeling a melodramatic, yet intense symbolism in that self hug. He pictured Clara running across the lawn distraught. Then he realized she wouldn't do that. The rule book said, no tears, so Clara didn't cry. He tried to cry for both of them, but he knew he couldn't. He wanted to rewind, to start over, to always tell the truth, but more than anything he wanted to keep his mother from strangling him with her celebration.

He remembered Christina cowering at the top of the stairs, two beers in her hands, watching him climb the kiva ladder to the roof, telling him not to go up there. He remembered the comforting pain the roof gravel caused when it cut into his toes. He remembered knowing his mom couldn't hear him when he yelled at her but wanting her to. He remembered wishing he could die too, if only to be closer to her.

Remembering how warm Cliff's hands were when they wrapped around him, pulling him back from the edge, forced him to open his eyes. The chair next to the bed was empty. Artie reached for the glass on the night table and drank the melted ice water, which had that funny metallic freezer taste. Even though he had dismissed all the other possible options, he was surprised when Liz spoke to him.

"You need more?" she asked.

Artie shook his head without turning to look at her.

"You want me to run you a bath?"

He managed to squeak out a "No," then he turned to look at her. "I'm sorry," he said. Her eyes were soft, not angry.

"Don't be. I love you."

Artie felt his nose tingle and his eyes welled up with tears. "You shouldn't." Much to Artie's surprise, Liz was teary too.

"Come here," she said, opening her arms to embrace him.

He crawled across the bed laid his head on her chest and let her circle him in her embrace. She kissed his forehead over and over, and she held him so tight that his breathing was labored.

"You're wrong. I should. I always should."

Through the fabric of her shirt, Artie could hear her heart beating.

THIRTY-ONE

*Cliff + Liz
refund each other*

Cliff went straight to Sissy's sink and splashed cold water on his face. Four hours of sleep had revived him enough to ease the aching in his neck, but he still felt groggy. He took a glass from the cabinet and filled it with ice. Then he put the glass down on the counter, deciding he wanted a beer. He pulled one can out of the blue and white cardboard case that took up the entire bottom shelf of the fridge. It was crap beer, the cheap shit that teenagers drink. He popped the tab, leaned against the refrigerator door, and rolled the bitter bubbles around his mouth.

Liz tip-toed down the stairs with her index finger pressed to her lips. She was telling him to be quiet. Once she was standing next to him she said, "He's sleeping, again." He thought she might comment on the beer, but she didn't. She just leaned next to him and rested her head on his shoulder. He didn't want her to touch him, so he moved, leaning in like he was looking for something to eat.

"I could make you something," she whispered.

"No, thank you," he said, closing the fridge and walking past her towards the stairs.

"Cliff, wait."

"What?" he asked angrily.

"Could we talk?" she looked scared.

"So you can tell me how to handle this situation or how little you respect me, or maybe you want to tell me again about how you don't really love me all that much."

"I deserve that," she maintained eye contact, and crossed to him. "Come with me, please. I don't want to wake him."

Reluctantly, he followed her into Artie's studio. The curtains in the studio were drawn, so it was pitch black. Cliff went to turn on the lights, but Liz stopped him, and he watched her pull up the shades. In the sunlight, she looked tired, weary. The knees of her jeans were still black from kneeling in the dirt the night before, and although she had tied her hair back, he could see that it was dirty.

"You should shower," he said as he sat down on the couch.

"I will, in a minute."

He watched her look around the room at the different pieces Artie was working on. Most of them were either half finished or discarded. She walked up to one and touched it, closing her eyes and biting her upper lip.

"What are you doing?" he asked.

"They're Clara," she said.

"What do you mean?"

"All of these," she spun around gesturing to all the art in the room, "I think they're Clara."

Cliff looked at the collection of abstract shapes. There were cracked clay sculptures, some wire pieces, a chiseled stone or two, and they all looked different to him, so at first he thought she was crazy, but when he looked harder he saw it too. There was no one piece that looked like Clara, but there were moments in each that reminded him of the small of her back or her wrist or the curve of her calf.

"He couldn't really make them look like her because if we saw them..." she trailed off.

Cliff finished her sentence, "We would know."

"I would know," she said. "You knew."

Cliff didn't say anything. He was not in the mood to argue or defend his choices.

"I wouldn't have told me either," she said, then she crossed and knelt down in front of him. "I'm sorry, please forgive me."

Cliff felt the muscles in his jaw slacken. She was looking at him, her chin tilted up, begging his forgiveness. In her eyes he saw their life. He saw their children and Sissy. He saw sorrow and years of stress. He saw her laughing and scowling. He saw how she loved him. He saw his wife, and he looked away.

"What do you want from me?" he asked.

"Simply, forgiveness. I want you to let me love you again. I want us to be a team."

He stood up and stepped past her. It was not that easy anymore. "I'm not so fond of your decisions these days, and you've never been a team player, Liz."

"I know."

"For weeks, I've been trying to figure out how to fix what's wrong between us, but this morning, with Clara, I started to think you were right. Maybe we just don't love each other anymore."

"That's not true."

"How could you possibly even consider sending Clara to New York?"

"I couldn't. I just didn't want you to yell at her."

"What?"

"I saw the anger in you, and I didn't want you to direct it at her."

"It's not your job to shield Clara. She does enough avoiding on her own."

"I know, but she was..."

"She was what? Upset? What?" He felt the rage from the morning building again. "God forbid, anyone feels anything around here.

She should be upset, shouldn't she? She obviously walked in on Artie with that girl last night, and then she watched that spectacle on the roof." He was yelling now, only in a whisper and it felt completely ineffective.

"That's just it," Liz said and looked at the floor, "she wasn't upset."

Cliff paused. He looked at Liz, sitting cross-legged on the floor. She was gripping the fingers of her right hand with her left and squeezing them over and over again. It was a nervous twitch that she had for as long as he knew her, but she only did it right before crying. He hadn't seen her do it in months, and finally he really took in that she had been crying, that she was about to cry right now. He controlled himself from going to her. It was her turn to suffer.

"She didn't even flinch," Liz said, her voice shaking.

"Well that's what you taught her to do. What did you expect?" He chastised.

"I was just trying to do what Sissy asked me to do."

"Well, she was wrong."

"I know, but I loved her," Liz started to cry. "I loved her so much."

Involuntarily, Cliff stepped towards her, but he didn't bend down. He didn't have the energy or the compromise in him, and he was surprised when Liz stood up. She locked her arms around his waist. He didn't reciprocate. Part of him wanted to, but he didn't trust it.

"We loved her," she said.

Cliff broke from her embrace and sat on the couch again. He pushed his hands through his hair, exhaling "I loved her too much." He hadn't meant it as a confession, but the guilt was thick in his voice.

"I know," Liz said. Cliff looked at her, lost and astounded by the reaction. She looked just as shocked and surprised as he felt.

"You know what?" he asked.

"I'm not sure. Michael said something over Thanksgiving about me living with your mis..." She shuddered and let the word evaporate, she took a deep breath. "I know how you loved her. Sometimes, I saw your face, when you were looking at her... I saw it in you," she paused, "...I looked at her like that too. And it's over now. Whatever we did wrong is gone." She was crying. "I'd do it again."

"Liz, I...." He wasn't sure what the right thing to say was.

Liz sat down next to him. She looked dumbfounded and her hands were limp at her sides. "I didn't want to know," she said, her eyes racing back and forth, like they always did when she was intently thinking. She turned to him, "Did you sleep with her?" She turned away and closed her eyes, waving her hands in front of her face. "Don't answer that," she blurted, "I don't want to know." She was silent for a minute. Then she said, "I loved her like that too. I think if I could have slept with her I would have."

Cliff's mind raced. He wasn't sure what to say and then he lied and because it was right, "I never slept with her but I wanted to." Liz looked at him. He thought she knew he was lying but better that she would never be certain.

"Thank you," she said.

He took her hand. It was rough, from years of doing dishes and sewing sutures. She had a scar on her thumb that she got slicing a stale bagel a few years back. He ran his finger over it. She had needed three stitches, and he held her other hand when she got them. He wondered how he ever let her get so out of control.

"I should tell you something," she said and he knew it was as prompt for a confession. She was going to tell him where she went everyday, and he knew if she was having an affair, he didn't want to hear about it. He wanted to love her again. To put the past behind them.

"It doesn't matter," he whispered.

"No, it does. I have a friend."

"Liz, please don't tell me this. I don't want to hear it," he was pleading.

"It's not what you think," she smiled. "It's a woman."

Cliff couldn't get his hands around what she was telling him. "You're having an affair with a woman?"

"No, we're just friends. Her name is Ruth."

Cliff laughed, "I really thought you were having an affair."

Liz didn't smile. "I think I was."

Confused, Cliff asked, "What do you mean?"

"I love her. She's part of me, like Sissy was, like you used to be."

"Used to be?"

"I lost track of you," Liz's voice cracked.

"We lost track of each other," he confirmed

She nodded, and leaned into him curling against his chest. It felt good to hold her again, like he had a purpose. The floor above their heads creaked, and they heard Artie calling, "Liz?....Cliff?"

They both stood. He put his arm around her as they headed for the studio door. When they were at the bottom of the stairs, he kissed her temple and whispered, "I got it. Go shower. Then maybe the three of us will go get something to eat."

She stepped away from his grasp, then she turned, "I love you, more than I ever have," and kissed him. When he went to speak, she covered his mouth. "When I've earned it," she said, happy.

Artie came towards them. "Earned what?" he asked.

They both looked, but neither one moved to speak.

"Ooookay, earned something that's not my business. I'm gonna shower." He pointed towards the downstairs bathroom.

He passed them and they turned to watch him go. He stopped and faced them again.

"I like when you guys get all gushy," he said, then he turned and hollered over his shoulder, "Can we eat soon? I'm F-in starving."

"Nice recovery, you little shit," Cliff hollered back.

"Cliff..." Liz scolded. Once Artie was out of ear shot she added, "We're going to have to talk to him about last night, about the drinking." Cliff eyed her. "Eventually."

"Eventually..." he put his hand on her waist and ushered her towards the door. "Shower. Maybe we'll go to Tortilla Flats?" She stepped over the door frame and started back to the house. He stood there with the door open and watched her walk, liking the sway of her hips. When she had gotten about ten feet away she turned back, breaking into a little jog in his direction. On her tip toes she gently kissed him again. Her lips were soft, giving. He pulled her close to him, turning a sweet kiss into a passionate one. He felt the intensity of his earlier anger begin to feed a hungry pent up lust.

"You look so sexy," he said.

She blushed a little and smiled brazenly, "You're not so bad yourself."

The gravel on the driveway behind them popped as Clara pulled up in the truck. She slammed the door, making her way to the house. She didn't see them, so Cliff called to her, "Hey, sweetie." He raised his hand and lazily waved. Clara's eyes pinched together.

"Hi, Mom," she said and then turned to go into the house.

Clara had never given Cliff the cold shoulder before, and the force of her anger made him feel nauseous.

"Well, that's a change," Liz said, teasing.

"That was awful."

"What are we going to do about her?"

"How could you possibly stand having that directed at you for all that time?"

Liz shrugged and looked at the space where Clara used to be standing. "Maybe, we should get her a place in town."

The suggestion startled him. "You're kidding, right?" He had just begun to feel like there was some glimmer of hope for his family.

"Well, no. I think living here with him is too much for her right now." Cliff felt the comfort dissipate and the rage thrive all over again

"She needs us. We just finished discussing how messed up your whole happy charade has made her, and now you want to let her run away from her problems?"

"Her behavior is not a direct result of mine. There are other factors." He thought some of the dictatorial coolness had returned to her voice.

"Jesus, Liz." Cliff couldn't believe what he was hearing. He knew it was too good to be true.

"She can't very well get better, if she has to see him at breakfast every day."

"Don't you think they should talk? We don't even know what happened last night."

"She's not ready to talk to him." Now, her tone was downright haughty.

"Yes, dear. Whatever you want, dear," he said in a condescending drone.

"Cliff, stop. I don't want to fight with you." Liz's voice had returned to calm, but Cliff didn't buy it.

"No, you want to patronize me. You want me to back down and let you do what you think is right."

"No, I want to love you, but right now, they have to come first, and what I know is that Clara needs to get away from Artie and really, I think Artie should move into Michael's old room. It's too nostalgic for him in here."

"So, let me get this straight. Your daughter doesn't need you, but Sissy's son does?"

"They both need us. US! God dammit! It's not about me anymore."

"It's always about you, Liz." He turned away from her, taking in the dry, emotionless delivery and hateful finality he embedded in his words. Out of the corner of his eye he saw Liz hang her head in defeat and then start her trek back to their house. He knew she wouldn't turn back this time, whatever ground they had recovered was lost again.

He put his hands in his pockets, sighed, and walked out of the foyer back towards the kitchen. Standing up for what he believed made him feel proud, like he was a man, the leader of his family. He wouldn't care this time.

When he got past the living room he found Artie sitting at the bottom of the stairs. His hair was wet and he had a towel wrapped around his waist. Cliff could tell from the expression on his face that he had caught the gist of the argument. Even if he'd only heard part of it and it hit him hard.

"You shower awfully fast, kid," he said trying to move quickly from one moment to the next. Artie stood, shaking his head. A little tuft of air escaped from his nose, as he crossed to the kitchen and pulled a beer from the fridge. "Don't you think you had enough last night?" Cliff asked.

Artie disregarded the comment, popping the tab. He walked over to Cliff, took one of Cliff's arms by the wrist and put the can in his hand. Cliff gripped the can feeling the wetness of the condensation on his fingers. "Cliff," he said, in a tone that reflected none of the previous evening's turmoil, "she's right about Clara and me, we can't both live here anymore."

Cliff didn't sip from the can right away, but once Artie left the room to get dressed, it was a comfort.

THE POOL

It took them eight years to finish the pool. They began building it long before they conceived of the idea that a child would be born in its depths. They started it with a garden shovel, and naturally a garden shovel grew up to be a bulldozer.

It was not a large pool, but it looked like a watering hole and it gave birth to a slate patio that covered half an acre of land. It was an abstract shape, and the cement they used for its floor was a gray green color. Rocks and shrubs were strategically placed so they could imagine antelope or mountain lions sipping from it, subsiding their thirst.

They hosted many parties by its side. In the summer, they ate Sunday brunch on the patio. They had fresh squeezed orange juice, bagels, and eggs or warm maple syrup and blueberry waffles. In the winter, they drained the water. They stood around and watched as the water seeped away until it had almost disappeared, and then they worked together and pulled the tarp cover tight over its surface.

Without fail, each spring they would find some young creature had drowned in its watery depths. It didn't matter the creature, a prairie dog, a desert mouse, jackrabbit or horny toad. What mattered was the way it made them feel. They would cry as they rescued the lifeless carcass from the water. Dead creatures never smelled or sat right with them.

The pool was a place where life pushed forward. It died each winter and was born again each spring, and they watched their bodies grow older in the dim light that radiated from beneath its waving surface.

THIRTY-TWO

A few days after Artie's breakdown, Liz called a family meeting. They all sat in the living room, Liz and Clara on the couch, Cliff in the armchair and Artie cross-legged on the floor with his back to the television. For the first few minutes no one said anything. Clara looked intently at her mother, waiting for her to speak. She could feel Artie's eyes on her. His stare was warm, as though he was pressing his nakedness against her skin, making her claustrophobic. The conversation started because Clara threatened to leave.

"If no one has anything to talk about, then I'm outta here," she said.

"No, I..." Clara was surprised to see her mother glance at her father, as though she was seeking his approval. Her father didn't look up. Instead he scowled, clearly offering no support. When Liz spoke, she offered up the option of moving out as though she were an auctioneer, "Clearly one of you needs to live somewhere other than here."

Artie spoke first, "It makes more sense for me to move out."

Clara was appalled. She turned to look at him and saw he had never taken his eyes off her. He trapped her with his stare and said, "Clara is your daughter. She shouldn't be forced from her home."

Cliff moved to the edge of his seat and reached out to touch Artie's shoulder. Clara couldn't understand how either of her parents could even look at him after what he'd done, let alone offer him support. As far as she was concerned, he was a traitor.

"Clara," Liz said, "does that work for you?" Clara narrowed her eyes, searching for words that would hit Artie hard. She imagined that she could breathe fire. Flames would roar forth with her words, forcing Artie to release her from his snare.

"Does it ever matter what works for me?" She asked. The only person who seemed affected by her bitterness was her father. He closed his eyes and dragged his hand across his face before he spoke. His voice was as cold and bitter as her own, only he directed his anger at her mother.

"Everyone is just doing their best," he said.

Clara tried to use her rebuttal to force him to acknowledge her, but her words did little to affect either man's gaze. "Well, I'm tired of all of you. I want out, so no, that doesn't work for me."

"I figured," Liz said, acting the part of the impartial mediator.

Liz had already found Clara an apartment through her mysterious friend, Ruth, so it was all settled. She moved into a little efficiency on East Devargas Street, which was right near her father's office and within walking distance to work and town, so they let Artie keep the truck. Liz helped her pack her boxes and move the following day. Artie tried to help them, but Clara wouldn't have it, so Liz paid a few of his buddies to do the heavy lifting. Cliff skulked in the shadows and didn't speak to anyone the whole time. Clara was not surprised that he didn't help her move. He clearly did not approve of the entire situation. She was angry at him and he was angry right back.

Liz made a big deal out of decorating the new place. Clara picked out a pale yellow paint that reminded her of an old dress in Liz's closet. The dress had some sentimental value, so it had always been wrapped in plastic, but when Clara was little, Liz let her play dress up in it. The two of them painted for hours, but it never looked quite like it would have if Cliff had done the painting.

When they finished painting, Liz went to the car and came back with three big, plastic bags from Bed Bath and Beyond. Without asking, she had bought Clara towels and sheets that matched the paint. She was so proud of her gift that Clara didn't have the heart to tell her that the matchy-matchy-ness made her dizzy, like she was caught in a pastel yellow tornado.

Clara didn't take to living alone like she thought she would. Coming home to an empty apartment made her feel invisible. The first week was awful. She was afraid to go outside. Afraid she might lock herself out or forget where she lived, so she sat on the couch in her pajamas and watched *Law and Order* reruns. She was fascinated by the fact that Jerry Orbach died, but through the magic of television he still seemed to be alive. She didn't bathe, rationed food like she was living in a fallout shelter, and called in sick to work everyday. It was a craving for chocolate ice cream that finally pushed her over the edge.

Things did not really get any easier once she braved the outside world, but at least she began to shower. Everyone she knew from high school was away at college and she was too lonely and depressed to go out dancing, so she walked up to the plaza and looked in all the stores, talking to every salesgirl she could find, hoping she might make a friend, someone, anyone, to spend time with. She couldn't call home and cry misery because who would she cry to? On the phone every morning Liz suggested she sign up for an interesting class.

"Maybe a ceramics class," she said. It was a ridiculous suggestion. Clara was never interested in ceramics. She didn't even get a kick out of Play Doh when she was a kid. Instead, she just moved through her routine. Set the alarm. Get up. Walk to work. Come home. Eat. Watch TV. Go to bed. Repeat. It wasn't much of a life, but it was working for her until she spotted the truck parked about two blocks from her apartment.

It was two months after she moved in. At first, she thought it was just a coincidence. She figured Artie was in town, eating a Frito pie at the Woolworths' counter or hanging out with his buddies on the plaza, scaring the tourists, so when the truck was parked in the same place the next day she was surprised. She tentatively walked up the small stone path that led to her apartment wondering where he was hiding. She looked over her shoulder as she went inside, scanning the courtyard for some sign of him. She could feel that he was there, somewhere, watching her. It was almost as if she could hear him breathing.

It took her a few weeks to find his hiding place. She was taking out the garbage. He had made a little nest for himself behind some shrubbery, halfway between the dumpster and her door. It was a big gulp cup and an empty wrapper from a package of Twizzlers that gave him away. She sat down, where he would've sat, thinking he must bring something with him to sit on, because she knew he was never comfortable sitting on the bare ground. From his spot, you could see every inch of her home, except the bathroom. Clara hated that he could see her suffering, but his mere presence meant he was suffering too, and she found so much joy in his possible struggles that she set out to torture him.

She started planning her day around him. She would hold her phone to her ear and pretend she was talking to someone for hours. She would prance around her house in a matching lacy bra and panties with the shades open. She would leave in the evenings, dressed to the nines, like she had somewhere to go. She even sent herself flowers like she was some pathetic heroine in a romantic comedy.

Clara made an effort to go on a "pretend" date at least once a week. She left the apartment wearing a little flouncy flowery dress that she knew Artie liked. She intentionally paused in front of the door, searching in her purse for the keys and holding her cell phone to her ear with her shoulder, saying something like "I'm running a little late," loud enough to make sure he could hear her, laughing and trying to sound flirty.

Her pretend dates often took her to Galisteo News. She knew Artie wouldn't follow her. He was too much of a coward to risk being caught, so she spent most of her time out imagining the distress he felt, not knowing where she was or what she was doing, and she often smeared her lipstick before coming home to ensure his imagination would get carried away. She tried to stay occupied until at least eleven, but most nights it was hard. She could only read so many magazines before she wished she were home, cuddled in her bed, watching T.V.

It was on one of her "pretend" dates that she met Gabrielle Matthews. Gabe, a fifty-three year old professor at the College of Santa Fe, was sitting at a nearby table, watching her. She hardly noticed him, until he started talking to her. She could see her reflection in his silver-rimmed glasses. He was eating a tuna fish sandwich. A piece of lettuce stuck in his teeth and every one of his words was laden with a faint fish smell, but he made her laugh. They spent a pleasant evening talking about Santa Fe and all its extremes, such as the population versus the number of galleries, or the best coffee and the worst sludge. He was a nice man and she found him incredibly entertaining, so after that first night she often spent her date nights chatting with him.

Eventually, Gabe invited her to audit one of his classes at the College of Santa Fe, and she went. It was a philosophy in literature class. The course asked whether or not an author could justifiably incorporate his or her philosophy in a work of fiction, and if he or she did, would the philosophic ideas be both more palatable and accessible to the reader? Clara quickly became engrossed and soaked up every bit of information thrown her way.

At first, she didn't have many friends, and she didn't want any lovers, so all she did was read. She convinced Gabe to ask his colleagues if she could audit their classes, and went to a different class every day of the week. She was openly argumentative and her new scorned sarcastic wit attracted a lot of attention. Eventually, her social calendar began to boil over. Without even knowing it, she stopped trying to actively torture Artie. There were no more pretend outings, only real ones.

Elizabeth thought her new friends were bizarre, but they weren't really. They were a mixture of wealth and rebellion. They wore expensive used clothes and had extensive educations, but no one seemed to have a real job. They were trust fund babies, busily writing the great American novel, or developing a "new" genre of music, and Clara felt at home with them. They seemed to understand her problems and told her that Artie was an ass who she should just forget.

Her closest friend was a girl named Kylie. Kylie was a five foot ten torso with ice blond hair and huge feet. She never stopped cursing, but she was smart enough to make Clara laugh. Kylie's medium of choice was presentational art. Most of her work consisted of chaining people together using their piercings. The whole concept of body piercings fascinated her, the more unusual or grotesque the better.

Clara initially found her work shocking and repulsive. For instance, she had a piece entitled "possession," where a young woman with a pierced clitoris was chained to a man with a Prince Albert. The chain between the piercings was only about two feet long, so neither person could move without causing the other pain. The first time Clara saw the piece all she saw was a naked hairy penis with a piece of metal through it. She giggled and turned away, thinking she might throw up.

A week later, she got it. "Possession" was a commentary on male/female relationships. On the ties between two people, the mixture of pleasure and pain. The complexity of social bonds was a major theme in Kylie's work and that drew Clara to her. The two of them would sit in coffee shops and theorize about human behavior for hours.

Clara loved her new intellectual life. She decided she was artsy and embodied her new persona in every way possible. She stopped dropping the "g" off her "ing" words, bought a ton of used clothes, and dyed a chunk of her hair black. For the first time in her life she thought her outward appearance looked as awkward as her inner turmoil, and in response people began to treat her like she was something special. At parties, they listened to her and responded with opinions of their own. She enjoyed feeling more sophisticated. After a while, she became a coffee house fixture and stopped attending her classes, except for phi-losophy in literature. There was something about Gabe.

The first time she was in his classroom, he spotted her right off the bat even though she was sitting towards the back of the echoing lecture hall. He smiled in her direction, a sly smile, the kind where you only lift one side of your mouth. He was wearing a pair of tattered blue jeans and a gray-collared shirt. He left the first two buttons open. His hair, brown streaked with gray, was tied neatly in a ponytail. His shoes were soft, suede, European-looking moccasins, which he wore with no socks. He was a creative, intelligent, witty adult, and that alone had sex appeal.

Gabe had presence. He commanded an audience but he wasn't pre-tentious like his colleagues. Every week he would strut into the room and take off his shoes. He couldn't sit still, and he bubbled over with energy about his teachings. He was still learning. He took in every-thing his students said, mulling their opinions over, and using them to expand his own thoughts, but it wasn't even that in the end. It was the way he looked at Clara. That look made her long for company. She wanted to be near him, to feel the strong solidarity of him.

There was nothing torrid about their affair. People speculated that they had been an item long before they were, but they weren't lovers while she was in his class. Clara stopped being his student the day after their first date.

She didn't realize it was a date. She was wearing her jeans and one of Michael's old ratty sweatshirts. Gabe took her to a little Greek hole in the wall that she didn't even know existed. The guy behind the counter was missing a volume gauge, so he screamed at the customers and into the phone. He even screamed the orders over his shoulder to the chef. The chef just rolled his eyes as he sliced long strips of meat off the rotating spigot. There were no tables, and it was practically summer, so they ordered two gyros and ate them silently, sitting on the curb, taziki sauce running down their arms.

When Clara finished chewing Gabe said, "A delicacy such as this can only be followed by one thing?"

"Oh yeah, and what could that possibly be?" Clara laughed.

"Peanut butter ice cream, hello?" He emphasized his words with a gregarious lifting of his eyebrows.

"Ahh...Clearly. How could I have been so foolish?" She turned to face him and smiled.

"You have a little something," he pointed to her chin.

Clara wiped her napkin across her face. "Did I get it?"

"Nope. Let me help you." He rested his left hand on her cheek and using the other hand wiped her chin with his napkin. "All better," he said quietly.

They looked at each other for maybe a minute before Gabe leaned in and kissed her.

When they broke apart, Gabe said, "Don't come to class anymore. I'm no longer interested in being your teacher."

Clara nodded her head, trying to appear mature. Gabe laughed.

"I was trying to be silly," he said.

"Oh." Clara swallowed. Gabe put his arm around her. His fingers cupped her shoulder.

"Laugh with me, so I don't feel stupid," he said.

Clara laughed nervously, but by the time they finished, their ice cream she felt silly and excited. Gabe drove her home and walked her to the door. Clara didn't even think that Artie might be watching when she let him kiss her. Instead, she was wondering if she should invite Gabe inside. There was a clatter, like a cat or the wind knocking something over, and immediately she knew he was there.

They both heard him fidget and whisper, "fuck." Clara looked right at his spot, and she could see him crouching, trying to stay hidden, shaking whatever he had spilled off his hands. She quickly looked back at Gabe. He was peering in Artie's direction trying to make out if there was someone hiding in the darkness. Clara turned his face towards her and kissed him again, knowing he would be distracted easily. When they went inside, she shut her blinds for the first time in months.

In the morning Clara stood in her doorframe wearing only an

oversized T-shirt. She had to get up on her tip-toes to kiss Gabe good-bye.

"Can I see you tonight?" he asked.

She nodded, sweetly touching his face. When he was walking away, he paused a few times to look over his shoulder at her. She just smiled said, "Go. You're late already." He skipped off and Clara was struck by how strange it looked for a man his age to be so giddy, like youth was trapped inside him.

When he was gone, Clara stared at Artie's perch. She didn't expect him to be there, but she was aware of his absence. Barefoot, she crossed to his spot and sat on the ground. Little bits of rock and dirt pressed into her thighs, ensuring that when she stood her thighs would be covered with little red marks and creases. A little breeze blew through the open door, making the closed blinds chatter. Sitting there spying on her own apartment, she was fairly certain that he wouldn't be back, and she missed him already.

THIRTY-THREE

Liz + Michael
Michael wants to propose
but issue w/ her father

Michael stared out the window of the Worthington's apartment on Fifth Avenue and Sixty-Eighth Street. Spring's warm weather drove more people into the park than the icy winds that had whistled past bowed heads just three months earlier. Michael enjoyed watching the people. The distance between him and the ground made them look like dollhouse miniatures. Central Park dolls. Dolls paddling boats on the lake, dolls loafing in the grass, dolls playing ball with their kids, dolls holding hands, strolling.

For Michael, Central Park was the coolest thing about New York. Not to say that he didn't love the city, but looking out at that huge expanse of nature nestled between row upon row of skyscrapers awed him. Whenever he was in the living room alone, he pressed his forehead against the glass and tried to see all the way up to One Hundred and Tenth Street. Sometimes, if he looked hard enough, he thought he caught a glimpse of Columbia or the slightest shadow of an older somewhat decrepit but still ornate building in Harlem, but most of the time he saw nothing, and nothing was a good feeling. He liked to think of the park as endless, a mysterious magical world, like C.S. Lewis's Narnia.

Ten stories below him, just across the street, the magnolia trees were in full bloom. Spring had come late. It was almost June, but the soft wispy color of the sky signaled the kind of spring day that makes you want to smile at strangers. There was almost no wind so the trees stood completely still, reaching and stretching their candy colored petals to the sun. Katie loved magnolia trees. She said the huge pink and white petals were romantic, in a sad way like a sappy movie or the last page of a great novel. They disappeared as quickly as they arrived, but they were never really gone because the following spring they would blossom again, inciting romance in their onlookers.

Michael had a specific attachment to the cluster of trees he could see from the window. The first time Katie brought Michael to New York, they were walking in the park when it started to pour. Michael took off his T-shirt and tried to cover their heads, but it was no use. They ended up soaked and cold, and when he saw the apartment across the street he was dying to go right in, but Katie stopped, grabbed his shirt, threw him a smile and knelt down by the magnolia trees. The rain had broken apart the flowers and scattered them all over the sidewalk. He watched her gently cradle a collection of magnolia petals in his T-shirt.

"Katie, what are you doing?" he asked.

"Saving it," she said.

"Saving what? The flowers are already dead."

She smiled at him. "Not the flowers," she said, "the day."

It was a cheesy moment that only readers of romance novels would find romantic, but even so, every time he passed those trees he was reminded of how much he loved her. Seeing her sitting there on the ground was the first time he realized Katie was soft and sentimental as well as smart and strong. Maybe it was the first time it occurred to him that she needed him, or it might have even been the first time he realized she loved him or was planning on loving him. Whatever it was, he owed those magnolia trees something, which was why he decided to use them as the backdrop to propose.

Michael realized he wanted to ask Katie to marry him on a night when they had driven all the way to New York to see some lecture on gender issues, some hoity-toity sociologist that Katie was absolutely enthralled with. They were running late, so in about ten minutes they parked the car, sprinted up to the apartment to throw on some decent clothes, and were pulling on their coats, when Elizabeth called, hysterical. Michael tried to calm her down, but it was no use. Katie rolled her eyes at him and said, "Give me the phone." He handed the receiver to her, and listened as her voice slipped into the sweet and sticky salve his mother needed.

"Elizabeth, it's Katie. What's going on?" He held his coat and tapped his foot, while she paced back and forth, nodding and occasionally saying something like "Oh," or "Um-hm." Michael could hear his mother on the other end of the phone, something about Artie freaking out. There was more nodding and sweet talking, while Michael watched the minutes slip away.

Michael's day had already been a breeding ground for aggravation and painful impatient moments. His alarm didn't go off, Katie took at least forty minutes deciding what clothes she needed to bring with her, and they sat in dense nerve-wracking traffic on the George Washington Bridge, so listening to this phone call would have been excruciating no matter what, but because he knew Katie was really anticipating this event he was unusually peeved at his mother for dumping the family problems on him.

The lecture was being held in some dank high school auditorium on the other side of the city. Even if they took a taxi they were going to have to sneak in the back door, disturbing at least one person and possibly the entire presentation. Michael hated having an auditorium full of eyes squinting in his direction, scolding his rude behavior, So he tapped his watch face, and made a "what are you doing?" gesture.

Katie didn't pay any attention to him. Instead, she pulled off her jacket, threw it over the back of the couch and sat down.

Michael was furious. He drove all the way to New York, sat in traffic, and stopped twelve times for Katie to pee, so they could see a stupid lecture, which Katie had not shut up about, until suddenly his mom called upset. And then, Katie couldn't care less. Lecture? What lecture?

He felt his cheeks grow red with anger and he paced furiously around the room. When he looked over at Katie, she rolled her eyes, shook her head and mouthed, "You're such a baby." The expression on her face made him feel stupid. Truth was he was dreading the lecture they were late for, and he was screaming mad because Katie was being nice to his mother. She was right. He was a complete baby. In the end, Elizabeth talked her ear off and they didn't go, but Katie never said anything about the lecture, and when Michael tried to apologize she said, "If my family was in turmoil, I'd want someone to listen too."

They had dinner at this restaurant on the Upper West Side, Rain. Katie loved the food. It was Asian inspired, Thai or something. Michael ordered what he always ordered when they ate there; a beef dish in a tangy sweet sauce. His motto was if it's good stick with it. Something had been on Katie's mind the whole day, but as usual, Michael had no clue what she was thinking.

When the waiter walked away, Katie said, "You should try something different every now and then." She was wearing a blue shiny top that was reflective in certain lights. She wasn't really looking at him and he could feel the distance between them.

"The beef is delicious," he treaded lightly.

"There are other things you'd like."

"I guess. Maybe next time." He stretched his hand towards hers, which was resting next to her plate. She looked up watching a waiter pass and shifted her position, dropping her hand to her lap. Michael wasn't sure if she had seen him reaching for her, so he tried not to feel rejected.

Katie said, "Sometimes I think you avoid anything that makes you uncomfortable or vulnerable."

"What's up, Kate?"

"I don't know."

"Yeah you do. You've been totally weird since you spoke to my mom."

"It's just," she paused, "It's not the food. It's your attitude about your family. I like your family. They're vibrant and interesting. You must have had such an unusual childhood, but you hide all of that so you can seem like your background is less interesting."

Michael started to defend himself, "You have no idea what it's like. I was..." but Katie interjected immediately.

"No, you're right. I don't know what it was like, but I know that you think you were slighted or something, and maybe you were. I don't know." She took a deep breath. "The thing is, it's something they did that makes you so appealing, to me at least. You're not just another wealthy brat. You're funny and confident. You know about art and opera, but you also know how to build things and how to do your own laundry. They made you something special." She was caught in a whirlwind of frustration and pity. "God, Michael, can't you see how lucky you are?"

Michael blew off the entire speech. He said something curt and obnoxious, which quickly caused all dinner conversation to evaporate. After dinner they walked down Central Park West looking for a cab. It was still cold out then and he could see Katie shivering, but when he tried to get close to her and use his body heat to warm her, she refused to touch him.

In the cab, she stared out the window, squeezing her body tightly to the door so there was as much distance between them as possible.

"Please stop this," he said.

"Me?" There were tears in her eyes, "You're the one who thinks I'm so shallow that I could never love anyone who wasn't born in a golf shirt."

"Katie. I never once," but that was exactly what he had thought, well sort of. "It's not exactly like that. I just want to be what you want." His nervousness softened her. It always did.

"I want you," she turned and curled into his armpit, "and them."

It was that "and them" that got him. Michael wasn't sure if it was the actual acceptance of his family or if it was an acceptance of something, some part of him that was like them, but whatever it was he knew in that moment that he wanted her too, forever.

A couple weeks ago, he told Elizabeth. He thought she would be skeptical, that she would make some "you're too young" or "we haven't even met her yet" argument, but she didn't. She had been acting very weird since Clara moved into her own apartment. Her voice always sounded distant and lost. It was unnerving.

She said, "She's a wonderful girl, isn't she?"

"I think so."

"Do you have the money for a ring?"

"Some of it."

"I'll talk to Dad about lending you the rest," she paused, "or maybe you should call him." Michael knew that his parents were hardly speaking. Since Artie had moved into his old room, he kept calling with nostalgic memories of their childhood and the conversation tended to drift to what was happening at home. He didn't know the details, but it was clear that his father didn't think Clara living on her own was such a good idea.

"I will," he said, trying to parlay his understanding of the situation without making her feel bad.

"Maybe you could get married here," she said.

"Maybe," then, shocking even himself, he said, "I'd like that." And he meant it.

He hadn't been exactly sure when or how he was going to propose until Katie said her father was going to be in the city this weekend, and she wanted to see him. He could ask Bill Worthington for Katie's hand and propose in Central Park. As they drove into the city, he spotted the late-blooming magnolias and almost busted his own surprise.

It should have been a perfect scenario, but he couldn't seem to nail down permission from Katie's father. Early yesterday morning, He was sitting across the table from Mr. Worthington, trying to work up some nerve. Katie was out buying breakfast, so the setting was right. Bill Worthington was barefoot and he wore jeans and an eggplant colored polo shirt. They were both drinking iced coffee topped with Rediwhip. Mr. Worthington kept the red and white can in front of him, so he could continually re-top his drink. Michael never had Rediwhip in his life until he met the Worthingtons. Elizabeth made fresh whipped cream.

"What's the matter, Mike?" Bill asked. "You look like you just swallowed some old bag's fart."

Michael half-smiled. Over the past few months, he discovered that in the absence of his wife, Bill Worthington was the king of lude inappropriate jokes and disgusting metaphors. He was never quite sure of the appropriate reaction. Mr. Worthington's kind of humor fell under the same heading as locker room gossip, only without the malicious intentions. The guy was nice, just gross. Whenever possible, Michael ignored the inane portions of his comments.

"No, It's just ... You see I was wondering..." he took a deep breath and spun his glass in his hand, "I was hoping you would agree to...." The phone rang.

"Hold that thought, kid." For a while, Mr. Worthington chatted with some business associate. At first he was pretty formal, but eventually the disgusting jokes and a little snicker slipped out. Michael couldn't stop staring at Mr. Worthington's feet. They looked rubbery, like dried Elmer's glue. Each gray toenail was flaky and mutated, really gross. Michael decided the whole world would be better off if they were eternally hidden beneath smooth black socks. His stomach knotted every time he glanced in their direction, and eventually he got up, quietly excusing himself, just to get away from them.

He thought he'd shower and then they could talk. It never occurred to him that no other like moment would present itself. By the time he got back into the kitchen, Katie had arrived with breakfast and his first opportunity had passed. He spent the entire day standing right next to Bill Worthington, but never once finding a solo moment long enough to pop the question.

He was still hopeful. It would happen today. That was the reason he had risen early. He turned from the window and listened to see if he could hear any signs that Mr. Worthington was awake. The muffled rumble of the shower signaled that he would have Bill Worthington's undivided attention in a matter of moments.

It was going to be a perfect day. He fiddled with the ring box in his pocket. He had a perfect plan. He would ask if she wanted to go for a walk in the park, the air would smell sweet and damp, and a light cool breeze would raise goose bumps on the backs of Katie's arms. He would lend her his sweatshirt. On the way back to the apartment, he would jump up and hit the branches of the magnolia tree. The huge pink and white flowers would tumble to their feet. Katie would be shocked, and ask why he did that. He would drop to his knee, hold out the ring and say, "So you could save the day."

THIRTY-FOUR

Artie crossed his arms and leaned back in his chair. The ticking of the clock drowned out the drone of his English teacher's voice. In exactly seven minutes and twenty-three seconds, he would be finished with Friday, and he could go home. He could curl up under the sheets and think about Clara. He just wanted to put the day behind him.

It was prom night, but he wasn't going. A few girls had lingered around him earlier in the month, but he didn't ask any of them. A girl he had never spoken to before asked him, but he made up a lie about a girlfriend from out of town. He just didn't want to go without Clara. His buddies kept pointing out that he was going to miss the best party of their high school careers, but he wasn't interested in that either. He just wanted to graduate.

He crossed out the days on one of those extra-large calendars. He hung it right by the front door so he could scratch off the day before he even put down his bag. As of today, he would have exactly fifteen school days left. He wasn't sure how finishing school would make things better, but he was certain it would. Maybe once he graduated, he would move out too or start traveling like his parents did.

When Clara first moved out, he thought he might die. When she announced that she was moving, not him, he thought he lucked out, but living in her house was awful. In the beginning, he often got home before everyone else, and no matter how hard he tried he always ended up lying in her bed looking at her ceiling, trying to smell her on the sheets or he went rifling through her drawers, trying to learn more about her, to feel closer to her. He always felt guilty about invading her space, and every day he panicked that he would fall asleep and either Cliff or Elizabeth would find him there.

After a few weeks, to avoid the unyielding pull of her room, he started driving around until it was late enough for someone else to be home. It was his aimless driving that led him to her new apartment. He hadn't gone there intentionally, but once he realized where he was, he couldn't help himself from taking one little peek.

He was surprised when he first saw her. He wondered why she decorated with so much yellow. The consistency of color made the apartment look like a staged room in a Bloomingdale's catalogue. She looked so miserable trapped in her little yellow cage, so without even questioning his motives, he started going there every day. He told himself it was because he didn't want her to be alone. He found a perfect spot to watch her from, one where she would never see him but he could always see her. He knew it was bordering on obsessive when he started going home for dinner and then going right back, but he couldn't help himself.

For the first month or so, she spent endless hours watching T.V. and eating junk food. She was even getting a little belly. He called it her microwave fat. One afternoon he thought she spotted him. She seemed wary walking to her door and she kept looking over her shoulder. After that she got happier. She started talking on the phone all the time and then one night she got dressed up and went out on a date, and that date was followed by more dates. He tried not to be devastated. After all, she thought he had been with Christina and he never said otherwise.

While she was out, he liked to imagine them living in her little apartment together. He spent hours thinking about what they would buy at the supermarket and on which days they would do their laundry. Because Clara always came home alone, he dismissed her dates as unimportant and was relatively unfazed by her new social life until it changed again. She stopped dressing for dates but she still went out. She was reading all the time. She changed her hair and her look and he felt her slipping away, like he didn't know her anymore. Then one night she wasn't alone.

She came home with a man who was twice their age. He saw her coming up the walk with someone and panic set in. When he realized how old the guy was, he sighed, thinking, no way that's a date, but then the old dude kissed her. At the sight of them kissing, Artie dropped his drink and Clara looked right at him. He could tell from the speed of her glance that she knew he was there the whole time. He closed his eyes until he heard the door shut.

When he opened them he watched her face in the window as she shut the blinds. It felt like good-bye. He waited a few minutes before he left, just keeping up appearances in case they decided to come back out, but he knew they weren't. Then, he stood, his pants sticky with Coke, and went to the car. He hadn't gone back since that night.

About a week after he stopped spying on Clara, it dawned on him that up until now Clara had always placed his feelings before her own. Well, it didn't dawn on him, it dawned on Cliff. The two of them were sitting downstairs in Artie's house watching a football game. Cliff spent a lot of time watching T.V. Artie knew it was because he was trying to avoid Liz but neither of them discussed it. She had been a little loony lately, joining drum circles and shit. That particular afternoon she was out at one of her housewife empowerment meetings, a.k.a, the reason for the new bumper sticker, "EVE was framed." Neither one of them was really interested in the game. In fact, Artie had been staring down the phone thinking, I bet Clara's home now. Cliff was sitting on the couch across from him, drinking a beer and staring at the T.V., when he said, "Ya know Art, Clara always did everything for you."

It wasn't some big epiphany but it started the gears in Artie's head. He started to think about how Clara had spent all those years loving him and living in his shadow. Initially, he had tried not to fixate on the image of her kissing the old man because it nauseated him, but now he had begun to worry that she had run out into the world and met a self-sufficient man, a grown man, a man who took care of himself. With these thoughts came the realization that he was an immature jerk, a floundering child, who didn't deserve her.

He couldn't shake the feeling. He lacked experience and responsibility. He didn't have a job. He didn't read the paper. United States' politics were beyond his understanding and global politics were as accessible as long lost biblical scrolls written in Sanskrit. He could make a bowl of pasta but French toast was beyond him. Clara and Michael weren't like that. His mother coddled him more. They all did. They blamed it on his artistic nature. He used to think it was a blessing, but now it was his burden.

He was pondering how he could combat his juvenile behavior when the school bell rang. Artie's English teacher shouted something over the clatter of the emptying classroom. Artie picked up his backpack. Jimmy Green, the slowest guy in the world, sat in front of Artie. There was no way around this kid. It was a wait or climb situation, and it got on Artie's nerves every Friday. First, Jimmy carefully folded a piece of paper and put it in his shirt pocket, then he started to reorganize the pens in his bag. Artie tapped his foot hoping the sound would create a sense of urgency. Jimmy only seemed to slow down. Artie rubbed hard on his temples with his thumbs and tried to let go of his frustration.

Fuck it, he thought. If Jimmy wouldn't get out of his way, then he'd go another way. He pitched his backpack over the desk to his left, and then climbed over. He quickly headed for the door, and once he had cleared the classroom, he broke into a full out sprint. He had parked the truck in the far right corner of the parking lot, so he had to run past almost every one of his friends. A few hollered at him, "Yo, what's the rush kid? Forget to rent a tux?" Artie threw up a hand, but he didn't stop moving. Once inside the car he peeled out, dirt and dust spun up from the tires, so he couldn't see anything behind him. He loved that moment. He waited for it every day. It was somewhat cliché, but chaos behind and clear skies ahead was a good feeling.

He rolled down the window and rested his left elbow against it. For a moment, he imagined his mother sitting next to him.

"Your daddy always used to do that," she said.

"What?" He was interested now, unlike when she was alive.

"Rest his elbow on the sill."

"Do car windows have sills?" He asked with half a smile.

"Always such a smart ass." He could hear her laugh.

By the time he turned out onto Rodeo Road, she was gone. He was amazed at all the little things he was starting to remember about her. In the beginning, he kept himself awake at night worrying that if he didn't think about her, his memories of her would fade. Lately, she was more real to him than she had been when she was alive. He heard things in his head that he had ignored when she was alive, things about life and experience, things about his father and her love for him, things about himself, and most of all, things about Clara.

His mother loved Clara, but not like Liz loved Clara or the way Liz loved him. She loved her without a parent's tainted sense of judgment. She didn't see Clara as flawless. She saw her as beautiful, intelligent, careful, frail, cowardly, silly and angry. They hung out together. Clara was her friend. Sissy saw Clara as a person with emotions and feelings, and Artie wasn't exactly sure if he ever saw her that way. He wasn't sick or anything. He didn't sleep with someone he thought of as his sister, but he didn't really see her. He saw safety, familiarity, comfort, and escape. Being in a relationship with Clara was not something to be taken lightly, and he just walked right into it, dick first. He was a selfish idiot.

He missed her something awful, and he hated the idea of her sleeping with someone else, but he wanted to win her back for the right reasons. He wanted to offer her something, to show her he wouldn't be a coward anymore. So far, he couldn't even call her, but someday he would. Someday he would be a man.

He pulled the car into the driveway and said the word "shit-head" out loud. As he shut the door, he noticed Liz sitting on the front stoop. He tilted his head and lifted his hand to say hi. He was surprised to see her. She wasn't usually home at this time of day.

"Hey, kiddo," she said with fake enthusiasm, "I was waiting for you."

"What are you doing home?" he asked.

"I've been home all day. Can't ya tell?" He assumed she was referring to her appearance, but she looked pretty normal to him. "I thought we could talk."

Artie and Liz had never talked all that much. Even though they were always close, they never really had much to talk about. Ever since he had moved into Michael's room they pretty much exchanged hugs and daily babble, the kind of stuff that doesn't matter in the long run. Certainly not the type of conversations that required waiting on the stoop for him to get home, so the idea of chatting with Liz made him uncomfortable, like he was about to be punished.

"What about?" he asked.

"About a lot of things," Liz's eyes drifted to the ground. "Why don't you sit down?"

"You wanna go in the house?"

"No, it's nice out. Let's just sit here." She scooted over and made room for him to sit down next to her.

Artie put his bag down and sat on top of it. He never liked sitting on the ground. He would if he had to, like he had outside Clara's apartment, but inevitably if he did, water seeped up from the depths of the earth and made his pants wet so it looked like he pissed himself. Liz looked out to the right, where the sun would set in a few hours.

"I ran into Jeff's mother today," Liz said.

"Clara's Jeff?" Artie asked.

"Yeah," she nodded her head, "she couldn't stop talking about how Chris...You know Chris, Jeff's little brother?" Artie nodded, Chris was a freshman. "Well, Chris got asked to the prom."

Artie crossed his legs, Indian style. "Yeah, I know."

"How come you're not going, Artie?"

He shrugged his shoulders. He didn't like where this was going. Pressure was building in his chest, and his ears were ringing. "Just didn't feel like it, I guess." If he held his breath, he wouldn't cry.

"Would you have taken her?" She asked.

He bit the corner of his lower lip. "I don't know. It would have been weird." He couldn't hold off the waterworks any longer. "God, I'm so emotional lately, like a girl." He wiped the tears away with the heels of his palms. "I don't know what to say, Liz."

"Just tell me what you would've done."

"I would've wanted to take her," he said forcefully. Liz turned her head further away from him. "But I don't know that I would've been right."

"No," she was crying a little bit, which Artie didn't expect, "she would have looked beautiful.

First he laughed, then he put his head in his hands and really started crying. Liz put her arms around him and kissed his forehead.

"I miss y'er mom," she said.

"Me too," he whispered.

"I've been thinking that we should throw her another party, a different kind of celebration."

"What do ya mean?" he asked

"I'm not sure yet, but something fun. You wanna help me?" She squeezed his shoulder and smiled.

"Maybe," he scrunched up his nose and shrugged his shoulders again.

"I'll invite Clara," she teased.

Artie knew Liz had no idea that Clara would bring a date, an older more together man.

THIRTY-FIVE

Elizabeth decided it was finally nice enough to wear a skirt and sandals. When she closed the door and heard a breeze rustle through the garden, she doubted her decision for just a minute, but the air that hit her skin was pleasantly warm. Summer had arrived late and sudden. With all the flowers in full bloom, she could hardly see Artie's bronze as she walked to the car. Just the small expressive crease of the young boy's brow and the end of his spear peeked over the pungent orange day lilies. The noon sun was high above her, and glared into the window, so she pulled down the visor before she turned the key in the ignition. She was headed to Mr. Balducci's pharmacy to pick up Clara.

Since Artie had moved into the house she had changed her routine. Her sleeplessness had passed, so she didn't hide in the pantry anymore. Sometimes she even slept past seven. Although Cliff and she hardly spoke, he spent most nights sleeping next to her and sometimes in his sleep he would pull her close to him, allowing her to believe his waking anger was not part of his subconscious. In the mornings he tended to skip breakfast, and she tried not to miss him. She wanted to give him time. She wanted to show him that she was willing to be a solid part of their life, whenever he decided their life should begin again.

Artie seemed a hundred percent better. He was doing well in school, and since the incident, he hadn't come home drunk once. They quietly ate their morning meal together. If they spoke, it was about his school assignments or their ideas for the celebration, but something about his demeanor was different. He seemed driven. And so, breakfast had changed. It had finally settled into just being the beginning of the day rather than an insurmountable chore.

When Artie went to school the house grew silent, and she liked it. She did the laundry and the dishes like she used to. She made the beds and took her time in the shower. Sometimes she stood in Cliff's closet and touched his clothes or watched the morning show in the living room. Her house had started to feel like home again, and the comfort of its memories made her languid and lazy.

Even though she stopped going to Ruth's house first thing in the morning, she still went almost every day, but the time they spent together was different. As things at home got better, things with Ruth felt strained. They weren't alone as much. They took classes together and spoke less. When Liz first conceived of throwing Sissy a second celebration, she thought she would invite Ruth. Liz loved her and wanted her to be part of her life. She thought they could be friends always. She daydreamed about inviting Ruth into her house. She pictured her sitting at the kitchen table, making Cliff laugh like Sissy had. She didn't think Ruth could replace Sissy, but she thought that another woman in her house might bring the balance back to her marriage and her family.

She decided the best way to combine her two worlds was to introduce Ruth to her family in stages. She hadn't talked to Ruth about the idea, but not because she thought she'd be opposed. Introducing Ruth to the kids and Cliff was a big deal for Liz. She thought Ruth would take it as a symbol of how much love Liz really felt for her. She wanted it to be a surprise, like a box of candy on a day other than Valentine's Day.

She decided Clara should be the first, so she had called her and asked her to lunch. Clara had to work in the morning, but her shift ended at 1:30 pm, and after that she was free. It was a little later than Liz usually went to Ruth's house, but Ruth didn't worry any more when she arrived late.

Clara was waiting on the curb when Liz arrived. Liz glanced at the dashboard clock. It was just 1:30, so Clara must have finished early. Liz was eager to get to Ruth's house, but Clara stood slowly, gathering her things. A couple of months earlier, she had dyed the hair that framed her face jet black. Liz wondered how she thought it was attractive. Even so, every time Liz saw Clara, she couldn't help but smile. They were finally speaking on a regular basis. They spoke each day before Clara went to work. Liz knew Clara had trouble when she first moved, but lately she seemed better. She often spoke of a professor at the College of Santa Fe named Gabrielle Matthews. Liz wasn't sure what the relationship was there, but she was trying her best to stay out of Clara's life.

Settling into the car Clara said, "Where to Mama? Is there a reason for this meeting of the minds or are we just getting a bite to eat?"

Liz wasn't exactly sure how to broach the subject. She tried to tell Clara why she wanted to have lunch the night before, but Clara abruptly hung up the phone, claiming she was late for dinner with friends. Clara knew about Ruth because Liz rented Clara's apartment from one of Ruth's friends, but they never discussed who Ruth was and if they had, Liz wasn't sure that she would have been able to explain their relationship.

"Well, actually, I wanted you to meet a friend of mine," she said.

"Ruth?" Clara asked.

"Yes, Ruth."

Clara raised her eyebrows. "Really..." she said drawing out the word so as to express jest and surprise. Liz smirked at her teasing and felt certain that she was doing the right thing.

"Don't act so surprised."

"No, you're right. I should feel flattered." She paused making sure Liz was listening.

"Yes, go on."

"It's just I didn't know Ruth was of the public domain."

Liz couldn't believe how Clara's speech patterns and her vocabulary changed since she moved out. She had grown incredibly intense and her wit was intellectual and riddled with sarcasm.

"I think you are going to love her," Liz said. Clara fished through her knapsack and pulled out a wine colored lipstick. Looking in the visor mirror she put the lipstick on and then smacked her lips together, making a puckering sound.

"I'm sure I will," she said, reaching over and squeezing Liz's hand.

When they got to Ruth's house, Liz got out of the car and walked towards the door. Clara was slower, forcing Liz to pause and wait for her. Waiting was hard. Liz anticipated the look on Ruth's face when she came through the door, and the burst of comfort that came with that look felt overdue. When Clara caught up, Liz opened the door and walked in. Behind her Clara whispered, "Shouldn't you at least knock?"

Liz just waved her off and crossed down into the living room. The door to the studio was closed, but Liz knew Ruth was there because the sultry sounds of Miles Davis crooned inside. Liz paused, listening for a minute. She looked at Clara, who was standing awkwardly behind her.

"Is she here?" she asked.

Liz pointed to the door. "She's painting," she said. Then she stepped forward and walked into the studio. Ruth was still in her pajamas. The piece she was working on was a portrait of Liz. The figure had Liz's features, but it was hard to discern anything else human about it. Liz had never seen Ruth paint anything like it. Most of her work leaned towards realism rather than the abstract. The colors in the painting were dark and angry, like Clara's lipstick, and Liz couldn't stop looking at it.

Her own eyes looked out at her, expressing everything she had put Ruth through over the past year. She could see how little she thought of Ruth's feelings, and feel all the ways that Ruth loved her that she never acknowledged. She could see her own selfishness. Every time Liz touched her or needed her was torture. Ruth was playing the role of mistress without any of the benefits. There was no way to merge this life with her family. The gravity of Liz's mistake and severity of her emotional blinders made her feel incredibly hysterical. Her ability to lie to herself, to manipulate the facts of a situation so that the truth of the thing was lost to her, was all too familiar. She thought she'd out-grown lying to herself the night Artie hollered at the moon, but clearly that wasn't true. Ruth was dying inside and Liz has just continued to bleed her dry, like a parasite.

Ruth turned, her face haggard with sleeplessness and her eyes bloodshot from crying. Liz tried to look into her eyes but Ruth was focused on something beyond Liz's shoulder.

"Hello," she said.

Clara stepped forward, jutted out her hand and introduced herself, "I'm Clara." Liz had completely forgotten Clara was there.

"Nice to meet you, Clara."

Liz watched them shake hands. Ruth looked shocked and Clara looked scared. They both turned their gaze on Liz, begging, "what now" with their eyes. It took Liz a second to speak.

"I thought we could all have lunch, but if you're working..." she trailed off, looking back at the painting. Ruth put down her paint brush and wiped her hands on her shirt.

"Just let me get cleaned up," she said.

She walked past the two of them and a few seconds later Liz heard the shower turn on. Clara stood next to her looking at the painting. "Is that you?" she asked. Liz didn't answer. "It looks like you," Clara said, tilting her head curiously, like a confused fox terrier.

"It's me," Liz replied, still in shock.

"Did you pose for her?"

"No." Liz whispered, embarrassed and feeling cornered like she was hiding a secret.

"It's dark."

Liz nodded, "Really dark."

"Is that what her paintings look like?"

"No, not usually."

Clara nodded knowingly, "Oh."

Liz put her arm around her, ushering her out of the studio. The two of them sat awkwardly on the couch in the living room. Liz noticed they were both sitting on their hands, and she was reminded of the discomfort she felt the first time she met Cliff's parents. She tried to relax, but she couldn't help thinking that Clara shouldn't have been exposed to Ruth's unrequited love, and the intensity of her love for Elizabeth was omnipresent. Clara couldn't not notice it, but there was nowhere to go. They couldn't just leave. Clara would notice the weirdness in that too, so Liz just started talking.

"Tell me about Gabrielle," she said. Clara blushed and swung her feet up and down, as if she was regressing before Liz's eyes.

"Not much to tell really."

"Are you dating?" Liz knew the answer.

"Sort of."

Liz couldn't help wondering if Artie knew, and then she remembered the young woman in the purple bra and panties. Clara deserved a little happiness.

"What does 'sort of' mean?" she asked.

"It's not that serious. He's older."

Of course, he had to be older. He taught college. Liz raised her eyes to the ceiling trying to decipher how young he could possibly be. If he went straight through grad school, he could still be in his twenties, but Liz figured early thirties, which was a little awkward, but not so bad.

"How much older?" she asked.

"Older," Clara said.

Ruth came into the room. Her hair was still wet and she was wearing jeans and a white tank top with no bra. The wet strands of hair dampened her shirt making see-through spots, and Liz found the choice completely inappropriate.

"Who's older?" Ruth asked.

Clara smiled mischievously, "The guy I've been dating." Ruth sat on the chair across from them to tie her shoes.

"What's he do?" Ruth's voice was familiar, like she and Clara were old friends. Liz forgot how forward Ruth's first impression was.

"He's a professor at the College of Santa Fe," Clara said proudly.

"Really, what's his name?"

Clara didn't speak, so Liz said, "Gabrielle Matthews. He teaches literature."

"Gabe? You're dating Gabe?" Ruth looked at Clara and raised her eyebrows. Clara nodded and looked at the floor. "Well, he certainly is older, but if I were your age, I think I'd be interested in someone much older too." Liz wondered just how much older this Gabe was, but she didn't stay with that thought for long because Ruth kept talking. "Of course, I'd be more likely to choose someone a bit curvier but..."

Clara jumped right in, "You're a lesbian?" She was clearly panicked by this bit of information.

"Does it bother you?" Ruth asked.

Clara tried to cover her shock. "No, God no. I was just surprised." Clara turned to face Liz. She looked her up and down, clearly wondering if she was about to announce that she was a lesbian too, and if she was, was this woman sitting across the strange modern living room her lover?

"Don't worry, Clara," Ruth said, "your mother is all about dick." The "ka" sound in the word dick violently penetrated Liz, tying her stomach in knots and vibrating in her chest cavity. She closed her eyes and swallowed so as not to cry. Clara did what any teenager would do in the situation. She laughed. Ruth laughed with her. Liz opened her eyes and was numbed by their smiling faces. Ruth stood, her laces tied and said, "Where to ladies?"

Liz tried to think of somewhere fast. She wanted to get this whole experience over with as quickly as possible, but she couldn't think of anywhere.

"I'm up for anything," Clara said.

"Guadeloupe Café?" Ruth suggested.

The Guadeloupe Café had the slowest service of any restaurant in town. In fact, if the food wasn't so good it would have been a complete failure, but there was nothing Liz could do. Clara said, "Oh, yeah. I love it there," and that's where they went.

Liz drove, while Ruth and Clara talked art and music and everything cultural under the sun. Liz was surprised by how much they had in common. Clara had a whole new slew of interests since she moved out, but Liz was unaware of the intensity of her passion concerning all things cultural and philosophical. She kept up with Ruth easily and often had things to add to the conversation that seemed insightful beyond her years.

By the time they sat down in the restaurant, Ruth and Clara seemed less uncomfortable than they were when they exchanged their first few words at Ruth's house, but Liz couldn't shake her dread. She added bits and pieces to the conversation, but she wasn't really paying attention. Every time Ruth spoke Liz wanted to cry. She was memorizing the coarse texture of her hair, the sounds she made when she chewed her food, the curve of her lower lip. She knew their time together was coming to an end and just like when Sissy was dying, Liz desired to trace all the lines in Ruth's face with her fingertips and tape all the rhythms of her voice, so she would never forget them.

The waitress had just put their food down, when Cliff came through the door with Gladys. Liz saw him before he saw them, and before he could turn and leave Gladys was on her way over to say hello. Gladys hovered over them, smiling like she was advertising toothpaste.

"Hi," she said, "God, I haven't seen either of you in such a long time. Cliff never stops talking about you though." Liz doubted that was true.

"Hi, Gladys" Clara and Liz said in unison.

Cliff stood behind her, not really approaching their table at all. Gladys stuck her hand out in Ruth's direction, "I'm Cliff's secretary, Gladys," she said.

Ruth took her hand and said, "Ruth, Liz's lesbian lover." Liz practically jumped out of her skin. Gladys pulled her hand away and looked to Cliff for confirmation. Cliff looked Ruth up and down with contempt. Liz prayed that Cliff would look at her, see her shaking her head vigorously, denying the words Ruth had just spoken. Clara laughed.

"She's joking, Gladys," she said.

"Oh, of course," Gladys blushed.

Clara looked over her shoulder and tentatively said, "Hi, Dad." For the first time Ruth looked over her shoulder, taking in Cliff. She stood.

"Cliff, I presume." Ruth was poised, but Liz sensed her sorrow.

"Ruth," Cliff bowed his head a little. They didn't shake hands.

"Nice to finally meet you. It seems this is a day for introductions."

"Well, we should go sit, let you ladies get back to your lunch," Cliff said. Gladys looked at him with confusion.

"Why don't you join us," Ruth offered. Eternity locked in a room with Jerry Falwell seemed more appealing than sitting with Cliff, Ruth and Clara noshing on burritos, but now that Ruth had offered, there was no way for Cliff to refuse without making a scene. Liz wondered if Ruth was enjoying the discomfort.

Almost immediately, Gladys, Ruth and Clara began talking about some foreign film that was playing at the Jacque Cousteau theatre. Cliff and Liz sat directly across from each other and said nothing. The waitress came to take Cliff and Gladys' orders and then Gladys excused herself to use the restroom. Once she was gone, Clara turned to Cliff.

"How ya been, Dad?" she asked.

Cliff's face was stern when he said, "You changed your hair." Clara's hand flittered up, tucking a black chunk behind her ear, and she nodded a little. "I don't like it." Clara bit her lip and anger flashed across her face.

"Thank you," she said, her voice cold and distant like the smell of astringent.

Ruth touched Liz's knee under the table and Liz jumped. Ruth smirked.

"What's wrong with you?" Cliff whispered.

Liz didn't answer at first and then she said, "Nothing. I just wanted Ruth to meet Clara." Liz was aware that Clara and Ruth leaned back as Cliff leaned in towards her.

"Are you enjoying this? Having all your anxieties at one table?"

"Dad, stop," Clara begged.

Gladys returned from the bathroom. "It smells great in there. I have to ask them what the smell is." No one spoke to her or even acknowledged that she had spoken. Cliff stared at Liz and her eyes started to burn. Ruth stood dropping her napkin on her plate.

"Well," she said, "I'm stuffed."

Clara followed her lead and managed to squeak out, "me too."

Ruth added, "I hate to eat and run, but I have an optometrist appointment. I'm thinking about lasik, and considering that these ladies are my ride..."

She smiled at Gladys, who said, "Oh you're kidding. I thought for once I was going to eat lunch with someone other than him." She rolled her eyes at Cliff. Liz forced herself to laugh a little.

"He's not so bad," Liz said trying to seem jovial but she couldn't look at Cliff.

Ruth and Clara stood, gathering their purses. From the standing position, Clara gobbled one more mouthful of food.

Gladys said, "It was really nice to see you both."

Ruth was already walking away. Clara gave Cliff a little wave. Liz stood wistfully watching her daughter try to move back into her father's good favor. Cliff didn't say anything or even acknowledge that she had waved. Once Clara started for the door, Liz stopped caring that Gladys was there and said, "Grow up. She loves you. You should let her know you love her back." She left before he had a chance to speak.

They were close to Clara's house, so Liz dropped her off first. Ruth hugged her goodbye. Clara hugged her back and whispered something in her ear. Liz walked her to her door.

"Sorry about your father," she said.

"Whatever. The whole situation was awkward."

"Yeah, sorry about that too." Clara took her keys out of her purse. "Do you have plans tonight?" Liz asked.

"I'm seeing Gabe."

"Right," Liz paused trying to stop herself from asking, but she was dying to know. "How old is he?"

"Too old," Clara said. Liz nodded, realizing Clara had no intention of telling her and wondering if that was what she whispered to Ruth about. Picturing Clara dressed for a date with a suspiciously older man, reminded Liz that she wanted to tell Clara about the party.

"Listen, I meant to talk to you about this last night, but I'm throwing a party on the anniversary of Sissy's funeral celebration. I want you to come." Clara looked back towards the car.

"She's waiting," she said ignoring Liz's invite. Liz knew that anything having to do with home or Sissy was still off limits, but she wanted Clara to know about the party. She wanted her to have time to mull it over because maybe gentle reminders would encourage her to show up.

"Okay. I'll see you." Liz turned to leave.

"Soon?" Clara asked.

Liz stopped and turned back to Clara, smiling, "Whenever you want."

"Mom?" Clara shifted like she was having trouble putting her words together. "I'm not sure I can come to your party."

"I figured, but maybe you'll think about it."

Clara looked at the car again. "She loves you," she said.

Liz looked down. The cement beneath her feet had a huge crack in it, reminding her of the childhood jingle, step on a crack break your mother's back. Liz nodded and closed her eyes.

In the car on the way back to Ruth's house, Liz didn't say anything and neither did Ruth. When they pulled into Ruth's driveway, Ruth went to open the car door and Liz stopped her by placing a hand on her thigh. Ruth dropped her hands into her lap and asked, "Now?"

Liz had never seen her look vulnerable before. Even when she had cried or gotten angry there was always a force inside her that was strong and impenetrable.

"I think so," Liz said.

Ruth shook her head. "I thought I was ready," she laughed nervously.

"I don't think you can ever be ready to lose someone you love," Liz said taking her hand.

"You know what your daughter whispered to me..."

Liz shook her head, no.

"She said, don't be sad. Celebrate."

Ruth started to cry. Her tears made Liz's arms ache so that she wanted to shake the anguish from Ruth's face.

"I'm so sorry," she said through her own sobs, "I didn't mean to hurt you."

Ruth looked at her and before Liz could realize what was happening Ruth leaned across the car and kissed her. Even though she was desperate to pull away, Liz stayed still. She took in the gentleness of Ruth's lips. The grace of her touch was distinctly feminine and so lonely. Ruth didn't make eye contact again.

Before getting out of the car, she said, "I didn't mean to love you, Liz."

Liz watched her walk inside. She didn't glance back. Her long blond, multifaceted tendrils grazed back and forth across the middle of her back. The door closed behind her. Liz stared at it, knowing it would never open again, even if she knocked.

THIRTY-SIX

Clara sat on the couch and looked out the only window in her tiny efficiency apartment. She had always teased her mother for staring out windows, but over the past few months she had grown to understand the window trance. When you didn't know what to feel or when you were consciously trying to feel nothing, staring at glass panes was mentally obliterating. Something about gazing out a window made thoughts suffocate and die.

Dating Gabe was nothing like being with Artie. Gabe took her to plays and poetry readings. He bought her gifts and wrote her love letters. Gabe was lovely. He was independently wealthy and taught school for kicks. He had a huge wall-less house in the hills that he called an artist's loft. It was decorated in a classic beige and gray minimalist style. It kind of reminded her of Ruth's house. In other words, the house felt crisp and clean in a vacant, sanitary way.

They didn't live together, but Clara stayed with Gabe a lot. She ate dinner there almost every night, and it was almost completely satisfying. Clara had invited Kylie to Gabe's house for dinner a few times. Each visit played out the same way. All three would eat dinner and drink red wine. Then, Gabe would get tired and retire, while Clara and Kylie held down the fort. Kylie always asked the same questions: What's it like when you're in public? Is he better in bed? Do you ever feel weird, ya know because of his age? Clara didn't really have any answers. Their relationship was incredibly comfortable. It was nice, but it wasn't tumultuous or exciting

Before dinner every night, Clara would watch him cook, a green apron tied around his waist, and honestly delighted in him. He was so intelligent and he supported her in a way no one had in a long time. He loved her. He looked at her with a quiet peaceful comforting gaze, and she loved him too. She loved the way he sat in the living room reading fat books while listening to classical music. She loved the way he thought about life all the time and the way he never stopped learning. Sometimes, she thought that she would always want to stay in his home, cozy under his large down comforter. Those were the facts, but Clara knew there was always something more than facts, something pliable. Reason and logic are dry and unrelenting. They leave no room for emotion.

Gabe was standing in the kitchen cooking dinner the first time Clara noticed how old he really was. He dropped a wooden spoon on the floor and as he bent to pick it up a familiar groan came out of his mouth. She could hear her mother like she was right there with her, bending and holding her lower back. She felt enlightened and homesick at the same time.

After that evening she started to notice the little things, the lines around his eyes, and the way his skin stretched and sagged. She tried to push him to go out dancing with her and Kylie. Clara wanted him to be spontaneous. She wanted to make love in the car and eat junk food in the middle of the night. He couldn't do those things. He was just too set in his ways.

Gabe's lack of spontaneity was not her only problem. She was constantly hassled by memories, which she thought she had filed away for good. Visions of Artie. She couldn't stop picturing his hands, moving over clay, or chiseling at stone. He haunted her. At night, hours after Gabe made love to her tenderly and sweetly, like she was breakable, she would wake, the feeling of Artie's skin still lingering from her dreams. She could still taste him, feel the little hairs on her forearms jump at his touch. He was always with her, making her lonely and uncomfortable.

Clara had tried to rationalize, to sit back and love Gabe and her new life in Santa Fe, but all she really wanted was to go home. She wanted to laugh at the kitchen table and tan on the roof. She wanted to swim in the pool naked, when no one was around and most of all she wanted to sleep in her own bed and wake up knowing that her family was nearby. She tried to talk to Kylie about feeling homesick, but she just didn't understand. She made suggestions like, "Why don't you get a drastic haircut or try a new look. You could go like totally platinum. That always makes me feel better."

It took all the courage Clara could muster to let her mother leave without her when she dropped her off after their lunch with Ruth. She wanted to scream and throw a temper tantrum like she did when they left her at sleep away camp years ago. Clara was ten. She had wrapped her arms around her mother's waist, screaming, "Don't leave me here." It took three counselors to pry her off her mother, and her father was so affected by her outburst he could hardly walk. You couldn't act like that once you're not a child anymore, and Clara was fairly certain that she couldn't bring her father to his knees no matter how hard she tried.

In the end, she wound up spending hours sitting on her couch, like she was now, staring out the window. She knew she had to do what any other well-loved, good child does. She had to call home and talk to her mom, but it had taken her weeks to get to the point where she could even consider the idea, and even though they were on good speaking terms, it took guts to ask Elizabeth for advice.

When she had gotten home from work a few hours earlier, Kylie called and invited her to hang out with a group of people at some up and coming artist's house. Clara turned her down because she had decided that even if it took her the whole day, she was going to call Liz and tell her exactly how she was feeling. If everything went well, Clara could move home before Liz had her party for Sissy and then maybe she wouldn't feel so strange about attending.

The phone rang three times and the answering machine picked up. Clara pictured the machine sitting on the counter in the kitchen. It was ancient. They bought it when Clara was six or seven. It was a big bulky plastic box covered in a faux-wood finish. The message was from a good decade ago. Elizabeth made them all stand around and record their own names.

"You've reached the Gordon's residence..."

"Cliff,

"Michael,"

"Clara,"

"Artie,"

"Sissy,"

"and Elizabeth can't come to the phone right now. Please leave a message after the beep and we'll return your call as soon as possible. Have a great day."

Clara's eyes stung and she almost started to cry. She had not expected to hear Sissy's voice and the sound rattled her insides. BEEP.

"Mommy? Mommy are you home? It's me Clara," she paused, "Oh well, please..."

"Wait." The machine's feedback screamed into the receiver and Clara held the phone away from her ear. "Clara? Are you still there? What's the matter?"

"I miss you." Clara couldn't help herself. She stopped speaking and began to shake with sadness. Her chest jumped and her breath grew short. The sound of her sobs was startling, loud and heavy like dropping a pan. Elizabeth started to cry too. "It's okay," she said. "It's all okay."

"I want to come home, Mommy."

Elizabeth was quiet. Clara took her silence as a negative sign.

"Please, Mommy. Please." Clara gripped the edge of the counter top with one hand and crouched, her head curling in towards her body, her abdomen constricted. "I'm so lonely. Please. I'll pretend he doesn't exist. We can avoid each other."

"That's not what I want Clara."

"I just want to be home."

"Did you fight with Gabe?"

"No." Clara sat on the floor and put her face in her hands.

"What is it then?"

"I don't know. I'm homesick, I guess."

"You miss him?" Elizabeth's voice was calm and patient.

"Mommy," warm tears ran down Clara's cheeks, "how come he never even tried to explain it to me?"

"I don't know baby."

"What did I do? Why didn't he love me?"

"Clara, don't be ridiculous. He always loved you."

"Not like that."

"I know but..."

"Forget it. You don't understand." Clara stood up. "Listen, it was stupid of me to call. I'll talk to you later, okay?"

"Clara, don't hang up."

"What?" Her voice was tight. She could feel her anger rising, and she wanted to hang up before she lost her cool. She couldn't believe that she had cried like that.

"If you really need to come home, you always can."

"Yeah, thanks."

Clara placed the phone back on the hook. Walked across the little yellow apartment, shuffling her slippers against the floor, and sat down on the edge of her bed. She flopped back and looked up at the ceiling. The air ducts had never been covered and even though Clara understood that through artistic eyes that should be industrial and cool, she missed looking at the uncool and placid flatness of a finished ceiling. Clara had built a life for herself, a life where she was her own person, not Elizabeth's daughter, or Michael's little sister or the girl that loved Artie. She couldn't go back, and her mother knew it. There was nothing left for her there.

After wallowing for a good twenty minutes, Clara showered and called Kylie. She didn't want to go to the party, but she thought maybe Kylie would come get her and take her to the mall. If Kylie still wanted to go to the party, then maybe she would at least drop Clara off at the food court. Inside, bordered by Orange Julius and Corn Dog Plus, was a huge carousel and whenever Clara was depressed in high school she would go there to see the pretty painted ponies and watch the kids go round and round.

THIRTY-SEVEN

Cliff - lonely

After seeing Liz and Clara at the Guadeloupe Café, Cliff couldn't re-member why he was angry, but he was certain that no one he saw during the day talked to him, and he was lonely. Gladys hadn't said more than two or three words to him since they ran into Clara and Liz. She sent him memos and e-mails, but no actual spoken words were exchanged. Liz and Artie spent every evening planning Liz's second celebration in honor of Sissy, and he wasn't really talking to Liz so he couldn't join them. He knew Clara would speak to him if he made an effort, so he decided to make an effort.

He didn't call before going to her apartment, hoping the element of surprise would work in his favor. He knew her schedule because he called Mr. Balducci every couple of days to check up on her. He picked a Wednesday morning in late July when Clara had the entire day off. He went early. If she was still sleeping he would wake her. He knew she would be there because if it weren't for her job, Clara would never leave the house before noon.

He picked up two large coffees on the way and parked the car on the street near her apartment. Outside her door, he couldn't believe his stomach was in knots at the idea of speaking to his daughter. He couldn't remember one instance of anger between them before this happened. It didn't seem possible that he had never been angry at Clara, but if he had no memory of it, then it couldn't have been any kind of worthwhile anger. Truth be told, he wasn't really angry with her now. He knew he acted like a child denied a lollypop. He pouted because he didn't get his way, and in the wake of his irrational pouting, Clara's anger for not letting her go to New York was so fierce that he had returned it with a vengeance. It was not his most admirable moment, but he had not acted cruel and immature intentionally. It didn't really matter. Cliff wasn't standing in front of Clara's door seeking forgiveness or acceptance. He just wanted her company.

He knocked tentatively at first, and when Clara didn't answer, he started slamming his fist against the door and hollering her name. He was still banging when she turned the doorknob, so when the door opened the momentum of his knocking pushed him through the doorframe. Clara took a little step backwards. She was in her pajamas and there was still sleep in her eyes.

"Daddy," she said confused, "is everything okay?" She had dyed her hair back to all blond and she looked like his little girl again.

"I just needed to see you."

"Come in." She stood back and stretched out her arm welcoming him. He felt good being invited, wanted. He moved quickly inside before she could change her mind and sat down on her couch, still holding both coffees.

"Is one of those for me?" Clara asked. Cliff handed her a coffee.

"Black, two sugars, right?"

"Right." Clara crossed to her little wall-o-kitchen. "You want a bagel?" she asked as though he was just her father, surprising her with a cup of joe on a sunny summer morning, but he could tell from her over the top pleasantness that she was waiting for the ball to drop.

"Okay," he said. He looked around, taking in the décor. "It's so yellow in here."

"It's awful, right?" Clara kneeled on her linoleum floor and shuffled through her fridge drawers.

"Why don't you change it?" he asked, thinking that he should turn the conversation from nuance to something more serious, while still reveling in the luxury of just chattering with her like everything was hunky-dory.

"Mom. She bought all this stuff for me, and she was trying to be so nice. I didn't have the heart to tell her." She held up a cream cheese container that was scraped to the bone. "Butter and jelly, okay?"

"Fine," he nodded, smiling. "You see your mom a lot lately?" he asked.

Clara sliced the bagels and put them in the toaster. She didn't face him while she spoke, "We talk almost every day, but I don't see her all that often." She paused and faced him, her expression grew serious and like Liz, the curl in her brow and the tightness of her lips said more than her words. "I see her more than you do."

Cliff examined his coffee, while he put together what he wanted to say. He loaded his coffee with milk, so much so that it looked more like cream than coffee and the light bouncing off its surface created no reflection, only glare.

"I see her. I just don't talk to her," he said.

"You don't really talk to me either, do you?" He heard the hurt in her voice, but she filtered it through a foreshadowing of forgiveness.

"I am now." He freed his gaze from the milky ripples of his coffee cup and looked her in the eye.

"Will you be tomorrow?" Her question was genuine.

"Yes. Listen, Clara, I don't know what to say. I owe you an apology I guess. I owe your mother one too, but sorry is hard for me. I haven't often had to say sorry."

"You don't owe me an apology Dad," she crossed to him and sat down on the couch. "I treated you like shit. I treat everyone like shit, but I'm working on that." She smiled and Cliff wondered how she was working on herself. He had never heard her speak of herself like a work in progress. Clara continued, "Mom didn't do anything to you. She did something for me. Moving into this apartment may not have been as easy a move as I thought it was going to be, but I couldn't stay home. I needed to be here."

"I know," he said intentionally looking her in the eye. "I get that now."

"She's not the same anymore. I still don't agree with all her choices, but I know she has everyone's best interest at heart. She's not forcing you or me or anyone to do anything." Cliff looked away but he put one hand on her back to let her know he heard her. He couldn't discuss Liz's behavior. He wasn't ready. Emotion rose behind his cheeks. He blushed whenever he felt emotionally uncomfortable. "We don't have to talk about this," she said, standing up. "It's okay Daddy. We'll all get there." Her voice was more grown up and grounded than he thought it could be, than he thought he could be, under the circumstances. She crossed the room and went back to work on the bagels.

He watched her make him breakfast. Every one of her movements felt like she was actively trying to impersonate her mother. She held the knife the same way. The sound she made when she scratched at the toast to spread the butter was the same. She went overboard with jelly, just like Liz. While he watched her, he ached for Liz for the first time in months. He wanted them all to eat breakfast together again. When Clara brought him his plate he asked, "Are you going to the celebration?"

She fidgeted with her nightshirt, while she said, "I'm not sure I'm up for that."

"Because of Artie?"

"Yes and no. I miss home. I miss Artie. I just don't think I can spend the evening thinking about Sissy without getting upset."

His brows squeezed together and his lips parted before he could control himself. He was shocked that Clara was still hung up on the idea that celebrations weren't allowed to be sad.

"So? All she really wanted was for us all to be happy. You think she never got sad over losing Robert. I consoled her more than once."

Clara maintained an almost meditative state of calm.

"Dad, let's not go there," Clara said collecting the crumbs around her plate on the end of her finger.

"Why not?"

"Because I'm happy to have you in my apartment, and I've missed you, so I'd rather not argue about my choice to be the only Gordon or Cornwall who is strong enough to honor her last wishes. I don't care how she dealt. I only know what she asked of me. She said "no tears," and I'm not going to shed any."

Cliff crossed to his daughter and hugged her. She felt fragile in his arms, but listening to her words and hearing the conviction in her voice, he understood that the actions he had taken over the past few months were just as wrong as Liz's choice to send Clara to New York. He had stopped listening to what Clara needed and started trying to impose his choices for her life on her. He had tried to do exactly what he had criticized Liz for, but unlike him, Liz had stepped in and saved him from himself. He realized that even if your intentions are good and selfless, you can't protect your children from their choices or their mistakes. You have to let them figure everything out at their own pace, and if you're paying attention, their mistakes can teach you things you never knew about yourself.

They didn't talk about their problems or his problems or her problems for the rest of the day. Instead, Clara told him she had been dating someone, but it was probably ending, and that she had called Liz begging to come home a few weeks earlier, only to learn that going home wasn't what she really wanted. She told him that she had no idea what she wanted, and she told him that she missed him. She talked about thinking of him as she watched kids on the carousel at the mall. He used to take her there when she was a kid. He'd buy her a corndog and let her ride the horsies until her fingers ached from holding onto the golden posts.

He told her how good everything was at work, and hearing that Gladys refused to talk to him made her laugh. She asked about Artie and he explained that he was doing well. He was working, trying to save money to take some nomadic trek up the Rockies into Canada. Clara got sort of pensive about that and started in with a thousand questions like when, where and how, but she immediately retracted them, saying she didn't want to know. He could tell it was easier for her that way.

When they ran out of things to say, she cuddled against him on her couch, and they watched bad talk shows with titles like my baby's daddy was an alien. Around five, she told him she had dinner plans, but she could break them. He stood and said, "No. You should go."

At the door she asked, "Will you visit me again soon, Dad?"

"Whenever you want."

Clara smiled, "That's what Mom said when I asked her to visit me."

Cliff felt slightly embarrassed by the similarity between him and Liz because he had spent the past few months pretending that there was no common ground between them. He kissed Clara's forehead, and felt like crying when she wrapped her arms around his neck. She stayed in the doorframe as he walked away. He didn't shuffle his feet as he trekked towards the car, scrolling through his knowledge of her schedule, wondering how soon he could visit with her again. When he got to the car he realized he was happier than he had been in months.

THIRTY-EIGHT

At just after eight Santa Fe time, Michael and Katie boarded a plane in Dallas and now they were less than twenty minutes from touching down on the Albuquerque runway. Because Michael had chosen a night flight, the plane was mostly dark and the swishing sounds of sleep and snoring were all around. In the light of the few tiny overhead bulbs and the computer screens of tireless business men, Michael watched Katie sleep. She had lifted the armrest, curled into a tight knot on her seat and laid her head on his legs. When she first started to get situated, Michael thought there was no way she could cram herself lengthwise into their two seats, but she'd done it and had been sleeping in his lap since about ten minutes after takeoff.

Michael could hardly wait to feel the dry New Mexico air in his lungs. It was nearly a year since he'd been home, and when his mom called asking him to please come to her celebration, he jumped at the chance. He had always thought bringing Katie to Santa Fe would be one of the more traumatic moments of his adult life, but it wasn't like that at all. He was excited.

Katie was actually more nervous than he was. For the past few weeks she had tortured him with clothing choices and a constant barrage of questions concerning his family's habits. What time do they get up? Do they wear their pajamas to the breakfast table? Should she bring a bathrobe? Should she bring individual gifts for everyone or one big gift for all? Did he think Clara would like to be one of her bridesmaids or was that too weird because they had never met? What kind of party was the party for Sissy? Was it black-tie? Casual? Semi-casual? Semi-formal?

Michael wasn't sure he really knew the difference between semi-casual and semi-formal, but he knew that all the effort she was investing in meeting his family turned him on. He couldn't get enough of her since he realized just how much of herself she was investing in him. Katie thought he was good enough to spend the rest of her life with, so much so that she was in a dead panic about correctly presenting herself to his family, and that was hot. He tried to tell her not to worry. He tried to tell her that they weren't formal types, that they would welcome her with open arms no matter what gifts she came bearing, but she was unsatisfied.

"Could you just ask your mom about the party, at least?" she begged, and so he did. He called home a few days before they left to ask Liz what "the dress" was for Sissy's second celebration. He was standing in the kitchen of the New York apartment that he and Katie were living in for the summer. After their engagement, Bill Worthington had helped Michael land a killer internship at an investment banking firm. Katie was interning for *Marie Claire* and had not gotten home when he made the phone call. When he asked, he was surprised by the answer.

"Formal. Black," Liz said matter of fact-ly.

"Black?" Michael asked, astounded.

"Yes, black."

"Why black?" Michael couldn't imagine his mother dictating that an entire room full of people should be wearing black "You mean it's black-tie? You're throwing a formal event?

"Well, no. Just nice clothes and all black."

He stood in the apartment in New York, shaking his head. "Okay," he said, "all black," and they hung up.

So he would remember to tell Katie, he wrote *Sissy's party-all black* on the notepad near the phone, and promptly forgot about it. Katie found the note the following evening. Michael had just taken off his shoes and was lying on the bed watching the Red Sox game. Katie was a Sox fan and over the course of their courtship she had created a monster. Once he got started, Michael couldn't think of anything else but the Sox. She came into their bedroom with the slip of paper in her hand and asked, "When you called your mother to ask about the party, did she tell you the attire was all black clothing?"

Without taking his eyes off the TV he said, "Shit, sorry. I forgot to tell you."

"Like black-tie?" Katie asked, sitting on the end of the bed.

"Hmm..." Michael tried to pay attention, but he was captivated by the game.

"Michael," Katie said, frustrated.

"What? Sorry." He turned in her direction, but gradually his eyes tuned to the game again. Katie grabbed the clicker and snapped off the T.V.

"Hey!"

"Just give me two minutes and then we can both lie here and love the Sox. Deal?" Michael was surprised by the seriousness of her tone.

"Deal." He focused in, wondering why she was so flustered by the dress code for Sissy's party.

"Did your mother say black-tie or just black clothing?"

"She said nice black clothing." He took her hand, trying to comfort her. "I'm sure whatever you wear will go either way. Don't stress this too much." Thinking he had conquered her doubts Michael slipped the clicker from her hands.

"She said all black?" Katie asked again.

"Yes," he turned to the T.V. waiting for Katie to give him a cue that turning the game back on was P.C.

"It's a funeral," she said. Michael looked at her. He was completely thrown.

"What?"

"She's throwing a funeral, Michael. That's why the attire is all black."

Michael couldn't believe he'd missed that. All black equals funeral seemed pretty obvious as soon as Katie said it. After their conversation Michael called home again.

"Are you throwing Sissy a funeral?" he asked.

"No, not really. Maybe, sort-of." Liz said.

"Does anyone know that you're maybe sort-of throwing a funeral?"

Liz sighed, "Artie does, but it's not really a funeral."

Michael couldn't help bordering on furious when he said, "How could you not tell me that? I'm bringing Katie there for Christ's sake. Don't you think I should at least have the opportunity to prepare her for something like this?"

Liz was quiet. Michael took a deep breath, trying to calm his nerves. After a few minutes he said, "Mom?"

"It's not really a funeral." Liz's voice was a tiny whisper, and Michael immediately felt guilty that he had gotten angry.

"Okay, fine," he said taking his tone back to rational, "Please explain to me what it is then."

"It's a goodbye celebration," her voice was weak and tired.

"What does that mean?"

"Well, I think it's the kind of party we should have had last year when she died. A time to honor her, tell stories about her, explain why we loved her and how we miss her. It's going to be emotional but not funeral-y, other than the all black thing. Artie and I decided on all black because we want the opportunity to say grieving is okay." Michael couldn't speak. His throat felt tight, like he was going to cry. Liz continued, "I should have told you. You're right, but we didn't want anyone to know, especially..."

"Clara," Michael squeaked out, just barely controlling tears.

"Right." There was a pause. "Michael? Are you crying?"

"No," he said, but he was a little. He missed his family, particularly Liz. Listening to her talk, the emotional ups and downs of her tone, he knew she had a really tough year and he hadn't stopped, not even for a minute, to care about what she was going through. He hadn't taken the time to check in on Clara or Artie, and he hadn't thought about what it must feel like to live there without Sissy. No matter what his relationship with Sissy had been like, he knew that even he would feel the void she left behind at the kitchen table.

"Mom," he asked, "should I have been there more this year?"

"Doesn't matter. We wouldn't have listened or talked if you were." She didn't sound disappointed, but he was. He wouldn't forsake them the next time they were teetering.

When they hung up Michael knew that it didn't matter at all that Katie was meeting his family when they were hosting Sissy's sort-of funeral. He was proud of them for facing their fears and because he wanted to be there for them, particularly Clara. In fact, it seemed like a great way for Michael to induct Katie into the madness that was his family because without knowing Sissy, she wouldn't know them at all or for that matter, him.

The captain's voice came over the loudspeaker, telling the flight attendants to please prepare for arrival. Michael shifted gently. He desperately had to pee but didn't have the heart to wake Katie. He was captivated by the way her eyelashes pressed into her cheeks, and even though the urge to urinate was growing stronger by the second, Michael was going to let Katie sleep until the flight attendant forced her to sit up because he was fairly certain that getting to know his family would keep her awake for the next couple of days.

THIRTY-NINE

On the afternoon of Sissy's second celebration, Clara sat on the curb outside her apartment tossing pebbles into the street. She was waiting for Kylie to pick her up and take her to the mall. Normally, Kylie just dropped her off and picked her up later on, but this afternoon Kylie decided to keep her company. Clara knew Kylie was hanging out with her because she wanted details about her break up with Gabe the night before. But considering the alternative, spending the afternoon harping on the party she wasn't attending, Clara welcomed the company. As Kylie drove up, Clara pulled a pair of dark sunglasses from her bag to cover her eyes like she'd been crying. She knew Kylie loved drama, and she didn't want to disappoint.

Breaking up with Gabe was less interesting than it sounded. Clara had known her relationship was coming to an end for weeks. Noticing that she was slipping away, Gabe tried to pull her back. He bought her flowers and told her how spectacular she was, but it didn't matter. She wanted something he couldn't be.

They were sitting in his kitchen over gray granite counter tops when Clara said she wanted to go home. Generally, when she was at his house she stayed for days or at least for hours, but last night she knew she wanted to leave before they even ate dinner. Gabe was squeezing wheat grass through a press and preparing to drink it.

"I'm going home tonight," Clara said. He looked up from what he was doing and Clara noticed that his fingers were tinted green. He knew right away that something was up.

"You're not coming back are you?" he asked.

Clara paused, but she didn't really need to think about it. "No, I don't think so," she answered.

Gabe walked around the counter, put his green fingers on her face, and like he was begging, said, "Can I ask you not to go?"

She didn't say anything. He looked deep into her eyes, searching, and Clara began to cry. She knew that she was hurting him. He said, "I understand. I love you."

They made love, and he drove her home. In the car outside her apartment she tried to say something to make him feel better, but what could she say?

"Gabe...I."

"It's okay kid," he smiled, "I'm far too old for you anyway."

"It's not that really." She looked at her hands.

"How 'bout we pretend it is." He looked ahead and kept his hands on the steering wheel.

She got out of the car and stood on the curb while he drove away. He didn't wave goodbye or look back and she understood why. Clara respected his bravery in the face of heartache. She knew that sometimes she'd miss him, but since the thrill of their first blush had burnt out, lying next to him in the darkness, listening to the wheeze of his sleep was lonelier than being alone. He taught her that love comes in so many different brands that it's hard to know which one works best for you, and sometimes your brand works really well for someone else, even though theirs keeps you up nights, longing.

Of the three men she had real sexual relationships with in her life, Gabe was the most comfortable, and that felt good for a while, but like old sneakers, sometimes the most comfortable ones are not the ones you feel best in. Sometimes the complicated ones are more appealing, even though you know your feet might hurt. It's that one pair of heels that are so high they require a choreographed ritual of teeter and totter, but once you've got them on, suddenly instead of comfort you've got sexy and powerful and you remember how cool you are, which is more appealing in the end. So, rather than drag things out, which wasn't fair, she set Gabe free.

As soon as Clara sat down in the passenger seat, Kylie started nagging her about what happened with Gabe, but instead of telling her the whole deal, Clara took on her most dramatic Jackie-O voice and said, "You know Ky, I'm not really ready to talk about it yet."

"My bad, of course you're not. We'll just head out to the mall and blow off steam. Sound good?"

"Sounds great."

Kylie fished a pair of red rhinestone sunglasses out of her purse and said, "Only one more thing to do before we go." She flipped open the glove box and pulled out a cassette, which she stuck in the tape deck. Clara laughed when Cyndi Lauper's "Girls Just Want to Have Fun" blasted through the speakers. "What are you laughing at?" Kylie asked. "The break up tape is the key to a speedy recovery, and the sooner you recover, the sooner I get to hear all the gory details."

"Nice moves, Ky."

"I'm a genius, right?"

"Sure ya are."

"Dude, there's Milli Vanilli on this tape. You're going to be laughing in no time." She put the car in gear and started singing at the top of her lungs. After a few bars, Clara took her lead and started singing too.

Santa Fe's Villa Linda Mall is not a haven for elitist shoppers, but armed with her parents' credit card Kylie was dangerous anywhere that sold merchandise. Clara's budget was drastically limited in comparison, so she spent most of the afternoon sitting on dressing room stools re-hanging the clothes that Kylie wasn't buying. Kylie kept trying to get Clara to try things on, saying that she would buy her anything she wanted because her parents wouldn't know the difference, but that wasn't Clara's style. After three and a half hours of intense clothing consumption, Clara said, "Jesus, Kylie, can we take a breather?" Because she wasn't stupid, Kylie knew Clara was giving her shit for her shopping habits.

She countered the comment with jest, "That's why malls have food courts, b-atch, so you can get a Coke and then go right on purchasing."

"Well then, it's definitely time for me to get a Coke," Clara begged.

"Two Cokes, on me."

"I can buy my own Coke, Kylie."

"I wasn't pitying your poverty. I was paying you back for my selfishness because today is supposed to be about you. You're heartbroken, remember?"

In the food court Clara looked for a table, while Kylie stood in line at Sbarro. It was pretty crowded because it was the weekend, so it took Clara some finagling to get them a seat. She had to hover over two teenage girls who were finished, but hadn't gotten up. They were maybe sixteen, possibly younger, but they dressed to look more mature. Both had pastel thongs poking out of their jeans. Clara couldn't help wondering if they were still virgins, and then she found herself wondering if they knew Artie. Did they talk to him at school? Did they have classes with him? Unconsciously, she moved a little closer, so she could hear what they were talking about.

The prettier of the two was telling her friend that even though her boyfriend had graduated, they were going to stay together. First, Clara rolled her eyes thinking they were so naive because everyone knows that never works, and then suddenly, her thoughts snapped as she realized that Artie had graduated. For the first time ever, she had missed a defining moment in Artie's life.

No one had even mentioned it to her. Everyone had come to her graduation, even Sissy. When she walked up to that podium and took her degree from the principal, there was an entire cheering section that stood and hollered her name. Who went to Artie's graduation? Did both her parents go? Did anyone go? She should have gone. Even if she had to hide in the back, she should have seen him in his cap and gown. How could she have forgotten?

She felt tears welling up in the corners of her eyes. The girls stood and even though she was so intent on grabbing their table moments before, Clara didn't make a move to sit down. She wanted to chase after those two naïve teenage girls, tackle them if she had to, and prod them for information. Did they go to graduation? What had the ceremony been like? Did they know Artie and could they tell her if anyone cheered for him? She didn't actually possess the courage to corner the two teenagers, so she just stood there panicking, staring at a crumbled napkin the two girls had left behind, and knowing she didn't want to be free of Artie, until someone tapped her on the shoulder and asked, "Are you waiting for that table?"

Clara breathed deep before she turned to confirm that, yes, that table was hers. However, she didn't get the words out because when she faced the girl asking the question, she was looking right into Christina Graves' eyes.

"Clara," Christina said, "Shit, Hi."

"Christina," Clara said, instantly icy and territorial, "Table's mine."

"Of course," Christina backed away.

Clara turned to sit down. Kylie was approaching her with two Cokes and pizza. Clara hadn't asked for pizza but she'd eat it.

"Who was that?" Kylie asked.

"Christina."

"The slutty-bitch who balled your man?" Kylie was excited to put a name to a face. She craned her head in Christina's direction trying to get a good look at Clara's nightmares.

"That's the one."

"Ewe," Kylie pointed a finger in her mouth, pretending to make herself vomit.

"Totally." Clara took a bite of her slice, and little drips of orange grease puddled on her paper plate.

"Yo, Dude. Don't look now. She's coming back." Of course, Clara looked. Christina was headed directly for her with determination on her face. Kylie thought the whole thing was fantastic, "Jesus, look at her. This is one brazen bitch."

When Christina got to the table, she said, "He didn't tell you, did he?" Clara didn't speak, so Kylie spoke for her.

"She saw all she needed to see."

Christina turned to Kylie, "No she didn't. She thought she saw something. I know. I was there."

"Okay," Kylie said, "It's true. You were the naked slut in bed with her soul mate, so explain it for us."

Christina breathed through her nose, controlling her anger. "Back off, okay. I'm doing the right thing here. Nothing happened, Clara."

"I saw you," Clara said, "My mother saw you, Christina."

"He didn't even invite me there. He was so wasted. He drank himself silly because he was upset you left." She emphasized her words with her hands and even though there was strength in her voice Clara still felt like she was whining. "I drove him home because he couldn't stand up anymore, and we both know I've always had a thing for him, so when I got him inside, I stayed, thinking that maybe he was so drunk he'd want me, instead of you. I took off my clothes and went to get us some beers. By the time I got back to the bed he had passed out." Christina paused. "I thought," she paused again, getting more and more uncomfortable by the minute, "I don't know what I thought." She looked at the floor and sighed, "Maybe I thought if he found me there naked when he woke up it might happen, but it didn't. He didn't even know I was there when he took off his clothes. He was trying to console me because I was crying from embarrassment when you walked in."

"Bullshit," said Kylie but Clara was inclined to believe her.

"Who are you?" Christina asked frustrated. "Why would I make that up?"

"I don't know. Maybe you want to kill your slutty-rep?" Kylie suggested

"Believe me, I'd have to wipe out the entire teenage population of Santa Fe to do that." Kylie laughed and Christina smiled. "I'm telling the truth," she said. "He loves you. Did you know he didn't go to prom?"

"He didn't?" Clara said, biting her lower lip.

"He doesn't drink or hang out with us anymore either."

"Really?" Clara asked.

"He's a total hermit." Christina crossed herself as proof.

Clara was unsure what to do with the information Christina was giving. Her first instinct was to run to Artie, but that felt too impulsive. She needed to think. She gathered her things and stood. "I have to go," she said and started to walk away.

Kylie hollered after her, "You're not going to get very far without a ride from me."

Clara stopped, turned back and impatiently said, "Well, come on then."

Kylie grabbed her pizza and rushed after Clara but not before getting in the last word, "Bye-bye, funny slut-girl." While Kylie was racing in Clara's direction, Clara gave Christina a little wave. Clara never imagined that underneath Christina's shameless exterior was a decent person. Kylie echoed her sentiments, "Who knew? Huh? A harlot with a heart of gold!"

When they got into the car, Kylie said, "Where to? Are we going to find your long-lost love and rekindle the fiery flames of passion?"

"No." The answer confronted her with force, sudden and heavy. Clara knew that what was between her and Artie was more than just her misconceptions about his tryst with Christina. She couldn't go to that place with him, not now. She had come too far to go backwards.

"No? Then why'd we rush out of the mall like banshees with our heads cut off?" Clara giggled at Kylie's reformatting of an old cliché. "God, I was so excited. I thought something really big was about to happen."

"Something really big did happen, Ky," Clara said.

"Yeah, yeah. I just thought we were in for a little happily-ever-after shit."

"Maybe we are, someday."

Kylie nodded. "Okay, so, now that we've left the mall, you want to come to my place. We could mix frosty, fruity cocktails." Although the thought was tempting, Clara knew she couldn't go to Kylie's house. It was time for her to go home, time to see her family.

FORTY

Cliff draped his tie around his neck and approached the bathroom where Liz was putting the finishing touches on her make-up. Standing in the doorframe, he wondered why she dropped her mouth open when she applied her mascara. She was leaning over the counter top so as to get her face closer to the mirror. He knew her eyes were not as good as they used to be. She couldn't read the ingredients on a ketchup bottle, but she still managed to apply her make-up perfectly. She had chosen a simple sleeveless black dress, which beautifully contrasted with her blond hair and tan skin. The look was meticulous and graceful, like Audrey Hepburn. Everything about her was flawless. He loved her more now than he had ever realized, but so far he'd been unable to muster the strength or the words to express what he was feeling.

Over the past few weeks he had started speaking to her little by little. First, he said things like, "Liz, have you seen my green polo shirt?" Her responses were unsettlingly easy and smooth, the natural rhythm of a wife interacting with her husband, "On the dryer." When these little interactions picked up pace and became daily occurrences, he moved on to more generous offers, "I'm making tea. You want some?" Again Liz maintained a state of calm, "Um... no, but thanks for asking." Her nonchalance left him baffled. He imagined they were like passengers on passing trains, standing in the windows, waving and smiling. Everyday he made an effort to show her kindness, but there was still a dull, unapproachable tension between them.

Liz spoke to his reflection in the mirror, "You need me to tie that for you?" He nodded and moved towards her as she turned to face him. He stood closer than he needed to, hoping that invading her space would act like a catalyst, and knowing that it would take more than his physical presence to heal the rift between them. As her hands moved tentatively to button the top buttons of his shirt, he looked over her shoulder, admiring the reflection of her silhouette. She had lost weight over the course of the year, so her dress hung loose on her hips and buttocks. He thought of that movie from when the kids were little where Lily Tomlin began shrinking and kept shrinking until there was nothing left of her. He didn't know which one of them had started disappearing first, but he was certain that together they could keep each other from becoming completely invisible. When she took hold of the two ends of his tie, he covered her hands with his and looked down into her eyes.

"I'm sorry," he said. She released the tie, wrapping her arms around his neck, and pressing her full weight against his body. His hands slipped easily under her arms, grazing her shoulder blades as they fell to her waist. He pulled her tighter against his body and felt her breath shudder. She tilted her head up to meet his kiss. Her lips were gentle, weightless, like tissue caught in the wind. Sadness gripped the back of his throat and he couldn't control his tears. They hadn't made love in almost a year.

He let his left hand drift down her body to the back of her thigh and she lifted her leg until his palm was nestled behind her knee, and her heel had locked him against her. Unsteady, they leaned back against the bathroom vanity as their kisses intensified. He grasped her other leg, lifting her up on to the counter. Their love making was almost motionless. He kept his hands fixed on her waist, always pulling her to him. Eventually, he grew completely still, cradling her, satisfied by the feeling that they were one.

"I love you," he breathed softly, like mist. Then, he curled his head against her chest, listening to her hushed weeping.

FORTY-ONE

Artie slipped out the back door, heading towards the house he grew up in. It was late afternoon. The sun perched on the peaks of the Sangre de Christos, waiting for the colored shards, which signaled its departure, to gain momentum. Unlike city vistas, New Mexico's view has no sense of limitation.

In Nantucket, Artie sometimes stood on the beach at the end of the day, usually with some intoxicant in hand, and wondered how people could find an ocean sunset beautiful. For him, watching the sun plunge into the water was like watching someone step off the edge of the Taos Gorge and plummet to their death. In New Mexico it wasn't like that at all. The distance yielded speckled shrubs, then soft hills, then mountains, then murky mountains, and beyond that the idea of mountains. There was never a moment when the foggy jade peaks lined up evenly against the cerulean heavens, so when the sun set in Santa Fe it traveled safely, sliding leisurely down those rocky hills, allowing the future to rise again tomorrow.

Across the lawn and inside his house, Artie found Michael lying on Sissy's bed watching a baseball game. Katie wasn't with him, but the shower in the bathroom was running. It hadn't bothered Artie when Liz suggested that Michael and Katie stay in his house, but seeing them use the space was unsettling. He felt like their sweat on his mother's sheets and their pee in her toilet were undermining any residual memories he had of the time before she died. Since they arrived he had done his best to avoid seeing them use the space.

"Can you help me with the screen?" Artie asked Michael.

"Do I have time to watch the end of the inning?"

"We're running late as it is." He paused, aggravated, "Don't worry about it." He started down the stairs. Michael was immediately on his heels, but he didn't catch up with him until they were back outside and crossing to the pool.

"Whoa, slow up, kid. I was just asking." Artie dropped his pace a notch, allowing Michael to fall in beside him. Michael's voice was light, supportive. "Give me tasks and I shall fulfill them," he said bowing his head subserviently.

"We have to set up these metal frames, and then tack the fabric to it."

"That doesn't sound so complicated," Michael said putting his arm around Artie's shoulder.

"We also need to set up the rows of chairs in front of it."

"It will probably take us like twenty minutes. Chill, it's all good."

Artie smirked, knowing that Michael was totally underestimating the complexities involved.

Setting up the screen actually took over an hour. The metal frames, which according to the guy they rented them from, "just snapped together," were designed to frustrate aeronautical engineers, and the screen was not just any huge sheet of fabric. It caught any little breeze, like the parachute that every gym teacher has in the back of the equipment closet for rainy day activities. Just unfolding the damn thing took at least fifteen minutes, and in order to hang it they had to enlist the caterers and the band members to help hold it up. It was dark by the time they finished. If production was measured by aggravation, then they would have had an entire multiplex in the back yard.

Exhausted and breathing hard, Artie wiped the sweat from his brow and stepped back to examine their accomplishment. Michael stood next to him, bent over like a marathon runner just after crossing the finish line.

"Next time you ask me to hang a little screen and unfold a few chairs, remind me to turn you down," he said.

"Not so simple, huh?" Artie replied breathlessly.

Liz and Cliff who had been circling the property lighting the luminarios strolled over to admire the handiwork. They were holding hands.

"Wow, Guys. I can't believe how great that looks," Liz said. Artie watched her slip her arm around Cliff's waist and curl into his shoulder. "Like a real movie theatre. It's amazing. Isn't it?"

"If we had those radio thingies, we could open a drive-in," Cliff added.

Excitedly, Liz jumped up and down a little. "I have the best idea. Let's watch the old footage, like the stuff from our wedding, over dinner tomorrow night. We can make a picnic."

"We should." Cliff kissed her forehead. They were completely in their own world, a glow-y, weird world, but a good one. Doe-eyed, Cliff looked up at the screen again, "Maybe we can even get Clara to come. Whatta you think guys? A little nostalgic pow-wow on the lawn?"

Neither Artie nor Michael said anything. They were too busy staring at the Kafkaesque metamorphosis. Cliff and Liz had hardly spoken over breakfast and now they were draped all over each other, like teenagers.

"Are you two high or something?" Artie joked.

Michael laughed and Liz blushed a little, but Cliff took the whole thing very seriously, "No, we just remembered how much we love each other and our family."

Katie came up behind them, "Wow, that's awesome."

Liz turned, gushing, "I know. Doesn't it look amazing?"

Rather than listen to the conversation repeat itself, Artie excused himself and went to get cleaned up. While he showered, shaved and combed his hair, he was excited, but when he got back to the bedroom he couldn't bring himself to get dressed. He looked at his suit, laid out on the bed and thought that his mother was hardly dead a day the last time he wore it.

They bought the suit together, at *Dilliard's* for Clara's graduation. The sales people told her over and over that she wasn't allowed to go in the men's dressing rooms, but every time they turned around, she snuck back in completely mortifying Artie. When he couldn't take it anymore, he told her he was old enough to try on clothes without her. Her face went slack like he'd slapped her.

"Okay," she said, tight lipped and cool.

Then she pulled a credit card from her purse, handed it to him and left. Of course, he had no idea what suit to buy. Empty handed, he found her in the car. He was surprised when she didn't chastise him for being fresh. Instead, she walked back into the store, her cheeks all puffy, and bought three suits in his size. Slapping the plastic suit bags on the back seat she said, "You'll give a fashion show for Liz, Clara and me and we'll return the two we don't like." He never apologized, and she never shopped with him again. A few days ago he tried the suit on for Liz and she said he'd out grown it.

"Pants are too short," she said, shaking her head and tapping her index finger on her chin. She offered to take him to buy a new one but he couldn't do it. It was just another thing, another ritual, that he would have to redesign to include someone other than his mom and he wasn't ready. Instead, he dug his father's big black biker boots out of a box in the back of the studio closet, thinking no one would notice short pants when they were overpowered by massive man boots, circa 1979. The mix-matched ensemble, formal-dirty boy, suited him, and made him feel more comfortable than he would have in loafers or dress shoes or whatever, but still he couldn't bear the idea of putting it all on. He wanted to grab something more free-flowing, something that would allow his body to breathe if his emotions got the best of his lungs. When he stood to look in the closet, there was a knock at the door.

"Come in," he said checking the security of the towel he had cinched at his waist. It was Katie.

"Sorry," she shrugged, smiling, "Liz wanted me to see what was keeping you." Artie liked her from the minute she got off the plane. She was warm and easy to talk to.

"I'm trying to figure out what to wear," he said. Katie glanced at the suit on the bed, and he answered her inner monologue, "I've outgrown it," Katie fingered the jacket sleeve.

"Outgrown or outworn it?" She asked.

"What do you mean?"

"Well, women often outwear clothes, which is different than outgrowing them, and when I say outwear, I don't mean wear out," she paused gathering her thoughts and Artie sat down to listen. "Let me give you an example. I have a shirt that I wore the first time Michael and I had a fight. It's a really nice shirt, so I can't throw it away but I can't wear it because it's sort of cursed. Do you see what I'm getting at?"

"It reminds you of the fight."

"Right, I've outworn it." Katie picked up the suit and draped it over her lap. "So, which is it, outgrown or outworn?"

"A little of both, I guess."

"Here's the deal. You can't spin outgrown, but if we put our heads together, we might be able to figure out how you could outgrow the outworness of this suit."

"You want me to tell you why I've 'outworn' it?" He asked, chuckling a little.

"If you feel comfortable."

He did, but he couldn't hide his emotions when he said, "My mom bought it for me."

Immediately, Katie smiled, looking right past his sadness "If she picked it out, it's the perfect suit for tonight."

"Why?" He was confused.

"Because you can be certain that you're wearing something she liked, something she liked seeing you in." Katie closed her eyes and held out the suit. "Put it on, and I'll help you with your tie."

When he was dressed, he stood in front of her, using one finger to hold his jacket over his shoulder, his best male model pose.

"That's hot," she said laughing, "If you had sunglasses you'd be Bono." She stood, "Let's go before Michael thinks I've fallen for..." Katie looked at him searching for what he wanted her to acknowledge him as.

"Don't ask me. I'm just as confused about where I belong as you are," he said cheerfully.

"How about you," she suggested. "Before Michael thinks I've fallen for you, Artie Cornwall," she winked.

When they got outside, Katie turned and said, "Nice boots, by the way."

"My dad's." he said with confidence.

A fair number of people were already gathered around the pool, sipping drinks and noshing on toast points. Katie made a bee-line for Michael and Artie followed.

"What were you two doing up there?" Michael asked. "Art, you making the moves on my girl?" Katie gave him a little smack.

"Just wanted to make sure the merchandise was top-notch," Artie joked. Katie turned, feigned shock on her face and smacked Artie too. Then she smacked Michael again because he was laughing.

As Cliff approached, Katie pouted, saying "You're both sick."

"Same twisted influence," Cliff smirked. They all laughed.

Not knowing what to do or who to talk to, they stood in a line off to the side, watching their guests. Like the year before, Artie was amazed at the number of people who decided to show up just because they heard mention of his mother's name. There was one couple by the pool who were dressed in black, fairly traditional, tribal garb and Artie would have bet his life on them having traveled from some far away native land.

As Liz started walking towards them, Michael leaned over and whispered to Artie, "Who are all these people?"

"Ask her," Artie said, waving at Liz.

"Ask me what?"

"Where you got the guest list?"

Liz looked back towards the pool. "Sissy wrote it," she said, "last year."

"Who are they?" Michael asked.

"People she cared about, I guess." She paused and then addressed all three men. "Listen, if Clara shows, make sure she stays while I'm talking."

"Why would she leave?" Katie asked.

"It's hard to explain." Artie said.

Grudgingly Cliff said, "We should try to mix in, I guess," but mixing in was easier said than done. After about twelve conversations with strangers that mostly concerned his future plans, Artie moved to the outskirts of the crowd and sat down on the edge of a pool chaise.

As soon as Clara came around the corner, he spotted her. She wasn't wearing black. Her blond hair was loose and she'd chosen a red and white sundress that made her look delicate, like a dancer. He had to control his urge to jump up and run toward her. The first person she talked to was Michael.

Their reunion was touching. Michael was standing with his back to her and Artie watched her tap him on the shoulder. When he turned to look at her, surprise crossed his face, and then he hugged her lifting her feet right off the ground. From where he was sitting, Artie couldn't hear their conversation, but it was clear that Michael introduced Clara to Katie. Katie showed Clara her ring and then both girls smiled. Gushing, Artie guessed.

Next, Artie saw Cliff spot Clara from the dance floor, where he and Liz were "cutting a rug." They approached Clara, hugging her, smiling, laughing. Artie stayed put and took in their interactions like he was a camera. They were a family, and Artie had a choice. He could be part of that family, right now, as Liz and Cliff's son, or he could choose to love Clara and maybe in the future that love would make him part of their family again. He had spent the entire year trying to avoid the choice, but there was no way to exist in both roles, and now that he knew he had to choose, the choice was simple. He loved Clara.

After a few minutes, Artie noticed that while everyone talked to her, Clara's eyes were scanning the crowd. She was looking for him. He didn't want to talk to her while she was surrounded by everyone else. There were too many things to say, personal things, that not everyone needed to know.

He stood, making sure that he was no longer in the shadows. Still and quiet, he kept his eyes on her, waiting to be spotted. He wanted her to know that he knew she was there, but that he wouldn't approach her if it was going to ruin her night. Michael said something and she laughed, throwing her head back. She was wearing red lipstick and something about her expression looked naked and vulnerable, like a child.

Katie and Michael headed for the dance floor and she turned towards him, watching them walk away. Once they started dancing, she found him. Her hands were clasped in front of her and although there was sadness, she was almost smiling. She put her hand on Liz's shoulder, said something, and then headed in his direction. He was startled by her approach. He had been fairly certain when she arrived that he would spend the evening skulking in the shadows.

When she got to him she said, "You wanna walk?"

Her voice was sweet and soft. Nodding, he pushed his hands into his pockets and let her take the lead. They walked down towards the garden and then around his house out into the uncultivated part of the property, where he had spent most the night a year earlier. When the noise of the band had faded into the distance she said, "You're wearing your father's boots."

He didn't look at her. "My pants were too short."

She made a little breathy noise that bordered on laughter, and he knew she was smiling. She stopped walking, staring out at the night sky.

"I saw Christina Graves today," she said, crossing her arms over her chest.

"Nothing happened between us."

"I know."

He glanced at her quickly. Her expression made him think of what it feels like to stand alone in a parking lot at three in the morning and watch the weeds blow by. Closing his eyes, he tried to still a whirlwind of emotions. He didn't want to cry. Crying would only push her further away. They stood quiet for a few moments, while he gathered his thoughts. A breeze picked up and she rubbed her arms.

"Cold?" he asked.

She turned to him, nodding, "A little." He took off his jacket, handing it to her. "We should go back," she said, turning.

He still had so much to say but he didn't know where to begin. Defeated he walked a step behind her until they got back to the garden. Liz saw them and waved, walking in their direction. Feeling his opportunity slipping away, he touched her shoulder and blurted out, "Will you ever see me that way again?"

With her eyes on Liz, distracted and under her breath she said, "I never saw you any other way." Then she walked forward to meet her mother's approach. Liz put her arm around her, leading her towards the makeshift theater, and looked over her shoulder signaling for Artie to follow.

Rather than join the Gordon clan, Artie stayed back, watching Liz seat Clara between Michael and Cliff. Liz's presentation was incredibly emotional and Artie wanted no part of forcing Clara to watch. Nestled between her father and brother Clara smiled, unaware that she was about to be trapped and coerced into feeling when she had chosen not to. Liz stood in front of the screen, holding the band's microphone. She tapped at it and the microphone screamed.

Laughing nervously, she said "Sorry," and took a piece of paper that contained her notes from her pocket. She held the microphone in her left hand and read from the piece of paper in her right. The paper crinkled and shook with her nervousness. "I brought you all here tonight to make a second go at honoring a woman who changed my life and the lives of my entire family."

A man whistled and hollered Artie's mother's name. Looking out at the crowd, Liz smiled, "Exactly." Buried back in her notes she read, "Sissy Cornwall's life and her accomplishments are endless. She taught me how to appreciate both my successes and my failures. She helped me see the celebration buried in all of life's moments, even those that make us cry."

Artie glanced at Clara. She was already uncomfortable, but when she moved to stand, Cliff put his arm around her, keeping her in her seat. Liz continued, "Before she died, Sissy asked me to celebrate her life and for a long time I thought that meant staying upbeat, swallowing my tears and avoiding any grief I felt."

Artie could see that Clara was in anguish now. She looked to Michael, pleading her case with her eyes. He kept his expression blank taking her hand and looking back at Liz.

"I know now that's not how one should go about celebrating the life of someone they loved." Liz began to cry as she spoke, "Sissy was my best friend. She helped mother my children. She listened to my secrets. She carried my sorrows, and she lives on in my tears as well as my laughter. I miss her every day, but I see her passions in my husband, her heart and conviction in my daughter, her unyielding determination in my son, and I am lucky enough to see her creativity and her smile every morning when Artie sits down at my breakfast table."

Many of the people in the crowd were teary eyed and Clara was no exception. Artie could see her chest rising and falling rapidly as she tried to gain her composure. Liz looked up signaling the man running the projector, and one of the caterers flicked the switch that turned off the outdoor lights.

"My family and I have put together a video dedication that we would like you to watch," she said turning to face the screen.

Artie had seen the dedication before. The first image was Liz and his mother feeding him. He was a baby in a high-chair, and they had brown goo all over their clothes. His mother's voice boomed through the band's speakers.

"Hello Gordons," she said. "Say hello, Artie." She took his miniature hand and waved it at the camera. Instead of complying, he started to cry. She picked him up nuzzling her face against his and rocking her hips. Liz sighed, smiling.

"He looks like his father," she said.

Sissy's words resonated with melancholy, "I know."

Watching her hold him on the giant screen was more powerful than seeing the same thing on the T.V. in the living room. Her face was more detailed. He could see her eyelashes holding back her tears.

The video progressed through a montage of emotional moments: his Mom dancing with Clara, helping Michael with his English homework, sneaking a beer on the back steps with Cliff. It didn't feel like her whole life. There were whole groupings of years that they had forgotten to film, but it was powerful. For fifteen minutes, she was alive, laughing, crying, loving. The final image was his Mom sitting by the pool, talking.

"Get that camera out of my face," she teased. Her teeth showed through her smile. She was wearing a navy blue bikini and it had to be towards the end of the summer because she was really tan.

From behind the camera Cliff said, "Not until you give us your life's philosophy."

She leaned forward, the skin rippling at her waist, blew a puff of smoke at the camera, and squashed out her cigarette in the ashtray on the table. Curling her finger she beckoned the camera to come closer to her face before she said, "Life is both good and bad. If you're lucky enough to love or be loved enjoy it. Cry when you hurt. Smile when you're happy. Embrace every moment because it can all slip away so quickly." She leaned back pulling another cigarette out of the pack of Marlboros on the table. "But most importantly celebrate every time you have the opportunity." Cliff kept the camera on her while she brought the cigarette to her lips and lit it. She shook her head and laughed at him, saying, "Go on, get outta here."

Written across the black screen were the words "We love Sissy." The film ran out and snapped in the projector. On cue, the caterer turned the outdoor lights back on, and slowly the guests wiped away their tears with their shirt sleeves. Some took hold of each other's hands and shared encouraging strength filled smiles, but there was very little noise, until Liz went to speak. Then, the clapping began. First, it was just one person, his hands cracking encouragement like a whip. Then, it was everyone, including Michael and Cliff, and as they stood to cheer, Clara saw her opening. She was on the run and without thinking about it, Artie chased her.

Cliff hollered, "Let it be, Artie," but he couldn't. He knew better. Even if she was angry, she needed him. She was fast and she was always the better athlete, but no matter how far she ran, tonight he would outrun her.

FORTY-TWO

Clara found relief in the pounding of her feet as they hit the dirt access road that led to Old Pecos trail. She knew that Artie was still behind her, and he was catching up. She could hear his labored breathing. If she wanted to outrun him, then she couldn't stop and she couldn't look back. The night air hit the wetness on her face as she ran, a constant reminder that she had cried in front of all those people. She wanted to run all the way to her apartment if she had to, but her body was tired from crying and it was hard to breathe around the congestion that came with her tears.

She understood why they had forced her to watch, but she wished they hadn't. Whether her choices were right or not, whether they were what Sissy would have wanted didn't feel like it mattered anymore. All she knew was that she didn't want to feel the pain that came with crying, but the more she tried to stop crying, the more she cried and the slower she ran. Artie called after her.

"Clara, stop," his voice was high and squeaky, "Clara, please. Let's go back and I'll drive you home. We don't even have to see anyone. I have the keys to the truck in my pocket." She kept running, thinking he was at wit's end now and would stop chasing her soon, but he kept on her, gaining. "This is ridiculous. You don't have to talk to me. I'll just take you home."

Unconsciously, she looked back over her shoulder. He was about thirty feet behind her. Watching him rather than the road, made her lose her footing and she slipped. Before she could get back to her feet, he reached her. Rather than try to stand she curled into a ball, like someone expecting a beating. Her sobs were loud and they shook her body. He kneeled next to her putting his hand on her side.

"Come on," he said, trying to make her stand.

"Go away," she spat.

"Nope," he shook his head.

She crawled to her knees, begging, "Please, Artie, leave me."

"Why?" Clara was surprised by the firmness of his voice. "So you can lie in the dirt and cry by yourself? It's not going to happen."

"I can't bear for you to see me." She hid her face in her hands.

He lifted her chin and she saw compassion in his eyes as he whispered, "Don't be so dramatic. I'm not strong enough right now. Just let me help you." Unwittingly, she gave up.

He lifted her to her feet and steered her back towards the house. Clara pressed against him as they walked, wondering if she could stand without him and worrying that he would force her to speak to her parents. When they got back to the driveway, he was true to his word. He opened the truck door and surprised her by actually picking her up and placing her inside. He pushed down the lock and didn't look at her when he shut the door.

On the drive back to her apartment, they didn't speak. She couldn't speak. She stared out the window, letting the images from the dedication flood her mind. Sissy's hair, her eyes, the sound of her voice, it was too much at once. Artie parked the car and walked her to the door. She tried to fish her keys out of her purse, but she couldn't find them. Her frustration mounted.

"They're in here," she said frantically, starting to cry again. He took the purse from her, found the keys and opened the door. When she got inside she turned to thank him for the ride, but he was shutting the door.

"You want tea?" he asked. She shook her head. "I'm gonna stay," he said.

She nodded, surprised that she wanted him to. "I have to call your parents and tell them you're okay," he said. "Shower. It helps." She didn't move. He crossed to the phone, dropping the truck keys and her purse on the coffee table. She watched him dial the numbers. He was so handsome.

"She's fine," he said without saying hello. "We're at her house." He paused, listening to whoever had answered the phone. He shook his head. "No, don't come here." This time while he was listening, he ran his finger over his lip. "I'll see you in the morning." She could tell from his expression that the other person had started speaking again. He interrupted, "I'm hanging up. I'll see you in the morning." He clicked off the phone and faced her, still holding it.

She managed to say, "Thank you," before she started shaking. He moved towards her, but he didn't take her in his arms like she wished he would. Instead, he took her by the shoulders and led her into the bathroom. When she saw his reflection in her vanity mirror, she couldn't help but think it was the first time he'd ever seen the inside of the bathroom, unlike the rest of her apartment.

He sat her down on the closed toilet and turned on the bath faucet, leaning over to test the water temperature. She watched him, making no attempt to do anything else. Kneeling in front of her he took off her sandals. He stood up and lifted her dress over her head. She didn't feel naked in front of him. She closed her eyes waiting for him to unsnap her bra and her breath quickened at the thought of his kiss. He didn't touch her. She heard him turn off the bath water and waited. Then, she heard the little click of the door closing.

When she opened her eyes he was gone. She could hear the T.V. from the other side of the door. She peeled off her bra and panties and stepped into the warm bath. The water covered her body, cradling her and reminding her of swimming in the pool a year earlier. She inched down, submerging her entire head. The sound of the drain slurping up the excess water echoed in her ears, drowning out everything else. She stayed submerged until her lungs burned, thirsty for air. When she came out of the bathroom, he was lying on her bed.

"Better?" he asked. She shrugged, moving to her closet. She dropped her towel, not to tease, just because she could, and pulled her pajamas from the spot on the top shelf. She thought she could feel him watching, but when she looked back his eyes were closed. In her pajamas she crawled into the bed. He didn't touch her. She lay curled with her back to him.

"I love you," he said, his voice trembling, "but that's not enough." She waited, listening. "It's too important." He didn't have to say anymore. She nodded, feeling the tears stream down her face again.

When he turned off the T.V., he curled up behind her, pulling her close, and they lay like that until she knew he was sleeping. Gently, she worked her way out of his grasp and stood, looking at him lying in her bed. His face was droopy with heavy sleep and he looked peaceful. She loved him, as always. She took a piece of paper from the notepad by the phone and jotted him a note. *Gone Swimming.*

FORTY-THREE

After the presentation and Clara's hasty departure, the celebration quickly dwindled. Liz stood in the driveway shaking hands and hugging guests as they made their way to their cars. There were so many people she hardly knew, people from Sissy's life before Santa Fe. She looked into their faces, seeing grief and understanding that they all felt they owned a part of Sissy. Sissy had touched them in some way that Liz would never know about, and she couldn't help but wonder if they all had stacks of yellowed letters addressed to *so and so, our family*. It occurred to her that Robert's death changed her life. If he had died somewhere other than Santa Fe, Sissy never would have been hers.

When they were all gone, Liz went into the kitchen to see if the caterer needed anything, but the refrigerator was already filled with tinfoil wrapped leftovers and the dishwasher hummed. The servers had gathered their things and were preparing to leave.

Outside, the band loaded their gear. Through the kitchen window, Liz watched Cliff settle up with them. He was smiling holding an amber drink in his hand. Scotch. Somewhere during the evening he'd shed his jacket and tie, unbuttoning the top buttons of his shirt, revealing the skin below. He was stunning to her, so manly. She wanted to dance with him.

With that in her mind, she went into the living room and turned on the radio. She wasn't sure how to make the outside speakers work, so she turned the volume up until it was near deafening and opened the window. Just a stone's throw from where she was standing, Katie cuddled against Michael on a chaise. Her mascara had run, leaving black circles under her eyes. Cliff sat next to them in a chair, nibbling on the ice cubes. They looked in her direction when the music started.

"Too loud?" she asked. They simultaneously shook their heads. All three looked spent. Lazy and eager to join her family, she popped out the window screen, rather than walk back through the house. When she stepped over the sill Michael smiled at her and said, "Very *Dukes of Hazard*, Mom."

She shrugged, "Just call me Daisy." Michael rolled his eyes.

"Artie called," Cliff said.

"Everything okay?" Liz knew the answer before she asked the question. If Clara was with Artie, then she was safe because he loved her. During their weeks of party planning, Artie talked about Clara. At first he was tentative, hardly answering Liz's questions at all, but as time went on he opened up. Through Artie's eyes Clara was everything Liz had ever hoped she'd be; strong, brave, poised, sexy, the list was endless. She knew they were lucky to love each other the way they did, even if it was hard for her to understand.

"Yeah, it's good. She's good." Cliff said, taking one last swig of his drink. He stood, spread his arms wide and shook his chest like he was a busty woman. Katie laughed and Michael covered her eyes with his hand. Giggling, she fought to free her vision.

"I cannot bear to expose you to the stylings of my father's seductions," Michael teased. Katie squirmed and squealed, wanting to see exactly that. In response Liz started rocking her shoulders and beckoning Cliff with both her arms.

"Oh come on, Michael," she said, shuffling towards Cliff and trying to work up a little something Latin, "he's so sexy!" Cliff paused, striking a stunning disco pose and Michael, overcome with laughter, released Katie.

"Devastatingly," Katie said, pulling Michael up from their chair and making him dance with her.

Just before Cliff took Liz in his arms he said, "I like her, Michael. She's so perceptive."

The four of them danced for a while, being silly and trading partners every so often. Liz had fun without thinking about it. She loved watching Michael and Cliff groove. Neither one was a good dancer, but they were so goofy and lighthearted that it was easy to overlook any rhythm they lacked. After about three or four songs when they had all worked up a sweat, she and Katie were laughing so hard that they collapsed and let the men take over. The duet was short lived. Michael being younger and still caged by inhibitions came to sit near them as soon as he became aware of their laughter. Cliff would dance all night if he could sleep at the same time.

"Don't you ever get tired, old man?" Liz laughed.

"Depends on my options," he winked.

"That's it for me," Michael said, throwing down his tie as though it were a towel, "when you two start throwing around sexual innuendos, I'm done." Michael stood, taking Katie by the hand, and leaning over to kiss Liz. Looking over at his father, he said, "Good luck with that."

Cliff paused and threw his arm out to add a little flair as he said, "See you two cats at the breakfast table." Once they were out of earshot, Cliff stopped dancing and came over to sit by Liz.

"She's nice," he said.

"I really like her."

"Funny, cute, smart. The whole package."

Liz nodded, watching them disappear into Sissy's house.

"Should we follow their lead?" Cliff asked, standing.

"I think I'm going to sit here for a little while," Liz said, hoping he wouldn't be insulted.

"You want me to sit with you?"

"No, you look exhausted."

"Okay," he nodded, understanding. He kissed her, letting his lips linger for an extra moment. Then, he walked backwards to the door, keeping his eyes on her until the last second.

Once he was gone Liz stood up and walked around the pool putting all the furniture in its rightful place. She wasn't certain how long she was going to stay outside, but she hoped if she gave it a little while, Clara might show up.

During their conversations, Artie told Liz about finding Clara naked by the pool on the night of Sissy's first celebration. He described her behavior in vivid detail, but Liz knew he didn't recognize its purpose. Dancing and playing naked by the pool was not something Clara was likely to do unless it was some sort of homage, and if it was, Liz wanted to take part. So, she sat in the stillness and relative quiet of the late night and waited.

Clara must have parked the car on the access road because Liz didn't hear her drive up, and they were both surprised when she came around the corner.

"Mom!" she said, startled, "I thought you'd be sleeping."

Liz decided to be upfront, "I was waiting for you."

"Waiting?" Clara looked confused.

"A young man I know told me you liked to swim in the middle of the night."

"He told you?" Clara whispered, looking at her fingers.

"I want to swim and dance...hum old Beatles songs and remember her with you." When Clara looked up her eyes were wet with tears. "Will you let me?" Liz asked. Clara nodded.

They stood next to each other on the edge of the deep end and peeled back their clothes until they were completely naked. Neither one said a word. Liz let Clara dive first, but she was quick to follow, splashing through the water's surface before Clara could even come up for air. The coolness washed against her skin, easing away the tension in her muscles and clearing her head. She dove and surfaced again and again, following Clara's lead. After a while they lay still, floating on their backs, right next to each other.

"I loved her," Clara said.

Me too, Liz thought and remembering that first evening with Sissy in Salt Lake, she raised her hands above her head in prayer and celebration.

Made in the USA
Middletown, DE
24 August 2020